Child Of The Pines
By H. S. McInerney

To all the individuals who didn't fit into the social norms… You'll find what you're looking for, and it will be a beautiful, wonderful thing.

Hidden Pines Press
Established 2022

Published by Hidden Pines Press
Copyright ©2023 H. S. McInerney
All rights reserved

ALEARIAN
Tara
Pernak
Raven Wood
Summer Set
Brendal Cove
La'Brog
Sapphire Bay
Anora

4

Table Of Contents

Chapter One: The Change. 7

Chapter Two: Gilded Mountains; The Silver Star. 51

Chapter Three: Tension. 97

Chapter Four: Gem Strewn Waters. 149

Chapter Five: The Secrets They Carried. 189

Chapter Six: A Truth to a Lie. 237

Chapter Seven: Immortal. 257

Chapter Eight: Magic be Thy Master. 273

Chapter Nine: The Burden of The Blade. 299

Chapter Ten: How Glitter Hides the Rot. 311

Chapter Eleven: What Binds Us. 317

Chapter Twelve: Darkness. 335

Acknowledgments: 343

Chapter One: The Change

Blood. It was what she craved, what made her belly ache, her mouth wet. Blood and the heat of the hunt.

She reveled in the musk of the mountain elk as they trampled the tender grasses of the glen. Below her, her pack wound through the sagging pines as they crept closer to the elks' mating ground. A heat seared through her before it settled in her belly. She crept from her perch, cinnamon-toned fur stark against the dense greenery. Her icy-blue eyes tracked the elk as they circled one another in their eagerness to mate. Her tongue lolled in the summer heat, the air so thick and sweet, it left a film upon her tongue.

Her nostrils filled with the ripe scents of beasts laced with blood. The rich, green grass was speckled with it, a temptation that led the wolves to the lone stag.

The elk stood, head slung low as he watched the rest of the herd, blood dripped from his sides. The bugle of the victorious bull elk sent a shiver through him as he backed further from his brethren, and his safety. Each wolf moved closer, forgoing the shadows to step into the clearing.

A soft growl trembled through the air. The largest of the wolves snapped at a smaller black wolf to his right. The smaller pack member laid back his ears, slinking behind his alpha. The bull saw them, his antlered head swung up as he turned to face them. His creamy tan hide twitched as blood dripped from his slashed shoulders. Flies droned around the wounds while the blood thickened, a thick crimson jelly that clung to his fur.

The cinnamon she-wolf glanced at the adolescent pup before she turned her gaze to the alpha. He towered above the others in the pack, each of them twice as large as the wolves of the south. The wolves fanned out; their jaws snapped eagerly as they lunged at the elk. Each lunge tested his fragile form. Weakness made his movements lazy as it threatened to overwhelm him due to his earlier defeat. Anticipation rippled through her, saliva dripped from sharp fangs as she edged closer.

The elk bellowed, his voice rose into a blood-curdling screech. A shiver ran down the she-wolf's spine, her hackles raised with excitement that shot through her. Rolling liquid eyes fervently looked for an escape that would never come as sable and silver wolves pressed him farther from his herd. The heavy brown fur of his neck swayed as he tossed his head. Throat extended, he called out once more; the sound dredged up from his belly, deep and low before it climaxed in a shrill, raspy note. His call echoed through the clearing, so hollow and alone.

The black wolf broke from the pack. He lunged for the elk, only to be turned away by twisted antlers. With a yelp the adolescent scurried to the side of a pack mate, tail tucked between his legs. They tightened their circle as they pressed their quarry closer to hungry mouths; expectant mouths demanding the rich flesh he promised. The alpha snarled, a savage note that sent a surge through the pack. Two wolves lunged for the elk's throat and shoulders, while three other wolves bit and slashed at hind quarters.

The white lupine's fangs sank deep into his trembling shoulder—a savage tug, and the cream hide ripped nearly to the bone. The stag bellowed and swung his head toward her in a feeble attempt to free himself. Crimson blood bloomed against his tender hide sending the wolves into a frenzy. The pack rushed the bull— silver, black, and sable bodies mingled in a savage blur as they attacked his shoulder and flanks.

Cloven hooves struck out, desperate to cleave a path, to fracture and break the bones of those that hungered for him. The she-wolf ran forward and leapt for the bull's throat. As her paws pressed from the earth, the frenzy of the hunt burned in her veins, the elk swung for her. With a violent twist she altered her course and caught the delicate velvet of his muzzle in her jaws. She tore at him, muscles flexed as salty blood pooled against her tongue. Heat burned deep within her as she swallowed his blood. The elk reared, and cloven-shaped hooves flailed as he strove to free himself. She released him, loping out of his range. A hunger burned through her, bright and vicious, as she watched his fearful eyes.

His tattered hide trembled as fatigue and pain overwhelmed him. Each puncture, each slash that he endured, released his precious life essence in scarlet spurts. It speckled his form, the very earth around him. The scent of blood filled the cinnamon wolf's nostrils to the point of intoxication. Her mind hummed as she watched for an opening. The largest of the wolves, a sable beast with amber eyes, leapt for the bull. The lupine filled her view as she watched him catch the elk's throat between his fangs. Each wolf ran for the animal, biting and tearing at his legs and flanks.

The alpha held on. Each breath was a labor while the sable wolf's nostrils filled with the thick mane of fur. Yet he held firm. The elk rasped as its throat collapsed under lupine fangs. His knees folded, his magnificent antlered head brought low as his body failed him. Only a whisper of air could reach desperate lung. Brown eyes grew dull as shredded muscles stilled. The alpha held on, the pulse against his tongue was weak, slow, yet he held on. At last the elk's heart stopped and the sable wolf released him.

He snarled at his pack, muzzle red with blood, then howled. The pack's voices mingled with his own. As the sound faded through the glen, its echoes swallowed by the shadows of the forest, the alpha ripped out the elk's jugular. Blood ebbed slowly as the wolves descended upon the kill. The body of the felled beast jerked as though it still lived. His flesh was tugged and torn from every side as the wolves fed. Blood pooled beneath him as the essence of his life turned the once-green grasses black.

The cinnamon-colored lupine joined them, icy blue eyes transfixed on the feast before her. She sank her teeth into the warm elk flank at last, and reveled in the taste of him. It was sweet; salty and sinful as it slid down her throat. She closed her eyes, and fed…

Kenna woke slowly while she savored the cool grass against bare skin. Blood streaked her human form in dark trails that cracked into small flakes as she moved and released a sweet metallic scent. The pack was still asleep, full and peaceful after the hunt. With agitation Kenna watched the darkness around her while she wondered what had drawn her from slumber. A soft growl escaped her while she delved into the copper magic that dwelled within her center; it pulsed, hot and eager, ready to be bent to her will. She shifted her weak human eyes to the icyblue of her wolf form, her magic making them pale and luminous, and the night bloomed with silver light.

Her lupine eyes reflected each glimmer of starlight as it chased away the shadows. Still she waited, unsure of what could be in the darkness. The moments trailed on as Kenna listened to the music of the night, the cry of nocturnal creatures, the whisper of the breeze through the pines… Slowly, she felt her body relax as sleep began to curl its dark fingers around her mind, only to be startled into wakefulness by a dull rasp from the woods. She rose, tense and careful as she wound her way through the pack to gather her loose gown from the tree. Kenna snatched her garment from a branch and pulled the slip over her head, then slipped into the woods.

Kenna moved through the darkness like a wraith, as one bare foot after another slipped silently through the leaf litter. She clung to the shadows while she waited for the telltale rasp, she was not disappointed. Kenna delved deeper into the trees and was again rewarded with another rasp. She altered her course, then swiftly gripped her gown as she veered to the right. With a small smile she leaped gracefully over a fallen tree, and landed with a soft thud in a small clearing in the woods.

Moonlight reflected in icy blue eyes, eyes that

glowed with magic, that marked her as other, and for a moment she hesitated. She drew in a deep breath and caught the mingled scents of churned earth, wild boar, and blood. Her mouth watered but her full belly protested at the thought of another meal. She pulled in the scent once more through altered senses as the realization washed over her like frigid water. The blood was human. Her pulse quickened as memories, dark and loathsome, swelled around her. She could not think of it, not now, but she did have to see. Kenna pushed aside the brambles with fingers that trembled and absorbed the carnage of the scene.

The earth yawned with deep wounds; dark soil spilled across the grass like stagnant blood. A broken spear mingled with the dirt and not far from it, slouched against the base of a pine, was a man. A man. A shiver twisted her frame while she watched from the shadows. It was so rare to see humans in the woods. The woman edged around the glen, each step hungry as she devoured the distance between. At last she stood, breath ragged, against the tree that he himself rested against. Now that she was closer the smell of blood consumed her. Fangs ached as they began to descend past pink, glossy gums. She pulled a breath through her mouth in a feeble attempt to sooth her desire for him. She could taste him; so rich and fragrant. He smelled of pines, of something spicy that wrinkled her nose in the most delicious way.

Her full belly clenched, and she winced. She delved into the copper pool that shimmered at her core and released some of her magic, her eyes returned to a soft aquamarine, her magic now deep beneath the surface. Kenna was relieved that she could no longer taste him, yet her excitement quickly dwindled. Carefully, she stepped around the pine and knelt by his side.

Black locks, so dark it consumed the starlight, hid his face—except for his lips. They were a pale blue that reminded her of those already gone. Slowly Kenna reached out, her breath stilled within taut lungs, and pulled the black fabric from his chest. The man drew a sharp breath. Kenna quickly released him then slipped into the safety of darkness. She watched him look for her weakly, his eyes glassy and unfocused. Within moments his eyes began to close once more, his head limp against his chest. A wetness clung to her, the slick texture a lure as she turned her gaze to her fingers. She paled; they were covered in blood. Her heart hammed, a manic metronome in her ears. She crept closer to again examine his wound and shuddered at the severity of it.

  His flesh was laid open to the bone, muscle flayed wide. Blood congealed in clumps along his exposed slick, white sternum. Looking around she found scattered objects, most of which were crushed and useless. Just as she turned her gaze back to him she caught a soft glimmer in the dirt. She crossed the clearing to find a dented canteen. She unearthed the item, half buried in churned soil and shook it. A wan smile curved her lips when the whisper of sloshing water met her ears.

  Kenna returned to the man and knelt in the dirt before him. She released the canteen and took a firm hold of his tunic. In. Out. His chest moved in a slow, hollow rhythm; lungs weak and bruised beneath shredded flesh. Kenna ripped his tunic open and poured the cool water over his wound. Within a breath the man was in motion. His calloused hand was upon her as he sharply yanked her hand away from him, his teeth bared in a grimace of pain. The canteen thumped softly, the only sound to accompany her heavy breath as she stared at his hand. Her eyes followed the line of his muscled arm smeared with dirt and blood, until she at last found his face.

  Pale with blood-loss, his face was taut as he watched her, a hint of steel in his once glassy eyes. As their gazes crossed, they measured up the other; the silence that stretched between them amplified by the nocturnal creatures around them. In the distance a wolf howled. Kenna's lips twitched, her call dead in her throat as he held her. The steel faded as the fog of shock consumed him. Kenna's body trembled as adrenaline pulled through her.

She knew he was dangerous, same as any wounded animal. Slowly she extracted her wrist from his grip and was relieved when he looked away. She watched him, muscles tensed as she leaned away from the small space between them, yet he remained limp. Kenna closed the void and reached for him, she paused a few inches from his arm. He did not respond. Ever so gently, she pushed his tattered tunic from his chest. The garment's weight pulled itself from his shoulders then fell in a crumpled heap around his hips. A small tug ripped the fabric wide, thus free to be pulled from his frame. Kenna tore the back of his tunic into long strips, and bound his wounds.

Kenna pulled loose a semi-clean strip of fabric. She stretched it smooth, then leaned toward him expectantly. She was ignored. A soft growl rumbled in her chest and she sat back on her heels. Just as Kenna pulled on her magic to add muscle to her frame, eyes aglow with pale blue light, before he softly rested his brow on her shoulder.

She released the change, the beastial presence once more slumbering deep within her. Kenna gingerly wrapped his torso and felt him tremble beneath her touch, his breath a soft caress against her neck. Her skin tightened pleasantly at his closeness, a flush hot beneath her skin as something in her belly stirred; desire or discomfort, she shied from it regardless. With quick movements she continued to wrap his broad chest in the cleanest linen she could. Once the knot was firmly placed above the wound, she pushed him back against the tree. Kenna shuffled back and watched as blood began to seep through his bandages.

"I can take you to a healer, she isn't far from here," she said, voice rough with misuse.

"I doubt I'll make it."

"How did you get here?" As she asked.

"I was hunting Gullinborsti. It was a bit of a dare really," he answered with the ghost of a smile. Kenna's eyes widened. *No one is fool enough to hunt them on their own! Even the pack won't touch them.*

"You were willing to die for a dare?" She did not keep the judgment from her voice, and even in his state he heard it. A sigh rattled through him.

"Honestly? I didn't think I would find one. I thought they were more of a myth like the rest of this place." He gestured around them vaguely.

Kenna nodded slowly, her mind filled with some of the otherworldly things she had seen beneath the heavy pines. There were so many legends about this place that many humans would not enter, or even name it. The closest village was a day's journey from Crescent Lake, where she and the pack dwelled. Blackwood was his only hope of aid, if they could traverse the forest in time.

"Do you have a horse?"

"I do, if the wolves haven't gotten to him." His eyes closed as he spoke. Kenna smiled with teeth that were perhaps too sharp.

"What is his name?"

"Zane."

She closed her eyes, reached deep within herself and pulled forth a thin shimmering wave of energy. Her skin tingled as she cast it out into the woods. Animals' souls flashed in the darkness like stars that brimmed with life, some so small they were like a memory of light in the gloom. She cast farther and felt the pull of a large life that blazed with the sun's radiance in her mind's eye. She crooned his name through the magical web and felt the stallion's reluctant response.

"Zane. Zane, sweet Zane…come to me…" she sang as she wove her magic around his mind. He resisted her touch, which only encouraged her more. She strengthened her call to match his will. *"Zane… Dear Zane. Come to me midnight wanderer. These woods are not meant for you sweet Zane. Come to me before the shadows take you away…"* Her sing-song voice burrowed her magic deeper into his consciousness until he succumbed to her call.

Pleased that the stallion would come she returned her attention to the man. His breath was shallow and his bandages bloomed black in the moonlight.

"May I know the name of the man I may soon bury?"

"Caleb."

Caleb… she hummed the name in her mind. *Caleb…*

She felt Zane before she saw him and stood to greet the stallion at the edge of the glen. His sleek black form slipped through the shrubs with ease, and as he drew near his nostrils flared with the scent of his master. His head tossed in agitation, the whites of his eyes vivid against his ebony coat. Zane had a lighter build than most warhorses, with long slender legs and sloping shoulders that promised blinding speed. Kenna took a step toward him and was stunned by his bronze eyes. *They seem so human,* she thought as she caressed his face.

"I need you to lay down as close to him as you can. I will help him on and then we have to get him to Blackwood." The stallion snorted, velvet nostrils flared as he strode to his master.

The stallion nuzzled him gently, then lowered himself so close to the man Kenna feared Caleb would be crushed. She walked around the horse and reached for the change. Once upon her, she grabbed Caleb. His sudden intake of breath made her flinch, yet she held on, with him braced against her, she lifted him haltingly into the saddle.

Caleb screamed when his sternum hit the saddle horn before he fell into the blessed relief of oblivion. Kenna shivered as she pushed him farther into the saddle, released her magic, ,then braced herself to look at his chest.

The bandages, though still in place, had completely soaked through with blood, which now stained both saddle and horse. Kenna could taste the hot metal, its thick scent a film upon her tongue. Nauseated by the hunger his scent pulled from her, she stepped away. Kenna sucked in fresh air and a blood-smeared hand wiped sweat from her brow and licked salty lips. Please don't... Her heart fluttered as she grabbed Zane's reins and turned toward the edge of the forest. Stars flickered through the branches as Kenna pushed the horse as fast as she dared.

Blood dripped languidly down Caleb's arm, his slumped body resting against the stallion's neck. Sweat streaked her sides as she once again risked a slow trot. Caleb's body swayed in time with every step Zane took; his labored breaths had shallowed, nearly inaudible between guttural groans of pain that punctured the stillness between each shod step. His pulse was thready, skin ashen and cold. She was going to lose him.

Long gone were the stars that guided them, replaced by the pale light of dawn; the journey had taken longer than she'd anticipated, longer than she'd realized. Fear reclaimed her, the relief she felt at the tree line forgotten. She tightened the grip on the reins and quickened her pace. Zane, with an unnatural awareness of the situation, matched her gait seamlessly.

They stumbled through the undergrowth, the trees young and slender and saw flecks of blue between the branches. When Kenna at last reached the tree line with Zane in tow her body turned to water as the knot in her chest released with explosive force. Just below them was the small village of Blackwood, to the right was Jan's cabin. A thin stream of soft gray smoke trailed from her chimney before being scattered by the breeze. Birds sang softly around them as they woke with the day. Yet, she found no joy in it. As Kenna hurtled down the hill she called for the healer, her voice strained at the sight of Caleb's ashen face.

She stopped at a small picket fence that suffocated beneath all sorts of growing things. The fence shone softly with magic that stemmed from delicately etched runes in each post. Kenna dropped the stallion's reins as she pushed through the small gate.

"Stay here," she yelled as she climbed the steps of the small, whitewashed cabin. "Jan?" Kenna called out desperately. "Jan!" An older woman with blonde hair threaded with silver rushed out the door, wood mere inches from Kenna's nose.

"Kenna what is it?"

Kenna grasped the healer's hand as she propelled them from the porch.

"I found him in the woods, he's been gored by a Gullinborsti."

Jan paled as she looked past Kenna to the slumped figure on the black horse, bitter fluid dripped lazily down his chest in dark streaks. Kenna shivered as the blood stirred a response from her once more.

"Help me pull him down. You get his shoulders, I'll grab his legs. Make sure to mind his head!"

With gentle urgency they pulled the injured man from the saddle. With great effort the two of them managed to bring him inside. Once they were within Jan's small dwelling they were able to rest him on a cot that was permanently placed by the fire; its crisp white linens soon dappled with crimson.

"Grab my bag," Jan demanded as she checked Caleb's pulse, then his breath. It was far too slow. She rested her palms on his chest; the healer's lips moved soundlessly, while a soft green glow engulfed her fingers. Slowly, the color returned to him, his breaths close to the calm of slumber.

Jan moved her hands, green light gone, and began to cut away the makeshift bandages. She proceeded to wash his wound with an herb-infused wine. Once clean, she took a thread of animal sinew, quickly laced it through a long, curved needle, then pulled it all through a clove. After a moment of careful scrutiny she returned to Caleb and began the slow, arduous task of stitching his chest back together. Kenna watched until all she could see was the soft glow of the fire against crimson stains.

When she woke she saw that Jan was gone and Caleb was asleep peacefully on his cot, his chest wrapped in fresh linen. The color had returned to his face, a soft golden tan dull beneath the blood loss. The room was quiet except for the soft crackle of the fire, which only seemed to lull her back to sleep until a deep growl erupted from her belly. With a sigh she got up and stretched, and a hunger-fueled wave of nausea washed over her. When she walked into the kitchen she was greeted with the familiar view of Jan with a long wooden spoon in hand. Dark liquid churned in a pot while she read from a book laid on a small table. The book was hand stitched with coarse, yellowed paper with inscriptions in various handwriting. Older entries were more charcoal pictures and symbols than anything. The worn tome had been with Jan for as long as Kenna had known her, yet she had never been given the chance to read it. Kenna leaned against the door frame, the corners of her full mouth tugged up as she watched her old friend.

    Jan had been like a second mother to her. Once she had turned five winters old the pack had taken her to the village healer. The older woman saw the young naked child at the edge of the wood, surrounded by wolves, and took her home. Every night, Finna, the alpha's mate and Luna wolf to the pack, came and checked on her human pup as the little girl learned the ways of humans. Kenna remembered many cold nights as she howled from the gate, her cheeks coated with icy tears.

    Jan had taught her everything: how to speak, read, wear clothes, and eat like a human. It had taken her what felt like ages to learn how to use words instead of growls to communicate her needs, not to mention a fork and knife instead of her hands and teeth. More than once she lost her patience. Jan had been kind, despite the occasional tantrums from her wolfish ward and the villagers trusted her enough to spare her new child. Though it saved Kenna from their hands, Jan could not shield her from them all. Her stay with the humans had been arduous, at times causing her to stay within the sheltered realm of the garden gate.

    Kenna stayed with Jan until she was fourteen, though it was not uncommon for her to leave with the pack for days at a time. Her return to the woods had been much more successful, with her lupine heart and human cunning. Yet the greatest gift that Jan gave Kenna was her ability to learn control over her magic.

Since she was a small girl, she had been able to hear the thoughts of animals and make them understand her own. The beasts of the forest lived within her mind, an ever-present comfort to her isolation. After years of rigorous practice and tutelage, she could turn into them.

Once she learned the ways of their minds, the feel of their bodies, and saw the world through their eyes, she could make an imprint. Then with that copper fire that always burned within, she would shift her body to the shape of any animal she wished. Her easiest one, or her "go-to shift" as Jan informed her, was that of a wolf. Her beautiful cinnamon-sable fur would ripple across a lupine form making her a true member of the pack.

She hauled herself from her thoughts and walked over to Jan. Kenna peered into the pot, steam and spices tickled her nose.

"It's just vegetable soup" the older woman answered her young companion's thoughts. "Did you have a nice nap dear?"

"I did thank you. I hope you didn't need my help with anything."

"Not to worry, I managed all right." As she talked she ladled soup into a bowl then sawed off a piece of bread. Kenna accepted the food with a grateful smile, then took her usual seat at the table. Her calloused fingertips roved the silken surface, her mind flooded with memories.

Animated conversations, tear-stained fights. It was all a tapestry of her time with her mother. Kenna caressed the mirror-like wood, then a small sound punctured her thoughts. She leaned over her bowl to see Caleb perched on one elbow as he watched them from his cot. She leveled a sharp look his way, then leaned back, eyes locked on translucent brown liquid laden with vegetables. The soft shuffle of bare feet grew louder, then silence. She glanced through her lashes, hand still as marble beside her bowl. Kenna could see Caleb, he wavered in the doorway unsure if he should continue.

Jan solved that dilemma for him.

"Come in, come in. Sit down and I'll get you something to eat." Without pause she bustled around the small kitchen along with the same fare as Kenna. As she set the food before him she rested the back of her hand against his brow in a matronly gesture. After a moment she nodded, a smile tucked into the soft folds of her cheek. She stepped away to get her own meal.

"Your fever is broken." Jan said. Kenna smiled into her lap, proud of her mother's skill.

Once she sat down they all ate quietly. Nearly finished with their meal, Caleb leaned back,

"So Jan, how long have you been in this village? You are a very talented healer, have you ever considered going to Pernak?"

"Oh no," she shook her head, sufficiently flattered, "I'm not much of a city girl and they need me here," she answered impishly. Kenna watched their interaction with curiosity. It seemed even the old dove was enchanted by his looks.

"Well that's a shame, they are missing out on a wonderful woman, city girl or no." He responded, giving her a sideways wink. Kenna rolled her eyes.

"Jan, is your bath house still working?" Kenna asked.

"Yes it is, there is plenty of wood and fresh water in the trough." The matron stood and gathered their bowls, then set them in a bucket near the kitchen fire.

"Before you take one though I would prefer if Caleb bathed first." She wagged her finger at him, "Make sure you don't get those bandages wet. Only fill the tub halfway. You'll find everything you need, it's outside to the left of the barn." She stooped to grab the bucket then gestured to the door.

Kenna rose from her seat and followed her outside. They walked quietly, side by side, to a small stream on the other side of a clearing to the rear of the cottage. Once at the edge, they scoured the bowls with sand, then rinsed them in the cool spring water. Task done, they relaxed into a companionable silence, the warmth from the morning sun a balm to the gruesome night.

"How are you? It's been a while since I've seen you."

"I'm sorry Jan, the summer is a busy time with the pack. The pups are growing so fast and we go on a great deal of hunts. I should visit you more often." Her voice dropped with guilt.

"That you should," the older woman admonished her, weathered fingers squeezed Kenna's.

She leaned over, her head rested on the healer's shoulder. After a short time Jan patted her knee before she returned to the house with the bucket of clean dishes. Kenna stayed behind.

She laid down, eyes closed, as the sunlight devoured every inch of her frame. Kenna enjoyed the heat-induced oblivion, her mind drifting languidly. A call broke her solitude, someone had called her name. Tired roved as she propped herself up on her elbows, movement drew her gaze to where Jan waved to her from the garden gate. With a groan Kenna rose from the grass; she slowly wandered over to the small garden overgrown with an abundance of greenery, herbs and vegetables. The scents that filled her nose were mild and pleasant.

A light nudge opened the door that leaned at an awkward angle, and she walked to where Jan vigorously pulled a carrot from the earth.

"Go ahead and dig up some of those potatoes." Jan said over her shoulder as she turned her attention to the cabbage. Digging stick acquired, Kenna aided to excavate the fresh spuds.

"So how are things between you and Caleb?"
Surprised, Kenna looked up.
"We are fine I suppose, it's not like I really know him, he was unconscious during most of the time since we met." She returned her attention to the rich soil.
"It just seems to me that there was a bit of tension between you two."

Kenna pushed auburn hair away from her brow, weight balanced on her heels as she crouched in the dirt. "It's not that exactly." She rubbed her hands clean. "I just don't really know how to deal with him. I don't understand the things he says." *That and the way he looks at me sometimes...* Kenna frowned at the subtle flutter in her abdomen. A sharp stab in the dirt eased some of the discomfort.

"Well that's what happens when a man is rescued by a beautiful wild woman."

"I don't know Jan... I don't know how to respond to him half the time."

"Don't think too much of it, you're young. There's no need to rush." Jan stood, then shook the soil from her wool skirts. "Go and take a bath dear, then come in for dinner."

Kenna opened the door to the small bath house with a sigh. *I can't remember the last time I had a hot bath.* Once her eyes adjusted to the gloom she couldn't help but smile. A small fire still burned in the hearth that kept the room warm and comfortable, fresh towels were piled near homemade soaps and oils. She peeled off her musty clothes and stepped into the tub with a deep sigh. Warm water swirled around her as she dipped beneath the surface, with a breath she submerged and ran her fingers through her hair.

Eyes closed she pushed long, wet locks from her

face; water dripped down her lashes and nose. She opened her eyes a fraction, lashes encrusted with water drops like rainbow-filled opals. Kenna snatched a bar of sage soap from the table and proceeded to scrub her body and scalp till it tingled. She rinsed the soap away with a dramatic splash, then drifted over to the table where a few bottles of oil rested. Nose wrinkled, she sniffed them delicately. Kenna plucked the rose oil from the small cluster, contentment a soft glow beneath her breast.

She poured a generous amount into her palm and began to massage it into her hair and skin. With her back to the edge of the wooden tub she hung her glistening tresses over the edge. Her sleek body floated with lazy soap bubbles in the oil dappled waters, while she allowed her gaze to soften. After a time Kenna pulled herself to the center of the tub, tilted back her head and rinsed herself of the oils, then swaddled herself in a towel.

She wrung the water from her hair as she sat before the fire. Once dry she pulled on a plain, undyed wool shift and walked slowly to the small steel mirror that hung on the wall. She gazed at her reflection, while she contemplated the sudden changes in her life.

Kenna didn't know what the standard for beauty was, that wasn't something wolves cared for and she had never gone to the city herself. As far as what the village thought of her… She shrank from the thought painfully, she tended to stay away from them. She examined her face critically, her image hazy in the silvered steel. She had long copper hair that fell around her shoulders, even in the dim light it shined softly. Her skin was fair due to her time under the shady pines. Long gold lashes framed blue-green now, beneath gently arched brows.

Beneath that was a straight nose of middling size over full red lips and a small chin. In her eyes she was just a person, neither ugly nor beautiful. With an empty glance

she walked away. Kenna poured water onto the coals, then returned to the tub and pulled a large cork from the base. Soapy water
drained into a small latrine while Kenna gathered her thoughts. She blew out the candles and abandoned the dark room.

The sun hung low on the horizon, its color rich and vibrant like an unbroken yolk. She quickly walked across the yard; the last rays of light cast an ungainly shadow before her. Kenna climbed the front steps to see Jan at the table, dishes set in their usual places.
"Oh good you're here."
Kenna grinned sheepishly and sat down to dine. A pot filled with a thick stew steamed in the center of the table that was filled with potatoes, carrots, cabbage, and chunks of seasoned rabbit. In a bowl beside it was wild rice with steamed tubers, and fresh bread and sliced apples rested farther along the glowing surface. Jan filled their cups with cool water then sat down as each person filled their own bowl. The sounds of spoons as they sloshed, or bread as it tore filled the void. Kenna watched through her lashes while she ate; Caleb observed her, expression thoughtful, eyes guarded. A frown creased her mouth and brow.
"Why are you watching me?"
"Kenna," Jan cautioned with a harsh look. Kenna ignored it, eyes locked on Caleb balefully.
"You clean up nice, wolf girl," he answered with a crooked grin. Her frown deepened as she returned to her food, jaw clenched hard with each bite.

While they ate Jan went over the proper treatment for Caleb's chest, when to put fresh bandages, what salves to use, what to do if he pulled any stitches, and so on. Kenna leaned against the table, overwhelmed by the past twenty-four hours. It seemed as though Caleb was in a similar position. Jan looked them over with a practiced eye.

"Well, it looks like time for some rest. I'll clean up here and pack your things. I'll leave it all by the door. You two go to sleep, there is an extra cot ready by the window for you, Kenna."
They were dismissed.

With a small sigh, Kenna crawled into her cot; soothed by the soft crackle of the fire. She watched the flames, nearly lulled to sleep when Caleb's voice reached her through the darkness.
"Goodnight Kenna, I hope you sleep well." She glanced over, surprised to see his bare chest. The linen still held him tightly. As her eyes wandered over its crisp edges she could not help but follow the line of his chiseled abdomen. Tight skin stretched effortlessly against smooth muscle that continued to his exposed hips. She could see the beginning of a deep cleft near his groin and quickly looked away. Heat rushed through her, deep in her belly, and lower between her legs.

She pushed her back firmly against the cot. Is he even wearing anything? He reminded her of a mountain cat, so smooth and lethal, even relaxed he looked ready to pounce on his prey.
"Goodnight."

Kenna rolled over, eyes shut tight. Though she could no longer look at him, she could still see his tan, muscular body in the fire light. The light played along his chest, his broad firm chest that was hardly obscured by the soft smoke of deliciously coarse hair. She ground the heels of her palms into tired eyes, yet the image blazed in her mind, and sizzled in her veins. Steeling herself, she glanced over her shoulder to see if Caleb had noticed. A sigh whooshed from her lungs. Those hypnotic eyes were closed in slumber.

She sighed, fingers pinched around the bridge of her

nose. The tension grounded her to herself, to her cot. Not his, with its soft linen warmed by his hard, smooth body. She stretched out as much as the cot would allow, soon her tense body eased loose with every moment that passed; until she too passed into a shadowy world filled with moonlight.

K enna sat up with a gasp, and pushed sweat-soaked hair from her face. Her heart still hammered as she looked into the dark silence around her. The fire had burned itself out, all that remained were garnet ashes that smoldered. She stood, every movement slow. Her muscles ached as tension filled them, her breath shallow as she strained to hear past her pulse. She walked towards Caleb's bed, and was knocked off her feet by a thunderous explosion. The room flashed red with such intensity it nearly blinded her. Light and shadow played across her eyes as she scrambled to her feet. Caleb made his way toward her when another explosion went off. He caught her as she fell, their bodies tangled against the hard floor. His arms shielded her head and neck.
"What's happening?!" she yelled over the noise.

They could hear the screams as they stood. Blood smeared her shoulder where she had struck him in their fall. "It's a raid Kenna," His hands were a vice around her arms.

"You need to get Zane. Grab the satchel by the door, and get Zane. We have to get out of here."

"What about Jan, we have to help her," she argued as she pulled away from him. His fingers tightened, soft flesh dimpled beneath his grip.

"Kenna! Listen to me, these are bad men. Do you understand?" He held her face, forced her to look him in the eye, "Do you know what happens in a raid?"

She shook her head.

"They do terrible things. I'll make sure Jan is okay but you have to get Zane. Now!"

Kenna nodded as she stumbled free of his iron grasp. She ran for the bag by the door, another small eruption went off near the cottage. Her world tilted while the home shook, Kenna faltered and slammed into the door frame; white hot pain laced through her shoulder, her vision wavered as she panted through the agony. Kenna regained her feet and rushed for the bag, yanked open the front door, and froze.

She trembled in horror. She had stepped into a nightmare. The world was painted crimson with fire, thick smoke choked the air, each breath a labored gasp. People ran in all directions, their faces contorted in grotesque masks of terror. Their screams mingled to heights that numbed her mind as they were chased down for sport.

Kenna felt the thunder through the soles of her bare feet. It rolled through her, distorted her heartbeat, as a roan charger emerged from the shadows. Kenna could hardly see the rider, she hardly cared.

Her gaze was riveted to a woman with tangled blonde hair, a child scrambled to keep pace at her side. Bow raised, the roan was spurred on mercilessly, in a blink an arrow was lodged in the boy. The woman screamed, voice shattered as she dragged her son to her. She stumbled over his stilted legs and pulled him close.

A second bolt flew, the smooth wood impaled them both. Kenna's sight blackened at the edges. An arrowhead protruded from her son's back, pinned together, they fell. The charger did not stop. Black fluid splashed across the roan's chest as arms and legs flailed like rag dolls. Bloody, and crushed they faded into the grass.

For a time everything was quiet, just slow movements in the darkness punctured with red. She could no longer hear the screams, the weeping, the prayers… Only silence. It was a relief, her body relaxed and swayed with the flames before her, pulse steady as her focus softened. *This is wrong*… A tremble overtook her, Kenna shook loose from her stupor. I have to move. The night roared into focus. Flames burned brighter, hotter, louder.

The screams echoed around her with cries of pleasure in a cacophony of torment. Kenna ran for the barn. All of the animals were in a panic, cows bawled in fear as chickens flew over their heads.

She covered her face with her arms and ran to Zane, who lunged violently in his stall. Teeth bare, he bludgeoned the door in rage, ebony hide slick with sweat. She slung the satchel over her shoulder, then yanked the war horse's bridle off the wall. Kenna tried to touch his mind as she edged closer, but was knocked away by eddies of energy.

The stallion's mind was a vortex she couldn't grasp. Kenna clenched her fists, claws bit into the tender flesh of her palm. A wet warmth slid between her fingers. There is no time. Kenna clamped down on the creature before her, and forcefully bound his will to hers. Sweat dripped down her face as she slid the bridle over his head. He instantly took the bit. She could hear the shouts, an ever-present roar in her ears suddenly punctured by his voice.

Caleb had called for Jan. Fingers thick and clumsy, Kenna stared at the leather reins in her hands. Everything in her told her to drop them and find her mother, but she couldn't. Caleb needed her to do this task. She pushed past the doubt, pulled the saddle from the side of the stall, and swung it onto the stallion's back. Kenna quickly saddled him as best she could, curses flowed as she dropped the girth strap for the third time. The screams were louder, the smell of burnt flesh stronger as it filled her throat. Her mouth watered, but not with hunger at the scent of charred meat.

She kicked open the stall door and was nearly dragged off her feet as Zane's hulking form took charge. He barreled through the barn doors, Kenna desperate to keep hold of his reins.

Caleb stood with a long sword, malevolent in the firelight, as he stood before the door. He was covered with blood that was not his own, eyes dark and broken as they fell upon her. Kenna couldn't breathe when Caleb strode toward her, hands outreached. His hands were low and open, they begged her to be calm. She shook her head, "No." Kenna dropped the reins. "No…"
"I didn't find her in time. I'm so sorry."
"No. No! You said you'd find her!" Another explosion fractured the night.
"She was gone when I found her, Kenna. She died trying to save a child. I'm sorry."

Caleb reached for her, calloused palms firm upon her shoulders then steered Kenna toward the horse. Her form was pliant in his hands, eyes vacant with loss. He adjusted the girth strap on the saddle, swung into his seat, then reached a hand down to Kenna. After a moment's hesitation she was pulled up behind him. He brandished his sword and spun the dark charger around. A moment of calm, then they dove into the mayhem.

Kenna could barely see through the smoke, everything was ablaze and she burned with it. She held Caleb tight; she looked around her only to see so many familiar faces dead, their eyes forever glazed and unseeing. With a shudder she closed her own and leaned against Caleb's shoulder as he maneuvered them through the corpse-littered village. A yell to their left made her skin crawl as she tried to find the source. All too soon a man with an ax raised over his head came into view. He screamed at them as he came, a madness in his eyes.

Zane turned toward the raider. Caleb urged the stallion into a canter and with one smooth arch lopped off the man's head. Blood spurted from the stump that was once his neck, hot gore covered them in crimson streams. Kenna screamed as the headless body fell towards them. With a grunt Caleb kicked the corpse away. He spurred the charger over the remains that crunched wetly beneath iron-shod hooves. Blood dripped off her lashes as the stallion galloped through the village towards the woods.

Kenna could not decide what would haunt her longer—the screams of the dying, or the hollowed silence of the dead.

They hurtled through the forest at a breakneck speed, a shadow-filled world blew by them in a blur of black and silver. Looking back, Kenna could see a soft glow above the trees ringed in greasy black smoke. She could only imagine the human fat that bubbled and hissed in the flames. She shrank from thought, her stomach heaved in revulsion. Tears streamed down her bloody face in silver threads. The steady drum of Zane's hooves lulled her into a trance as he bore them deeper into the forest. Kenna felt something familiar rub against her mind; she cast about the woods with her consciousness and felt the pack around her like beacons in the dark.

A smile softly cracked the gore upon her cheeks.

Relief flooded through her when the pack formed a circle around the stallion, silver bodies danced through the darkness. The wolves kept pace with Zane as the trees grew thick and gnarled, the underbrush a tangled mass beneath the bows.

The lupine guardians tightened the circle, a steady pressure that forced the sweat-lathered horse in a new direction. They veered off the main path, then wove into the trees, broad paws sounded against the soft soil of a small game trail.

The trail wove deep into the woods; they lost sight of the village and its ominous glow. Zane began to slow as the undergrowth thickened around them. Round another bend in the path the wolves eased into a trot, tongues lolling as their pants rasped in the dark. Finna led the pack, and horse, through a shallow stream, while Throv watched the path they left behind.

The alpha padded through the water, muzzle low as he lapped its chilled surface. The party stumbled into a small alcove hidden by brambles. Once inside they were completely concealed, even with Zane's added height Kenna could not see over the wall of shrubbery. She sighed a heavy breath through her nose. A tremble in her core threatened the use of her limbs. She sucked in a breath and pushed it back. There was no time. Kenna prepared to dismount but hesitated when she saw Caleb sway. She grabbed him, yet his weight was too much. In a desperate attempt to right themselves she tried to pull on the change, but her magic snuffed out like a candle. They fell.

Her cheekbone slammed into his shoulder and her vision was shot through with sparks. Stunned, she laid on top of him, her lungs heaved heavily. It was his hands, calloused palms that cradled her face that made her move. She pulled away quickly and regained her feet. Caleb stood slowly beside her, face pale in the starlight.

"I'm sorry." She reached for him haltingly, fingers closed on empty air. The distance between them closed and Caleb took her hand. It seemed a comfort, that touch, a lifeline in the dark. A warmth crept over her, overriding the hot pulse of pain that had bloomed across her cheek.

The silence was palpable. She decided to hazard a glance at Caleb, and could see the fatigue etched across every line of his body. This is no time to be a child, she chided inwardly while she scanned the secluded glen. There, in the center of the glade stood a weeping willow surrounded by thick, emerald-green moss; the closest thing to a bed they would find. He still held her hand. Kenna flexed her fingers, a soft reminder that he had to let her go. Caleb had followed her gaze, fingers still clasped around her own. A sigh escaped him as he released her. He walked without a word, bloody sword loosely grasped with absent-minded ease. Kenna couldn't follow, not yet.

She turned back to Zane, and her heart reached for his. The stallion's sides were lathered in a thick layer of sweat. Foam gathered at the corner of his mouth, only to be shaken loose as he tossed his head at the wolves that slunk into the clearing. She rubbed his neck and murmured, "It's all right boy, they're friends." She slid the tack from his weary frame. Kenna slipped the bridle over his ears, then slung it over her shoulder. A smile tucked the corners of her mouth when the stallion rested his brow upon her breast.

Once he was free Zane dropped to his knees with a groan, and swiftly fell into a roll. The pack watched him from the edge of the small glade. Kenna eyed the wolves warily. She turned and brought the saddle to rest behind Caleb. He leaned back with a grateful nod, even while she moved him his eyes stayed closed. She opened his shirt and gently peeled back the bandages to expose the great wound on his chest. Mouth suddenly dry she leaned closer to inspect his chest; the metallic tang of blood drifted through her nostrils, and down her throat.

She pushed down the desire that bloomed in her chest, swallowed the spit that filled her mouth. Kenna bit her lip, the flash of pain reeled in her senses and cleared her mind. Bandages removed, she could see the devastation that laid beneath.

The wound was swollen and red, the stitches nearly consumed by angry flesh. Blood oozed slowly from the tattered edges of the laceration. Kenna eyed the liquid, a liquid she knew would taste like heaven upon her tongue. She shook her head, copper hair flared around her as she fought the wolf within. How long had it been since she exposed herself to humans? Too long it would seem... *Focus!* She raged within the confines of her mind. Just focus... Kenna reached for his wound, softly laid her fingers on the hot, pinched skin. She was relieved to find that none of the sutures were broken. Small blessings, she thought sullenly as she grabbed a salve from the satchel beside them. She smeared the ointment over his chest and watched with wonder as the redness faded away; the swollen tissue soothed and released the stitches beneath. *Magicked.* She put the jar away and stood.

Caleb rested at her feet, his eyes closed as his chest rose and fell peacefully. Kenna scanned the glen, ears alert for any sound in the shadowed brambles that surrounded them. The gentle babble of a nearby brook drew her gaze. Through the trees she could made out the hazy curve of a game trail. She strode for the woods, then hesitated. Kenna cast a glance over her shoulder to Throv who dipped his head in acknowledgment; his words growled through her mind.

"We will watch your human."
"Thank you father." She slipped into the woods.

She was a wolf, at least at heart, and enjoyed the

darkness of the night. This night was different. Every shadow seemed to hold a demon with an ax, behind every tree was a mad man; under every bush the body of the dead. She cursed, her heart raced as she angled toward the stream. A ribbon of silver caught her eye, it gleamed between the dark branches. Kenna stepped through the shrubs, her bare feet crunched lightly against the river stones. It sang to her, and muttered happily of all it saw, oblivious to the horrors of the night as it twisted out of view.

She stepped into the cold water, a shiver ran along her entire length while she lowered herself into the shallows. The water turned red around her, the frigid stream pulled the blood from her body. It rippled in muted crimson, more black than red in the moonlight. She laid herself flat, icy water raced down her back and froze the air in her lungs. Jaw clenched, she reached above her head and gripped the rock that protruded from the stream bed. She stared at the star-bedecked sky, eyes vacant as she let the stream wash away the blood, and her pain.

Her body was numb; the cold that was once her salvation a brutal reminder of her mortality. With lungs that ached, Kenna crawled out of the stream in a stilted crawl. The stones bit into her frigid limbs, yet she crawled on, fingers like claws against the gray rocks. Her hair clung to her face and swung in twisted tendrils, water pouring from every strand. The soft brush of tender grass tickled her fingers, each blade a slender milestone. A sigh eased from her as she rested in the grass on her belly.

The night cradled her, there on the shore while her muscles thawed; she looked to be asleep, so still and calm. It belied the turmoil that raged within her mind, raged within her broken heart.

She felt a presence that rasped against her mind. Kenna lifted her face from the grass, eyes unfocused as she blinked away tears. Leara, her ivory pack sister, watched her, golden eyes gleamed in the moonlight. Kenna rushed toward the wolf. *"She's gone, Leara. Jan is gone."* Silence weighed heavy between human and wolf. The only human mother Kenna had ever known, the only human she had ever loved was dead. Leara didn't have the words. She nuzzled her human sister, her cold nose a soft pressure against her throat.

    Kenna panted past the tension in her throat, the tears that slid hotly down her cheeks. Leara's scent filled her nostrils and stilled her mind. The ivory wolf pulled away and raised her muzzle skyward. Her howl echoed through the night, a rich alto that carried the unspoken words of a tattered heart. Kenna joined her, her own voice cracked as tears slid down her face. The pack picked up the call; voices mingled in velvet baritones and wind-swept sopranos. Their ballad was mournful, broken, and filled with all the things they longed for.

    Kenna shuddered, her song had long since ended but there she sat, face stiff with dry salt. Her icy blue eyes glinted in the moonlight as she faced where Blackwood once stood.

"We should get back" she whispered. Kenna stood, joints stiff with stillness. She plucked grass from her night shift, then rubbed her face with the cool, damp hem. Leara stood, her warm coarse fur a comfort against the human woman's thigh. "Let's go."

    They returned to the clearing to find everyone was asleep. The pack was spread out among the trees in a protective circle, sable, silver, and black forms subtle masses in the shadow. Zane rested near the entrance, head slung low, velvet muzzle mere inches from the ground.

    Kenna walked towards the willow with lazy steps. Her body was absolutely spent. Caleb's evergreen eyes met hers, and she was startled by the burst of pleasure that bloomed in her chest. He was awake.

Her mind raced as she scrambled for something to say. Not for the first time, her words failed her. She padded across the glen on silent feet to sit beside him on the carpet of moss. It was soft beneath her, and cradled her sore body with its spongy texture. Silence lingered between them, heavy and loathsome as words bubbled up within her, then died against the barrier of her lips.

Kenna slipped the canteen free of the saddle behind Caleb, and took a long drink of water to soothe her swollen throat. Caleb looked at her then quickly glanced away; he cleared his throat, his stubble dark against pale skin.
"Can you pass me the canteen?" He would not look at her, instead he reached out his hand. Without a word she passed him the water, her shoulders tight, she felt snubbed. He took a deep swig then passed it back to her. Kenna dropped the canteen on the grass, it landed with a soft thump.
"Have I done something to offend you Caleb?"
"Of course not, it's just..." he trailed off awkwardly, his eyes scanned the grass, the trees; anywhere but her.
"It's just what?"
"You can't tell?" He flashed her a sheepish smile, "Your shift is see-through Kenna."

He looked away, his skin held a rosy hue. Kenna's brow furrowed; she was nearly nude beneath the transparent gauze of fabric, its cream color lost to the moisture of the stream. From head to toe she burned. Kenna looked down, jaw set; her shift had lost all trace of color and clung to her like a second skin, every curve caressed with cool cloth fingers. Her breasts were the most visible, the cold made her nipples erect beneath the sheer fabric, full breasts heavy and taut against the chill.

She turned to leave, then changed her mind. *I will not be ashamed.* Her chin rose in a silent challenge. Kenna leaned back on the heels of her palms, nails burrowed in the moss, aquamarine eyes locked on the tree line before her. A chill crept over her as her body cooled with stillness, the damp fabric clung to her breasts, her flat belly, and smooth thighs. Caleb eyed her in a sidelong glance, a sudden look she saw from beneath the veil of copper lashes. Something in her stirred under his gaze; they both looked away.

Kenna plucked absentmindedly at her shift, and cleared a throat tight from tears and unspoken words. She did not utter a word, again silence prevailed. The sounds of nocturnal animals wove sweet tunes through the night, blissfully unaware of the humans that had suffered beneath the silver of the moon.

"I don't blame you. It would be easy, but I know Jan. She would never leave someone that needed her." Again, bitter silver trailed her face.

"She was out of reach, I tried to run to her but…" He gestured helplessly toward his chest. "I wasn't fast enough. I've never seen someone face down their own death with such calm. It was beautiful, but it will haunt me nonetheless. I'm so sorry."

Kenna listened, eyes focused on something only she could see.

"I know. I don't even think I could have pulled her away."

For some time they sat in silence, a sort of peace between them. His voice sounded in the darkness. The blissful, silent peace over.

"Have you been to the city Kenna?" She shook her head in response, the muscles in her neck shrieked at the movement.

"I would like it a great deal if you came with me. Pernak is a close friend's family holdings."

"I don't know Caleb." Kenna shifted uncomfortably, memories nagged at her, she shoved them away. Again that sweet silence, punctured only by the sounds of the forest. Then, it was lost once more.

"Would you at least promise to stay in Pernak with me for a few days? I would like to get to know you better, especially since you saved my life." He leaned over and gently pushed a copper strand behind her ear.

She watched as his fingers blurred before her, his touch sent trails of lightning through her; each point of tender contact left a thrill that tingled down her neck. She answered slowly,
"I will think about it."
"I'm sorry if I offended you earlier Kenna." He said, suddenly serious. "I just don't want you to think I'm trying to take advantage of you in any way." She waited for him to continue. "I like you Kenna, but you are younger than me." He took her hand, his thumb trailed along her fingers gently in soft circles. His touch was warm and tingled pleasantly as it thawed her icy skin. Kenna looked at him with a sidelong glance; his face was serene, his eyes soft as he waited for her answer.

A lopsided grin cracked the coldness of her face. "Well, it will be interesting to see the friends that sent you into the forest in the first place."
His eyes flashed with mischief as his crooked grin mirrored her own.
"Indeed you will."
"We should get some sleep. It's late." She gently disengaged her hand. Kenna stood, every muscle burned and shrieked, it nearly brought tears to her eyes.

She blinked rapidly while she brushed away grass that clung to her damp form. Without a backward look she left him to lay beside Leara. As she curled up beside her sister she saw that he still watched her with that wonderful smile.

Kenna sat up and gasped, she barely managed to stifle a scream. Her body was covered in a thick sheen of sweat. She plucked her gown from her slick chest and stood on legs that shook; icy blue eyes roved the darkness around them. Everyone was asleep, peaceful in the moonlight surrounded by shady green walls. The grass was cool and moist as she quietly walked through the small clearing toward the stream. She was parched, spit sticky as her tongue stuck to the roof of her mouth. She was startled to hear Caleb's voice behind her.

"Did you have a nightmare?" He watched her as she turned to face him, concern etched in the lines of his weary face.

"Yes." Her throat was tight from a smoke she could no longer taste.

"Do you want to talk about it?" He patted the ground beside him softly.

"No." she responded, then walked over to him despite herself.

She shifted uncomfortably on the moss, leaning back against the willow, comforted by the rough bite of bark in her back.

"I'm sorry Kenna, I wish I could have kept you from seeing those things. It will get better after a time, I know that's hard to believe now but memories do fade."

The darkness curled between them. Kenna began to slump over as exhaustion took her.

"Will you sleep beside me tonight?" Her spine straightened. "I only mean sleep Kenna, just so I know you are safe. It will help me rest."

Laughter danced at the edges of his voice; she glared at him which only made him laugh in full. It was rich and deep, a tumble of sound that echoed in her ears. Despite herself she smiled in return, though it quickly faded as she laid down beside him. Kenna stared at the six inches of velvet moss that stretched between them, counted in time with Caleb's soft breaths. She glanced up, his eyes were closed, he had fallen asleep. Her body tensed to crawl further away, her shift hissed as it peeled from her skin. Eyes closed, his arm flashed out and pulled her close. She slid across the ground, closing the space between them with a soft thump against his side. She peered over her shoulder, his tight lips twitched before they gave way to a smile.

A soft growl escaped her as she pressed her hot cheek to the moss. Muscle by muscle she relaxed. Her body cool, she enjoyed the warmth that radiated off of him tinged by the faint smell of his sweat. She matched her breath with his, then drifted into nothingness.

Birds chirped softly above as they fluttered from one branch to the next. Kenna squinted against the pale morning light that filtered through the trees, her memory fractured as she looked around. For a moment she thought she was back with the pack sleeping in their hidden glade until she realized who exactly was beside her. Breath hitched, her movements slow with intent, she took his arm from around her waist. She slid forward on her belly, toes dug into the moss as she propelled herself forward in little spurts.
"Leaving so soon?" Kenna froze as his deep voice drifted through the cool morning air.
"I was just getting up, we should probably get moving. Are you hungry?" she asked, her tone hesitant as she stayed belly down on the ground like a pup. His gaze roved over her with an easy grin that put a wicked gleam in his eye; the look was mischievous enough to make her wonder if he would pounce at any moment. A breath whooshed from her in a ragged burst when he began to move closer, smooth muscles propelled him up and toward her.

Kenna scrambled to her feet, turned away to grab the canteen in the grass near them, and swallowed greedily. Water dripped past her lips and she gazed at the willow, cheeks hot against the cool morning air. Container drained, she rushed towards the tree line; belly full, she sloshed away from the clearing. She called over her shoulder, "I'll be back with water for tea." Her heart pounded while she slipped away toward the shelter of mist-filled trees. Kenna paused in the shade, still heavy against the watery morning light. Caleb rolled onto his back, stretched his arms before he neatly tucked them beneath his head; raven black hair spilled over tan, muscled arms.
"We can't have a fire, Kenna," he responded, voice soft and clear. Caleb's eyes closed against the golden dawn, and for all the world he looked like a cat content to sun himself.

With a soft growl she disappeared. Caleb leaned against his charger, broad hands rubbed the stallion's crest as he snorted anxiously. Kenna trotted toward them, the full canteen a heavy weight against her hip.
"Is everything all right?"
"I thought I was dreaming, but I guess not." Caleb gestured at the wolves. "Have they been here the whole time?"
"Well, yes. They helped us find this place. Without them Zane would have run till he fell."

Caleb nodded and mumbled quiet words to Zane. The stallion lipped his shirt, ears tilted forward as he listened to his master.
"How is your chest feeling?" Kenna took a step closer; she offered her palm to the horse and rubbed his velvet muzzle, her body taut as she waited for Caleb's answer.
"Better than it was. Take a look for yourself."

Caleb unbuttoned the collar of his tunic, then slid the bandages apart to reveal the grizzly slash beneath. The edges of the wound were no longer red, but a soft silver inlaid with pink. Kenna's brow furrowed as she examined the wound. Jan's salve across his wound.
"I've never seen anything like it," she whispered, pale fingers reached for him only to stop a mere inch away. She could feel the warmth of him beneath her fingertips and suppressed a shiver. Their eyes met as she silently asked his permission. Caleb flashed her a wry smile,
"Go on wolf girl, I don't mind."
She snorted softly at his nickname for her, but touched his wound nonetheless. The edges of the slash were cool wherever the silver was present; as though the flesh had frozen beneath the tusk of the immortal assailant.

Her fingers grazed the sutures, the warm pink flesh that they bound, and she saw his pectoral flex.
"I'm sorry." She pulled away.
"It's all right, just a bit sensitive."

Heat warmed her face. *Well of course it hurts. What was I thinking?* She brushed her fingers against her gown, an awkward silence heavy between them.

"I think you have to put more of that salve on." She pointed to the saddle bag already secured to Zane's back.

"I suppose you're right."

He turned from her, the corners of his mouth turned down in a soft frown; eyes shuttered and thoughtful. Kenna longed to touch him, to trail her fingers along his arm and voice the question trapped in her throat. Yet there it remained, as she watched him dip his fingers into the medicinal jelly and smear it across his chest.

The red tissue soothed to be replaced by a dull sheen of silver. Jar returned, Caleb gazed across the glen. The wolves watched from the ample shade as the humans hovered around the war horse.

"There is no time like the present. We had best be off."

His eyes rested upon her expectantly, a query arched his dark brow. A tentative smile curved her lips, Kenna gazed at her ward and found herself more drawn to him in the morning glow than she had in the gentle shine of the moon. His hair gleamed like raven wings, so dark and lustrous compared to his gold-dusted skin.

"Yes, let's go."

Her smile faded when she turned to where Blackwood had once stood. A breeze had blown away the columns of fat- and flesh-fed ebony smoke; now only the soft smudge of gray marred the pale horizon. The muted rustle of fabric pierced by creaks of leather brought her back to the glen. Kenna watched as Caleb mounted Zane, then joined him behind the saddle. Kenna held him loosely, her mind an endless loop of shadows.

"How long will it take us to reach your friend?"

"Pernak is still about two, maybe three leagues from here."

"That sounds simple enough."

Despite the confidence of her voice she still carried reservations about going to such a large city. Kenna never fit into Blackwood, something the village people and their sniveling children made abundantly clear. She could still hear their laughter, a hollow echo in her ears. Only now the sound was replaced by the raucous call of crows and popped cinders. Kenna shook herself free of the past and focused on the road before them.

The sun rose steadily higher, and carried with it the smothering heat of midsummer. The minutes turned to hours, lethargic beneath the morning heat, and with that time brought impatience. Kenna was thoroughly tired of riding behind the saddle; any dip in the road was instantly felt as one half of Zane's hind quarter would drop away. Kenna was left to perch precariously on the ebony hide that remained.

She growled under her breath, then rested her least chafed cheek against Caleb's back. Kenna watched the world go by in languid shades of brown and green, her mind adrift with birdsong.

"I think you owe me," her voice cracked between them.

"Do I now?" Mirth shivered in his voice as he suppressed a deep chuckle.

"You do. Have you got any idea how sore my ass is? At the very least you owe me for that."

Laughter erupted from them both, a blessed release of the tension that lingered in their muscles.

"Indeed I do, and I promise once we get to Pernak that I will lavishly reward you in return for all your care; and your tender ass."

Kenna rolled aquamarine eyes, an unbridled smile upon her face as she forced false sternness into her tone.

"I could do with a hot meal, and a bath."

"Getting a bit ripe?" His shoulders shook with silent laughter.

"How rude you are!" Kenna giggled despite herself, his deep chuckle quickly joined hers.

By mid-morning Kenna was restless. The pack had grown tired of the slow pace; they had fanned out ahead of them to scout the land. They would grab a snack if the opportunity so charmingly presented itself, and Kenna longed to join them. A sigh escaped her; she could not leave Caleb alone and injured, so she had stayed behind. She reached up to tap his shoulder.
"How much longer?"
"'Bout another league, maybe less. We are making good time under the circumstances."
"Is there anything I should know about the city, or the people maybe?"
For a long moment he was silent, the rhythmic thud of hooves on soil the only sound between them; then he answered.
"The city may be too much for you to take in at first. It has great walls around it that were built hundreds of years ago to protect the people from creatures of the forest. At that time, this forest was running thick with magic so the people created a barrier. Past that, the interior is fairly normal, though the citizens can be a bit eccentric or over suspicious due to the location. Once we are at the main estate you will meet the noble family that resides there.
"Lord Randal of Pernak is my friend and our host. His older brother is watching the estates while their parents take their little sister to a boarding school for her education as a Lady. Then there is my cousin Von, our friend Aden, and my aunt Ressa. They will treat you well."

Kenna absorbed the information quietly. Her curiosity about the city dwindled at the list of names, titles, and responsibilities. Her stomach tightened as she watched the horizon grow near. A new city didn't necessarily guarantee trouble, yet doubt crept in. Blackwood was small minded in every way, and had made life there dangerous for anyone who was different. She could only hope Pernak was more open minded. She pulled away from her thoughts and listened to the hum of sounds around them. It droned softly in her ears as she was rocked by the stallion.

Kenna's slim figure slumped against him, her clothes damp with humidity, while fatigue claimed her. Zane meandered down the road with easy strides that bore them closer to humanity. To and fro she swayed, her body limp, warm, and relaxed. She tilted sideways, her thighs slicked with sweat that slid her all the faster toward the road. A smooth step, and the black-furred body moved away from her to leave her off balance frame afloat in mid-air. Caleb grabbed her elbow and threw his weight to the other side of the saddle.

His sutures burned with the force as he righted them both, a sheen of sweat beaded his brow. Kenna started awake, her body ablaze with the heat her panicked heart pumped through her. Too embarrassed to speak, Kenna pressed her brow into his back. Caleb's callused hands encircled her wrists, then with a gentle tug he pulled her close. A small smile creased his face when she sighed against his shoulder.

They had stopped, the small group clustered on the crown of a small hill that overlooked a valley. The pack broke from the tree line; sable and silver pelts gleamed in the late morning sun. They padded toward the horse and riders, tongues lolling in the thick air.

Kenna brushed her mind against theirs to quiet the hum in her veins; magic rippled in her gut as the beast within shivered. A thread of magic worked its way through her to alter her senses; the scent of man washed over her in a dense wave. She quickly released the magic, and surveyed the valley below them. The forest had fallen away to reveal a crystalline blue sky speckled with ivory clouds.

Green grasses mingled with amber bent in a warm breeze, it whispered softly while it ripened under the golden sun. Kenna's gaze roved the land hungrily; she devoured every inch only to pause at a mountain of stone punctured with drops of ice that shimmered like broken glass. She sucked in a breath, then wiped sweat from her brow with the back of her arm. Her eyes squinted against the sunlight, her mind transfixed upon the wrongness of the ice-bedecked mountain below.
"What are we looking at?"
Caleb didn't answer, only stared at the mountain flecked with frozen shards.
"Are we waiting for someone?" She pressed further.
He stayed quiet; her curiosity transformed into annoyance as she inhaled, a sharply worded question on her dust-coated lips. He twisted in the saddle to face her.
"You have to look closer."

There was a gleam in his eyes that made her second guess herself. Brow furrowed, Kenna leaned around his shoulder to take a closer look at the strange mountain. Realization struck her, a gasp parting lips that trembled.

Chapter Two:
Gilded Mountains;
The Silver Star

Kenna slipped from Zane's back and stumbled forward on stiff legs. She squinted against the haze at the mountain of snow and ice, yet it wasn't a mountain at all; it was a city. Its walls shifted from one shade of gray to another, one section deep and rich, then added into a soft powdery gray only to shift color once more.

Thousands of small glass windows dazzled the sides of the buildings like scattered diamonds that shone in the summer light. She was awestruck by the massive bronze doors, stark and brilliant against the drab gray of stone. Fantastic designs of dragons and winged women danced on a breeze eternalized within the bronze sky. She looked up at Caleb, aquamarine eyes glistened with wonder, and gratitude.

"This is Pernak? This is a city?" Her voice was breathy. She slid from the saddle, a dull thump on the dirt echoed her movements. Caleb's presence washed over her, the breeze laden with his scent.

"This is Pernak. Would you like to see the inside?"

"Yes, I think I would."

She grabbed his hand, a smile upon her face as she pulled him toward the stallion. Caleb glanced at their interlaced fingers, a gentle smile touched his lips and set his face aglow. They strode toward the stallion, filled with a new vigor, a new sense of hope and direction. Caleb swung into the dark leather saddle, flakes of dried blood cracked free and floated to the soft soil of the road. Kenna watched each burgundy flake fall, then glanced at her pack; her gaze then shifted to the man before her, hand outstretched. A broad smile creased the corners of his eyes, the joy that seeped into them set them ablaze.

Kenna wondered at the small fleck of gold that settled there like dappled sunlight. For a moment she hesitated; in that smile she could see the promise of another world and some small part of her said no. Kenna pushed it down, the fear that threatened to hold her to the shadows, and took his hand.

They descended the hill and wove their way down the dirt and shale slope. The wind began to shift, a hot breeze turned into a wind that switched directions endlessly with sudden bursts of frigid air. Kenna breathed in the thick, soup-like air and quivered with excitement. The storms of the north were violent, sheets of silver rain and ground-shaking thunder would soon rock the valley with unprecedented fury. Caleb adjusted his grip on the reins, then spurred Zane forward. Kenna gripped Caleb, white bone of her knuckles sharp against translucent skin, as clouds of molten steel bore down on them; eager to wage war upon the land.

The wall loomed ahead of them, a beast that grew

with each thunderous hoof beat. Rain pelted their backs to seep through their clothes in frigid streams. The dust settled to pool against the ground, in place of gilded plums it settled into thick puddles of mud. Stone walls towered above them, when Caleb at last released the charger into a gentle canter. Kenna leaned around his shoulder, a shiver ran through her at the sight of men in gold and red that sprawled across the castle grounds. A dozen soldiers ran across the battlements towards the bronze gates that led to the belly of the city.

Somewhere deep within the walls a horn sounded, its brassy notes swallowed by the thunder that clashed and roiled at their heels. City gates swung wide to reveal a shadowed tunnel that soon filled with a cavalry squad. The pair drew close, muddy water dribbled from their hair, their sodden clothes, down their faces in a garish mockery of tears.

Kenna swiped them away as she eyed the human soldiers. The armored men watched the mounted pair with eyes like steel, their faces taut with mistrust while they encircled them. Kenna watched their smooth movements and leaned closer into Caleb. A shiver ran through her as she shifted, her thin gown sheer where it clung to her flesh. Kenna glanced back at the woods, her view narrowed to a slim slash of freedom, then nothing but bronze when the doors shuddered closed.

The shrill scream of bolts struck the air while they were slid into place, secure against the outside world; and secure against escape. *Thank Divya the pack stayed behind.* A small pain bloomed in her breast at the thought of her family. She turned back to Caleb, her wet lips close to his ear.

"Who are those people?"

"They are the soldiers that defend Pernak. Conner must have sent them to greet us once we were spotted."

She squinted against the dust that was now pelted down by the first splatters of rain. The soldiers were mounted atop heavily built horses, muscles rippled as they pawed the ground eager to move. Each soldier carried a weapon; long steel swords sheathed in well-worn leather, or heavy crossbows that rested easily in the confident cradle of their grasp. *This is a welcome party?* A pang of doubt, and she hoped the only thing that would be pelting against her was the rain.

There was no breeze within the city, only the dwindled splatter of rain. Kenna eyed the mighty walls, a growl rumbled in her chest as her hackles rose. She was stifled in the thick humidity, circled by deep stone. Sweat slid down her sides, her pulse raced.
"I need to get down."

Before Caleb could respond she slipped from the saddle to land in the road. The guards watched her suspiciously, but made no move to stop her. Thick gold dust clung to her throat, an earthy film that made it difficult to breathe. Kenna surveyed what she could see of the city while Caleb talked softly to a man whose ebony skin gleamed beneath a sheen of mist like rain. The road doubled back on itself like a snake, it narrowed at every bend as it led them toward the castle at the town's center. Baffled by the serpentine design Kenna stepped closer to Zane.

Caleb finished his discussion with a curt nod.
"Captain Remus will take us to the main estate."
Kenna nodded slowly, her eyes full of questions. *They talked far longer than needed if that's all that was said.*
Remus signaled to his men with a sharp gesture, then led them toward he road. His men dispersed around them in an escort that made Kenna's spine rigid.
"Would you like to ride with me?"
Rain dripped from Caleb's nose as he looked down at her.

"No," she rested a clammy palm against the stallion's warm, slick shoulder. "I will walk."

The deeper they trod into the city the more Kenna felt trapped. Everything was stone, the walls, the roads, the houses; the farther from the gate they traveled the more she missed the dust that lingered near the gate. A reminder of the outside world. There was no plant life anywhere, only a plethora of stones in every shade one could imagine. The only adornment a select few homes hosted were decorative tiles, painted with delicate ivy bejeweled with soft blooms. The roofs also added color with varied shades of blue, red, and burnt ochre ceramic. They wound closer to the city center, and the quality of life grew steadily more luxurious.

Small humble homes with little to no decoration gave way to graceful structures with grand arches, and glazed tile displays. Even the tombs that clustered between dwellings were polished and speckled with stained glass. One house was so extravagant as to boast a detailed mural of a young forest, butterflies suspended in a whisper of a breeze, a buck grazing on tender grasses. The delicate skin of the deer's nose so alive it nearly quivered with their scent when they marched past. What care the artist had given to render such a masterpiece; it gave Kenna a glimmer of hope, perhaps not all who lived in the stone city were lost to the world outside its somber walls.

The party stopped beside a great fountain, it bubbled merrily in a granite garden. The shallow bowl looked soon to overflow with fresh rain. Carved into the fountain were water sprites and fish of all types, all of whom spouted liquid from their mouths in a whimsical display.

A knot in her chest slowly unfurled within her at the sight. Kenna walked forward to trail her fingers in the cool water, it rippled and glittered beneath the splatters of rain and scattered clouds. She closed her eyes and opened her mind to the world around her. Within a moment she saw a sea of stars, each one an animal's life force and at once she did not feel so isolated. Kenna was not alone, trapped within this mountain of stone. Warmth spread through her at the realization, only to dim beneath the hard weathered faces of the armed men that stood before her open eyes. Rain drops clung to her lashes, she blinked them away, the feeling quickly snuffed out.

    Caleb dismounted once they passed through a smaller gate that led to the castle grounds. He passed the reins to a young man, with a firm pat on Zane's shoulder. "Be good." He murmured then took Kenna's rigid arm. He flashed her a wry grin, "You will be safe, don't worry. No one will dare lay a hand on you."
The smile had faded from his lips as he spoke, his eyes dark as his gaze drilled into hers. Kenna nodded, words lost somewhere deep within, and let him lead her into the cool dark recesses of the ancient structure.

    A short man in burgundy silk near the door waved them in, and announced grandly,
"Welcome to Dragon Stone Keep, Lord Conner of Pernak will see you in the great Hall." He turned sharply on his heel, then led them deeper into the keep. Caleb leaned over, his breath tickled the damp strands of her hair.
"The great hall is a customary place for a Lord to visit any guest."

    Kenna blinked in the gloom; uncertain what to say she flicked a glance at the knight beside her. His shoulders were loose, his gait easy within the confines of the corridor. She sighed to herself as she followed the portly man. Torches that contained a flameless light glowed against the stone walls; each bobbed in its iron domain. The mage lights kept the chamber aglow, like a tunnel leading to a cavern underground; a mountain indeed.

They came to a pair of massive oak doors stained a rich amber, that gleamed in the opaque light. Carved into the face in stark relief were elaborate, detailed dragons. Each scale a coarse ridge beneath one's fingertips, each claw sharp and smooth. They danced through a brass and bronze sky. Kenna was mesmerized by the craftsmanship before her. The butler stepped past her, a sneer twisting his thin lips as his eyes roved over her mud-splattered legs and arms, the thin drab fabric of her night shift. Kenna returned his look with a baleful stare.

Disdain for her clear, he straightened his silk tunic, grabbed the gold door ring suspended beneath a dragon's talon, and pushed the wooden beasts into the great hall.

Kenna inhaled sharply as she stepped back, her eyes dazzled by the brilliance of the room. The dark corridor had not prepared her for the splendor of the great hall and perhaps that had been the goal. It left its guests wide-eyed and breathless, the scene before them otherworldly. Kenna stepped into the white marble room, bare feet cold against the polished floors. She looked down to see her reflection in the tiles, and the shimmer of art around her. Kenna looked up, at a loss for words.

Dragons of every color flew across the walls, their scales only enhanced with precious jewels of a matching shade. Tendrils of gold had been laid into the marble in such a way, it gave structure to the wind that the great beasts glided on. Great ivory pillars lined a path through the grand hall, each monolith hoisted a bronze torch on either side of its four faces. A thick, red carpet sprawled out before them, like blood on snow, its rich texture enticed them toward the throne.

"It will be fine, Conner is a good man." Caleb encouraged, he took Kenna's hand and gave it a pulse of pressure. Her only response was a slight nod before she slipped her hand free.

Conner was a shadow framed by light, his dais rested before an unbridled fire that blazed behind him. His seat was hewn from stone so dark it was nearly black, a bold contrast to the purity of the chamber. Kenna touched her magic, then let it go as her eyes flashed with ice, only to dissipate to a sea blue after a single blink of copper lashes. The Lord would stay in shadow as he intended until they drew close.

Caleb stopped her with a small gesture, an open palm mere inches from her left hip. Kenna halted, her eyes locked on his mud-flecked fingers, then down to her feet. She curled her toes into the thick red velvet of the carpet. "Kenna," Caleb's voice pulled her eyes up. "This is Lord Conner of Pernak, and an old family friend. Conner, this is Kenna." His gaze shifted from the lord to her, his hand brushed hers as he spoke. "A true blessing, and my salvation personified." Heat rushed through Kenna's veins at his words and the light that flickered in his eyes. She looked away, at last to gaze at the lord of the mountain city.

He was a man in his late twenties, languid in a throne of molded stone. His hair was a pale gold, long and thick down to his broad shoulders. Honey eyes shimmered against dark lashes as he watched them approach, an alertness in them that belied his restful body. As they neared the lord, Conner stood from the throne and with two long strides grasped Caleb by the shoulders. He pulled the dark knight toward him in a firm embrace.

"Caleb! What happened to you? I hear you went after some magic pig?" His voice echoed off the marble walls. Caleb laughed as he pulled away.

"I don't know if I would call it that exactly, but yes." Caleb turned to Kenna and gestured or her to come forward. "This is the woman who saved my life, I would have died without her."

He clasped her hand, pulled her closer to the pair,

then slid his warm palm to the small of her back. The Lord of Pernak stepped forward, and took her hand to lay a stubbled kiss upon her earth-stained fingers. Kenna's breath hitched, and she quickly withdrew her hand. Before she could speak, he announced to the guards and guests in the room.

"Our friend and ally, Caleb Devoney of Tara, needs to rest and mend after his ventures in the dark woods. Please escort him to the healer's wing at once." He nodded at Kenna, then grasped Caleb's wrist in a warrior's farewell. "Try to be more careful," he turned to Kenna. "Enjoy the keep."

He nodded to his guests, only to disappear behind the throne and into the flames. The introduction had been brief and left Kenna with a sense of concern. As though he had felt her discomfort Caleb informed her,

"Conner is a military man, he isn't much for drawn-out affairs."

"All right then."

They walked down the crimson carpet, back through the amber doors, and into the gloom of the mage-lit hall. Returned to the grand halls entrance, they were welcomed by a woman in her late thirties with long brown hair held back by a thick, green ribbon. Soft eyes framed by small crow's feet squinted up at Caleb. With a small nod she curtsied, her crisp white gown crumpled around her ankles,

"Lord Devoney, please follow me at once so we may dress your wounds."

She turned sharply on her heel without a backward glance. Caleb winked a farewell to Kenna then followed the maid out of sight. Kenna felt at a loss in the strange castle, bereft of her companion.

Her eyes lingered on the dark hall they had once entered until she heard someone distinctly clear their throat behind her. Kenna whirled, muscles rigid to find herself face to face with another golden male. He resembled Lord Conner, and it quickly became clear to her that they were related.

He had the same sunshine hair, though his was cut shorter. He also was graced with topaz eyes and caramel lashes. The young man seemed to be in his early twenties, perhaps even the same age as Caleb.

Lost in thought over her sudden company she didn't catch the first words uttered from his upturned lips.
"I'm sorry, what did you say?"
"I said it is lovely to meet you."
"Oh yes, it's nice to meet you as well..."
"Randy," he filled in with a soft laugh. "I'm here to give you a tour of the estates, to make you feel at home while Caleb mends a little. Also, I will have the pleasure of introducing you to his aunt, Lady Ressa Devoney of Tara, the Silver Lady herself."
"The Silver Lady?"
"Yes, she is called that because all lady knights in the Devoney family wear only silver. A symbol of their virtue and honor as protectors of the realm."

Kenna stared at him while her mind devoured the information he had so readily provided.
"You are Lord Conner's younger brother." It was more of a statement than an inquiry.
"Indeed I am. Now please, let me escort you to your chamber."

He gestured her down the hall with a graceful flourish, toward a dim corridor decked with nimbuses of light. They walked in silence, their footsteps reverberated against the cold, hard stone. Kenna shivered, her toes ached; this was not the grass and soil she normally roamed.

She eyed Randy's supple leather boots enviously. The pair mounted a narrow stair that spiraled up into the keep. It was not until they had passed the final step that he asked, "Is there anything you would like to know about Pernak?"

"Yes… Why is the entire city made of stone? It's so cold here." She glanced at the walls, her skin pebbled beneath her thin shift.

"Ah yes, the fabled city of stone. Well it's a bit of a story really if you're interested?"

"I am." Kenna listened to the hollow echo of their tread as Randy gathered his thoughts.

"Well in that case…" he took a deep breath, "When Pernak was young, it was really more of a village being built against the base of the mountain. The original families that settled here were miners, as well as a few millers due to the proximity of the forest. For a time the village prospered and began to grow. Unfortunately, they were not the only ones well settled in the area—there were also dragons." He paused, honey eyes bright in the darkness.

Kenna stopped, brow furrowed as she looked up at the lord.

"I don't understand. I thought dragons were myths."

"Myths come from legend, and legends from truth." He resumed their upward journey; Kenna padded behind him, her bare feet quiet. "Haven't you ever seen a myth personified, dear Kenna? A myth you could believe?" His voice was rich, it floated down to her and set her mind ablaze.

A memory drifted through her thoughts. She had been so young when she saw it, one of the Durga. The giant white wolf, larger than a bear, near the pack's lake. Its golden eyes had locked on her, and her fragile child's heart threatened to explode beneath that gaze.

The Durga had watched her, its black lips glistened with water, large ears tilted forward as though it could hear her rapid pulse. Then the mighty wolf turned away, slipped back into the shadow of the heavy pines. She never saw the Durga again. She reached the final step and turned to her guide.

"Yes, I have seen myths made flesh and bone."

"Then you can understand the shock, the admiration, but mostly the terror of those who settled here." He nudged her elbow and led her down the left corridor. "The dragons didn't take kindly to the humans living in their territory, so they burnt it down. Now most people of sound mind would have left, but not the people of Pernak. They were outraged that their precious village had been destroyed and vowed revenge. So they rebuilt, all the while trying to fight the dragons off, but what a futile effort it was. Mere mortals cannot fight off armor-covered beasts with ancient wisdom, and bellies full of flame."

His face was thoughtful, perhaps he imagined the torment those long-ago people had suffered. Blackwood flashed in Kenna's mind. She shook away the pain fervently.

"Why not leave? Any wolf worth their teeth knows when a hunt isn't worth the meat." Randy's laughter filled the hall.

"It would seem wolves are smarter than men."

"I agree."

He glanced at her sidelong, her bitterness had not been lost on him. Concern marred his features, only to be tucked away beneath the hospitable mask of a noble host. "So the people gave up on fighting and focused on building. They crafted a home that the dragons could not destroy, at least not with the ease of before. They demolished all the plant life nearby, and constructed everything in stone. When the dragons passed over and let loose their punishing flame the stones would glow, pulsing with heat, but never burn. After a time it is said the dragons lost interest and a truce of some sort was worked out. In time the village of Pernak became a great city framed as a fortress of glittering stone, a man-made mountain that would bow to nothing. Not even immortal beasts. "

"When did this happen?"

"A few hundred years ago."

"Are there still dragons in the area?"

"No, they left these parts long ago." His voice was solemn, perhaps even a little wistful.

They turned down a final corridor to stop before a pale pinewood door. "Here is your room. I will call on you later." Randy bowed to her, his golden hair slid forward, a soft gilded screen around his face. Kenna took a step back, her face clouded with confusion. He straightened with an easy smile. "See you soon."

Kenna watched Randy disappear into the shadows of the hall, his golden crown flashed in and out of focus of the mage lights until he was consumed by shadow completely. Standing alone before her chamber she found herself troubled by the Lord's tale; the thought that great dragons had once lived here filled her with a sense of loss. *To touch such a mind.* She glanced over her shoulder while she turned the thick brass latch, then walked through the door.

The room was humble, but to Kenna it was a room she hardly dared touch. The stone walls were covered in a white wash to combat the mountainous interior. The false sense of a bright, airy chamber made her eyes ache after the shadows of the corridor. She stepped deeper into the room toward the overstuffed bed pressed against the wall. Kenna ran her fingers against the green velvet coverlet, with a tentative push she felt the feathers beneath. A sigh whispered through her, her gaze roved to the window in the far wall, and the forest beyond. Kenna examined the castle grounds from her perch, a swirl of emotions clanged through her chest. She turned sharply, rushed back to the feather bed, and flopped down. Kenna burrowed close to its downy surface as doubt gnawed her tender innards. She rolled, her face bathed in golden sunlight; dust motes glittered in the beam, to float and swirl before her silver-lined eyes. Kenna sat up, her fingers trembled while she swiped away her tears. *I'm sorry Jan, I just can't...*

Guilt filled her, smothered her broken heart. She looked around the room desperate to evade the pain within her. It was then that she saw a curtain suspended from the ceiling, its heavy velvet billowed softly towards her.

Kenna rose, her bare feet tapped softly on the stone floors and colorfully embroidered rugs; she buried her fingers in the weighted fabric, gingerly peeled it back to reveal a heavy copper tub resting before a small, crackling fire. A small window lay open to the afternoon air, each gust wafted thick steamy ribbons of air to her. "Holy Divya." Kenna whispered breathlessly. She dipped her fingers in the delightful steaming fluid, a ragged sigh rattled from her. A fraction of the pain within her drifted away with the ripples her touch created, her presence undulated across the gilded waters.

She slid the straps from her shoulders, tattered cream fabric slid down her frame, caressed her breasts, her belly, her thighs, to fall in a crumpled heap around her soil-smudged ankles. Her breasts tightened with the sensation. Kenna shook back her copper tresses, to tickle past her shoulders, down her spine. Shivers shuddered through her as she slipped into the warm water. She submerged and succumbed to the heavenly waters, each tight muscle grew limp while she melted away with the dirt.

A sharp knock was her only warning. Before she could lurch from the tub, a small woman burst into the room, a pale blue dress in hand. Kenna drew her knees to her chest, her sodden auburn hair covered her breasts. "Oh don't be so shy dear, I've seen it all a hundred times

over." The woman chided cheerfully. "Now get out of that tub and get over here so we can get you dressed." Kenna stared at the small woman; her dark hair piled high, held back by a starched, white linen headscarf. The maid firmly gripped Kenna's water-slick arm and pressed a heavy cloth into her hand, then turned her back.
"Well if you're that modest, put that on while I work on that hair of yours."

Kenna slipped from the tub, wrapped herself firmly in the warm cloth while she eyed the bold woman. The towel was rough against her skin, pleasantly abrasive; she rubbed herself down. The maid turned, saw her charge and clapped. Kenna jolted at the sound, she suppressed a snarl when the woman spoke.
"Now that you're out we can get to work. You've been soaking the day away girl and Lord Randal should not be kept waiting."
"I'm sorry." She wasn't, not in the slightest but it seemed this matron expected as much.

Her solemn head nod confirmed Kenna's guess when she rattled on.
"Oh don't feel so bad dear, he won't be upset, now come and sit down. By the way my name is Marion."
"Kenna."

She sat before Marion with a rigid spine, only to be soothed by the practiced ministrations of the older woman. Peaceful, this woman with her motherly touch. It awoke an ache within Kenna that she clamped down on ferociously. *Now is not the time.* She gazed at her reflection, blinked back the at the vacant stare that met hers; so cold and haggard that face had suddenly become. Kenna swallowed past the unbearable constriction in her throat, and willed the pain away. Copper lashes fluttered, then met the woman in the mirror once more; the frigid exterior had melted to leave behind a pale, tired woman with far away eyes and a soft mouth. She closed her eyes and leaned back into the firm fingers of Marion.

Her hair was dry; brushed and pinned back away from her face in a casual way that flattered the long, smooth planes of her neck. Marion stood her up, then pulled away her towel with a forceful tug. Kenna staggered, eyes wide as a thin white shift was pulled over her head. The under garment was quickly followed by the soft blue dress made of cotton. Her clothes tugged into a desirable position, Marion passed her a pair of supple leather shoes, more akin to lambskin slippers. They had been dyed a darker shade of azure to stand out from the gown. Marion stepped away to beam at Kenna.
"Now look how lovely ye' are dear. The Lords will be most pleased."

Kenna glanced into the tub and was startled by the reflection she saw in the tepid waters. Though her dress was simple to most ladies due to its plain cotton blend, Kenna was enamored with its smooth texture. There were no coarse areas, or irregular hemlines to affect the quality; it flowed as the sky on a clear summer day, pale and delicate. The gown had long fitted sleeves and a gentle sloping neckline to allow a modest view of her cream skin tinged with the faintest golden sheen stretched taut over full breasts. Her head tilted while she watched her copper tresses slide forward to flash against the soft blue. Kenna turned from the stranger before her.
"We should go."

She trailed Marion through the keep, and examined the world around her. The castle was not filled to the brim with courtiers, and their ladies that dripped with gold and gems; nor were the walls covered in treasures from generations past. The corridors of this castle were drab in comparison to the unknown glories of her mind. There were no windows, they walked through an unending darkness pierced briefly by the glow of mage lights encased in steel. The maid no longer spoke, the only accompaniment to their steps was the whisper of fabric against stone.

Kenna's eyes roved the castle's interior as they descended to the lower floors, mildly dismayed that the only anomalies were large paintings of some long-departed relative. Dust clung to the corners of the paintings, subtly coated them, cracked ancient canvases, in a silver sheen. They entered another sweet halo of false sunshine, where Kenna noticed the mage torches were held in place, not with simple steel as she had guessed, but dragon talons. She marveled at the silver cast scales, garishly displayed as decoration on their descent to the parlor.

Her mind flashed to the spectacular great hall, with its dragons that glittered, and an inferno of fire… It made her wonder at the outer halls, shrouded in darkness; their only adornment the delicate, silk-woven tapestries of spider webs, and severed dragon claws. Lost in thought she nearly trampled her guide.

"I should have been paying better attention," she said sheepishly, thankful for the dark halls that hide her crimson shame.

"Pay it no mind. Now go in there, they are waiting for you."

Before Kenna could ask who exactly waited for her, the elder woman was gone around another bend, swallowed whole by the velvet shadows. She drew a breath that quivered. *You can do this, you can handle them. You managed to make it through the woods with a wounded noble; no reason you can't survive a parlor room with a few of them.* She stepped through the door.

Her eyes landed first upon Randy. He was the only familiar face, if she could really call him that, in the decadent room. Caleb was still in the healers wing which meant she would face these strangers alone. An uncomfortable tightness bloomed in her chest at the thought, her breath evaporated in her lungs. As though he had sensed her inner turmoil, Randy strode across the room to meet her.

"You look wonderful and rested. Did you find the room to your liking?" he asked, his warm hands firm upon her shoulder when he steered her toward the small gathering.

Kenna scanned the room with the vigilance of a hunter; every entrance, every exit, any threat, she cataloged them all. Despite the predator that writhed within, the woman in her admired the beauty of the parlor. It had large windows that faced the inside of a walled garden full of delicate flowers. Small blooms of yellow, dusky pink, and the deepest violet that became black at its center, clung to the walls as they mingled with luscious ivy. Carefully manicured roses adorned with storm-strewn diamonds gave curve and shape to slender gravel paths. A graceful rose-quartz fountain bubbled merrily in the garden center, eager to draw one near. Kenna was shocked to see plant life, and found herself instantly drawn to it.

Unfortunately, she was not graced with a better look, instead she was turned towards the other two individuals in the room. They both seemed to be knights as far as she could tell, with one being a man with a large red dog. The creature looked up at Kenna's entrance, a familiar anchor in an unknown world.

She smiled fondly at the canine, while she impatiently awaited the time that she may greet him. The other knight was a woman, which Randy first led Kenna to. His sweet voice began the introductions.

"Kenna, this is Lady Ressa Devoney of Tara, Lady Knight of The Silver Star." Ressa bowed her head graciously at his words. Randy continued, "Lady Ressa, this is Kenna, your nephew's savior."

Kenna surveyed the woman before her. They were

around the same height, perhaps the noble woman was even shorter than Kenna, yet her stature was not diminished by it. She was beautiful, Kenna noticed, when she examined Ressa for any resemblances to Caleb. They looked nothing alike; where Caleb's hair was raven-wing black, hers was a pale blonde gently kissed by the sun. Her eyes were also different, a bright blue with a sharp gleam to them akin to precious gems. Kenna had no doubt that those bright eyes captured every detail of any space she entered. Her lips were thin and delicate, and at that current moment pulled into a soft smile over straight, white teeth. Kenna smiled in return and accepted a small hand that the Lady Knight extended.

"Our family is eternally grateful to you. My nephew is still a bit reckless at times."

"I'm just happy that we made it here."

Ressa chuckled in response, voice warm, gaze guarded. Kenna turned away, her hackles pricked her spine when her back faced the silver woman. Randy gestured toward the young man, who patiently waited, figure draped against the mantle. He was handsome, close in age to Caleb and Randy. Tall, with thick, wavy chestnut brown locks, cheerful gray eyes, and a long nose with a bit of a bend in it; as though it may have been broken once or twice. He shrugged away from the mantle to meet Kenna.

With a flourish he took her hand, slowly bowed over it, misty eyes locked on hers, all the more vivid against tawny skin, while his lips caressed her fingers. She watched the taut burgundy fabric of his tunic stretch across his muscled frame, her breath stilted as she managed not to pull her hand away. A sultry pause hung between them; he straightened, his hand still upon her own, and greeted her in a rich, melodic voice,

"My name is Aden, I hail from the southern coastal city of La Brock." His smile was slow and

smoldering. Her own lips twitched in response, fingers warm where he still held them.
"Hello Aden of La Broc."
"And where do you hail from, sweet savior?"
"The north."
"How mysterious," he rejoined, his right brow raised. Kenna slipped from his grasp, and those ravenous eyes.
"Who would this be?" She knelt to welcome the red canine in favor of his almond skinned master.
"That would be Dane."

Kenna could hear the fondness he had for the animal cool his sensual tone. She leaned forward and stroked the canine's long face and large, stand-up ears. He was a mix she had not seen before, but a lovely mix it was. Long legs reached their way to a deep chest and sloped shoulders. His face was what charmed her the most.

It was his beautiful amber eyes, so familiar and kind. With a final pat she stood to find that they all watched her, a bemused expression on their faces. Her checks grew hot under their scrutiny until she blurted out, "Why are you all staring at me like that?"
"We're sorry Kenna, where are our manners? It is just uncommon to see a lady get on her knees to pet a dog." Aden explained in a rich baritone.
"Well I am no lady."

They all sat, proceeded to pour drinks, and pass delicate morsels of little substance. The conversation wandered aimlessly for some time from one topic to the next. Kenna paid little attention, she did not know any of the people or places they spoke of. Instead she turned her attention to Dane while she stared towards the garden. The sun was ready to set, and bathed the garden with crimson light that faded into shadow.

Delicate ivy blooms shuddered in the darkness, before they closed velvet eyes to the evening sky. She saw without seeing, her mind adrift with memories of the woods and her pack. They were safe, deep in the woods, yet she missed the coarse, familiar touch of their minds within hers. Unfortunately they were out of range for her to communicate with, and deep pain shot through her in the absence of their mental touch.

Lost in her thoughts she did not hear her new companions say her name.

"Kenna?" Randy repeated, a perplexed expression on his face.

"I'm sorry, what were you saying?" she started, her mind scrambled to pick up and put order to the snippets of conversation that had flitted to her.

"We were asking if you would be joining us on the trip back to the capital?"

"I haven't decided. Will all of you be going?"

"Yes," Ressa responded. "A few guards shall join us but that is all. Once the healer clears my nephew we will leave, hopefully within a few days."

"Is that really safe to leave so soon?"

"Caleb is, along with the rest of us, a Knight of the Realm. We serve the King and with that duty we must stay close at hand unless told otherwise. As for Caleb's safety, he has already been healed by a green mage. He only stays in the mending wing to regain his strength." Aden's words purred through Kenna's mind, smooth and warm like velvet.

She had heard of green witches with this high level of skill before and was relieved to hear that Caleb had received such care. Her mind shifted back to the conversation.

"How many days will it take for you to get to the capital?"

"Well," Randy responded, his ankle crossed over his thigh, "If we set a nice pace without too many stops we can reach the capital by midday on the eleventh day. The road we will be taking is well cared for, it should be a simple journey."

His amber eyes watched her over the rim of his goblet as he took a sip of chilled wine.

"How much did Caleb tell you about me?" Kenna leaned towards the table, a furrow in her brow.

Glances were exchanged between the small group; the subtle shift and sigh of fabric shouted their discomfort to her delicate ears. Kenna sucked air between her teeth in a low hiss. "I need to know exactly what you know."

Ressa broke the tenuous silence, shoulders stiff as she turned to Kenna.

"Caleb didn't go into great detail, but he said you possessed some sort of beastial magic. That you can speak to animals and well..." she trailed off, thin brows knitted together. Kenna's knuckles were white around the stem of her glass, the wine a sour taste upon her tongue.

"And?" Kenna demanded, voice low.

"Well he said he swore he saw parts of your face change one night. I'm sure the lad was delirious with pain." Ressa concluded quickly.

Kenna leaned away from the table, the wooden chair a rigid form against her spine. *I can either tell them that Caleb was right, if only to a small extent... or I can keep the truth to myself and hope they don't press the issue. Though that may prove difficult since Caleb must have seen part of my change when I found him.* Her breath was slow, even, and deep as she observed the nobles before her. Caleb had been trustworthy and kind, and it was her hope that his friends and family would be of the same character. That leap of faith left her with a deep ache, the wings of her soul hesitant to unfurl.

"Caleb was not delirious. What he says is true, I can speak with animals with my thoughts."

Her hands trembled slightly against the linen table cloth, she eyed them with disdain. Kenna grabbed her wine goblet and drank deeply, her thoughts raced with every bittersweet drop that passed her lips and tongue. She glanced up though heavy lashes, ready for the hatred, the disgust, the fear. *Beast. Abomination. Forest trash...* The names followed her like her own shadow. Only when she was alone, hidden under the stars that glimmered without prejudice, without judgment, did she cast that shadow aside.

She learned at a young age to keep her mouth, and her heart, shut tight, lest the rest of her take the punishment. Secrets; secrets kept her safe.

Ressa spoke, her tone neutral while she gauged the truth in Kenna's words.
"Those are very rare, and interesting abilities you have. What of the shifting? Is there any way to prove them?" She watched Kenna with suddenly bright eyes.
"Well I won't change for you if that's what you're asking." *I'm no bloody show pony,* she thought vehemently.
"I didn't really expect that you would."
"You will meet my pack though. They will travel with me, if I decide to go with Caleb. I expect that won't be an issue?" A growl rumbled deep in Kenna's throat.

She had not missed the sharp glint in the knight's eyes at her reference to the woman's nephew.
"Your pack of what?" Aden asked, that easy grin danced in his eyes.
"My wolf pack. They are family to me and we always stay together."
"That will be most interesting, I look forward to it." Ressa replied before either of the young men could ask the questions that flew to their lips. Kenna stood and announced,
"I would like to see Caleb. Would you mind Aden, if I take Dane as my guide?"

Aden gulped down his wine, a blush appeared beneath his olive-gold complextion. Like the well-groomed

noble he was, he recovered quickly.
"Yes of course, Kenna. I'm sure he will know the way."
"Thank you."

Kenna's heart beat a staccato rhythm while she fled the parlor, Dane padded softly at her side. Once they were far enough from the chamber that she could no longer hear their voices she leaned against the wall. Dane whined when he looked up at her.
"It's alright love, it's just stressful for someone like me to talk to people like that." She spoke aloud to calm her nerves. As Jan says, 'saying what bothers you often helps it lose its hold." Her chin trembled at the recollection. "Best we are off then. Lead on."

The red hound slid into a languid trot that quickly drew her down a corridor she had yet to see. It bent back on itself, made them wind around till they were on the far side of the garden. Kenna glanced out the window and drew strength from the darkness. Dane sat beside a green door, a small gold sign inscribed with 'Healers Wing' hung from brass hooks. She pushed against the door, her body taut as she strained to hear past the thick wood; it swung open at her gentle touch. Kenna stepped into the healers hall, air heavy with the scent of medicinal herbs, tension seeped away and her shoulders lowered.

The air was cool and heavy with the scent of herbs, linen, and scented wax candles to keep away insects. An open window welcomed a cool breeze that trailed through the chamber, friendly plants swung lazily from the rafters overhead. Soft light filtered in through shuttered lamps beneath a thin haze of sage smoke. Her gaze roved the room, lungs tight while she searched for him. Three beds away on a narrow cot, Caleb slept.

Kenna waved her hand, motioned for Dane to stay

as she drew closer. He slept on his back, dark hair feathered against the cream pillow. It gleamed in the dim light, so lustrous that she could not stop herself. Kenna stroked the hair from his brow, smooth and peaceful while he dreamt. Caleb's breath deepened to a great sigh as he responded to her touch; Kenna's lips twitched, and she withdrew her touch.

She leaned closer to examine his now restful chest. The tip of the scar jutted past the edge of the blanket, and unwilling to disturb him she leaned away. As though he sensed her absence he shifted, dark brows furrowed, then smoothed when his thigh pressed against her hip. While he shifted, the sheet had slid away to reveal a long, silver scar that gleamed against his tan skin. She remembered the cold silver skin around his wound while it healed, and found that the scar was frigid beneath her fingertips.

Kenna pulled away, quietly began to rise, then smothered a gasp. A large, rough hand trapped her own. She turned and met his gaze, it smoldered and held her fast; Kenna felt herself burn beneath such heat.

"I'm sorry, I didn't mean to wake you. I just wanted to make sure you were well." His languid gaze rippled across her skin like sweet sunlight. Caleb released her hand, with a grunt he propped himself on his right elbow.

"It's all right little wolf, I'm doing just fine. You don't have to worry, the healers here are truly talented." He paused, a shadow over his face as he contemplated his next words. "I told Conner about Blackwood. He sent out riders to go to the village and help clear out any scum that stayed behind. He will send money to help them rebuild, or welcome them to the city. He will leave the choice to the people" While he spoke his thumb slid across her fingers in a slow circular rhythm; it relaxed and excited her all at once.

Her toes curled in her slippers, she breathed deeply through her nose. For a moment all Kenna could do was watch their overlapped hands, her pulse feathery and light. Slowly, she disentangled herself then stood.

"I met your aunt and a few of your friends. Actually, I just came from there." She took a small step beck, in desperate need of the physical space to steady her thoughts. He raised his brow at her comment.

"Oh? How did that go?" He sat up, swung his legs from the bed. She felt her eyes wander to the thin sliver of sheet stretched over muscular thighs, hard abdomen... she cleared her throat and looked away.

"Well enough I think. I told them that I am thinking of going to the capital with you."

"Really?" His grin lost its flirtatious edge, now it shined at her.

Kenna quickly turned her back as he began to stand. The soft whisper of fabric brought on a varied sensation of relief and disappointment.

"I am glad that you are coming, Kenna. It is going to be a wonderful experience."

"I hope so..." She didn't hear him step from his cot, only felt the heat that radiated off him in waves. He grabbed Kenna gently by the shoulders, turned her to face him. His gaze met hers, his voice a slow rumble in her ears,

"You don't have to stay but I do want you to know, I'm glad you came. Waking up to see you reminded me of our night in the woods."

Caleb leaned closer, his lips mere inches from her soft mouth. Her breath hitched, their lungs heavy with mingled air as he drew closer still. His hands slowly slid from her shoulders, his fingers massaged her softly, knowingly. Each firm pulse untangled every knot while they roved down her arms, down her waist. Caleb drew her close; her chest pressed to his, he cupped the back of her neck with a calloused hand, tilted her face up with a gentle pressure under her chin. Her eyes were closed, yet she could feel his gaze on her. Their lips so close her own trembled.

Then his were upon hers, a soft, slow, demanding kiss. His tongue grazed her full lower lip and she opened herself to him. Caleb explored her, took his time with her while he deepened the kiss. A small sigh escaped Kenna as she pressed closer, her thin gown scorched to cinders at his touch.

Without thought she reached up to wrap her arms around his neck, to lose herself in their embrace. She was breathless, her lips slightly parted as she gazed at him. Just as she began to remember where they were Caleb kissed her again, this time with hunger and desire. He drew out each moment with tender attention that ignited a heat deep within her. It was not till they heard a throat clear behind them that they pulled apart as if they had been doused with cold water. Kenna was shocked to see a matronly healer stood at the door with hand on hip, a dour look on her face.

Kenna quickly pulled away from the knight despite his sound of disappointment, his fingers trailed off her arm. She did not look back at Caleb.
"I have to leave, I'm sorry." She rushed from the chamber and nearly fell over Dane in her flight to the corridor. Kenna could already hear the healer lecture Caleb when she regained her feet and fled.

Back in the safety of her cozy room, Dane sprawled across her feather coverlet; her mind tumbled to the kiss that still set her lips ablaze. A whine interrupted her tangled thoughts, swiftly followed by a muffled thump from her bed. Dane watched her, his tail wagged merrily.
"You'll bat the feathers from my bed if you keep that up," she chided softly as she crossed the room to join him. She flopped on the bed beside the hound. "What do you think I should do?" For a moment the dog did not respond, then she felt his mind slide against her own.

"You should follow your instincts."
"Instincts," she muttered aloud. "I'm not sure where those went." Kenna curled up with the canine, fingers buried in his tawny red coat, and was soon lulled to sleep by the sound of his breath.

His fur against her cheek was so familiar it caused a pang to shoot through her; only to be lost to the shadows of dreams, filled with the whispers of eternal pines.

She later woke to a gentle tap on her door.
She sat up, the weight of the blanket she had rolled under in her sleep slithered from her chest with a sigh. Memory of where she was rushed in, her eyes adjusted to the pale light of dawn that shone through the leaded window pane. Dane leapt from the bed, Kenna's bare feet touched the cool floor and she shivered. She ran fingers through her snarled copper tresses, a distraction from the flutter of nerves that roiled within her stomach. Kenna opened the portal to find Aden in the hall.
"I was wondering if you intended to give me back my dog, or should I just get a new one?"
"I apologize, I fell asleep and didn't realize the time that had gone by."

Dane leaned against her, a heavy weight to brace

and steady her. She rubbed his ears before he returned to his master; Dane greeted him with a firm press of his muzzle into Aden's open palm.

The air against her now-vacant thigh felt frigid despite the warmth of summer, each current of air that swirled around her a reminder of her solitude.

"I actually came to tell you that you had missed dinner; and breakfast." His eyes, gray as storm clouds, darkened with concern.

"Did you want something sent up?"

"No, I plan on leaving the castle for the day to go to the woods."

Aden leaned against the door frame, a frown creased his face while he peered down at her.

"Is that a problem?" Kenna growled.

"You can't leave the city. They haven't opened the gates since Conner got the news about your village."

"It's not my village..." She muttered, then rushed to the window, disappointment blooming in breast as she gazed at the stone walls consuming the keep.

She pushed open the iron-bound glass, leaned out desperately, and longed to be free of the stone cage she found herself in. Kenna glared at the wall, her mouth hardened into a thin line. There were just too many emotions here, too many things to see, and hear. Her senses reeled, utterly overwhelmed under the constant onslaught. She needed the calm of the woods.

It was at this moment a thought formed in her mind, when a hand on her shoulder pulled her from its final form.

"Are you well Kenna?"

"I am. Please don't send any food up, I would like to be left alone."

"Yes, of course." His lips were tight, the corners of his wry mouth turned down at the corners. His tread was heavy, slow, when he at last turned toward the door and crossed the small chamber.

She heard his steps pause at the portal, yet she would not, could not turn to him.
"Thank you," she said quietly. A soft click as the door closed behind him; she waited but a moment before she rushed to the door herself. Kenna pressed an ear against the cool wood, she listened intently until she could no longer hear his steps against the flagstones. She stepped from the portal, kicked off her slippers while she simultaneously pulled the pins from her bed-mussed hair, then shook loose her tresses with animalistic pleasure.

She strode to the window, her knuckles white as she gripped the gray stone, and she leaned into the opening. Wind tugged at her hair, her gown, as she squinted against the gilded light of dawn. Her gaze roved across the castle grounds; no guards were in sight, and thanks to the high walls, the city was shrouded in a predawn dusk. She calmed her nerves and slipped off her gown, it rippled to her feet in a pool of blue.

Kenna delved deep within herself and felt the soft glow of her magic, how it eagerly awaited her touch. She pulled bronze threads from the source, wove them around her body in tendrils that pulsed with warmth, a heady caress from beneath her skin. What care should she have for walls when she could simply fly above them?

Raven wings spread wide to catch the thermals quickly, her wings snapped wide and swept her from a free dive. She loosened a rebellious call, while she beat her wings with vigor against the sky. Kenna swept the dawn-kissed clouds with her midnight feathers, her body light and joyous like the stars that had twinkled overhead; now hidden by the golden nimbus that rose at her back. Soon she soared over the city wall, the small rotation of guards like insects below her.

Currents swirled around her ebony form as she

angled herself toward the woods, she opened her mind to the shrouded realm beneath the pines. It took but a moment to locate the pack, their bright minds glowed in the darkness that dwelled between consciousness.

Kenna adjusted her flight, tilted her well-built form toward a lush section of the woods, her wings pumping faster while she gleefully flew to her family. It was hard for Kenna to be away from the pack, more than it was for someone to leave their family home. Especially her mother Finna, who had nursed her since the very first night alongside her own pups. The wolves were family, friends, and confidants. They were Kenna's whole world. With each wing beat that took her from the glass-bedecked mountain behind her, Kenna found herself. Found herself in the freedom, in the magic of the change, in the sanctuary of sagging pines. Thoughts of her pack brought other, complicated thoughts to mind. Her rhythmic flaps against the wind faltered, if only for a moment.

Tonight she would tell the pack that she planned to go to the capital with Caleb, and his companions. She had to go. The thought of another world fascinated her, and Pernak had awoken an insatiable sense of wanderlust. Blackwood was a thing of the past, which sent a pang through her heart that she forcefully set aside. *No more tears.*

Her feathered form dropped inside of an air pocket, she embraced the nothingness with a quick dive. Kenna's heart thundered while the world below rushed to meet her; eager to snap her feather neck. *Another time perhaps.* Kenna snapped open her wings, her joints groaned at the strain, then she banked to the right to catch a cross current. Perhaps they would rebuild the village, or they would leave to another. She wobbled on a draft of air. The raven clenched her talons; no matter how hard she tried to put the village behind her, she could not help but feel the same vicious ball of rage grow within her belly.

All the jeers and slurs that had been hurled her way, despite the fact that she had only been a child. How the boys, and even the men had whispered behind her back; that she laid with wolves and other beasts while she lived in the forest. The scorn that the girls had shown her no matter how friendly her advances were. A cry escaped Kenna, she plunged through the lavender and rose sky, while the wind roared around her. *The Capital will be better. It has to be*

She cast about in a lazy circle, mind turned inward to the magic that tethered her to the pack. Above the tree line she caught sight of a small glade, the same glad that had rippled through her mind from the wolves' eyes. In an instant she folded her wings, and dropped from the sky like a meteorite. Wind streamed past her in a blur, her body taut with strain. The ground rushed toward her, Kenna banked, her dive evening out into a tight spiral that soared towards the glade's center. A foot above the ground she slipped her wings, shifted back into her human body to land on the soft grass. It tickled the soles of her feet when she padded to the trees. Kenna rolled her shoulders to relax the joints, her muscles quivered from the rigorous flight.

Under the shade she rested her naked frame in the dew-coated grass, then raised her face to the pale-blue sky. A howl, deep and rich, rang from her full lips. Long and slow the melody floated through the forest, an echo of her call returned to her. A mass of many voices; her pack would come.

Satisfied, Kenna stretched languidly in the morning light, her pale body gleamed against the darkness of the trees. For a moment Kenna kept her eyes closed, she listened to the sound of the forest, the cool air wafting over her. She was not left alone long; she heard her pack rush through the shadows toward their human member. In mere moments she was surrounded by the massive mountain wolves.

Everything was a blur of fur and voices. She could feel each of their coarse bodies rubbed against her bare form, their minds a ripple of color and sound within her own. Kenna knelt in the grass, her eyes traced with silver while she watched the pack around her. Contentment, warm and sweet settled over her. She leaned against her mother while she asked after her family.

"How are all of you? I've missed you! I can't believe the pups have made such a journey already." Kenna laughed aloud and stroked Calla's satin ears.

The wolf, somewhere between a pup and full grown, thumped her tail heartily against the grass.

"When will you return with us to the forest?" Baylor asked.

"Well..." Kenna twisted a blade of grass, held it reverently, then tore it apart and shifted from thought to vocal communication. "I agreed to go with Caleb to the Capital, and I want you all to come with me." More than one wolf raised their hackles, fur bristled as they looked between human and alpha. Her words hung heavily in the mist. "I've told them all about you, and I was assured that you all would be welcomed. Please... come with me."

Kenna's stomach twisted while she awaited his response. Throv watched her intently. A deep growl rumbled faintly in his chest, while the great wolf thought over her proposition. It was Finna who spoke first.

"Is this really what you want?" Her golden eyes darkened to molten amber with concern.

"It is."

The Luna Wolf looked at her mate. *"Throv."* He laid his ears back. *"Throv,"* Finna continued, *"she is not a pup anymore, but she is still our daughter. We should go with her."*

"What of our territories?" he snapped, fangs glinted in the watery morning light.

"We can reestablish them once we return." She stood before him and slid her delicate ivory muzzle under his heavy jaws. It was an intimate gesture between mates, and the pack looked away.

Kenna gnawed her bottom lip, her eyes locked on the grass between her toes. Her father's opinion affected her deeply no matter how hard she tried to move past the puppy notion of parental approval. Throv embodied so many of the things that she wanted to be; strong, steady, confidence that could not be swayed by fear or self-doubt. All qualities she admired and struggled to attain; yet she worked hard to keep those doubts from others.

She chose instead to lean into her fear and snarl her way past it. At last the alpha spoke.

"We will travel with you as long as the pack stays safe." A sigh rushed from her lungs at the words, she looked up into tawny eyes. They glowed ominously, devoured each ray of light that slipped through the branches as his gaze bored into hers. *"If this journey should bring any harm to the pack we shall leave, with or without you my daughter."* He did not look at her, only turned into the mist. The pack vanished like wraiths with him, Leara waited at the edge.

A shiver ran through the length of the silver tipped-white wolf. Kenna flashed her a smile that trembled.
"Go on, I will see you soon." She whispered down the bond, then broke the connection before Leara could respond. A whine slipped from the young she-wolf before she disappeared beneath the pines.

Kenna sat alone in the grass and shivered despite the warmth of her skin. She felt as though she hovered on the brink of an abyss; with one wrong step she would lose her pack forever, and become a Sigma. A lone wolf; a living nightmare. She tilted her face to the sky and sucked in a shaky breath.
But I want them both.

Kenna swooped through her window in a blur of black feathers, shifted in mid-air and tumbled across her bed in a sweat-streaked heap. She heaved with arms that trembled, and flopped on to her back; she stared at the ceiling, her emotions nauseated her in their endless motion. Kenna's head tilted to her right, eyes listless while she ran pale fingers through tangled hair.

Her gaze caught on the soft gilt of the tub; how it glared at her balefully, challenged her, taunted her. Yet it was as hollow as she felt. Full lips peeled back in a feral snarl; Kenna turned her back on the copper monster and the life it promised. The hollow tread of steps roused her from her thoughts; she sat up with a start, her soft breasts peaked against the cool breeze that drifted through the window. She clamped her thighs together while she cast about the room. Her gown laid in a crumpled heap on the floor; Kenna lurched for the garment, seams popped in her ears as she yanked the thin fabric overhead. Her chamber door opened while she jammed her arm through the final sleeve.

Her pulse thundered against her breastbone, she stepped around her chamber door to find Randy within the oak frame. His expression was sheepish as he observed her mussed hair, rumpled gown, wild eyes…

"Sorry to come by, I know it's early but I thought I would check on you. The guard mentioned some strange animal behavior… I thought it may have been you. Are you well?"

Her eyes widened a fraction when she realized her mistake. *I forgot to check for a guard on my way in!* She mentally kicked herself; the last thing I needed is some guard babbling to the town that I'm a shape-shifting demon. She'd had her fill of that nonsense before.
"Yes, I'm fine. I just needed to see my family."
The mere thought of them brought back Throv's foreboding words. She bit the inside of her cheek, eyes cast down.
"Do you want to talk about it?"
"What?"
"You seem upset is all. I'm guessing this is all a little much for you at the moment."
Kenna laughed weakly,
"It is a bit hard to get used to."

Randy walked across the room to sit cross legged by a fire that the maid had started, then looked at her expectantly. Kenna laughed at the way he had so clearly made himself less of a threat. She closed the door, walked to her bed and sat down; her tired frame slowly sank into the feather-stuffed covers. They stared at each other, one wild, one tame; both unsure who should speak first. Randy broke the silence.
"You have dirt on your face."

Kenna licked her palm, eyes slanted while she rubbed her cheek vigorously. "Thanks," she mumbled. Randy nodded, obviously making a point to ignore her strange habits.
"So you went for a fly?" he asked, his tone low and casual while he stoked the embers.
"Yes, I needed to see my family, and Aden said the gates were closed."

Randy dropped a fresh log onto the coals. "How did

it go?" Flames licked the edge of the wood provocatively.
"I told them to come with me to the capital."
"And?"
"My father, Throv, well he is the alpha. The Lord of the pack in human terms. He makes all the decisions, though my mother Finna has a great deal of say so… My uncle Baylor puts his thoughts in as well." Kenna rambled, her voice dwindled to a whisper, then silence.
"So what did your father say?" Randy faced her once more.
"He said that they would go with us, but if anything went wrong they would leave."
"Is that really so bad?"
"You don't understand. If they leave it means they are leaving as a pack, and if I don't go with them I am no longer Pack." Her voice was low as she contemplated the nightmare of being truly alone.

    Randy was silent, his expression clouded, thoughtful, while he turned over her words. In the silence that lingered, Kenna agonized over the ultimatum her father had presented. They were the only family she had left.
"I can see how that could be a hard choice for you. It would be like my family exiling me?"
"Yes, exactly like that. I want to be with my
family, but I also want to see more. Blackwood was small; the people there only thought of what was right in front of them, and that made them happy I suppose. It never bothered me to stay with the pack, Jan was the only human I cared for." She paused, gathered her thoughts. "Seeing Pernak was like seeing another world, with art, fancy houses, and strange people. It's all so new and honestly a bit stifling at times, but mostly exciting. I don't want to spend my life in Blackwood; never knowing what the world has to offer. I just don't know where that leaves me when it comes to my family." Loathsome tears had spilled down her cheeks at her words, streaks of ivory skin laced the dirt

on her face.

Droplets clung to her lashes, and framed her world in gold while she looked at the knight beside the fire. Randy stood and sat beside her on the edge of the bed, his gaze never left hers while he masterfully produced a small handkerchief. He passed her the small square of cloth, his knee lightly pressed against hers.

"The best I can do is help provide you and your family with safe passage." His response disappointed her, and she could see that register with him; his brow furrowed, his lips tight, the corners tucked down in a reserved frown. "I don't know the ways of a wolf," Randy continued, "but I can say that I will help you and your family stay safe so they will have no reason to leave you behind. You shouldn't feel guilty about wanting to see the world Kenna, it's a wonderful place. I hope your family will feel the same."

He patted her shoulder gently in farewell, then left her alone in her room, the door clicked shut behind him. Kenna stared at the semi-permanent wall of oak, her palms harshly scored her cheeks. *I could have sworn I said no more tears. Humans make me soft.*

In the woods there was never a reason to cry, life was simple, it made sense; but not here. Here, there was too much emotion, and yet… She felt lighter and less afraid after her talk with Randy. To have someone to listen and understand was an experience she had never encountered with someone her own age. *Perhaps this is what it's like to have a friend…*

The maid had filled the belly of her copper beast later that morning, and informed Kenna while she bathed that their party would leave Pernak early. They would be on the road to the capital by mid-day. Kenna thought excitedly while she adjusted her new garment. She surveyed her reflection, jaw clenched. Her hair was braided from brow to tip; she now exposed a delicate, perfumed neck that shone like fresh cream above her evergreen gown. The dress she now wore was a modified riding habit that fell somewhere between dress and tunic.

    She wore a long sleeved white shift beneath it all, her arms clad in fitted sleeves that tapered to her wrist. Small white cuffs, which she feared would become horribly filthy on the road, accentuated her every gesture; a soft white gleam at her peripherals. The gown went down to her knees, with long slits on either side which exposed light-tan riding breeches. Her calves were clad in dark-brown boots that loosened slightly just below the knee, and also added a polished look to the attire that ensconced her in heat. *Does it really matter what I wear while I ride?* Her finger tips grazed a rigid seam of embroidered ivy. *Frivolous.*

    She stepped away from the mirror and strode to the window. Kenna leaned into the thick breeze, while she cast her mind out like a net in search of the pack. She wasn't really sure that she would find them so close to the city, but she missed the closeness between their minds. To her dismay she only felt the animals that dwelled within the city, a heaviness sank through her.

    She began to pull back her magic and felt the pack, a faint light that glimmered at the edge of her mind. She honed in on the vibrant energy, called them closer, a smile played across her face while their light bloomed brighter. She could hear the rumble of their paws, the rasp of breath between fangs, through the heady connection of their bond. A wildness thrummed with in her, eager as it unfurled from its copper-gilded center.

    Her concentration was broken by a sharp knock on her chamber door. Kenna growled, she turned icy blue eyes

toward the door and snapped,
"Yes, come in." The last syllable hardly left her lips when her door swung open to reveal a sarcastic dark knight.

Caleb leaned against the frame, a crooked grin slowly curved his sinfully full lips. For a moment Kenna watched him, impressed by his transformation. He wore brown britches so rich in color they were nearly black, and firmly tucked into supple leather boots.

A cream tunic stretched across broad shoulders in a feeble attempt to mask the powerful muscles beneath. The front of his tunic lay open, thin leather cords trailed down his chest, and subtly drew attention to the soft silver scar; a scar she knew would be cool beneath her fingertips. His face had been freshly shaven, she could still smell the soap on his skin as though he was right beside her.

Kenna was enthralled with his scent, yet remained rooted to the flagstones. Caleb's raven black locks were brushed away from his face, revealing a high brow above lustrous green eyes, no longer ringed with shadow.

He stepped into her room; languid as a hunter, he stood before her. His head bowed as he gazed at her. Kenna's eyes lingered over his lips, hungered to taste him despite herself, ready for the pleasure his touch could provide. No greeting passed between them; the air was so taut she hardly dared breathe for fear it would tear her asunder.

Caleb slowly raised his hand to her face, calloused fingers rough, he held Kenna close with fragile restraint. His thumb traced lines back and forth across her cheek bone, a rhythmic sensation that lulled her deeper into his hold. Caleb bowed his head further, their lips so close she could feel a heat thrum within her. Her breath hitched when his lips met hers; fire laced her veins, desire seared her core. His tongue flicked her lips, soft, gentle in his eagerness to explore her.

Something in her shuddered, and at the last moment Kenna pulled away. Flustered, she stepped back, one, two steps while adjusting the front of her riding habit. The heat between them cooled to dull embers. She turned her back on the room, on him, and leaned against the window frame, quietly pressing her flushed cheek against the leaded glass. Kenna heard him draw close, the whisper of cloth, the sigh of her name on his lips; she did not respond, only kept her eyes locked on the horizon.

"What's wrong?" He leaned against gray stone opposite her.

She glanced at Caleb for a moment, the way the sunlight softly caressed his shoulders as he turned his back to the world beyond.

"I just don't know if I'm ready for this," she answered quietly. He only watched her, his brow creased, his firm hand twitched then fell still against his arm. Kenna took a deep breath then said,

"It's just so much that is happening so fast, and I don't mean you, it's everything. The village, here, now the capital." The words were bitter somehow. Caleb's eyes softened as he tucked a stray strand behind her ear.

"Change can be challenging, but it's worth it."

"How can you be so sure? What if I go there and it's a disaster."

"It could easily go that way, yet it could easily be the best experience that you'll have. You've seen so little of the world Kenna, don't let yourself become afraid." He turned, his arm a light pressure against her shoulder.

A cobblestone courtyard lay wide and clear before then, speckled at its edge with stone buildings, cradled by the wall. In the distance the horizon was smudged in dark green, rich brown, and wisps of blue-tinted gray. An avenue to another world— if she were brave enough to take it. In that silence that nestled between them she found an unexpected sense of companionship. She glanced sidelong at Caleb, watched the way he viewed the world with an openness she'd never had the courage to give. Perhaps one day she could. A small sigh escaped her while Kenna leaned her head against Caleb's shoulder, and took comfort in his calm.

Kenna watched while the small company finished their final arrangements to depart. Caleb talked with his aunt, both heads bowed, deep in conversation. Caleb leaned against his charger, both horse and master were equally matched; rich like midnight, powerful figures, so beautiful in their darkness. His hand stroked fur black as ink that gleamed in the midmorning light, intent on his aunt's words. Kenna shifted her gaze towards Lady Ressa; she saw that she was paired with an impressive mount of her own. The gelding by her side was purest white, each muscle rippled under velvet skin while he shifted behind his rider. *It seemed nobles liked to match.* Kenna shrugged off a spear of jealousy.

She leaned her weight front one foot to the other, gravel crunched beneath her heel, and gave sound to her impatience.

"His name is Frost."

"Excuse me?" Kenna was startled to see Randy by her side.

"Lady Ressa's charger, his name is Frost," he explained with a grin. "I saw you admiring him, but enough of that. I have someone for you to meet."

"Who?" she asked suspiciously.

"Come along and I'll show you." Without delay he walked across the courtyard, Kenna quickly followed. "All right, turn around,"

Kenna frowned, spine rigid, yet she complied and turned her back on the golden lord.

She stood there, a sense of foolishness crept over while the seconds ticked by, but she waited. At last the moment came. "Okay, take a look." His voice called to her enthusiastically. She faced him and shock rippled through her; she beheld Randy beside a small bay gelding, with black socks and a short, stiff ebony mane. A smile tucked the corners of her mouth while she looked the animal over, but did not dare to put to words what she thought Randy implied.

"Well come on, come and meet him. His name is Shren, he is going to give you a ride to the capital." Shren tossed his head at the sound of his name, a soft nicker followed the action when he eyed the human that held him.

Kenna stepped closer to the horse and slowly reached out a hand that trembled. For a moment she thought that he may refuse her, but his umber eyes were kind when he placed a delicate black muzzle into her palm. She stroked his wide cheek and opened her mind to the horse. While Kenna looked him over she realized he was not nearly as tall as Zane, which gave her some comfort since she had never been taught to ride. If she did fall from Shren it was at least much closer to the ground. Kenna glanced at the dark leather saddle, her brows knit together. "I can give you a lift up if you like."

Kenna smiled shyly. In her excitement over her new companion, she had forgotten that he was still present. "Thank you."

Randy stepped around her to stand beside the horse, then bent forward and clasped his hands, palms open to form a step with his woven fingers.

"Go on, step up." Doubtful, Kenna put a hand on the Shren's withers, then lifted her right foot into Randy's palms. "Not that one, give me your left. You swing over with your other."

Heat prickled her neck as she quickly gave him the

appropriate foot. Once she had placed her boot firmly in his grasp he boosted her up with surprising force. She nearly slipped over the other side, belly strapped roughly against leather, before she caught her bearings against the saddle horn. She grasped it tightly and glared down at the knight.
"You said you would lift me, not toss me." Kenna growled.
"Sorry about that." He laughed, his cheeks bright while he rubbed the back of his neck. "Good thing Caleb didn't see, he'd knock me right over. Now here, take the reins, Shren will do the rest. All you have to do is try not to fall off." He tossed the strips of leather up to Kenna and walked away.

She leaned forward and rubbed the horse's neck, a plea sang down the newly forged bond,
"Please be gentle with me, I really don't want to fall in front of all these people." The gelding's ears flicked when her mind met his.

Lady Ressa's voice rang clear as she announced their departure. Kenna's knuckles turned white, bones strained against translucent skin while she gripped the reins. This was it, this was her moment. She reached out with her mind and contacted the pack, she let them know that they were at last on the move. Kenna thought back to earlier that morning.

Caleb still leaned against her window, expression thoughtful while he gazed at the wilderness beyond the wall. Kenna sat on her bed, anxious for his words.
"What is it?" She had longed to join him against the stone, to lean into his warm, solid frame; she stayed seated.
"I only wonder how this journey will go with your pack."
"They agreed to come, and Randy said they will not be harmed."

A silent question lingered in the silence left by unsaid words.
"Of course," he turned to her, "I only wonder how the men will handle it. Perhaps—"

"I will not leave them behind."

Her fingers clenched into fists around the fine velvet covers, her hackles tickled their way down her spine. Caleb crossed the space between them, and stooped to one knee. His touch was light as he disentangled her fingers from the blanket.

"I wasn't asking that of you, I never would. I was only wondering if it may be best that they follow us in the trees. It may be easier on all of us."

Kenna watched him, examined every inch of his open, earnest face; the tension in her eased.

"Yes, that may be better. I will let them know to stay in the woods, and not be seen until
the time is right."

He squeezed her hand, gratitude in his evergreen eyes, in that broad smile.
"Thank you."
He pressed a chaste kiss to her temple, then stood and left the room.

Kenna pushed down her concerns, she had to remain focused. She turned her attention to the string of riders that trailed ahead of her; it had also been decided that she would bring up the rear, a new and entirely distasteful change in her travel style.

The party moved with painstakingly slow steps, an overgrown beast lazy to move, and in that languid gate Kenna grew familiar with the faces of her would-be companions. The group consisted of five guards, three young knights, Lady Ressa and lastly Kenna herself. Definitely the odd man out. She released a hitched sigh.

Shren pulled her from her thoughts when he leaped into a fast trot, black-tipped ears pinned to his stiff mane. *Don't like the back either, can't say I blame you.* A rough chuckle barked from her while she sweated with the effort to stay seated.

Kenna leaned forward to stroke the agitated geldings neck while he struggled to make his way farther up the line, his neck already warm, the deepest layer moist. She straightened in her seat and swiped her brow with those puffed white sleeves. *I knew this outfit would make me hot.*

Chapter Three: Tension

She was sore all over, and quite positive that her bum would never gain back feeling. Kenna straightened legs that were determined to stay bowed, she glared at the row of horses that grazed on grass innocently, as though they knew nothing of the abuse they had given her.

"That bad huh?" Caleb's voice was cheerful despite the glowering expression he desperately tried to keep in place.

"Yes!" Kenna snapped. "I'd much rather walk."

"You can, but I'm sure your feet will fall off before we're halfway there." Caleb responded drolly. Kenna flashed him a glare that scorched.

"Come now woman, don't look at me like that! Let's change the subject, when will your pack be here?" The corner of his lips twitched as he fought his own gleeful smirk, the conversation tactlessly changed to a slightly less tender direction.

"They have been here the whole time, they are just waiting to be seen." Kenna turned a softer gaze toward the trees, and indulged in the silence between them.

A nearby guard busied himself with the fire, sparks and tendrils of pale smoke curled in the evening breeze, then scattered away in the golden glow. Sparks took hold of the wood and filled the air; the subtle tension in the small band seeped away, tense shoulders loosened when that age-old scent of humanity wafted through the camp. It invoked a sense of safety, of civilization, that soothed the tension of the woods; so full of hungry mouths, sharp claws, and savage fangs. Kenna glanced around the camp, aquamarine eyes thoughtful in the dim glow. In that calm, Caleb's voice drifted to her.

"Call them over."

"Now?" she asked incredulously, fingers clenched.

"Yes, why not?"

"I really don't think they are ready for it."

She waved an ivory hand, not at the woods, but the humans that clustered at its edge. A weighted silence filled the void between the pair, they watched the small fire consume its evening meal of dry oak and pine, the way it grew with each morsel.

"Tell them to come, I'll tell Ressa to keep everyone calm."

Kenna watched as the knight strode away into the shadows that stretched across the camp. His stride long and smooth, no hint of a long ride hampered his muscles. She growled softly and rubbed her palms into her own tender thighs, undeniably jealous of his comfort.

Kenna inhaled deeply, her eyes unfocused as she gazed vaguely at the horizon. A lazy sun settled on the edge of the world, a world to which she closed copper lashes in a cascade of rainbows followed by darkness. Kenna's gaze turned inward, toward the reservoir of magic that glowed like embers at her center. She spun slender strands from the pool, wove them into a net, and cast it out towards the woods that hid her lupine family.

Within a breath she felt the wolves, their souls shined bright in her mind's eye. Without words she pulled them close, passed them images of the camp down their bond, of the men that dwelled there. Soon the shadows took form; voice by voice the camp fell quiet, each human felt the eyes of hunters upon their backs. Whispers passed between the small company, and though they had been warned to stay calm many a hand grasped their swords.

Most men thought themselves the apex predator, a confidence man-kind claimed with the knowledge of tools, manipulation of flame and earth, and the ever present flow of technology.

Nonetheless, when man-kind trod the woven paths deep in the woods, with only the moon as witness, even the bravest fell prey to fangs that flashed in the starlight. Kenna watched them, her hackles rose at the sight of gloves on steel. It was Caleb's voice that soothed her.
"Tell them to come out," he whispered.

She swallowed past a dry throat and encouraged the pack to come forward. First to leave the trees was her father, Throv. The powerful wolf held his head high, eyes rebellious in the firelight, hackles raised in a majestic mane. Men murmured in astonishment at his sheer size, and Kenna could not help the satisfied smile that curved her lips. Finna joined her mate, her snow-white fleece glowed against the fires that gave it a golden kiss. It was Ressa who sighed in admiration as she laid eyes on the wolf, one silvered alpha that admired the other.

The alphas stood, a lethal reminder of a world that lived beyond the light of human fire and walls. Their presence invoked awe and fear in the hearts of every human in the camp, all but one. Kenna watched with pride while the remainder of the pack followed the alpha and Luna wolf to the edge of the wood. Wolves stalked from between the trees, sable, black, and silver fur stark against the greenery. Heads low, ears pinned, they flashed fangs tipped with firelight in defiance.

No one dared breathe, the air so taut one could have reached out and strummed it like the finely woven strings of an instrument. They stood face to face, man and wolf, in the semidarkness of dusk. Kenna watched it all unfold, her body tense to the point it ached, yet she waited. Neither man nor beast was willing to make the first move, until the stillness at last shattered. Caleb strode from his place beside Kenna and made a straight line toward the alpha pair. Kenna nearly jumped out of her skin at the sight of Caleb while he walked so brazenly toward her pack. She feared how the wolves would respond.

Her eyes shifted from the pack to Throv; a deep growl rumbled from his chest, black lips pulled back to reveal fangs that dripped with saliva. She dared not tear her eyes from the scene, even when she heard the dreadful hiss of steel. Sweat slid down her sides with silken fingers that made her quiver despite the warmth of the night. Caleb stopped his reckless walk two steps from the wolf, a distance Kenna knew he could cover in one effortless leap. As though they were of one mind, the alpha's muscles tensed in preparation to strike just as Caleb dropped to his knees. Muffled cries of horror greeted his gesture of submission, then fell deathly quiet when he bared his throat.

Throv paused, his snarl faded from in his throat and the panes of his face smoothed. He looked critically at the man that knelt in the dust before him, and hair by hair the wolf's mane relaxed. A begrudging curiosity overtook the wolf, his amber eyes alight with intrigue. There would be little Caleb could do to stop him if he tried to rip out the man's throat; every being with breath in the camp knew this, and shuddered when the great wolf stalked closer. Monstrous jaws parted with power enough to shatter bone, and cradled Caleb's throat. Caleb closed his eyes when pressure dimpled the delicate skin of his jugular. Just as gently as he had taken the man's life into his grip, the alpha let him go.

Kenna lost her breath explosively, the tension drained from her body so suddenly that she felt she would collapse. Caleb slowly rose to his feet, his face pale and dewed with sweat, he smiled at the camp. She rushed toward him, soreness forgotten, and gripped his arm roughly.

"What were you thinking?" Kenna's voice rose, panicked even though the danger was gone.

"I took a leap of faith, I figured your father wouldn't kill me outright."

"That was a stupid thing to do." Though she was angry that he had taken such a risk, she could not ignore the flicker of approval that flashed through her. Kenna shook her head, then looked at her pack with relief; her family would stay with her.

She turned toward the humans she traveled with, many still stood in shock, and announced,

"I would like to introduce you to my family." There was no answer. Nervously she looked to Caleb and found a smile already upon his face, kindness in his eyes. She cleared her throat while her pulse pounded in her ears. "This is the pack alpha Throv, and his mate Finna." She gestured to the regal pair. "His second in command, Baylor." The sable wolf growled in affirmation. "The pups, Varg, Leara, and Cana. Then there is the heart of the pack, Veyel." The omega preened at her words.

It was Lady Ressa that stepped forward first. For a

long moment the woman said nothing, only stared at the wolves. Kenna worried that some sort of dispute would ensue if she did not say something, anything, soon. The way she was staring was seen as a threat in the lupine world, which had not been lost on the pack as the high-ranked members raised their hackles in response to her gaze.

"I am honored to welcome you to our camp as our guests. I assure you that you will be respected among our humble company." Her voice was light as though she spoke to a courtier at a gala, not a pack of forest wolves. Some of the guards looked at one another, furtive glances passed between them in question.

Ressa felt their doubt behind her, she turned to face the camp, blue eyes blazed in the fire light.

"Is there something confusing about my invitation to you captain? Do I need to explain it further to your men?" her tone, laced heavily with honey, deepened the sense of danger; a sweetness nestled deep within a trap.

The captain was not immune to this, and cautiously answered.

"I'm sorry my Lady, but they are wolves. Why do you speak to them as you would a man when they are beasts?" A surge of anger scalded Kenna at his words, yet before she could respond, Ressa answered,

"Are we not all beasts Captain?" her voice dripped candied venom.

"I suppose you could say that." His answer was slow.

"In that case should I thrash you like a disobedient dog?"

"My lady?" his eyes widened.

"I didn't think so."

She looked at each and every man with eyes like crystal, she continued. "These wolves are my guests, and if I see a single one of you even think of threatening them... Well, you will have worse than a wolf to deal with." Ressa turned from the camp then strode to Kenna and Caleb. "Make your family comfortable, Kenna. If any problems should arrive I'm sure my nephew can handle them for you. Good evening."

She turned toward her tent, then paused; the glacial frost thawed from her beautiful face, only long enough to slip Kenna a small wink, the corner of her firm mouth tipped up, before she walked away. Kenna watched Caleb's aunt leave, her auburn brows knit together. Beside her Caleb laughed softly.
"She isn't that bad, she was just making a point."
"She is alpha here then?"
"Yes, exactly. That was just her showing a little fang if you will."
I can respect that. She was pulled from her thoughts by Aden and Randy, both grinned from ear to ear.
"What a show!" Aden exclaimed, his broad hand clapped Caleb on the shoulder.
"I thought you were done for, for good this time." Randy added, laughter hid the worry in his stiff shoulders.
"If it wasn't the boar it would be something else no doubt." Aden quipped. The three men laughed, while Kenna watched them, her lips pressed into a firm line against the mirth that threatened to bubble over. Kenna shook her head and she walked away. *A bunch of pups.*

She turned towards the woods, her steps quick, the encampment at her back, and dropped to her knees among the pack. Surrounded by coarse fur and tongues that lolled with merriment, she opened herself and touched their minds collectively.

When the wolves calmed she was overwhelmed by the silence, only punctured by the crackle of campfires. She looked up slowly, body taut, and found every pair of eyes on her and the wolves. A blend of expressions, adorned their faces; fear, confusion, awe, amusement… disgust.

She dared not look at her human companions, memories of Blackwood flitted through her mind, and she shoved them away. She rose to her feet, shook the dust and hair from her riding habit.

Silence settled between the denizens of the camp, unable to cross the chasm their difference in species had caused. Kenna was the only bridge between beast and man, a task she wasn't sure she was entirely capable of. The tension was broken mercifully by Caleb, he walked forward to extend a hand to the pups; Kenna frowned, her embarrassment made her words sharp.
"They aren't dogs Caleb."
"I know that." he responded, and shot her a slight frown. "But I have to introduce myself somehow."

They settled back and watched to see how the young wolves would respond to the noble. Varg, much like his father, had no trust for any human besides his sister. His smooth black face wrinkled savagely when he snarled at the young man before him, fangs white like fresh bone.
I'm done with this. Kenna thought as she strode forward, exhausted past words. She paused when Leara walked to Caleb who still knelt in the grass, open palm extended.

Each step was moderated as if she was undecided about the man before her. Kenna watched, her head tilted to the side while she tried to observe the feral meeting. He kept his hand extended, his long fingers splayed while he reached towards the wolf like a child. Leara breathed in his scent, soap, sweat, and horse; Kenna's scent feathered into his own, and Leara released a small whine at the recognition. Then, they touched.

Caleb ran his hand down Leara's slender muzzle, a look of wonder danced across his features. Her soft fur tipped with coarse guard hairs sprung up beneath his fingers, his touch revenant while he buried them in her thick coat. Never had his hands touched a living wolf; the way her body radiated heat, the thick scent of her filled his nostrils. He felt wild, and connected to the earth beneath his boots. Caleb's gaze cut to Kenna's, an understanding in their evergreen depths.

Kenna beamed, a light deep within her breast ignited by the compassion before her. She could only hope that others would find such openness, and that her pack would be able to join this new life with her. Caleb stood slowly, his hand still open at his side while he watched Leara go to Kenna's side.

"She is beautiful." His voice was a low rasp, raw and thready.

"Yes, she truly is."

"Well, it's getting late and I don't know if any of you have noticed but we missed dinner."

Aden huffed behind them. Lightning flashed through Kenna's veins, she had not heard him walk back to them with Randy in tow. She turned slowly, but not before she saw the smirk spread across Caleb's chiseled face. The four of them laughed at his moody expression, a petulant child that somehow wielded a sword. Her lips twitched at the thought, and she pressed her lips into a thin line. It was clear the large man did not like to miss a meal.

"My apologies, let's grab that dinner," Caleb responded while he slung his arm around his companion's shoulder.

Despite the long day, she felt no hunger, only the need for silence.

"If you don't want to go with us you can go to your tent." Randy said. Kenna quirked a copper brow at him.

"You read my mind."

"There is enough room in yours for your wolves I think."

Kenna watched him for a moment, unsure of how to respond. She didn't exactly like his reference of the pack as her wolves, they were not pets. With a mental sigh she pushed the thought aside.

"Thank you, Randy."

"Well, it's that brown one right over there." He pointed to a plain brown tent at the edge of the camp; it was delightfully close to the woods. "See you in the morning."

He patted her arm then he joined his companions near the campfire. Kenna watched him go, a deep sigh rattled through her, the weight of exhaustion no longer a burden she could bear.

Besides the dreadful ride that she would undoubtedly be subjected to again in the morning, the merge between wolves and man had taken all the strength she had left. Her soreness returned quickly, her adrenaline a distant memory. Kenna groaned, her hands pressed to the small of her back, then hobbled to her tent. Each wolf followed her inside, the dark fabric akin to earthen walls; Kenna dropped the flaps behind her, a barrier between her and the outside world.

Kenna opened her eyes to a brown sky; her heart hammered against her breastbone, panic sizzled through her. She had been swallowed by the earth. *No, no… I can't*—Then it all made sense; she was in a tent, not trapped underground. She rubbed her eyes and sat up in her narrow cot, her tent floor covered in fur carpets. Despite the close quarters the pack had determinedly piled into the small shelter, not an inch of space unused. Kenna slid from her bed, cloth rustling against her, then carefully stepped around the wolves. She made a haphazard escape, desperately avoided tails and paws while she went.

Kenna stumbled through the flaps, a burst of pure light filled with the song of larks and woodland birds. Her eyes rose, her stiff palm above her brow to admire a brilliant blue sky. Kenna stretched, every fiber of her being embraced the sweet sun that radiated warmth across her tender body. It was then that she smelled it; the delicious, savory smell of breakfast meat that crackled happily in a pan. Kenna's stomach snarled in response.

She rushed back into her tent, danced around her wolves, half of whom had risen, and found her filthy riding habit. A snarl ripped through her followed by a ravenous growl deep in her belly. Kenna crumpled up the soiled garment and tossed it away. *I could shift and hunt...* She looked down at her abdomen, thinly clad in a soft cotton shift. It growled mournfully in response when they both realized food would be delayed. In the turmoil of last night she hadn't realized her saddle bags had been empty of any, and all supplies. Lost in her thoughts she was startled by a tap on her tent flap. Kenna was still, she did not respond; not until she saw a hand reach between the flaps to discreetly knock on the fence post.

Kenna pushed aside the flap to find Caleb in a fresh cream tunic and light brown breeches. He smelled delightfully of soap and fire smoke; his hair still damp from his morning wash. An image of his lethal body, the way it must have glistened in the river beneath the sun, flashed through her mind. Kenna stifled a shiver, forced herself to focus on his pleasant face. His hands were tucked into his pockets, his eyes unreadable despite the easy smile that curved his lips.

"Good morning wolf girl."
Wolf girl, little wolf. What's next? There was no anger in her thoughts.
"Hello."
"I thought you might need a change of clothes. It would seem that the servants accidentally packed your things with Aunt Ressa's. Here." He swung down and scooped up a plump saddle bag that rested at his feet.

A small cry of relief escaped her before she reached up for the satchel and retreated to her tent; Caleb's chuckle rippled through the rent flap behind her. In her desperation for food she upended the saddle bag, she covered her small cot in a rumpled pile of clothes, hygiene products, and a comb. Kenna snatched away a light brown riding habit, tossed it to the edge of the bed away from her belongings, and slipped off her night shift. Finally dressed she proceeded to run a comb through her tangled hair, Kenna winced when it caught on a particularly nasty snarl; she muttered a curse while she untangled the knot with impatient fingers.

Strands popped in her hurry, she rolled her eyes at the now curled copper tendrils. Last of all, and most needed, was a small stick fresh and ready to be chewed. Kenna grabbed the twig, peeled back the thin moist bark, and vigorously mauled it, fine bristles were released which she used to brush her teeth and tongue. Refreshed, albeit sore, she found herself presentable enough to go out to breakfast. By this time the pack had left her modest tent to stretch their legs in a traditional morning run, only one remained; Leara.

Kenna tenderly rubbed her sister's ears, a smile revealed her fresh, white teeth.
"You are lucky Leara, you wake up so beautiful." The pup opened her jaw in a soundless wolf's laugh, mirth twinkled in her aurelian eyes. They left Kenna's tent and found

Caleb had waited for her, his face cool and calm, his posture relaxed.

He casually leaned against a nearby tree, his gaze attentive, hands diligent, while he cleaned a small dagger with a kidskin cloth. His chiseled face tilted up at the muted thwack of canvas that followed Kenna and Leara's arrival; a wry grin lit his features, he slid the knife into a small sheath in his boot. His gaze flicked to Leara, and he shifted his shoulders in the barest hint of a shrug.

"Are you ladies ready to eat?"

"Yes, we are."

"He is very happy." Leara commented, her ebony-lined eyes slid to the human beside her slyly. *"Like a cute puppy."*

"Says the pup." Kenna chuckled at the wolf's jest, though Leara's teeth were sharp on her thigh.

Caleb looked at her, brow raised curiously. "What's so funny?"

"Oh nothing." She refused to look at her sister, her lips pressed into a thin line to suppress the laughter that shuddered through her, and walked ahead.

All of the pack had abandoned Kenna to the slow, arduous trudge down the royal highway, except Leara. The silver-tipped creature was woefully dull, a thick layer of grime covered her once-pristine coat. Kenna watched her sister, red tongue long as it lolled from her parted jaws while she followed dutifully beside gelding. A glimmer of a thought crossed Kenna's mind. Reaching out to the gelding's mind she proposed an unusual idea; Shren immediately rejected it, ears laid flat against his skull.

Kenna's brows knit above aquamarine eyes, a tension in her gut flared while she pushed her will on the horse; gently at first, then with more force when she again felt his resistance. She never liked to force creatures to do as she bid, yet she could no longer stand the sight of her sister filthy in the road. The gelding relented, a ragged blow through delicate nostrils the only testament of his frustration. Kenna leaned forward to rub his brown-bronze neck in gratitude, then stopped him. She ignored the strange, suspicious looks from those that rode past, ignored the warmth that pricked its way up her neck towards her dustflecked cheeks.

She pushed herself farther back in the saddle, her stiff muscles shrieked in protest, and readied herself. Within a moment Leara sprang from the ground and landed squarely on the geldings shoulders, between Kenna and the saddle horn. Shren tossed his head, white-ringed eyes rolled wildly while he fought the urge to flee. Human and wolf quickly settled themselves in the saddle, Kenna's mount shook violently between her thighs; guilt bit at her innards at the sight of his fear. She brushed her mind against his, and sent him waves of calm reassurance and she squeezed him into a slow walk. She rode up the line. Many in the party stared at Kenna like she was a mad woman, yet she paid them no mind. Her sister no longer walked in the dust like a common dog, and that was all that mattered to her.

At midday the sun was a merciless disk of gold in the sky; it beat down on their backs with a heat that made each member of the party slick with sweat. The captain called for a short rest, and the air whooshed from Kenna's parched lips. She lightly pulled Shren to a halt near the side of the road, and wrinkled her nose at the thick humidity that clung to the air above the deep green grass. Leara leapt from the saddle with a grace that earned her a scowl from her human sister; once clear Kenna shimmied forward in the saddle, braced her hand against Shren's stiff mane, then slipped from her perch with stilted legs.

She waddled from the road with her gelding and Leara in tow, and took refuge beneath a shady pine. Kenna slid down the tree, coarse bark bit into her back pleasantly, until she slumped to the ground. Hot, swollen fingers fumbled at the cap of her canteen, before she greedily drank its cool contents. Water tickled her chin and she rubbed it away, her hand brushed her lips and she could taste salt and dust. Eyes closed against the noon-day glare, she was startled awake by a boot that roughly kicked her own. Kenna snarled as she glowered up at the figure before her.

It was Lady Ressa; the growl slowly faded in her throat.

"What can I do for you my lady?"

"None of that, call me Ressa." The knight answered briskly.

"What can I do for you then Ressa." Kenna continued, still mildly annoyed while she got to her feet.

"Do you know how to fight?"

"Excuse me?"

"Do you know how to fight, how to use any weapons?"

"Only my fangs and claws." Kenna answered slowly.

"Well that may be quite potent in the woods, but that simply won't do for where we are going."

"Is the Capital that dangerous?"

"For someone like you, it can be." Ressa answered, a contemplative look marred her oval face.

For a moment they stared at one another, evaluated each aspect of the other for any sign of weakness. Ressa's eyes flashed, her decision made.

"What weapon would you like to learn? Whatever it is, I'll make sure you can access it." Kenna watched her, unsure if the entire conversation was a test; or worse, a joke. Kenna shrugged with one shoulder, a half-hearted gesture, and decided she could no longer resist the opportunity given her; joke, test, or whatever it may be.

"What weapon is the most useful?"

"Useful?"

"Yes, useful. Which one can I do the most with, in life and battle?"

Ressa stood before her, thoughtful while her crystalline eyes scanned Kenna critically.

"I would have to say that the bow is the most useful, in your sense of the word. You can shoot an enemy from a distance, or from the saddle, and you can also hunt with it."

"I would like to learn the bow then." Kenna answered, excitement crept into her voice.

"Let's get to work."

At Ressa's direction, two guards produced a practice target in the rough shape of a man padded with extra clothes. Awkward as the target was, it would give Kenna a clear direction to focus her energy. She shifted her attention from the men to the weapon in her hands. The bow itself was longer than she was tall, its narrow form reached six feet in length. She felt strange, her hand clumsy and slow while she wore the leather glove.

She had protested the item once, and was swiftly rebuked by both Ressa and the guards; the protection, bulky and bothersome as it was, was necessary.

"Now lift the bow with your left hand, bringing your hand level with your sight." Ressa instructed.

Kenna lifted the bow to its designated location, her breath stilted in anticipation.

"Now slowly pull back the string with your right hand." Kenna complied. "Only use two fingers." Kenna relaxed the tension of the string, then adjusted her grasp; Ressa continued in a low voice. "Good, pull the string back slowly… anchor it near your mouth." Again Kenna obeyed, her hands trembled against the strain of the weapon, and the tension in her chest.

Sweat beaded her brow, then traced languid lines down her face; she blinked the salt away. "Relax, breathe in... breathe out... keep your eye on the target. Once you are ready, you may release." Ressa's voice was a whisper on the summer breeze. Kenna relaxed the string and felt the smooth caress of feather fletching between her fingers; she wasn't ready, not yet.

Ressa's eyes were gentle when she examined Kenna's face, the slight hunch of her shoulders while she held the bow with slack hands. "Begin when you are." Ressa concluded, then left her to her own devices.

Kenna waited until she was well and truly alone, then held the bow up with eager hands. She stroked each curve of smooth wood, and marveled at its lack of texture. Her fingers then ran the length of the string, her nimble fingers felt each delicate fiber coated with traces of wax. She tugged on the string and was pleased by the resistance, a wolfish grin creased her features at the challenge. She stood in a mockup of the proper position, her mind and body fumbled with each gesture, and pressure of the stance.

Kenna flushed with effort, her arm trembled while her palm grew slippery within the leather glove; despite her strain the string would only bend partially to her will. She could not draw it, the realization was a slap to her senses. She glanced around furtively and loosed a sigh at the bustle of an oblivious company. Kenna rolled her shoulders, eyes closed while she harnessed the change, she only allowed a trickle of her magic to flow and enhance her.

She swung the bow up and into firing position, inhaled deep, then she drew the weapon and released. When the string left her fingertips the air filled with a thunderous crack, splinters burst in her face, the briefest warning before she ducked as the top half of the bow flew at her.

"What was that?" exclaimed Caleb from behind her.

He held a fragment of her bow in one hand, its tattered string hung uselessly. Kenna wiped sweat from her brow with the back of her sleeve, then swallowed painfully, her throat dry as words escaped her. She released her magic, felt that copper fire seep from her limbs to settle in her belly; she licked her lips and answered,
"I…I couldn't draw it at first, so I tried a bit harder." Her cheeks warmed with the lie.
"A bit harder? Really? I haven't even seen men twice your size do that!" Caleb tossed the wood aside while he spoke. "Let's try it again with my bow this time."
"No." Kenna dropped her half of the once-was-weapon.
"No?" Caleb rubbed his chin softly while he watched her, the coarse hair rasped with each thoughtful stroke.

Kenna fidgeted under his stare then snapped,
"I don't want to break it!"
"You'll be fine. I'll guide you this time." He ignored her protests and strode back to camp, to the shadows within his tent. It didn't take him long to return with a large black bow that was longer still than hers had been. She looked at it skeptically.
"I won't be able to draw that."
"Turn around," he ordered gently.

Kenna faced the tree that propped up the cloth-man target. Caleb pressed his bow into her stiff hand, then slid an arrow into the other.
"Now get into a firing position." She responded to his request, her muscles rigid while she held the stance. His touch was warm, the calluses of his hands dragged pleasantly against her skin. His breath a whispered caress against her ear where it stirred her hair in gentle bursts.

Kenna resisted the shiver that stirred inside of her; she thought of the last time he had been so close. Her cheeks warmed uncomfortably, she wiped her face against

her shoulder in a halfhearted attempt to clear sweat that was no longer there. Without a word he encased her hands with his own, gradually pulling the string back until she felt her fingers graze her lower lip.
"Breathe with me."
His voice, a sultry growl in her ear, made her heart skitter frantically.

Caleb's chest expanded, seared her back with his merciless heat, her own lungs filled hastily; her every sense was heightened, her back ached with his closeness, her breasts tight against her tunic while she matched his breath. Kenna's arm wavered, the arrowhead swayed wildly until his other hand came around to brace her own.
She stood encircled in his embrace while they breathed together, exhaled together, held the long supple shaft of the bow together; his hands experienced and gentle, his voice a muted caress while he guided her.

The heat of their bodies mingled until she could no longer feel the air around them. The way it swam with damp heat, the drone of voices now dulled to the hum of fireflies while she stood suspended in his hold.
"Now release." His command was gentle breath against moist skin, she released and shivered with the freed tension of the bow that quivered in her palm. The arrow met its mark, burrowed deep into the no-man's false flesh. A soft growl of approval rumbled from his throat, her knees weakened; she was almost undone by the feel of him, then that primal sound... Kenna bit her lip when his hands once again moved against her.

Caleb lowered her arms then deftly pulled the weapon from her stiff fingers, while his lips traced wet lines through her salt. *Release...* It seemed so easy when he touched her that way. Kenna leaned back slowly and braced herself against his chest, her chin tilted up in quiet submission while Caleb sent shivers through her limbs. He traced his fingers down her arm and drew her deeper into his hold, grazed his teeth against her throat in a way that made her pant. Her hips pressed into his fractionally, her body overtaken by instinct; by the pull he caused in her that throbbed hot in her belly, and down between her thighs; a pull that demanded satiation. Caleb's body hardened behind her, pressed close with a new intensity while his teeth captured her earlobe.

Kenna felt the girth of him, that sensuous length that pressed into her behind, and balked. She stepped out of his arms and was washed with a rush of fresh air, it filled the void between them and quickly tempered the heat that had enthralled them. The moment dulled to an ember while the world around them acquired focus, Kenna saw the guards had nearly dismantled the camp with admirable speed.

"It looks like we are moving on." Her mouth was dry, her throat tight; Kenna could not meet his gaze, though she felt it heavy upon her brow.

"We should get moving then," Caleb answered, his voice smooth, collected; he sounded as though the moment had not existed.

Somehow it stung her and she looked at him quickly; the fire dulled in his eyes, and she questioned his touch. Kenna looked away while she passed him his bow. Silence grew between them, taut and strenuous.

"I'll get Shren for you."

"Please don't make me get back on that animal, it's so uncomfortable." Kenna pleaded. She could hear the whine in her voice, but she didn't care.

Kenna could not imagine another moment of being mounted, she would rather walk. A looked of startled amusement gleamed in his eyes, his lips twitched, and the emotionless mask he wore quickly evaporated. At the sight of his smile the tension in her chest eased.

"You can ride with me then."
"But I smell," she protested.
"Don't we all?"

The small encampment had been broken down with a speed born of practice and efficiency; Caleb had managed to get the guards to take Shren, which left Kenna to stand on the heat-wilted grass. She stepped forward, eyes focused on her hand while she patted Zane's midnight-black neck.
"Are you sure?"
"Yes, it will be like old times," he answered, and reached a hand down to her.
"Old times were only a couple days ago." she responded haughtily while she grasped his broad hand. Caleb chuckled as he pulled her into the saddle before him, once she was settled he wrapped his arms around her, then gently pulled her back against his chest. She could smell the slightly musky scent of his sweat mixed with leather, and could not help but find pleasure in the tang.

Leara, weary from her time in the sun ambled towards the trees, and her pack beyond them. Kenna watched her go while she relaxed into Caleb's hold, muscle by muscle until she swayed in rhythm with the stallion between her thighs.
"Are you comfortable?"
"Yes, very." She could feel his lips curve against her hair.
"I'm not bothering your scar?" Her head rested in the cleft between his neck and shoulder, while she spoke she turned toward him, her brow pressed lightly to his warm throat.
"Not a bit." Caleb responded. He pulled back a fraction, then kissed the side of her newly exposed neck. Her skin prickled with pleasure and she released a breathy sigh, which only encouraged him to kiss her again.

Warmth spread across her body when she felt his lips part, his tongue playfully licked the sweat from her collarbone. A small moan escaped her before she bared her neck further to his ministrations, her body glowing with pleasure. Kenna held her breath when she felt his teeth rake the tender curve between her neck and shoulder, her skin tightened deliciously; she loved the feel of his teeth. Caleb slowed Zane's gait subtly, the fellow riders unaware while they chatted, until they were at the back of the party, which allowed a modicum of privacy from watchful eyes.

With deliberate motions he slid thin leather reins across Kenna's thighs, drew the back of his hand against her abdomen in a slow graze that burned a path across her belly, before he released the reins to dangle across her legs. Caleb leaned back in the saddle, his boots kicked clear of the stirrups, and opened his legs wider. Kenna felt the space between them with a pang of annoyance, until his hands tilted her hips and turned her closer to him. Her smile, though hesitant and shy, mirrored his own. Caleb gazed at her lips, while his hands trailed lazy lines up her abdomen, torso, then the swell of her breast.

His thumb grazed her peaked nipple, and his eyes grew glazed with desire; his lips met hers in a languid kiss that burned through her. The flavor of sweat and dust mingled between them while they explored each other eagerly. Kenna's earlier shyness was gone, she was utterly consumed by the hunger within. While Caleb kissed her, he stroked her thighs in lazy circles with his index and second finger, slowly igniting fire as he went. Kenna wanted more, she did not want his hands to leave her, not with the way they made her feel.

She followed her need, moved his hands higher, briefly hovered over the center between her legs, before she slid his hands up her belly. His thumb grazed her waist band, which evoked a low growl from him while he caressed her supple skin. His body hardened against her, his grip on her breast was firm. Caleb began to speak, his voice husky in her ear,

"Kenna," he rasped her name, "we shouldn't—"

Zane whinnied loudly, tossed his head and pranced hard enough to sway the pair in the saddle. His hands left her frame while they looked up, one of the guards was headed towards them at a brisk pace. Kenna's heart raced, she thanked the stallion.

"That would have been rather embarrassing."

Caleb seemed less pleased with the interruption than she was, his voice cool as he addressed the guard.

"What seems to be the problem?"

The man, Ronald if Kenna recalled correctly, seemed uncomfortable, as though he knew he had interrupted but wasn't quite sure where to go from there.

"What is it?"

"Your aunt wanted me to inform you that we would be staying in the village tonight, sir. There has been word of an issue, and her assistance has been requested."

"I see, so my aunt's reputation precedes her. You may return to your place then."

Caleb dismissed the man with a small nod. With Ronald out of earshot Caleb laughed, Kenna's own voice soon joined his.

"Well that was a close one," he said, his voice full of mirth. "A little too close."

After that they rode in companionable silence, small conversations cropped up here and there while she rested in his arms. As the ride wore on Kenna drifted in and out of her own consciousness, and that of the wolves; she savored the way the woods looked through their eyes, and wished she was on her own paws beneath the pines. Caleb pulled Kenna from her ethereal state with a gentle kiss on the cheek once they reached the inn. She looked around tiredly and noticed the sun now rested like a fat hen on the

horizon. She twisted in the saddle,
"Where are we?"
"We have stopped at The Rooster Roof Inn."
He tucked strands of copper behind her ear.
"Rooster roof?" The question had no sooner left her lips, when she was answered by a particularly vocal bird.
"Well that makes sense I suppose." Kenna laughed softly then straightened in the saddle.

A sigh escaped her while she stretched, Caleb's strong hands rubbed the arch of her lower back.
"What happened to your aunt? Didn't that guard say someone requested her?"
"Yes, she rode ahead of the group so she could get it taken care of. She doesn't like to leave people waiting."
"What happened?"
"Apparently a man stepped out on his wife, and the woman he slept with is with child. His wife found out and wants to dissolve the marriage, then make the husband leave the property. He of course thought that would be unfair; he didn't see adultery as a problem. The town was split on the issue, so when they heard that my aunt was coming they sent a rider to settle it."
"I agree with the wife, she deserves the house. You should not step out on your mate." Kenna answered, clearly agitated by the situation. "What do you think?"
"I'm with you wolf girl. A man like that doesn't deserve a wife, let alone put her on the street."

While he spoke, he carefully climbed down from the saddle, then reached up to help Kenna dismount. Normally she would avoid the assistance, especially in plain view of others, but she was tired and sore; her pride would survive the chivalrous care.

His palms were warm when they wrapped around Kenna's waist, the pressure firm, yet gentle while he lifted her from the saddle. She landed in the courtyard on feeble limbs, and stumbled forward a step into Caleb's chest. His deep chuckle filled her ears, she wrinkled her nose with half-hearted annoyance, then stepped free of him on stilted legs. Kenna surveyed their surroundings while her mind connected with the pack. A vision of thick greenery nestled deep within shadows filled her mind, the vision overlaid with the sights before her. A smile tucked the corners of her mouth as she let the connection fade. Her attention returned to the establishment before her; the inn was a two-story affair of gray and nude cobblestone and mortar, with a large stable and paddock behind it.

A group of chickens babbled among themselves while they crossed the courtyard, entirely unperturbed by the group of men and war horses. Besides the large amount of chicken droppings, The Rooster Roof Inn was quite nice, busy and alive. Kenna looked at the windows, dim light within battled with the remnant glow of the day, a welcome reprieve from the heat, dust, and grime of the road.
"When will Ressa be back?"
"It could be a while, she sent a representative from the village to purchase us rooms which usually means a late night for her," Caleb answered, while he pulled saddle bags from Zane's ivory-streaked flanks.

He tossed them over his shoulder, a smooth motion born of habit, then steered Kenna toward the inn's double doors. The doors pushed open on well-oiled hinges, and they were hit by a wave of laughter, raised voices, food, and smoke. Music wove its beautiful notes through the menagerie of sounds, Kenna's eyes widened while she shivered at the explosion of life before her.

After such a long day she no longer had the stamina to handle so many people; she quickly stepped back and jarred herself against Caleb.
"I think I'll just go sleep in the woods with the pack. Maybe I will take my tent."

Caleb grabbed her shoulders, his fingers cupped around the joint and halted her retreat.
"Now now, you need to rest. Just go up to your room, you will be fine."
"Where are our rooms then?"
"Let me ask. Stay put."

A firmness crept into his voice, despite the twinkle of amusement that glittered in his gaze. Before she could protest further he strode through the crowd; many of the villagers parted before him like water around a stone. Within moments Caleb was at the counter, flashed a grin that dripped with charm while he leaned closer to the barmaid. The young blonde blushed and giggled under his attentive gaze, and did not miss the opportunity to show the lord her full figure, plump breasts so easily revealed by a low neckline. Kenna watched while the maid leaned forward, her pale breast inches from Caleb's forearm, her lips parted expectantly. Whatever words were spoken encouraged her, and she slid the knight a ring of keys before she whispered in his ear.

Caleb was unruffled by whatever she had said, picked up the keys, and strode away; her cornflower blue eyes watched Caleb merge once more with the crowd hungrily. Returning to Kenna's side, he pulled a key from the ring.
"Did you have a nice chat?"
"Excuse me?"
"With that tavern maid I mean. She was clearly interested in more than your room key."
"Were you jealous?" he asked, that wicked smile returned in an instant.
"You're such a mangy dog. I should have left you in the woods." Kenna snatched the key from his hand.
"Don't be that way." Caleb took her empty hand, his expression serious. "I was only being friendly, I have no

interest in that girl."

Kenna wavered, felt foolish, confused. *Why should I even care? He isn't mine,* another voice deep inside of her posed the question she was not ready to hear.

"I mean it Kenna, I'm not that kind of man." He took her hand, then raised it to his lips for a chaste kiss; his expression filled with concern. "Let me walk you to your room." Caleb looped his arm through hers and navigated the room with ease, and quickly brought her to the stairs at the back of the tavern's hall.

They walked up in silence until they stood before her door; a poorly crafted iron number four hung crookedly from a rusty nail.

"This room belongs to you and my aunt," Caleb said while he took the key from her, a muted click followed the release of latch and tumbler. He nudged the door ajar, then returned her key. "I'll leave your things by the door." His voice was soft while he dropped a saddle bag to rest against the frame. "Goodnight little wolf."

He turned from her chamber in search of his own. Kenna twisted the edge of her shirt, it was obvious she had offended Caleb, and that was the last thing she wanted; somehow he had become her friend, and the experience was new and unnerving. She reached out, her fingertips closing on his tunic with a firm tug as she pulled him into the room, then closed the door. He looked down at her, his green eyes not unkind, ebony brow raised in question.

"I'm sorry Caleb, I had no right to get upset with you like that," she said earnestly. "I just... don't have any experience in this sort of situation."

Caleb stroked her cheek, pushed her tangled hair from her upturned face. He leaned forward and kissed her softly, his lips feather light against her own. They parted, their breath mingled while he whispered,

"Forgiven." Kenna reached up hesitantly then pulled him

down for another kiss. This one deeper than the last, yet still gentle, unhurried. They looked at one another and he spoke first, his voice rasping slightly,

"Good night Kenna." Caleb stepped away, the lines of his body etched with desire while he opened the narrow door. With one final look he stepped from the room, the door firmly closed behind him.

Clean and refreshed, Kenna slid under the covers, eager for sleep to take hold; she was disappointed. All she could do was lie awake, gaze locked on the worn timbers of the ceiling.

The revelry from below could still be heard even though the sun had long since set, which only caused her to toss and turn further. Lost in thought, Kenna was startled when Ressa burst through their chamber door. Kenna sat up in bed, unsure if she should greet the knight or leave her be; it was clear the woman was in a foul mood.

Ressa pushed back hair shot through with silver, her callused hands steady despite the exhaustion that lined her face.

"Was everything settled?"

Ressa sighed deeply while she pulled her leather breastplate from her weary frame.

"It was an unpleasant affair. The man did not wish to lease his property to his wife, but finally I annulled the marriage." Ressa strode to the wash basin to run cool water over her dust caked neck. "He will have a hard time with things." she continued, "The man is a well-off blacksmith, but he now must make a new home for the woman he philandered with, and the new child on the way. He has many mouths to feed. A wife with three children and one more to come."

The blonde shook her head at his folly while she stripped off her sweat-stained garments. Kenna listened quietly, Blackwood had been a small village, and affairs

were difficult to conceal; yet she had never heard of something as scandalous as this blacksmith's story. Ressa kicked her soiled clothes toward the wall, then tugged on a long linen night shift; a hearty sigh escaped her while she slid into the narrow cot across from Kenna.
"What a relief."

Ressa's breath deepened, her body eager for the comfort of slumber. Kenna shifted back under her covers, uncomfortable sharing a room with a near stranger. Kenna wearily examined the room for the hundredth time, this time her gaze caught on sliver steel that glinted in a muted light. Her attention slid to a still-lit candle beside the wash basin. Loathsome as the concept was, she knew she would have to crawl from her cozy den of scratchy blankets.

Kenna slid back the covers, then crept across the hard wood floors, more than one creaked beneath her weight. She blew out the candle and paused while her vision adjusted to the gloom of the chamber. Star light filtered through a slit of a window, so dim it surely promised stubbed toes. Kenna gathered a spark of magic, changed her eyes into that of a wolf's. The room flashed with clarity as her lupine eyes gathered the starlight and reflected it into her large pupils. She strode across the room then climbed back into her bed, still warm from her occupation.

Her limbs were heavy, sleep lapped at the edge of her consciousness like dark waters.
Ressa's voice drifted to her in the darkness,
"What are your motives with my nephew?"
"What do you mean?" Kenna glared at the ceiling. "I have no motives."
"It just seems a bit odd, the way you found him and decided to stay. I'm sure things have been much better for you since then." Ressa's voice was even, emotionless.
"You are lucky I found him, or your nephew would be

nothing but scattered bones." Kenna snarled back.

Ressa's laughter was light, like silver bells despite the cruelty of her words.

"Calm yourself girl. I only needed to see how you would respond."

Kenna seethed, her fingers hooked and tangled in the cotton sheets. A soft snore filled the cramped chamber, Kenna growled at the sound; she tossed and turned after that, bound in bondage of cotton, her thoughts troubled by Ressa's words. *Is that how the others think of me?*
Kenna felt a pit yawn open deep in her belly, she began to doubt the decision she had made to leave her forest.

D ays passed in a hazy blur of sweat, sunshine, and leather that creaked with endless friction. Summer was merciless, tempers were short, and words were few and far between. The wolves abandoned their daily trek beside the road; instead they found shelter beneath the sagging pines by day, and made up the distance by night.

Beige dust coated the party, coated Kenna's dry mouth, filled her nostrils; she licked her lips and regretted the earthy taste. She had to admit, her companions were determined while they trudged down the road; still efficient despite the fatigue they all endured. Kenna kept to herself while she rode, instead she focused on her seat, or the world that gradually changed around her; despite each discomfort Kenna soon developed riding muscles, and found she actually enjoyed the saddle. She grew familiar with each member of the party, found the monotony of the day almost a comfort. From what she had gathered from Remus, their group was only one day from the Capital. The closer they came to Sapphire Bay the more populated the countryside became.

Every day they passed more towns, each larger than the last, its citizens filled the road, thick with traffic. Kenna was eager to see Sapphire Bay, from all accounts it was a majestic city, diverse in both weather and culture; yet each night that brought them closer caused the pit in her stomach to grow, if ever so slightly. Her only plan had been to go there, and that had been at Caleb's request. She was not sure what she would do from there. *Would I just leave? Turn tail and walk the entire way home?* The thought made her feel hollow.

Kenna pushed Shren farther up the line until she drew abreast to Caleb. A flutter went through her when she took in his sun-kissed bronzed skin. His lips always had an upturned tilt as he rode, just being in the saddle gave him pleasure; she was thankful for the weeks on the road that had brought them closer with each moon that passed overhead. Caleb felt her gaze and smiled.
"How can I help you, milady?"
"I'm no lady."
"So I've been told," he answered, unruffled by her rebuff.

They smiled at one another before he continued. "Now that we are so close, do you think you will stay?" Though a grin still graced his lips his eyes were guarded. Her own cheer evaporated while she considered the prospect of the city, but more than that, she thought of what

remnants of a home she could go back to.
"I don't know if there is anything there for me."
"There is something there for everyone."

Silence fell between them, only punctured by the rhythmic clip of hooves against soil. It did make Kenna wonder, perhaps Caleb did not want her to leave; she glanced at him beneath copper lashes, then back at her hands, white knuckled around leather reins. What could she do in such a place, she had no way to provide for herself. In Blackwood she hunted what she needed, and from what her new companions told her, it was treason to hunt in the Royal Forest without the permission of a monarch. Once more the pit grew, fed like a seed; her doubt waters that nourished, her fear the sun.

Shren slowed his pace in response to Kenna's hesitation, her turmoil, and attracted Caleb's attention.
"Is everything all right?"
"Just thinking of what life would be like there."
"It can be whatever you want Kenna, and I can help you. No matter what you decide."
He reached across the space between them and grasped her hand, for just a moment they enjoyed each other's touch. It was quickly interrupted by a dip in the road, the horses' differing heights pulled them apart with a suddenness that nearly pulled Kenna from the saddle. She squealed involuntarily before she righted in her seat.

Her face burned as she glanced up and down the line, hopeful that no one had witnessed her near disaster. Something sputtered beside her, Kenna looked at Caleb.
"Don't you dare." Kenna warned, further discussion forbidden.
"I would never." His voice was tight with concealed laughter, a slow smile spread across his stubbled face.
"I mean it!" she exclaimed, her own voice wobbling with laughter.

Caleb's eyes danced, his lips pressed into a firm line that mirrored her own. It broke upon them like a wave, that laughter that eased every ache, every tension in them. Kenna swiped tears from her cheeks, and attempted to breathe deeply past the joyous glow beneath her breastbone.

She winced at the stitch in her side while she nudged Shren into a trot. The pair rode in companionable silence while they enjoyed the cool, crisp breeze.

"We should be nearing the next village soon." Caleb informed her.

"No more tents?"

"No more tents." Caleb responded with a chuckle.

Kenna hummed with relief; at first the tent did not bother her, but after too many days in the heat, sweat and dust caked to her body. The tent was dreadful—its heavy fabric held in the warmth which suffocated her each night. The thought of a hot bath made her skin tingle with future delight. Caleb grinned when he caught her dreamy expression.

"Are you actually starting to like people?"

"People? No."

"That's rather harsh," he quipped.

"But I do enjoy hot baths," she continued cheerily.

"You had a bath at Jan's, and Randy's."

"Yes, but not like the ones at the inn. The copper tubs are so smooth and stay warm, it's much different from the wood tubs. Did you know I got a splinter before?" she asked incredulously.

She almost laughed at the memory her words invoked, then felt her mirth evaporate. It was at Jan's that she had gotten the splinter, and Jan who removed it for her. Pain and loss were a vice around her heart, she blinked back the string of tears and plastered on a smile.

"Where?" Caleb raised a brow suggestively.

Kenna opened her mouth to respond, then thought better of it.

"Never mind that, the point is you can't get a splinter from a copper tub." She had lost all interest in talking. It was clear Caleb wanted to push the issue further, but Kenna didn't give him the chance. She nudged Shren into a trot and savored the breeze in her damp hair.

She was unaware of his tender gaze, and that innocence drew him to her all the more. The evening sun glinted on her hair, set each copper strand ablaze. Her blue eyes gleamed vibrantly against her sun-kissed skin. Kenna hadn't realized, and most likely never would; but she had taken Caleb's breath away. He cleared his throat softly, careful not to draw her gaze, and returned his attention to the road while Kenna's hum filled his ears.

Their party clattered into the town square; the small troupe rode directly to the largest inn's courtyard. It was a three-story structure made primarily of stone with wood panels painted a pale blue. White shutters framed expansive windows that gave the inn a free, airy feel. Kenna pressed Shren to quicken his pace, despite his fatigue he complied. Caleb caught sight of her eagerness, a lopsided grin crossed his face with mischief. He called to her,

"I'm sure they have the smoothest tubs."

"Oh hush." Kenna tossed back while she slipped from the saddle.

A stable boy quickly took the gelding's reins, then walked the sweat-streaked bay toward the welcome comfort of the stable behind the inn; another child led Zane away. Caleb stood wearily with the saddle bags slung over his broad shoulder.

"Welcome to the Dragon Wing."

"I wonder what it's like inside." Her neck craned to get a better view of the establishment.

"Let's take a look." Caleb encouraged, his arm around her

shoulders.

The Dragon Wing was a swirl of motion, loud music and louder voices erupted from its dim belly. It held a level of cheer that nearly knocked Kenna off her feet. Caleb on the other hand seemed swept up in the good mood, his road weariness forgotten at the threshold. The smell of smoke and cooked meats made Kenna's mouth water, nerves forgotten. She could not stand the thought of the Captain's gruel, let alone the taste.

Rosemary and sage lingered in the air, a welcome scent, after the heavy tang of sweat and leather. Within moments they were greeted by a woman, a harried expression on her lustrous face, dark curls tumbled against her cheeks. Large brown eyes were weary, yet friendly when creased into a smile.

"Welcome to the Dragon Wing, are you here to dine or stay?"

"We need rooms for the night, three personal suites, and three more rooms, two beds each. If you could set up a fresh bath in each suite, that would be wonderful."

"Just a moment then, I'll see what I can get ready for you." The tavern maid bustled away, burgundy and cream gown lost in the crowd.

They ambled toward an empty table tucked into a quiet corner of the tavern's main level where the soft light dampened the hearty sounds around them. Caleb dropped their bags in a worn wooden chair, the thick gloss rubbed away where a multitude of backs and asses had rubbed it raw. Kenna slid into a chair beside him and gazed up at Caleb with a weary smile that didn't quite reach her eyes.

"It looks like the guards are wasting no time."

Kenna nodded discreetly toward the men.

Caleb turned at her words, movements slow, reluctant to remove her from his sight. He quickly located their companions in time to see them sit down, hands firmly grasped around tankards of cool ale. He laughed heartily and turned back to Kenna.

"You can't blame them. Nothing clears the dust from your throat like a cold ale." He sat beside her, their knees lightly pressed together, warm with summer heat.

Caleb watched Kenna; her back was rigid, it always was when she was around more than two humans at a time. Her long braid was loose and casually tossed over a slim shoulder, angular aquamarine eyes scanned the room in long, slow sweeps. He nudged her with his elbow, and grinned at her small start. She looked at him, auburn brows knit together.

"Yes?" She drew out the word in a venomous arch.

"What has you wound up?"

The fire in her eyes cooled, her shoulders rounded while she looked away.

"I just don't find the same comfort here that they do."

They, such an ambiguous word; he knew what she really meant. Kenna did not refer to just the company they traveled with, but the entirety of the room. She may look like the others, but she would never truly be a part of them; the shadows of the woods were ever present beneath those golden lashes, a wildness hardly leashed in every movement of her lightly muscled frame. He leaned back in his chair, fingers laced behind his neck. Kenna grew restless while she waited, her eyes occasionally became glazed when she made contact with the pack to soothe her jangled nerves, then snapped back to the room at any sudden sound.

Time slid by lazily while they watched the room, until the maid returned, her expression troubled.

"I'm sorry for the wait, but it seems we don't have all of the rooms you requested available."

"What do you have then?"

"Two chambers, with single beds."

Sweat beaded on her brow, her fingers wadded in her smudged apron. Kenna could taste her anxiety, and wondered at the type of people the maid dealt with.

"I see, perhaps you have—"

Heavy footsteps sounded behind them, and Caleb and Kenna turned at the rapid tread. Ressa strode toward them covered in the grim of the road.

Tendrils of clean skin, dirt washed away by sweat, snaked their way over her features, and deepened the wrinkles around her mouth and eyes.

"I will have a room to myself, thank you."

"Aunt Ressa, there are only two. It would be more reasonable to have you and Kenna share." Caleb glanced at the maid, "Perhaps you have a cot available?"

The woman's mouth opened, yet it was not her voice that filled their snug corner of the inn.

"Your mother raised you with such manners," Ressa patted Caleb's cheek with a fondness that madehis eyes roll. She flicked his nose, they both grinned when he swatted her hand away. Ressa turned to Kenna, hand on hip.

"I'm sorry to say this girly," Kenna's hackles rose at her tone. "But you make some rather odd sounds at night. If you snored that would be one thing, but I swore more than once an animal was in our chamber the other night."

Heat seared Kenna's throat and face, she looked away from the group.

"I dream vividly sometimes," her words were muted.

"Dreams or no, I am exhausted." Ressa returned her attention to the maid. "I would like my key please." Relief washed over the woman's face at a task within her realm of comfort.

"Of course, my lady." She quickly passed over an iron key into Ressa's open palm.

"Thank you," Ressa stepped away from her nephew.

"You're a smart lad, make it work."

The tavern maid gave Caleb the other key, bobbed a quick curtsy, and was gone. Caleb rubbed the back of his neck as he gazed at the key, so small in his grasp.

"So much for the cot," he laughed, an awkward forced chuckle most likely for Kenna's benefit. She slid into her seat, and he joined her a moment later.

"I can sleep outside," she glanced at the window, the sun a dim glow beneath the horizon.

"The pack is fairly close."

"No, I can go back to my tent." Ever chivalrous; now it was Kenna who rolled her eyes in exasperation.

"I handle the outdoors much better than you, my lord." A wicked twinkle glinted in her eyes.

"Is that right?" Caleb leaned across the table, his lips so close their breath mingled.

She could smell and taste the sweet herbs he chewed while he rode, smell the sweat and dust on his stubbled face. Her gaze rose from his lips to his eyes, eyes that still watched her soft mouth.

"That's right, my lord," she whispered.

"How funny to hear that term come from you, I think I'd prefer my name on those sweet lips." Heat washed over her; his name, when had she last used it? She couldn't recall.

"I'll just grab my things," Her voice was soft while she slowly reached for her saddle bag across the table.

Caleb reached out, his hand consumed her slender wrist while he held her fast.

"Aren't you forgetting something?" His voice was low, predatory.

"What would that be, Caleb?" His eyes flashed at the sound of his name.

"Your key." He gently twisted her hand, palm toward the ceiling, and pressed cool iron into her fingers. Caleb released her, hands fisted against the key and smiled; such a satisfied male smile. A growl rippled through her, annoyance... and pleasure? Pleasure at his wicked games perhaps.

"Fine, I will take the room." Kenna stood, and he rose with her. "You should at least come up and clean off a little." She wrinkled her nose. "You reek!"

Laughter bubbled up between them.

"Very well, I will follow you then." He gestured gallantly toward the stairs that were tucked into the back of the room.

"I'll have food sent up after us."

Kenna wove between the patrons of the tavern, eager for food. Caleb had swiftly located the maid and ordered, then made his way back to her. She sidled past a large group that argued loudly; its loudest participant, a rotund man with a filthy beard stumbled into her path. The scent of hot ale washed over her while she passed them, her mouth went dry. *There goes my appetite.* Face pale she shook off her revulsion and quickened her pace to the stairwell. Halfway up the first flight Caleb caught her with a gentle tug on her elbow.

She glanced at him and grinned, she had caught his scent while he'd climbed the stairs. A companionable silence settled over them while they walked, a calm that had been cultivated over hours and days in the saddle, side by side. Kenna stepped into the hall of the second floor and scanned the doors. She hesitated in the entryway and felt Caleb's body heat creep over her as he mounted the final stair.

"There is usually a small number etched onto the key." His words were kind, free of judgment. The tension in her shoulders slackened when she saw the number scratched into iron. *Room eleven.*

She glanced at the oak portals with polished steel numbers attached and found their chamber missing. Kenna

turned to Caleb with a frown.
"I don't understand." The key was warm in her hand, loosely caged by her fingers while she once more turned toward the hall; recounted each number with care.
"It seems we have more stairs to climb." Caleb stepped past her, his tread light on the floor boards while he strode down the hall. Tucked into a corner to the left of the final room was a narrow staircase. It hugged the wall, each step steep as it guided them to another floor.
"I didn't realize there were rooms up here." Kenna muttered.
"I don't think this one usually counts as a room for guests."

They crested the stairway to find themselves on a small landing before a slender door. There it was, that elusive iron eleven nailed to the chamber entrance. Kenna edged around Caleb and slid the bolt into the lock, tumblers whirled and a soft click released the tension in the lever.

A gentle push opened the room to them. It was modest, her tent was far more spacious; a narrow bed was tucked into the far-right corner, the metal bed frame braced against the molding of the door. A small night stand stood before a small window, on the opposite wall was a table with a wash basin, and an even smaller dresser. Kenna strode to the bed and sat, her back stiff and straight despite the ache of long hours in the saddle.

Caleb closed the door, dropped the saddle bags beside the wash station, then sat on the floor beside it. He faced her with a boyish smile.
"Well, at least I can clean up a little."
Kenna's nose twitched while she inhaled his scent.
Delicious.
"What's mine is yours." She spoke in a tone she had heard the nobles at the keep use, gracious and patronizing.
Caleb's laughter rang through her ears, and drew a modest chuckle from her.

He stood, peeled off his dust-coated tunic, then crumpled it into a ball in his palm. His motions were slow, deliberately slow as he evoked a sense of casual calm, yet his tense shoulders belied his steady hands. Kenna lit a candle with matches from the nightstand as the final rays of sunlight faded in a plum and navy sky. The light danced across his tan skin, rippled with him while he moved.

Water splashed over his fingers into the basin; his shirt was soaked, and he rubbed his face, neck, and chest with long, firm strokes. A knock on the door broke her fixation, and she lurched for the door. Her stiff legs tangled in the thin comforter, and she nearly tumbled onto her face. Caleb caught her, righted her atop the bed, then opened the door. The maid stood with a tray of dishes that steamed softly against her oval face. Her dark curls gleamed with moisture in the candle light, then bobbed while she nodded to Caleb.

"Thank you. I find myself half starved."

Her eyes slid over Caleb's well-muscled form, her lips parted slightly, her eyes hazy. Kenna suppressed a growl that rumbled in her chest. *What do I care? He isn't mine, it means nothing to me if she wants to bed him.* Yet the frustration at the other woman's desire remained.

"Not a problem at all, my lord."

"What was your name?"

"Helena."

"Well thank you, and let me know if any rooms open up."

"Of course."

Helena bobbed a curtsy, then turned toward the stairs while Caleb closed the door; Kenna didn't miss the glance that passed over the maid's round shoulders.

They settled on the floor together, the tray laden with meat pies, roast chicken and a small pile of steamed greens between them. An iron decanter with two cups rested on a small pile of cloth. Kenna grabbed a meat pie and bit into it; its flavor was simple but it was warm and had a decent amount of flesh for her to chew. She drank from her cup, and felt it slosh heavily in her belly. Caleb ate silently with her, though his gaze flitted to her more than once.

When they at last finished Caleb set the empty tray on the dresser, while Kenna washed her face and neck. She slipped off the soiled outer layer of her clothes until she stood in a thin tunic that hung just past her behind. Her fingertips grazed the edge of the smooth fabric while she walked to bed; her legs folded under her as she nestled into the corner of the mattress. Silence enveloped them while the candle burned, golden and hungry, ivory wax thick as it dripped from eager flames. A dizziness overtook Kenna, her muscles relaxed after a day beneath the sun. It was his voice that made her stir.

"How long were you in those woods?"

She sat up straight, aquamarine eyes blinked slowly while she focused on his face. He was solemn, eyes hidden in shadow while he watched his idle hands.

"For as long as I can remember." Their voices were hushed, it seemed wrong to speak fully in this tiny chamber.

"What about the village?"

"The village, well I…" a deep sigh escaped her while untangled the mass of emotions that knotted around her heart. "I tried to keep my time in Blackwood brief the older I got. When I was little I was there for a few years straight, Jan didn't think it was safe for me in the woods. Which is silly since my infancy there weren't perfectly well—"

"Infancy?" Caleb leaned forward, forearms braced on drawn in knees.

"Yes. I was a newborn when I came to the pack, and then spent most of my childhood with Jan. As I got older, and became a woman, being part of the village became harder. I would spend weeks, sometimes months alone in the woods with the pack. When I returned the villagers were suspicious, hostile, like I was some witch that had crawled out of darkness. Even with that, I had a woman's body, and men… they have their hunger to satiate."

Kenna stared at her palms, eyes vacant while she delved deeper into her past; Caleb's knuckles were white, his fists clenched so tightly his joints ached.
"That was the first time I used my magic against another human. I grew fangs and bit him, then claws to strike at him. He was bloodied and ran in terror from me, right out of the barn and into the village square. He accused me of being a witch, and that I should pay for what I'd done to him. Though my fangs and claws were gone, my mouth was still full of him, my fingers still stained. No one cared what he had tried to do to me." Her voice was low, her chest heaved deep, long breaths while she steadied herself.
"He deserves everything you did, and more Kenna."

She looked up, eyes filled with pale blue ice, the wild beasts within her thinly veiled.
"Perhaps, but it was easier to leave. I stayed away for two years, just running wild with the pack, using my magic to become one with the woods. I saw such beautiful things, things I couldn't begin to explain to someone," a smile quivered upon her lips. "And such terrible things as well." Silence lingered, heavy and loathsome; Caleb wanted to cross that void, comfort her against those fears that lingered in her eyes.

The floorboards creaked beneath him when he stood, and her eyes, a soft blue-green once more and framed in gold lashes, gazed up at him with trust. He sat beside Kenna on the bed, his palm warm on her knee.
"But you went back."
"I did," an answer to his statement. "I missed Jan and hoped that things would be better. In some ways there were, the men never dared touch me, but all of the villagers

hated me. They sneered whenever I walked by, so I stopped leaving the garden gate. It didn't seem fair to subject Jan to that." Kenna's heart twisted at the thought of her human mother; she clenched her fists tightly around the thin cover. Caleb grabbed her hands and gently untangled her grasp from the fabric.
"I'm sorry."

She knew what he really meant, not just sorry for her past, but sorry for her mother.
"It's all right, there was nothing that could be done." A tear rolled down her cheek, and Caleb kissed it away, his lips a brush of gossamer to her skin.

Her breath hitched when their gazes met, the swirl of emotions she saw there; Kenna pulled her hands free and sidled down the bed, her back to the wall while she sat on her pillow. Caleb stayed at the foot of the bed, a kind, patient smile curved his mouth.
"Tell me about yourself," her voice was breathy.
His smile broadened, and he complied.

They talked for long hours, sometimes laughter ricocheted around the room, other times a solemn silence, heavy with loss and regret. The night was dark outside the window, a heavy pitch beneath a star-studded sky. Kenna glanced at Caleb, her eyes so heavy she at times spoke with them closed.
"What made you go into the woods?"
"Besides the dare?"
"Besides the dare."

Caleb rubbed his face, his raven-black hair spilled across the bed where he had laid back, his booted feet still on the floor. Kenna longed to run her fingers through his hair, instead she laced them together, her arms encircled around her knees.
"I suppose I was looking for something, I didn't know what it was but I knew with all the places I had been, I'd never

come close to finding it." He turned his face to her.
"Are you still looking?"
"I don't think that I am."

Kenna's heart thundered at his words, and the rawness in his gaze. She cleared her throat and shook her fingers loose.
"Well I think it's safe to say no other rooms are coming up available."
Caleb sat up and stretched before he rose to his feet. Kenna looked up at him, a heat burned beneath every inch of her skin.
"I should put my tent together."
"Don't be ridiculous." Her pulse now buzzed in her ears, and she fought to keep her voice steady. "We have slept beside each other before, we can do it again."
"Are you sure?"
"Yes! Stopping being such a pup." Kenna peeled off her long socks, then her vest. "Turn around so I can get into my nightgown."

He complied, slowly; his eyes roved the lines and smooth curves of her body, pupils large and dark with desire. Kenna shivered despite the heat of the small chamber. Once his back was turned she quickly slipped free of her dirty riding clothes, then pulled on a shift.
"Okay," her voice cracked.
Caleb smiled at her, with her arms crossed over full breasts, her waist trim, and those legs; so long and thick he knew how firmly he could grip them when he pulled her close. Caleb clamped down on his imagination while he kicked off his boots.
"Crawl in and I'll blow out the candle."

Kenna did as she was bid, the sheets cool and thin when they fell around her. A sigh escaped her while each muscle relaxed against the soft mattress, then Caleb blew out the small flame. Silver filled the chamber in its absence, and her eyes locked on him as he drew near. His movements were slow while he lifted the blankets, when he slid into the bed beside her. They were silent while they laid shoulder to shoulder. *Is he as nervous as I am?* She glanced over and saw his eyes locked on the ceiling. *Maybe he is.* The thought sent a wave of surprise through her, that tingled and taunted her. *Touch him. Touch him.* A voice crooned within her mind. *Just reach out and touch him.*

Her mouth was dry, her mind dizzy with the song of that sultry voice; Kenna reached for him. Her fingers grazed along the long line of his silver scar, so smooth and cool beneath her finger tips, so beautiful in the moonlight. His lungs stilled at her touch, and she began to pull away, fear burned her veins until he grasped her hand. His fingers twined with hers, then he pulled her closed as he turned to face her.

His lips were soft upon her own, the kiss slow and gentle, his hands warm around her waist. She felt her body soften against his, and she wanted to draw closer, to cleave to his hard body and feel his heat sear her. Caleb responded to her need. His kiss depended, demanded more while his tongue caressed hers; he pulled her close then shifted on top of her, his knees slid smoothly between her legs and parted them.

Kenna's breath came fast, her body tight, but she held him close when he leaned away. His lips parted, his brow knit with concern but she pressed her mouth to his. Silenced, and soothed by the eagerness in her kiss he leaned against her. She hooked her legs around his, her rounded calves tucked behind his knees. Caleb's callused hands slid down her frame while he kissed her, squeezed her tight when she shivered against him. His lips trailed down her jaw, her neck, her collar bone, just as his fingers found the hem of her gown. He drew up the dress, his back arched while he dragged the gown up and over her hips and flat stomach, then over her firm, full breasts.

Her nipples peaked against the gentle graze of fabric, and heat throbbed in the apex between her parted thighs. Celeb bolstered himself on his elbow, his mouth on hers while his hand drew lazy circles up the inside of her thigh. Kenna's back arched, he was so close, mere inches from the slick space between her legs. She moaned when his mouth descended on her breast.

A light sucking pulsed through the tender flesh, his other hand cupped her, massaged her while he sucked, flicked her nipple with his tongue, grazed her skin with his teeth. Kenna moaned again, the slick wetness unbearable, how it ached for his touch. Her hips ground against him while she opened her legs wider. She could feel him, hard and long, his shaft strained against the laces of his breeches. He groaned against her breast when she stroked him through the thin layer of fabric, and felt him surge against her palm. His mouth took her as his finger slid inside of her, delved deep and stroked her. Such heat flooded her, consumed her while he slipped another finger inside. His hand pumped and her hips rocked in rhythm to his touch until her pleasure crashed through her.

Kenna cried out and held Caleb tight, moisture pooled in his palm and a deep, satisfied growl rumbled through him. He backed off the bed until his knees hit the floor boards, then grabbed her thighs and yanked her to the edge. Her legs were flung over his shoulder, toes curled with pleasure, as his mouth descended on her slick, hot lips.

She could hardly breathe, her moans long and drawn out like the smooth, long strokes of his tongue. He kissed her, opened her wider, then slid his tongue inside her. A sound of satisfaction, muffled by her body, mingled with her cries. He licked, and kissed, then slipped his fingers within her again; his tongue slid to the bundle of nerves and licked in time with each pump of his long, broad fingers. Caleb devoured her, drank her in as she came again and again against his mouth.

His other hand cupped her bottom and squeezed, held her against his lips while she shuddered through another orgasm. Kenna's legs trembled uncontrollably, her breath hitched when Caleb pressed a gentle kiss to the inside of her thigh, then lowered her legs to the bed. He rose to his full height and her eyes locked on the impressive bulge against his thigh. He crawled into bed beside her, curled around her while he slung his arm across her waist.
"Caleb—" her hips pressed into him.
"Not here," he kissed her neck below her ear. "Not in some inn. When I bed you Kenna, I want it done right. You deserve so much better than this crumpled little room." He kissed her, and pulled her close despite her sounds of protest. "Just rest darling." Another kiss. "Rest."

His breath was even, and the solid pressure against her back side was removed, if only so it would not touch and stir her desires. His thumb drew small circles against her arm, and the sweet satiation turned into a deep calm. Kenna's legs drew up as she nestled closer to him, her own breath heavy, and slow. Sleep overtook her, dark and tender until she was swept away by dreams.

Pale light filtered through sheer cream curtains, her room lit with the soft glow. Kenna stretched, the sheets crumpled pleasantly beneath her hand, and found the bed empty. Confusion and dread filled her veins with fire. Brow furrowed, she sat up slowly, then turned to face the room while her stomach twisted.
Was last night a mistake?

Her eyes alit on Caleb, dressed in only his breeches, his feet bare and propped up on the dresser. He watched the cobblestone square of the inn, then turned to her; his hair was rumpled, his grin soft and peaceful. Relief swept through her while she returned his smile.
"How did you sleep?"
"Wonderfully," she answered, then slid her leg free of the blankets.

The air between them purred, a physical thing that rubbed and slid against their skin. Caleb stood slowly, each sculpted muscle in his chest rippled, smooth beneath taut sun-kissed skin. Kenna's breath hitched when he strode towards her, then stooped to the ground; the memory of his midnight crowned head between her thighs made her ache where his lips and tongue had been. His fingers grasped his rumpled socks near a large pair of black leather boots.

Her breath rushed from her explosively, and Caleb looked up, still on his knees; his eyes glinted as they slid from her face to her womanhood before him, then back to her eyes. A feline smile curved his lips while he regained his feet.
"You look hungry little wolf."
"Starving."

Her lips were dry, and the tip of her moist pink tongue slid over the delicate skin; glossed and plump, they gleamed in the morning light. Caleb's gaze was transfixed on her mouth, he stood so close their breath mingled.
"Are you hungry?"

"Ravenous." His voice was a dark purr that rubbed over her skin.

Her nipples peaked, a warmth bloomed between her thighs. She remembered his words from last night. *"Not in some inn. When I bed you Kenna, I want it done right."* The heat in her blood cooled, tempered by his declaration. "Let's get dressed then."

Kenna stepped away from him and was revived by a sweep of cool air, a blessed barrier. She wasn't sure she wanted the quiet inn to echo with her shattered moans of ecstasy. The thought brought heat to her face while she donned her clothes, and readied for the day. Caleb stood by the door frame, his body relaxed and casual while she finished. No words were spoken, only a slight dip of his chin before he opened the door, grabbed their belongings, and descended the stairs with her in tow.

She paused on the bottom step and scanned the room for her companions at the same time as Caleb. Randy's golden mane was a beacon where he sat beside the main hearth at a small table; Ressa and the guards were nowhere in sight, but Aden sat beside him, and when they drew near Kenna saw his glassy eyes fix on her in misery.
"You look like hell."
"Oh Kenna, why?" Aden dropped his head in his hands with a groan. "You cleave my heart from my breast with such words."
Kenna slid into a chair with a snort.
"Try drinking less, it may make you live longer."

His dark brow arched, one hazel eye viable, his rich skin held the green hue of too much liquor.
"What a miserably dull existence," he muttered into his palms. Randy rolled his eyes, then grinned at Kenna.
"Foods over there, take whatever you like. We paid the tab already."
Kenna stood, but not before she threw him a look of

gratitude.

Mornings at the Dragon Wing were much more pleasant from Kenna's perspective. Calm, quiet, the cool clean air scented with fresh baked goods. She walked towards a long amber counter polished smooth by years of use; a large pile of buttered bread still soft and warm from the oven, apples, porridge, and a thick brown jar filled with honey. Beside the simple fare was a blue pitcher filled to the brim with cool, frothy milk. She took a small plate and mug, selected a piece of bread, then drizzled it generously with liquid amber.

Her cup full, she returned to her seat beside Randy. Aden now cradled a cup of tea that steamed softly against his face. Eyes closed he inhaled a rich herbal scent.

"Hopeless."

He glared at her declaration.

"Indeed." Randy chuckled beside her. Caleb returned to the table a moment later with two plates laden with food, then nudged the smaller one toward Aden.

"Eat and shut up."

"Savages," Aden took a bite of bread that dripped honey and butter. "My friends are savages." His muttered words were ignored while they ate; Kenna dug into her meal with gusto while she listened to the group converse about their past, specifically their childhood. From what she gathered, Randy was the unfortunate recipient of Aden and Caleb's practical jokes. Despite herself she could not help but laugh at their antics.

"You were the worst, I should have pushed you down that well!" Randy exclaimed at Aden.

"You are just too sensitive."

"You cut my girth strap!"

"Oh come on, you didn't fall off."

"I was upside down, I'm lucky I didn't get my brains bashed in."

Caleb who had quietly eaten, lost in thought while his companions bickered, stepped in when the mood shifted.
"Let it go, there is nothing you can do about it now." Randy sighed.
"Prick." He tossed his apple core at Aden, which landed in his teacup with a splash. Aden eyed his cup balefully, then drank down the liquid.
"Delicious."

Their meal finished and plates deposited on the counter, the small company gathered their belongings. Kenna trailed them, her breaths deep and slow while she crossed the threshold. This is it, we are almost to the capital. Kenna touched her mind to the pack, alerted them that she and the humans would move out soon, then severed the bond. There was still tension, and mistrust heavy in many of their thoughts and she could not stomach the weight of it, not yet. Kenna herself was eager to finish their journey; by this afternoon they would be in Sapphire Bay.

Sunlight poured down on her, warmth radiated from the crown of her head, her shoulders, and chest. A shiver of delight swept through her while she marched into the morning's warm embrace. Kenna swung into the saddle and directed Shren to the road, shadowed pines called to her in sweet whispers, but so did the sea.

Chapter Four: Gem Strewn Waters

White birds swirled above the riders with wings tipped in stormy gray. Bright yellow beaks parted and loosed a shrill cry while they kicked their webbed feet on eddies of coastal air. Kenna had never seen such birds, and even more strange was the air; the thick taste of it that coated her tongue, that filled the wind with its moisture. Such a cool, heady tang caressed her senses; Kenna stood in her stirrups, her nostrils flared to take in more of the intoxicating scent. She could feel the pack's minds as they roiled with curiosity, the smells and sounds grew stronger, a low roar hummed at the very edge of her hearing.

She glanced at the others, baffled by their calm faces. *Did they not hear the roar?* Her gaze slid to Caleb, his lopsided smile and over bright eyes.

"What's going on? What is that sound?" The low roar grew

louder with each step of shod hooves, her heart pounded at the sound.

"Just wait for it wolf girl, just wait."

Her brows furrowed, but she stemmed the flow of questions that threatened to drown her. The crest they mounted was covered in grass, flower-bedecked clover, and moss-covered stones; all so green and rich while fed by the mist. Just a few more steps and they would crown the hill, and she would see whatever being called to her from such a distance.

Then Kenna saw it, a mass that glittered from here to the horizon. White-crested waves strewn with diamond-like brilliance until the world fell away, lost to the curve of the earth. Tears seeped between her lashes while she strove to stare against the shine, it sang to her, overwhelmed her with its unabashed beauty. A pure cerulean sky arched above them, each to touch that precious field of blue; Sapphire Bay was a wonder to behold. Kenna reached for Caleb, leather cracked beneath her while she clasped his calloused hand.

"What is it called?"

"It's the ocean Kenna, we call that particular ocean Sapphire Bay, and our Capital."

"The ocean… It's beautiful."

"The moment we get a chance, I will take you there so you can swim."

"Swim? In the ocean?" she asked, her gaze flicked quickly between him and the water.

"Yes, you can swim there. It's a body of water like a lake but at some points unending, and laden with salt. I don't recommend drinking any of it."

Caleb squeezed her hand then let go, his chest ached at the look on her face; clouded with wonder and curiosity. The voices of her companions faded away into a soft hum accompanied by the base rhythm of hoof beets. Soft soil, rich like honey in color, floated around them in a haze that shimmered while they passed. Kenna looked back toward her travel companions, at Caleb; his shoulders tense with laughter, Randy recounted some event with hands that gestured wildly.

His reins were slung across his mount's neck in abandon while he talked, his teeth bared by upturned lips. She looked ahead again when they turned down the road, Kenna's mount edged around a bend shrouded by deciduous pines, only to be startled by yet another site of wonder.

The gilded road on which they walked wound its way gently through lush fields and pastures. Vibrant crops added shades of golden wheat, yellow corn, and the deep green of leafy vegetables. Herds of cattle roamed in pastures framed with white cross-railed fences that lead to small homesteads surrounded by smaller livestock. Farms gave way to the city with reluctance; small homes in varied shades of cream, tan, or pale rust grew into two- and three-story estates.

Each estate was a small palace in Kenna's eyes, and she marveled at their individuality. They were a myriad of colors, soft tans, whites and brown topped with rose-colored roofs. Green foliage added a gentle, earthly touch to the city from this distance, that nature had not completely lost its hold on the now-cultivated land. Sapphire Bay grew increasingly dense; it also rose in elevation until its colorful buildings were sprawled across the massive hill like a quilted blanket held in place by the castle itself.

Ivory stone reflected the sun in soft waves of light. Graceful arches gave way to soaring towers with windows that glittered like ice against the surface, some flashed with polished iron inlay, while others gleamed in a multitude of colors. A flag snapped in a coastal breeze over every tower, its movements were boisterous, almost proud, as though it was alive beneath the royal crest it bore. A black sword slashed through the middle of a deep-blue field, while a delicate white rose wrapped around its midnight-dark blade. To the west of the castle stood a thick forest, large trees gnarled with age and tangled branches braced against the winds of the shore.

Pines, oaks, and elms embraced one another in their shadows, a welcome sanctuary from the sprawl of humanity before them. The ocean filled the skyline behind the castle, where it perched precariously along the cliff, its outer walls built into the limestone rock face itself.

Her fellow riders turned the bend and were invigorated by the sight of the capital, for many of them those walls were home, and they urged their mounts to quicken their pace. The pack sensed their energy through Kenna's connection, and a surge pulsed down the magical line. She could hardly stand the wait, anticipation a worm in her belly. No matter how fast the horses devoured the earth between them and the city, Sapphire Bay loomed out of reach. Exasperation overtook her excitement and Kenna turned her thoughts from the behemoth in the distance.

Instead she focused on the things around, each little place that was within her reach. She gave up on reaching the city and distracted herself with the world they rode though. The countryside was a rich green sprinkled with trees and boulders blanketed in velvetsoft moss. Moisture from the sea thickened the air, left a thin translucent vale over the greenery that grew thicker beneath the shade and shadow of trees. As the party drew closer to the coast

Kenna was soothed by the constant dull roar of the ocean, its infinite sound lulled and shaped her imagination. *What does this dark water hold? I wonder how deep the water is, what type of creatures lurk in its depths?* Images of enormous beasts that swam through murky, bottomless waters filled her mind, then her body with a delighted shiver. Kenna was suddenly determined to immerse herself in the brine-filled substance. Her thoughts shifted from the depths to the trees around her, and the wolves that ran beneath them.

"Father, how are things in the forest? I believe you are in the King's Cloak." For a moment there was no reply, then his deep voice rumbled back.

"As far as we can tell there is no pack in the area."
"That makes sense, there are regular hunts."
"It will do."

Kenna cut the connection.

The road turned from soil to dust-covered cobble stones, each irregular shape made to join around the structure of mortar. Her small party clattered into the city, which despite its beauty from afar was marred, exuberant and melancholy, new and decrepit; Kenna shuddered at the swirl of sound that rattled against her ear drums. The city walls had a soul of their own, each street echoed with hundreds of voices. If Kenna could cover her ears without attention she would have and she wished desperately for the dew-covered glade, yet it was a world away. The primary road ran slowly through the city, turned like a serpent in the grass—in many places it nearly doubled back on itself.

The indirectness put Kenna on edge while they pushed through the thick crowds of the lower districts.

"Keep an eye on your things, mistress Kenna."

Captain Remus kept his musical voice low, ebony skin gleamed with sweat beneath a merciless sun. She frowned in response, unsure of what to say.

"The folks in this area can be rather desperate."

"I see… thank you," she answered slowly,

altogether uncomfortable with the image he painted of the people. If these people were desperate, perhaps it was due to the unbearable conditions they lived in. Filth was abundant, the roads crowded, and stray children with skinny dogs ran rampant. Hunger burned in so many of their eyes, it gave a sharpness to them that even the smallest child bore. Her heart ached at the sight, and Kenna could not understand a person's need to live within the city walls if this was the cost.

It was abhorrent, the sight of those children, thin and filthy in the streets; beggars on the corners, elderly alone beneath tattered shawls. There were those that did their best, heads down, threadbare clothes clean. She stirred Shren around a man with a stained tunic and bare feet, he did not look at her when she mumbled an apology. Kenna once more caught sight of Remus, her gaze drawn by the soft glint of coin while it slipped from his fingers to the palm of one street urchin after the next. She watched the children run away on spindle-like legs before she met his eyes. There was a soft kindness there and he gestured for silence, then turned his mount further up the road. Kenna nudged her gelding to follow the line, the Captain's secret a mark upon her heart.

Deeper into the city they traveled and slowly, poverty slipped away into the luxury of wealth. The streets were lined with delicately manicured trees and brightly colored shops. Many of the shops had living quarters above them, mostly inhabited by owners or merchants. Even the smell was different; it lacked the pungent reek of desperation, filth, and stale urine. Instead Kenna detected perfumes, wafts of floral scents, and delicious meals sold by street vendors. The crowds that mingled along the paths were as lovely as the flowers in the valley, each lord and lady garbed in silk, satin, velvet; veils fluttered in the noon-day breeze. Kenna was startled by the number of city guards, faces guarded, spines erect.

Heavy leather coated their chests, rawhide at their throat. Black gloves braced by gauntlets held thick batons, while a sword thumped against their thighs. Kenna's hackles rose when they walked past her, the man closest to her reeked of arrogance. *One would expect them to cluster in the lower levels with its high crime rate, not the decadent halls of the upper class. If they did that, then where would they swagger?* Her thoughts were a savage snarl in her mind, in her wild heart that raced. The harsh differences in living conditions bothered Kenna, in the village there was the poor and the better off, but there was a much larger number of people that lived somewhere in between. More than that a child would not have been left to starve, or never had been while Jan had dwelled there.

Kenna's thoughts shifted to the village that was now charred rubble, of that poor boy shot and ran down in the arms of his mother. Blood splashed through her mind, and she flinched. There was no village, and there was no Jan.

A darkness wrapped around her heart while she rode. Her thoughts lost to the memories that haunted her while she slept, that still clung to the shadows around her. Kenna glared at the city, and could only hope they would soon push their way through and reach the castle.

"That's my kind of place!"

Kenna was yanked back to the present by the outburst. She turned in her saddle and saw an animated Aden who shoved Randy with his elbow, a rakish grin on his face. Randy rolled his eyes as he leaned out of reach.

"Come on Randy, you know we have had a good time there. Don't be a snob."

"Shut up Aden." Randy snapped, then pushed his gelding further up the line. Aden waved his hand after the blond, a guffaw on his sarcastic lips.

Kenna turned back around to scan the streets for the

famed location.

"It's over there." Randy explained, his normally smooth brow creased with annoyance.

"The Silver Sparrow."

"Isn't it a bit classy for him?" Kenna asked, one thin brow raised. Randy laughed despite himself, and tension eased from his shoulders.

"Don't let it fool you, it tends to get a bit rough at night. Mostly due to Aden, but still."

Guess that explains the nose.

Dust clung to their sweat-encrusted clothes, and even their horses' coats were dulled by the fine substance. Kenna rode in silence, her eyes drifted in and out of focus while she kept in touch with her lupine family. A final gate separated the castle from the city with a guard at each side of the massive portal. One stepped forward, his brown beard cropped short, eyes narrow from years in the sun. After a brief conversation with Remus the guard waved a signal at a man in the left tower.

Moments later, the thick oak and iron doors swung open on well-oiled hinges and allowed their company to enter castle grounds. Kenna swallowed, her stomach again tight with nerves while she laid eyes on the elaborately manicured grounds. Ponds accented with waterfalls and graceful swans glittered among the rich emerald fields. Crushed rose stone wound intimate trails between the hedges and gardens that bloomed with a mage-made vibrancy. It was a place of wonder and comfort, nature and man joined together to create an escape from the cold stone. *This is it, I can do this.* Her body did not respond to the mantra, instead her heart beat even faster against her breast bone until she thought she would cough it out onto the road.

Randy leaned closer to her, aware of her nerves. "It really isn't that bad. Not all nobles are terrible I promise." Kenna could only nod mechanically. "I'm sure Caleb will help you through it." Kenna looked at him sharply. Randy laughed, "Thought that might get your attention."

By this point they had reached the gravel swath before the castle doors where a handful of young grooms waited for them patiently. She swung from the saddle and gathered her things, slung both bow and saddle bag over her shoulders. Kenna walked towards Shren's head, then stroked his velvet muzzle.

"I'm going to miss you boy, thank you for getting me here," she whispered into his ear. He nickered softly, umber eyes gentle while she stepped away.

"Take good care of him." Kenna instructed, passing the reins to the groom.

"Yes mistress, of course."

Kenna turned her back just as the bay was taken from sight. Caleb walked beside her, and in a smooth motion relieved her of her saddle bag.

"I thought you didn't like horses?"

"I do, I always have. I just didn't know it would hurt so much when you first start riding them."

"Don't worry, you can go and see him whenever you like." Caleb assured her. Kenna walked mutely beside him, but she had heard the understanding in his voice. Now that they were truly at the castle steps she was not sure she would be able to cross the threshold.

Her pulse pounded mercilessly against her temples. She rubbed them softly, slowed her pace while the pale oak doors loomed above her. *Perhaps this was a mistake.* Caleb put his arm around her shoulder, to bolster her or hinder her retreat, she could not tell.

"It won't be that bad, first thing's first, you go up to your room and refresh. You won't have to meet anyone until tonight," he informed her, one corner of his mouth pulled down in a lopsided grin.

Kenna focused on that mouth, so warm and inviting. Then her mind caught his words.

"What do you mean about tonight?"

"Well it just so happens that the court is having a small gathering. Princess Ena is finally of age to marry so her parents have been hosting to allow her a good look at her suitors. It's a perfect time to meet the King and Queen since you will be provided for at their expense."

"I never agreed to that!"

"Oh hush, it's not a problem at all. Where else would you live?" Caleb asked, a crease between his brows.

"I don't know… I didn't expect all this though." Kenna responded lamely.

She fell quiet after that, not sure what more she could say on the subject. They passed though the main doors and were greeted by a small cluster of servants, and pages. A page quickly attached itself to each noble, their boyish voices filled the hall with the soft hum of muttered words. Caleb excused himself from Kenna's side with a grin and a squeeze of her shoulder, then left with the young boy, and passed her saddle bags to a young female servant while he walked.

"This way mistress."

A girl with a long, brown braid now stood beside Kenna, her eyes were curious while she took in her clothing and assumed status; it seemed she was unconvinced. The guards under Remus's command went one way, and Kenna another, quietly escorted by the slender maid.

They headed down a western corridor in silence and soon came to a long stone staircase, covered with a thick colorful rug. Without pause Kenna's guide mounted the stairs with rapid steps. Though bright with opulence the inside of the castle was cold, frigid in its ivory beauty. The gloom of Dragon Stone had shown age, the will to endure, and in some instances decay; Sapphire Bay was a jewel that glittered, frozen in its splendor and indifferent to the lives that dwelled within.

Kenna followed her guide to the top of the stairs, then down a corridor that curved along the outer edge of the castle. Tall arched windows broke a pattern through the pale stone, each glass pane cradled by thin bands of iron that were polished mirror-bright like silver. Beyond the glass Kenna caught sight of the King's Cloak and felt a pang go through her, she longed to be with her pack beneath those heavy branches, grass cool beneath her feet, sky hidden by greenery above. Her attention returned to her path through the castle when a group of courtiers walked past, their perfumed scents so thick and pungent it was an assault on her nostrils. Kenna coughed, cologne cloyed to the back of her throat, and kept a closer eye on where she walked; more than once she held her breath when nobility passed.

Tapestries hung from the walls on silver or gold rods to depict hunt scenes, or woodlands creatures; heavy gilt frames displayed the faces of monarchs past, silver wall-mounted candelabras on either side to illuminate their faces, eyes glazed as they pretended at life.

Lost in thought Kenna nearly trampled her guide who had abruptly stopped at a honey gold door. It was tucked closely into the corner of the hall, exclusive or purposely forgotten, Kenna could not tell.

"This will be your room mistress." Her tone was light, though it fell flat at the use of "mistress." The maid was most definitely unconvinced.

Kenna shrugged, her eyes not on the girl's face, but the brass key she pulled from her stark white apron. The door unlocked and swung open on silent hinges to expose a small chamber with the curtains open on the other side of the parlor. Kenna entered the room slowly while she took in her new dwelling, then followed the maid into her new room.

"My name is Eliza, if you need anything else please call on me." Eliza deposited the key on a small table, curtsied, then left the room; her luminous eyes never left Kenna's road-stained figure.

Alone, Kenna explored her new home. For a moment she was puzzled, her eyes roamed the chamber in a slow assessment. Smooth white walls were adorned with tapestries and art, all of which consisted of animals, domestic and wild, and beautiful nature scenes. A small fireplace crackling softly, two luxurious sofas with plush pillows adorned with tassels, a large rug and a table; yet there was no bed. Kenna took off her boots and stockings; she enjoyed the feel of the amber floors beneath her feet, cool after the confinement of leather. She sat on the sofa and bounced once, it was pliant beneath her weight.

The sofa would be comfortable enough, though a bit cramped. She rubbed her neck while she eyed the thick rug under her feet. *Or that may be better for me in the long run.* Kenna walked across the room toward a wall of glass, only small sections of wood paneled the wall between sheets of iron framed glass. In the distance lay the forest where her family would dwell, closer still was a pasture speckled with the warm colors of multiple horses. Directly beneath her was a small garden bejeweled with flowers of all possible colors. At that moment she desperately wished her windows would open, that the soft fragrance of summer blooms could waft through the gauze curtains.

She inspected the garden from her perch and noticed a steel stairwell that spiraled while it clung to the wall, thick tangles of ivy embraced its frame. Kenna followed the wall of glass, fingers shifted one curtain after the next, so light and soft she barely felt them. Where the glass met the opposite wall, tucked into a corner, was a narrow door covered with a thick tapestry of a tree. She peeled the tapestry back to reveal a latch, thrilled she pulled it and found it unlocked. Kenna pulled the door open on oiled hinges and was met by a wave of floral-scented wind.

Her laugh was bright and joyous while she fought off translucent curtains that billowed in the breeze, then closed the door with a soft click. *Once it's dark I can have the pack join me.* Encouraged by her discovery she turned a curious eye to her room. On the other side of the parlor she found another door, this one was oak. Kenna slowly stuck her head through the portal and squinted against the gloom. She pushed the door open farther, then located the curtains on the other wall to her left.

They were thick and heavy, made of velvet backed by canvas that blocked out both the sun and its insufferable heat. As she pushed them aside, her eyes ached against the light, but quickly adjusted to the pale green walls, soft and vibrant like new oak leaves. Kenna ran her fingers across its cool surface while she surveyed her sleeping chamber.

The floor was the same warm amber as the other, which she now realized was her own personal parlor. There was a large chestnut wardrobe with a table beside it made of the same wood. On the table lay the odds and ends of a lady; a box of ribbons and pins, a small chest of simple jewelry, a bottle of perfume, and a small hand mirror with birds painted on the back.
Kenna frowned, unsure what she would do with the objects.

Her bed was much more to her liking; a thick forest green comforter with amber ivy trim stretched across a plush mattress. Feather-stuffed pillows in green and fawn colored cases were piled decadently across the head board, luring her closer with the promise of unimaginable comfort. She shook her head slightly, resisted the pull in order to see what lay beyond a small door on the other side of her bed chamber. *How many doors can this place have?* she thought with a frown.

She strode briskly towards the small portal, and pulled it open to reveal a white stone room with one slender window. It held no decoration of any kind beside a large tub filled with water that billowed steam to collect upon the white stone of the ceiling. Cool drops of water dripped down to splash on the tile of an ivory floor. Beside the tub was a small table with soaps, towels, and a rather large candle. *Great Divya, what a way to live.* She would have never thought she would have access to a personal bathing room. She closed the door behind her, then peeled off her filthy riding habit. Kenna tossed it into the corner of the chamber, a stained, crumpled mess against tiles that gleamed.

A knock echoed through her chambers, clear and vibrant while it demanded her presence. Kenna left the window with its gilded view of the pastures, forest, and mountains beyond; each ridge brushed with amber, every dip saturated in black and umber. She expected the wide eyes of Eliza, suspicious and fairly judgmental, yet it was not the slip of a maid at her door. Kenna's breath hitched at what the heavy oak portal revealed.

"You look lovely little wolf."

Kenna smiled despite herself.

"Thank you."

"Are you ready to go?" Caleb extended his hand.

"Go where?" she responded, her smile gone.

"To the gathering, dear." His tone was mild and indulgent, her eyes narrowed slightly, a tension in her spine.

"I thought that would be this evening," she protested, not ready to once again immerse herself in a crowd.

"It started early, now stop fussing and come with me. Don't forget your key."

Kenna growled at him, in a black silk shirt that gleamed with the same obsidian shine as his hair; she growled at the pants that clung to the muscles of his legs before they tapered into supple leather boots. His eyes danced with amusement at her frustration, and her admiration of his form.

In two strides she was at the table that held her key, she grabbed the brass item, and unsure where to tuck it she closed it in a clammy fist. She nudged Caleb from her doorway, back rigid with indignation, and turned the bolt sharply. It clicked into place while Kenna inhaled through her nose. Key in hand she followed Caleb down the corridor, the opulence of the castle once again glared at her.

Caleb led her through the castle with ease, chatted casually about its tenants and history, Kenna hardly listened. Her mind could focus solely on the fact that in a few short moments she would be in the same room as the King and Queen of Alearian. Her pulse quickened with each twist of the hall that brought them closer, and she did not hear Caleb's voice over its frantic hum.

"Are you in there wolf girl?" He lightly tapped her shoulder, and though his words were tinged with laughter, his mouth was tight, his gaze shadowed with concern.

"What did you say?"

"I asked if you were all right, you look a bit pale."

"I'm fine."

"Deep breath," Caleb slid his touch from her shoulder to her hand, a soft caress that trailed fire through her limb, then squeezed her hand. "Let's go in then."

A servant opened the door for them with a gracious bow, and with Caleb at her side, she stepped into the great hall.

She stopped in her tracks, limbs rigid as she took in the chamber around them. So warm and alive, this heart of the pristine palace made of moonstone and ivory limestone. Caleb stroked her hand gently then gave her a subtle tug. "It's all right little wolf, I will protect you." There was a twinkle in his evergreen eyes that drew a laugh from deep in her belly, a joy that eased her frame into motion.

The floor was patterned in honey and amber wood, each plank alternated in a splendid display; it was polished to a high finish that looked like a thin layer of liquid rested over its surface, a translucent pool on which the dancers glided. Ladies dressed in every shade of silk and velvet, like jewels that whirled and shimmered of their own volition. Precious stones graced their necks, wrists, and fingers; a spark of light, so sudden then gone as the dancer was spun away by a well-groomed Lord. The last rays of sunlight filtered through windows that stretched from the floor to the ceiling, the top of each panel decorated with stained glass. Music drifted through the air, its sweet notes delicate while nobles swayed to its rhythm.

Caleb and Kenna ventured deeper into the hall; she was tantalized by the rich scent of seasoned meats, pastries, and spiced wine. Candles flickered among the food and bestowed a soft light against each succulent surface.

"Are you hungry? I can get you something."

"No, but I would enjoy a drink." Kenna lied, though hunger gnawed at her belly, the tension there would not allow the thought of a single bite.

"Of course."

He sketched a bow that lowered his velvet lips to her fingers, slipped her a discrete wink, then stepped away. Alone she surveyed the crowd, unsure of her place within it; a lone wolf, a forlorn Sigma. Her solitude did not last long.

"Kenna!" Her name reverberated off the polished walls. She turned to see that Aden and Randy headed toward her, both dressed in finery that reminded her of the titles they held.

"Hello boys."

"Boys?" Aden protested, his broad chest heaved with an indignant breath. "You mean men!"

Kenna and Randy rolled their eyes, yet Kenna could not help the fondness that filled her for Aden. Despite his jokes and the way he reveled like there was never another sunrise, he had a kindness in him; that smile was a shield, not for himself but for those he loved, a shield to keep the hardships of life at bay.

"Who are you kidding Aden?" Caleb asked, laughter in his voice from behind Kenna's shoulder; she started at his voice.

In the crowd she had not heard his approach, a realization she found unsettled her deeply.

"You are just a dog on his hind legs." Caleb continued.

Kenna suppressed a laugh at Aden's stricken face.

"How dare you insult me so, and in front of such a beautiful lady," the brunette protested.

"Indeed she is beautiful." Caleb's voice was a low growl behind her, its sound skittered down her spine.

"How do you like your rooms, Kenna?" Randy's smile was soft, genuine.

"They are wonderful, thank you for asking," she responded, a wave of affection flowed through her towards the sun-kissed knight, perhaps it was the wine. Aden's gray eyes twinkled.

"Best watch yourself Caleb, little Randy here will steal your girl."

"I would never!" Randy protested, a flush replaced his tan.

"I've nothing to worry about, Randy is a good man unlike some fellows here." Caleb answered pointedly. This made both men guffaw with laughter.

"I don't know why I bother with you Caleb, you're just heartless."

Aden's eyes were plaintive, mockingly wounded. Kenna only half listened to their banter while she watched the crowd swirl around them; it was then that she caught sight of a lovely pair.

The man was tall and willowy, long strides carried him through the crowd with ease, his dark wavy hair cascaded to his shoulders. A dark beauty swayed in his arms in time to the music, she shared his features with remarkable closeness, her own frame graceful while she gripped his arm. Long raven locks rippled down her back in obsidian waves, so stark against her pale-green gown that matched her angular eyes. The pair looked incredibly familiar, though Kenna could not place why; she knew so few humans it made no sense that she should think anything of them.

They finished their dance with a flourish, then headed toward their group. Kenna watched their arrival with curiosity.

"Kenna, I would like to introduce you to my cousin, Von Devoney of Tara and his twin sister Sophia." Caleb said. She could smack herself; how could she miss such a resemblance? Sophia watched Kenna with a cool detachment, her gaze undecipherable. Kenna fought the urge to adjust her gown, and when that jade stare lingered she smothered a snarl. She was soon distracted by a charming smile and outstretched hand.

"It's a pleasure to meet you Kenna." His voice was like velvet.
"It's nice to meet you as well."
"Is that so?" Von asked, his lips quirked up at her words.
"Sophie, say hello." He did not look away from Kenna.
"A pleasure I'm sure."
"Should we sit then?" Randy asked.
"Yes, of course. Join us at our table." Von invited.
They ambled toward the twins' table, a circle bedecked with fresh wreaths of flowers, candles, crystal goblets, and gilded plates.

    Kenna watched Von and Sophia part while Caleb escorted her through throngs of guests. Sophia whispered into Aden's ear, her moon white skin a sharp contrast to his richer tones. He grinned while he leaned down towards her; laughter drifted from the pair before Aden pulled free her seat. *Not so chilly then.* Kenna slid into a chair that opposed them. Within moments their plates were laden with food. Kenna nibbled at her meal while she listened to the group of friends talk, and despite her best efforts she could not keep up.

    So many of the stories they shared were things they did as children; when they swam at their favorite lake, stole the neighbors' horses, or ran through fragrant orchards only to sit in a circle, young faces covered in fruit while they told stories of fairies and elves. It was magical, that sweet and vibrant childhood, and it was clear the noble children had grown up blessed by the sun and all its glory. Kenna herself preferred the cool caress of the moon, yet she could not help but smile as their laughter filled her ears.

    At times they included her in their conversations, but she would soon be left behind by the rapid current of their words, forgotten by all but Caleb. Throughout the dinner he kept his leg pressed against hers. He would touch her often, even in small ways; his fingers would brush hers while he passed her a drink, or napkin. He would stroke her cheek to clean it, or whisper sweet nothings in her ear. Boys in the village, if they did ever dare approach the wild wolf girl, had always been crass. Caleb made Kenna glad she was human, a feeling that was bright and unknown, and unsettled her to her core. More often than not she had shunned her human pelt in favor of a wolf's blessed sable, but with Caleb she did not feel the need to hide.

It was then that she noticed the way the crowd grew still and silent around them, men and women bowed and curtsied one after the other; silk, and satin sighed while it rippled around their forms, the only sound in the great hall. When her companions left their table Kenna stayed in her seat, her fork tight in her grasp.
"Who is it?"

He looked down at her while he reached out a hand to lift her to her feet. She stood beside them, his body a steady warmth beside her, their lips so close her heart skittered in her chest. Caleb's expression was thoughtful while he looked at her, then her vision blurred as he laid his lips upon her own. So light that touch, a gentle pressure of soft flesh that stilled the air in her lungs; then he pulled away, Kenna's lashes fluttered open and the sight of him grew clear. A smile reached his eyes, light reflected off a gold fleck near the edge of his iris while his gaze consumed her.
"It's the Princess Ena, she is greeting the court before her parents arrive on the dais."

Kenna nodded mechanically, her thoughts far away from the court she stood in. Princess Ena was sixteen and by the laws of the world she lived in, ready to wed and breed in the name of bloodlines and politics; it was her responsibility, and no matter that she was still a child, or that she had never been touched by anyone, let alone a man, she would do this for her crown. Kenna touched her magic when she caught sight of the shadows behind the young girl's smile, and with altered senses could taste her anxiety in the warm air of the hall.

She could smell that she was still a maiden beneath the sweet perfumes dabbed along her collarbones, nearly taste the sweat that clung to the pale silk of her gown. Kenna released her magic and slid her hand free of Caleb's; a storm brewed in her heart, and ached against the bones that caged it. Ena strode towards Kenna and her companions, her hair long and thick where it rippled over her shoulders, golden in the candle light. Her gray eyes were kind while she wove through the crowd, where she occasionally disappeared behind courtiers and their ladies' skirts.

Then she would appear, a soft smile upon her thin lips that revealed teeth that were moderately crooked; the imperfection took nothing from that smile though, instead she shone all the brighter.

"It's so good to see all of you. Randy, Aden, Caleb; I'm glad that you are back at court. It's rather dull without you." A number of greetings were exchanged. "And Caleb, you look dashing after that horrible wound I heard you received from a Gullinborsti was it?" Her voice was light, still young despite her manners and vocabulary.

"Yes, if it wasn't for Kenna my bones would be resting in those woods."

"Oh my, how terrible." Her gray eyes focused on Kenna with curiosity. "Please introduce us."

Caleb guided Kenna forward to meet the young monarch, his fingers cupped her elbow.

"This is Kenna, she hails from the northern woods and is my savior."

"Mistress Kenna, it's a pleasure to meet you."

"Thank you Princess." Kenna bowed her head, eyes averted.

"Please, call me Ena, we are all friends here. Have you met my parents?"

"No, I have not."

"Then let's remedy that." Ena answered cheerfully. Kenna felt like a cornered rabbit, her heart beat so hard that she thought it would burst.

Luckily fear had burned away all traces of her wine, which in hindsight may have been more hindrance than aid; there was nothing to relax her rigid shoulders, nor her restless hands. The royals were already seated on their dais, voices low while they spoke to one another. At their daughter's arrival they turned their attention to their guests, unruffled by their disturbance.

"This is my father, King Alaric Vimcor, and my mother Queen Calla." Ena introduced. Alaric Vimcor was a man in his mid-forties, dark brown hair fell down to his shoulders, with just the slightest bit of silver glinting at his temples. His beard was clipped short, hiding any gray that peeked through around his thin lips. Steady eyes watched them from above a long, straight nose.

His inhaled breath stretched the elegant sapphire blue velvet of his tunic while he greeted his daughter. "Hello Ena, have you seen your brother at all?"

"No father."

Kenna saw Ena's blonde lashes flutter. *A lie perhaps?*

Kenna looked away, unconcerned. The King's brow furrowed but he did not press the issue; relief rolled off the princess and Kenna stifled a grin. Calla sat beside her king with poise, her hair plaited and piled on her head in a delicate crown of gold, curls fell loose to frame her tawny brown face. Amber eyes held a restrained fire, full pink lips were tucked in the barest hint of a smile.

"My brother Osric is around her somewhere. You may meet him later." Ena said offhandedly. "Mother, father, I would like to introduce you to Kenna." The royal pair nodded at her kindly, Kenna nodded in response, her hands firmly clasped behind her back.

"Welcome to our court Kenna, I hope your accommodations are to your liking?" Alaric asked.

"They are, thank you, your Majesty." Kenna answered, throat hoarse; she fought the urge to rub her nose. She blinked when the royals looked away, a strange sensation tickled her, perhaps not from her nose but inside her head. Kenna looked up at the dais and caught sight of a woman with midnight hair; she whispered to the King. His face was intent on her words, and the woman flashed a pointed smile at Kenna while she spoke soundlessly.

She squinted at the strange woman and felt the sensation in her head strengthen. It was similar to the pull she felt when she made contact with an animal mind, yet subtly different; more powerful somehow. She brushed against the well of magic at her center, and again looked at the King's companion; it was not a velvet-clad woman that stood beside the ruler, but a slender black cat. The realization was a jolt through Kenna's consciousness, a jolt that snapped the tether to her magic.

It was a challenge not to openly gape at the shifter before her, not to climb that dais and ask the ivory-skinned woman to explain what she was. *Is she like me? What do others see when they gaze at me?* Kenna frowned, her fingers clasped so tight they lost any semblance of sensation. Whatever the woman was, she was not quite like Kenna, but something close perhaps.

Alaric's whisperer had said something of note that drew all of his attention. He held up a hand to her, then looked to his guests.

"Kenna, please enjoy the party. My Queen and I will be sure to call on you soon."

They had been dismissed, and Kenna followed Caleb and Ena when they returned to the rest of the court.

Caleb saw the distraction in her gaze while she turned over the glimpse she had caught of the woman.
"What's on your mind?"
"Who was that woman? The one standing by the King." Kenna fought the urge to turn around.
"That is Lady Isabella Faoleen, she is the adviser to the King. Why do you ask?"
"Nothing really, just curious." Her mind still tingled at Isabella's touch.

Seated once more at their table the small gathering of friends greeted her warmly, most of them that is; Sophia's spine was rigid, yet Kenna could not place the smell that came off the temperamental woman, it was not rage that tinged her scent.
"So how was it?" Randy asked.

His question drew Kenna's attention from the other woman, her mind rushed to process his words.
"Rather terrible actually." This made the others at the table laugh, even Sophia.
"So we are all dying to hear how you met our dear cousin," Von interjected, black brows wriggled like raven wings.
Aden sputtered at the words and red wine dripped down his stubbled chin when Caleb flashed his cousin a wicked look, then elbowed Aden for silence. The twins looked between the pair with a sense of horror.
"You didn't?!" Sophie exclaimed, her refined features distorted with shock.
"Come on love," Aden gasped for breath, "I didn't force him! It was just a little dare among men."
"Men? More like overgrown children if you ask me," she countered, obviously displeased.

Von shook his head and raised his voice over the clamor of Aden's protests.
"So how did you find Caleb?" His gaze had pivoted from his family to Kenna, his narrow frame leaned

towards her over the linen-covered table. She fought the urge to squirm in her seat, Kenna cleared her throat with another sip of wine; wine that she had meant to ignore.
"I found him cut to the bone and near death."

Her ominous words caused the group to quiet, each member glanced at Caleb, concern or confusion marred their features.
"Don't scare them, Sophie will tell my mother and I will never hear the end of it." Caleb flashed his cousin a vulgar gesture
"I would not!" she protested indignantly, cheeks pink while her eyes flitted from his face to the hand he had gestured at her with.
"Well it was bad," Kenna countered. "Yet as bad as it was he still managed to make a fool of himself." Her lips twitched. Von slapped the table with a laugh.
"That's our cousin. I bet he tried to charm you didn't he?"
"I think that was what he was going for, but I can't say he made his mark."

The group roared with laughter as they could clearly see the knight injured, yet flirtatious in their mind's eye. Kenna could still recall the look of those blue lips, how they had tried to smile in the face of death. It had seemed then, that he had accepted his demise; the shadows of the forest had grown thick and cold around him, and had seeped the warmth and life from his limbs. Kenna could still taste the metallic tang of his blood on the air while it had mingled with the soil. Such a fool he had been, to risk his life, then laugh at death's ready embrace.

Caleb grabbed her hand and pulled her from her thoughts, his eyes filled with mock pain.
"And here I thought I had won your heart?"
Kenna blushed when everyone gave knowing smiles.
"You haven't captured it yet," she whispered.
"You will have to work harder than that to catch that little

wolf my friend." Aden stated with a wink. Sophia elbowed him sharply.

"You mind your manners, you little tramp."

Aden grinned with more teeth than necessary, grabbed her lovely face, and kissed her soundly. At first she resisted, her hands pressed firmly against his chest, but it soon became clear that she enjoyed his embrace. Her slender arms wove around his neck while she returned his kiss, and a low roar reverberated across their table. Their group cheered and banged their glasses against the circle of wood on which they ate.

Aden released Sophie and raised his hands in an exuberant display of triumph, it drew a ripple of laughter from those in attendance. Amused as they were, Caleb and Von pelted Aden with fluffy rolls of bread; Aden caught a delicious projectile and took a large bite, his brows wiggled all the while. Kenna leaned back in her chair with sides that ached, she swiped joyous tears away with the back of her hand while she took in the faces around her.

All were gilded with smiles, their voices raised in merriment, yet one gave her pause; Sophie's eyes were downcast, her frame rigid while she tore a piece of bread to dust. She felt Kenna's gaze and looked up, for a moment rage twisted her face, then as fast as it came, it was gone. Her long-boned hand intertwined with Aden's, while slim shoulders shook with laughter. Kenna looked at the food that still filled her porcelain plate, unsure of the stranger before her.

Once back in her room Kenna contacted her family, it felt so good to meld her mind with theirs. She sent them images of the garden beneath her room, coaxed them closer while their shadowed bodies slunk across each pasture; her magic was like a beacon, it drew the pack closer to her with every moment that passed. Kenna watched the night, her brow pressed against the cool glass while she surveyed the grounds for humans. The wolves moved swiftly through the sweet grasses like wraiths, they moved as a unit, each member had its place while they shifted directions in the night, around a dip, hill, or a horse that spooked.

Her breath was tight in her chest, lungs stiff with excitement as they fought her command to widen and consume air. At last Kenna heard the clack of their claws against steel while they spiraled up the staircase. She rushed for the door and let them in amongst ivory gossamer curtains that billowed with a nocturnal breeze. Within moments she was surrounded by delightfully coarse fur of black, sable, silver and white. Tears sprang to her eyes while she immersed herself in her pack's loving embrace. The wolves whined and yipped loudly around her, ears laid flat in affection while they rubbed their jaws against hers;

Kenna laughed through the tears.
"Hush, no one knows you are here."
"Your cave is large, they will not hear." Argued Varg, a mischievous glint in his aurelian eyes.
"Where is your mate?" Leara asked, mouth agape in a wolf's laugh; Kenna swatted at her.
"He is not my mate!"
"You want him to be." Chimed in Cana.
"Oh Cana, not you too!" Kenna collapsed on the floor under an avalanche of paws.
"Enough children, settle down." Finna's sweet voice washed over them like cool water.
"Yes mother."

Kenna looked at her mother tenderly, how she loved her; their pack could not be more blessed than to have the Luna Wolf that they did, more than once she had brokered peace, had extended kindness over punishment. Finally calm, the pack gathered on the plush cushions of the sofas, many of the wolves rubbed their faces into the velvet and cloth pattern embroidered with heavy threat, such a delightful sensation over slender muzzles. *The cleaning lady isn't going to like this.* Kenna's lips tucked into a grin while she watched her family savage a common luxury without remorse.

She at last felt like herself, no other human in the room, only her pack near her while moonlight filtered through iron-framed windows. They traded thoughts until the moon was high and glimmered brightly with the reflected lights of a forgotten sun.

A sharp knock at the parlor door woke the pack, which induced a savage growl from the groggy creatures. Kenna breathed deeply where she lay on a plush rug from the east, her eyes focused on the ceiling while she waited for the person on the other side of the door to go away; again there was a knock, and this time Kenna was roused. She rubbed her face while she sat up to glare at the large panel of polished oak. *Who in the world could it be this early?*

She glanced at the pale daylight that streamed in between the curtains, and winced when her eyes ached at the adjustment. Kenna rose to her feet and picked her way through the furred bodies that bedecked her parlor floor.

She pushed back her sleep-rumpled hair, then strained her over-long tunic, a blessing as it were since it was the only garment she wore. Leara was at her side when she drew close to her door and paused; a soft buzz took form in the root of her mind so familiar, yet alien all the same. She took a step towards the door and felt the internal hum increase. Her brow furrowed when she placed the sensation, the King's Whisperer, Isabella.

Kenna opened to the cat that masqueraded as a woman, and for a moment, Kenna was at a loss for words. "Lady Faoleen, how may I help you?" Her fingertips found her temple and massaged small circles, the pressure staved off the buzz within her skull.
"Good morning mistress Kenna. I have a proposition for you."
"Excuse me?"
"May I come in?" Isabella glanced briefly at the white wolf.
"Yes… come in." Kenna opened the door wider to allow the strange cat-woman in then quickly informed the pack through their connection. The two women were settled, each on a sofa with a wide table that hugged the ground between them; a no-man's land. Leara settled at Kenna's feet, a comfort against her bare skin.
"Like I was saying, I have a proposition for you." Isabella smoothed her thick burgundy skirt.
"And that would be?" Kenna asked, her belly tense as she scented the other woman.
"I know that you have a magical gift, and from what I see and have heard about you, it lies with creatures." Again she looked at Leara. "I can help you cultivate that magic."

Kenna was unsure of what to say; this strange woman had come to her with an offer of powerful magic, it seemed far-fetched, like a fantasy one would dangle before a child's eager eyes; except Kenna was no child.
"I know this may seem strange Kenna, but I have a great

deal of knowledge and experience that I could offer you. Not only that, your abilities could prove very useful to the Crown." Kenna suppressed a growl. *Me, useful to the crown? Now that is far-fetched.*

"What would I owe you for this knowledge?"

"If you find your studies under me worthwhile, I would like you to go under the employ of their Majesties." Kenna pulled back but stayed her response at the sight of Isabella's raised hand.

"The King is a good man, so is his Queen. I have been with them many years and I can assure you that they are fair and just rulers."

Kenna settled against the sofa cushions, her expression purposely vacant while she nudged the ivory wolf's mind.

"What do you think sister?"

"I smell that she is different, but I do not smell a lie."

Isabella sat quietly on the satin-embroidered couch, her long-boned hands delicately folded in her lap. Her gaze had been vacantly focused on one of the arched windows that displayed the pastures, and the forest beyond; Kenna could feel that she waited for her to speak, if Isabella had any inclination that she spoke to the wolf she gave no sign. Kenna took the leap, though her gut clenched with the drop.

"I accept your offer then."

"Wonderful."

Her angular face creased in a smile, then she rose to her feet with a boneless grace. The floor was clear of wolves, they had slunk away to rest in the shadows while Kenna spoke with the King's Whisperer, so her path was clear while she walked to the door. She gripped the latch then looked at the woman still seated on the couch, a silver-tipped ivory wolf at her feet.

"I will return soon to start your studies."

The door closed with a soft click behind her, a

gentle finality. Leara stood and laid her sleek head in her human sister's lap; Kenna stroked the snowy fur while she stared out the window, a sense of detachment heavy in her bones. *Where is life taking me now?*

Kenna roused herself from the stillness that had seeped into her limbs, and released the pack onto the garden stairs; except for Leara who sat curled upon the cushions, nose buried in her tail. The pale light of predawn gave way to glorious rays of deep yellow, blush pink, and blue that chased away the shadows of night. Kenna went to her bed-chamber to freshen up, and returned minutes later in a cream tunic over fawn breeches, and knee-high leather boots. While she walked across her parlor she plaited her hair loosely over one shoulder, a subtle weight against her collar bone that provided a fraction of comfort. She headed for the door while she snatched her key from a round end table, then collected her bow quiver and shrugged it into place.

Kenna swung the door open with a newfound vigor to reveal a skinny boy with dusty brown curls; he stared up at her, hand raised and ready to knock. His brown eyes widened slightly while he lowered his hand.
"Good morning mistress, I am here to bring you to the King and the," he inhaled shakily, "the Queen." His voice lilted in a note so high Leara's head tilted to catch the sound; the whites of his eyes gleamed while he stared at the wolf. Kenna struggled to keep a straight face and guilt tempered amusement when she saw his young face bead with sweat.
"Thank you. Would you take me to them?"

He would not respond, the blood had drained from his face and his small mouth trembled.
"She won't hurt you, I promise." Kenna assured him. Her tone was gentle in the way she soothed a frightened animal. To prove her words true, Leara laid back her ears, head tiled with a soft whine while she wagged her tail like a

sweet puppy. The boy's eyes flicked back and forth between woman and wolf.

"Leara is just a young girl herself," Kenna said, then knelt between them. "You two could be playmates." That struck the boy as funny, his lips curved into a small, if fragile smile.

"That's it, go on and pet her. She likes it." Kenna encouraged.

He reached out with a hand that trembled, then stroked Leara's shoulder. With each pass of his fingers his grin grew until he smiled openly, gapped teeth revealed with joy.

"Why do you have a wolf in your room mistress?" The lad asked while Leara licked his cheek.

"She is my sister."

"She can't be your sister, you aren't a wolf!" he protested, then wrapped his arms around the young she-wolf.

"On the outside, no. Not always." Kenna answered with a wink. The boy's eyes grew wide again, though he did not release his new friend.

Kenna watched the two of them, hip braced against the doorframe. In children, wonder and curiosity could outweigh fear; her hope was that some of this boy's wonder would rub off on the adults, and let her pack be with her in peace.

"Would you take me to their Majesties then?"

"Yes, I suppose I can." He looked with mournful eyes at Leara, Kenna's heart went out to him. "You may walk with her if you like. She won't mind if you hold on to her."

"She won't?"

"She won't." Leara licked the child again in encouragement; the boy stood and quickly grabbed Leara's scruff with dimpled hands.

"My name is Tom by the way."

"I'm Kenna," she responded while she locked her chamber

door.

"Oh I knew that." Tom answered, completely disinterested in the human in favor of his new lupine companion. Kenna snorted with amusement as she followed Tom down the hall.

They accrued no small amount of stares, in addition to a fair number of panicked women and servants, on their walk to the King and Queen. Kenna stifled her snarls and accusations of ignorance, and at last Tom led them to a pair of polished oak doors framed by guards on either side. A great tree was carved across the glossy surface of the wood, unhindered by the seam which ran down its middle. Kenna pulled her gaze away with some effort when Tom stood on his toes to speak with a guard. The man then turned and knocked twice on the portal that echoed deeply, then the world tree cracked in half as the doors swung inward on silent hinges to reveal the Royal throne room.

The room was a work of art, the architect had managed to place the chamber in such a way that it had a whimsical stained-glass window that ran down the length of the room on both sides. Rose gardens filled one's view if they chose to look out of the gem-like glass, beyond those fragrant floral beds was the protection of stone walls.

The craftsmen had shaped each supportive beam in the walls to look like oak trees, the rafters' branches that intertwined like slender arms. Between these soft brown beams were walls of green painted with murals of creatures both mundane and magical. Kenna stepped onto the floor that was a high-polished silver-toned wood, the branches above glimmered in a subtle reflection on its surface.

A deep blue velvet carpet rested before the thrones where the King and Queen awaited Kenna with ease, their arms gracefully draped across the heavily decorated gilt leaves and cushions. Though their faces remained posed in a polite display of interest, Kenna did notice their gaze shift to Leara more than once. Kenna suppressed a small smile and devoured the final steps between herself and the throne. When she drew near she caught sight of Isabella, her small figure tucked into the deep shadows behind the thrones. She looked as lovely as before in her burgundy gown, so rich against her ivory skin, the only difference in her appearance was a pearl net that gathered her thick locks into a pile at the nap of her neck.

Kenna kneeled before the monarchs, which Tom had explained was appropriate on their walk, then bowed her head. Her jaw twitched as she lowered her gaze; these people were not her alpha, but they were alphas in their own right. The seconds ticked away while she waited, and Leara began to growl beside her. Finally the King's rich voice washed over her.

"Please rise mistress Kenna."

"Thank you my Lord," she murmured as she regained her feet.

"We have summoned you," Queen Calla began, "because Isabella tells us you have potential to be quite useful. You are a powerful mage."

Her umber eyes once more flashed towards the white wolf. Kenna bristled slightly at the term useful. *I am not a pawn.* Alaric analyzed her, the tension in her shoulders, her rigid spine, and Kenna knew he wondered if she was worth the trouble.

"Isabella has an impeccable sense of character. She has a great deal of… experience in the matter." Alaric said cryptically. Isabella grinned from behind the King's shoulder, Kenna sniffed an inside joke.

"So we are going to trust you, but first we would like to know the extent of your ability." Alaric said.

Kenna balked at his request, the nonchalance in which he asked her to expose herself so utterly. Never had she openly shared the full extent of her gifts with any human besides Jan, even then she had been hesitant. Leara leaned against her, a warm source of comfort in an unknown world.

"My magic is still changing, your Majesty. As I grow, so do my gifts. As of this moment I can heal small wounds on beasts, I can communicate with them through a mental connection, and share the shapes of many creatures if I so wish," she paused for a moment then continued. "I can also see what the dead have seen." The last words came out in a rush, their taste still lingered on her tongue, so bitter like bile.

Alaric raised a brow.

"Would you care to elaborate?" He leaned his elbows onto his knees, his calloused fingers formed a peak on which he rested his bearded chin.

"What I mean is, I can see what an animal saw before it died. It has rarely been useful, except once when we hunted a rabid bear that was killing the woodland creatures in its madness. The fresher the death, the more I can see. The mind holds onto the memories for as long as it can, perhaps until the soul is ready to leave. I don't like to talk about that particular skill."

Silence filled the throne room, a tangible thing that blanketed them while they watched one another. Kenna ran her finger tips through Leara's fur, and found comfort in its familiar texture. Isabella leaned in to speak into the King's ear, her voice so soft it did not disturb the stillness around them. Alaric's face was an indiscernible mask, and when she had finished, he leaned over to speak with his wife; whatever he had said she seemed to agree. Her ear bobbles swayed as she nodded in accord, her eyes locked on Kenna.

"Your gifts are unusual and spectacular. It is impressive for one so young, and with Isabella's help you shall fine tune it. She says you have potential to be a great mage."

Flattery is nice but can we get to the point.
"We shall trust you with this task. Alearian is at odds with our northern neighbor Vontrakal, and as much as we wish to avoid it, war may be in our future. Our concern lies in the fact that the ruler of Vontrakal, King Hrothgar, seems to be gathering valid information about us. We know about a fair number of spies in our midst, yet none have access to the information Hrothgar has been given. We need you to seek out this spy, and bring them to me."

Alaric drummed his fingers lightly on his throne. "You will study beneath Isabella, hone your craft then use it to find this spy. Do you understand?"

She bristled at his tone of voice. *I don't like the idea of sneaking around. It's dirty.* Leara touched her mind. *"Don't think of it as sneaking, think of it as stalking one's prey. You must be swift and crafty. You can do this sister."*

Kenna pulled a deep breath between clenched teeth. "I can do that, your Majesty."

Alaric smiled, his keen gray eyes calculated everything about her, a strategist the likes of which she had never known.

"Your gift will give you the advantage. You may be a bird on a branch, a cat in the window so to speak. I have a great faith that you will serve the Crown well."

She was dismissed.

The door swung shut behind Kenna with absolute finality. Just like that, she was in the employ of the Crown, a spy that would safeguard secrets for a kingdom she hardly knew, or cared for. It wasn't until Tom grabbed her hand that she realized she still stood before the door with her pack sister. The guards watched her with suspicion, their fingers curled around the hilts of weapons, Tom eyed them nervously while he tugged on her arm.

"We had better move on, mistress." Tom whispered.

"Of course, can you take me back to my room please?"

"I can't do that mistress, I have to take you to Lady Isabella."
He flinched at her sharp gaze. "Then take me."

Isabella's quarters were in a western tower that overlooked both the depths of the bay and land. Once they had reached the top of the stairs, Tom bowed.
"I leave you now, mistress. I hope to see you soon." His eyes were on Leara while he spoke, and the soft look eased the rigid tension in Kenna's spine. *The boy is just too sweet.*
"I'm sure we will see you again."

With that the child trotted away downstairs. She watched him go, then turned back to knock on the door that now stood open. A frown creased Kenna's brow while she stepped past the threshold.
"Hello?" her voice echoed against stone and plaster.
"Come on in," a voice called from the gloom of the chamber. Shoulders stiff, she entered the room, silver-tipped wolf in tow. It was fairly simple, besides lush carpets that smothered the sounds of one's steps and a satin couch, all that really decorated the room were paintings and books. The paintings were not of fashionable topics, but of far-off places, many that seemed unreal.

Kenna strode towards a dark canvas and stroked the glossy surface with the barest tips of her fingers. The castle was cast from midnight, slender towers spiraled towards the stars. Most of its structure was swallowed by mist, a shadowed forest lurked behind it like some faceless beast.

It made the hairs on her arms stand on end, a tension in her muscles readied her for a swift escape. That castle was a forbidden place that held malevolent secrets; Leara whined beside her, her hackles raised.
"I see you found one of my favorites, I was wondering

what held you."
"This is your favorite?" Kenna asked skeptically.
"Yes, it's a place I went to long ago." Isabella's eyes were dreamy while she spoke.
"You painted this?"
"I did. Enough of that though, let's begin your studies." She clapped her small hands.
"Follow me."

She led Kenna across her parlor into a small room that had a spectacular view of water on one side, and the forest on the other. The room was a perfect circle with a large table set in its center. On the table was an assortment of devices and objects—plants and vials, charms and grimoires, odd bits of hair, bone and precious stones. Kenna could sift through the objects for days and not know all of their worth. Above them bundles of dried herbs and charms dangled from the rafters on slender leather cords; against the wall, shelves held books that looked as though they would fall apart when touched.

Kenna wandered through the room, her hands clasped firmly together to curb the desire to hold and marvel at each object. Isabella busied herself among the weathered tomes, unaware, or perhaps unbothered by her new pupil's curiosity. Kenna jumped when Isabella dropped a stack of literature on the table with a resounding thump, trinkets chimed excitedly in its wake.
"You had best get started with your studies."
Isabella announced, hands on narrow hips.
"All of these are for me to read?"
"Yes, you do know your letters don't you?"
"Yes, Jan taught me my letters and some figuring but I've never read anything like this."

She ran her fingers along the spine of a leather-bound book with auriferous letters that read: *Bodies of Beasts and How To Define Them.*

Isabella watched Kenna in silence.
"It will be challenging, but with practice you will get faster at reading. I do expect you to apply yourself," she paused for a moment, "as in now." With that she walked from the room.

Kenna's hackles rose at the order, she began to protest but was stopped by Leara's gentle words. *"You must stay patient."*
"I agreed to help the King not be controlled by her."
"No," Leara paused while she gathered her thoughts, *"but you know she is his right paw. You should listen to her. I think she is only trying to help you."* Kenna sighed sharply through her nose, then brushed her fingers lightly against her sister's jaw. "You're right," she answered quietly while she sat down before the large table. She slid the closest book towards her and she opened it, determined to succeed in the world of man.

Chapter Five:
The Secrets They Carried

Kenna rubbed tired eyes as words began to blur together in a swirl of ink and parchment. The past two months had flown by, her days consumed with both studies of the body and mind. Her mornings consisted of armed lessons in the training ring in archery and hand to hand combat, her evenings were dedicated to riding lessons in the arena; she learned how to properly jump a horse, shoot from the saddle, and direct her mount with a swift hand. Despite this, the bulk of her day was dominated by studies with Isabella. Kenna could hardly remember the bird song from her beloved forest, it had simply been overwhelmed by the hum of words.

She snapped a book shut and pushed herself back from the desk with exasperation. Isabella glanced at her, her manicured index finger held her place in a detailed scripture.

"Is something the matter?" Her tone was cool as she addressed her pupil.

"I can't do this any longer Isabel, I'm going mad!" The sable wolf at her feet whined softly.

"I find that unlikely," her mentor responded while she carefully closed her book.

"You know what I mean." Kenna ran fingers through her hair for the hundredth time. "I need some freedom Isabel, I need to be outside."

"You are outside every morning and evening, I see no reason to interrupt your studies."

Kenna opened her mouth to argue but Isabella overrode her.

"Look how far you have come with a bit of knowledge and discipline. You can take on twice as many shapes, and your healing abilities are quite remarkable. You must press yourself if you wish to succeed here."

"I know that, and I appreciate everything you have done, but this was not my life. You can't possibly expect me to change so quickly. Just because I can change the shape of my body does not mean I can change who I am at my core."

Isabella's eyes softened as she watched the woman before her, a smile tucked into the corners of her mouth.

"Perhaps I push you too hard, I simply see so much potential and you have yet to prove me wrong. Not to mention the Crown expects you to ferret out a spy. One needs a proper education and control over their gifts for such work."

Kenna sighed and pulled her book back, resigned to the fact her mentor would not let her leave.

"I do see your side, Kenna. You may have the day to yourself," she raised a finger when Kenna leaped to her feet, "but I expect you to be diligent when you return tomorrow."

"Thank you Isabella." Kenna fled the room with the sable wolf close on her heels. Isabella shook her head then she gently restored the books to their places on the shelves, her parlor door swung shut with a loud click behind the woman and wolf.

Kenna and Baylor ran through the ivory halls of Sapphire Bay, ignoring looks from noble and servant alike. Their figures were a blur of color, an adornment to the frosty halls that echoed with the rhythmic pounding of her breath and boots.

"Would you like to go for a ride?" She asked her furry companion, her face glowed with joy.

"Would you not like to see your new mate?"
Baylor responded. Kenna stumbled to a halt at the thought of his evergreen eyes, so familiar, so gentle.

"I don't know what he's doing, I don't want to disturb him."
Kenna answered, her chest tight while her heart drummed against her sternum; it did not thunder from the run.

"As you wish, though I don't think you could bother him."
"What makes you say that?"
"We have all seen the way the dark one watches you. You are his moon."

She smiled but did not respond, simply walked towards the stables while she resisted the urge to hunt the castle for him. Kenna sent her thoughts ahead of her towards Shren and found the bay gelding willing; she could sense the earth beneath his hooves while he surged toward her, it rippled through their connection in waves.

At last Kenna was free of the castle, her long legs carried her swiftly across the grounds towards the paddock.
"We are leaving the castle." She sent him images of trees and streams that wove beneath bent boughs of pines and oaks. Kenna picked up her pace to trot alongside Baylor; she rounded the final bend and found that Shren waited

patiently by the fence.

She leapt the weathered posts and sprinted towards the gelding; at the last moment she pushed herself from the ground while she tangled her fingers in his mane, then vaulted onto his wide back. Without a bridle or saddle she urged him forward through the pasture and leaned close to his neck, her cheeks wiped by his midnight mane, and laughed with abandon. Her mirth smoothly turned into a howl as the trio sailed over the final fence between them and the King's Cloak, between them and freedom.

Kenna returned to the castle grounds with a gentle glow that seeped from every pore while she and Shren meandered through the fields. Wreathed in its embrace she glanced at the castle, and soon caught sight of a figure who leaned against the rail. He called something to her that she could not quite make out, and her head tilted when she called back,
"What was that?"
He only smiled as he waited for her to come closer.
"I have a gift for you." Caleb informed her, his voice a seductive growl. Kenna's toes curled in her supple leather boots at the sound.
"I don't have anything for you."
"Don't worry about that love," he answered, then kissed her softly.

His expression changed slightly when their lips parted, no longer hungry and dark with desire, but curiosity.
"You're a bit salty." His grin widened.
"Yes, it was quite the ride. So what about this gift?" Kenna bent around him and saw his empty hands.
"I see I've got your attention then."
"You do." Kenna purred, wet lips revealed fangs that glistened, her eyes glittered in the sunset's glow.

"Patience little wolf." His voice was low, he stepped close. Lightning raced through her veins when his fingers encircled her wrist and drew her limb toward him. He kissed the pale blue lines that branched beneath her skin, then stood as he held her. Caleb whistled a long, low pitch, though his gaze never left her lips, or silken throat.

A copper stallion trotted through the stable's open doors with long, elegant legs and inquisitive eyes. Kenna watched the creature's movements; the masterful arch of his neck, his slightly dished head held high until he stood before them, nostrils flared to take in their scents.

Kenna stepped forward and reached both body and mind towards the animal. The stallion's thoughts were warm and wild like a summer breeze, he longed for the hidden places just as she did. She gripped his halter and pressed her brow to his, their connection deepened while she memorized the shape and color of his mind.

She pulled back and looked at Caleb with eyes that shone, her lips parted in a breathless smile.
"He is your summer solstice gift, a small way for me to say thank you for everything you have done."
Kenna released the stallion and stood on tiptoe to kiss Caleb, their lips lingered, soft and tender.
"What is his name?"
"Finn."
"Finn… That's lovely. Thank you." His only response was to press his lips against her temple while she admired the horse, her horse. "Poor Shren, we have grown close."
"You can always ride them both." Caleb comforted.
"I suppose so."
"So how did you break away from Isabella? I hear she is a hard teacher," he asked, then stroked Finn's back to ease his restlessness.
"Well, she wasn't particularly happy about it but she let me go for the night."

"That's perfect then."

"Why?" Kenna's hands stilled which caused Finn to bump her roughly, she gently pushed his head away then repeated her question.

"Why is that perfect?"

"Because you may now join me at tonight's gathering."

A pitiful groan escaped her, she looked up into Caleb's shadowed face. Here I thought I would have a nice quiet night to myself. All the while Caleb watched her with a charming smile on his face, amusement danced across his features as he acknowledged her struggle.

"Well, I suppose after such a lovely gift I should accept your offer." Her tone was falsely cheerful.

"Now, don't be like that." Caleb crooned, then swept her into his arms. She laid her head against his chest, her nose tickled by the opening of his tunic.

"You should go get changed, I'll gather you after I tend to Finn." She quickly laid her lips to the bare skin of his chest, his delicious scent of soap, leather, and pines filled her nostrils before she pulled away.

"I am a bit smelly aren't I?" Kenna patted the chestnut stallion with a childish grin, then howled for the pack who had patiently waited at the forest line for her call. Caleb watched, an odd expression altered the smooth lines of his face.

Her chest twisted at his look, she averted her eyes towards the wolves that sprinted across the pasture, but could not ease the tension beneath her breastbone. Without a word she retreated with the pack to her chambers, the iron-wrapped glass a cold barrier between them.

Alone in her chambers she quickly washed and combed her hair, aquamarine eyes clenched tight against a nest of snarls around the nape of her neck; finished and turned her attention to her wardrobe. Kenna sifted through the gowns until she laid eyes on a moss-green garment made of a finely spun cotton and silk blend. It reflected candle light in emerald arches that shifted and bowed with each bend of fabric, she ran her fingers across its smooth surface, enamored by its touch. She donned the dress quickly then added the last touches before she strode to her parlor door. Leara peeled off from the pack to join her in the night's affairs.

When she opened the portal she was pleased to see Caleb waited for her in the hall. His dark frame leaned against the wall, a wine-colored tunic stretched taut against his broad shoulders. Ebony tresses brushed back from his brow to display high, broad cheekbones.
"You look lovely," he greeted while he took her hand.
"Thank you." She pressed her body against his, it was warm and hard, and utterly delightful. It was unfortunate that they would not be able to spend the night together without the bothersome company of the court.

Kenna ran her fingers up his arm, so hard beneath thin silk, and relished in the arousal that burned in Caleb's gaze. His lips curved in a feline grin as he pulled her closer, his hands firm on the swell of her rear. Heat flooded her senses as tension stirred low in her abdomen. She wanted him; wanted to feel his skin against hers, to feel his lips and teeth at her throat. Kenna arched against him when their lips met in a press of tender flesh and desire.
"I want to rip this dress off you." Caleb's voice was dark with lust, it sent a shiver through Kenna that found its way between her legs; legs she pressed together and felt a pleasurable ache against slick skin. She clenched her thighs harder, then rubbed them back and forth, her hips rocked against Caleb and the friction at the apex of her legs built.
"Rip it then."

Caleb answered her with a growl—his hands like

iron on her waist, he strode into the room and pressed her to the wall. He kicked the door shut and as it slammed into place, a shiver rippled through the wall that she was pressed against, a feral excitement took hold of her.

His leg pressed between hers and her silken gown slid against the wet folds of her center. Kenna moaned, her pulse raced and seared her veins in a delicious heat. Caleb's lips branded her skin, down her jaw, her throat; his shoulders bowed as he pressed his lips, then slid his tongue in the cleft between her full breasts. A shiver rippled through her, made her pant while she curled her fingers into his clothes.

Caleb's mouth captured hers as he slid his palms down her sides in a languid caress, then wrapped his hands around her thighs. His lips curled with primal pleasure while he hefted her up. Without thought Kenna pulled up the skirts of her gown to bunch around her hips, then tightened her thighs around his waist. She looked down into his eyes, her back pressed to the cool wall, her center and stomach flooded with his heat. Caleb's knee pressed into the wall beneath her and freed his left hand to slide along her creamy thighs. Her breath hitched when he grazed the bend between her open and bare flesh, and the curve of her leg. Their gaze met, pupils large, eyes dark with desire; Kenna licked swollen lips.

"Touch me."

His lips met hers with a fervent need while his index finger slid inside her wet opening. Kenna moaned, her hips bucked and ground against his hand as pleasure consumed her. Their tongues explored each other's mouths, lips, and throats while she rode his hand; his calluses a torturous fracture that drove her need mercilessly. Caleb pulled back and a whimper of protest escaped her. His lips tilted up against hers.

"Patience." She nipped his lip. "Naughty little wolf." He

growled into her mouth.

His ring finger joined his middle to slam back inside of her, and yanked a cry of ecstasy from her core. His fingers plunged into her again and again, she ground her hips against him until release crashed over her in dizzying waves. A fractured cry escaped her lips as she crumpled against his broad chest, her fingers tangled in his tunic. She could feel the tip of his hard length nudge the bare skin of her rear, then slide against the slick folds of her spread legs when he gently lowered her to her feet.

He cradled her against him while their bodies calmed. The fabric of her gown was smooth and cool, it slowly soothed the shiver of heat that echoed through her limbs. She smiled up at him, eyes bright with concealed laughter.

"I think we are going to be late."

His laughter shook through her and she relished the sensation.

"Yes," his lips brushed the crown of her head. "But a moment with you is always more precious. I would be late to the crowning of the gods if it meant I could stay by your side." His lips touched hers once more in a slow, gentle caress. A kiss of comfort, friendship, and affection. Her heart squeezed at the joy that washed through her, she took his hand.

"Let's go."

The great hall bustled with gilded individuals laden with silk, satin, and jewels in a gaudy display of color that boggled the mind. More and more nobles threw their eligible sons into the ring as word of Princess Ena's potential marital status spread through the country. Word had also reached Alearian's neighbors; courtiers and noble sons from other lands now mingled with the crowds as they vied for royal power.

Kenna sat quietly with her companion, Leara, at her

feet while she waited for Caleb and Randy to return. Due to his high status as the future successor of the Devoney holdings he was often hassled by his elders at court, while Randy played the delicate role of savior. Kenna sipped her apple cider while she ignored Von's words; her friend, as sweet as he was, had Kenna on the brink of madness. Much to her woe she had found that Von was in a one-way love affair with her mentor, Lady Isabella.

The moment Von had heard who her tutor was he began to ply her with questions about Isabella in the hopes he would find some way to her heart.

"She is just beautiful, we are a perfect pair, perfectly matched."

"She looks just like you." Kenna answered.

"Well there is nothing wrong with that." Kenna rolled her eyes, then shoved her seasoned potatoes around her plate for the tenth time.

"We are like a pair of elegant horses picked for one another for our sameness." Von continued with his usual attempt at poetic flattery. Kenna strongly considered if she had the fortitude to impale her hand with a butter knife to escape, with a defeated sigh she abandoned the thought. *He would just wrap it and keep talking.*

"I don't know if being called a horse is flattering," she said aloud instead. "Honestly she looks a lot like your sister, don't you find that odd?"

Von snorted as he dismissed her words.

"Nonsense, she looks nothing like Sophie."

In fact she did, but his lover's eye could not see the resemblance. A retort ready on her parted lips she caught sight of Randy and Caleb while they slipped through the crowd to join them. She stood quickly, and her relief outweighed the tinge of guilt she had at her excitement to leave her friend. "I'll check back with you later Von."

He hardly noticed her exit, his attention locked on

an unlucky fellow that had needed a seat to dine at. The man chewed vigorously while Von rehashed his ridiculous love scheme with a single-minded devotion. Something about Isabella truly sent the sense from that man's head; normally playful with a wicked grin at the ready, he was utterly hopeless where the werecat was involved. *Love makes fools of us all it would seem.*

Caleb's gaze roved her face, and a smile spread across his own.

"Is that mooncalf cousin of mine at it again?"

"Oh he never stops, especially since he knows I'm always with his 'beloved,'" she gestured at the word Von so lovingly intoned for Isabella, her face a mask of revulsion. Caleb laughed at her misery which only annoyed her further.

"It's not funny, he is an absolute menace."

"He's not that bad."

"You didn't have to sit with him! Now he is just tormenting that poor man."

They turned to look at the table where Von's new companion shoveled food into his mouth at a rate that warranted a healer.

"You left him to the wolves."

Kenna laughed, "The wolves would have been kinder."

Caleb took her hands, his fingers laced between hers then squeezed gently.

"Perhaps that's true." A lopsided grin settled over his features.

"The resemblance is uncanny though, you must admit. I understand Von and Sophie are twins, and you are cousins, but you all look so alike." Kenna said, a small crease formed between her brows.

"Well, the Devoney line has a very distinct look."

"Is Isabella related to you by any chance?"

"From what I understand, no, we are of no relation. I don't

think Von would be courting her so desperately if she was," he responded with a chuckle.

"I suppose that's true."

Doubt crept over her when she glanced over her shoulder at the familiar face, now alone and forlorn at the table. Guilt trickled in and she slowed her pace, ready to turn back when Caleb interrupted her thoughts.

"Enough of that, there are people you should meet." Kenna stifled a groan as she mentally prepared to add a name to her hazy list of nobles. If it wasn't for Randy she would have made a fool of herself ten times over at these useless events.

They were everywhere, with their lands and titles, and Goddess forbid you mistake one for the other. She shivered at the memory of the elder woman that had nearly burned Kenna alive when she had mistaken her for a less wealthy land holder. *Damn nobles are so touchy.* Leara bumped against her leg, a warm comfort in a crowd of strangers.

Caleb steered them toward a small group deep in discussion about some bland subject Kenna was sure. Randy elbowed her in the ribs which drew a scowl.

"Fix your face," he whispered, merriment bright in his honey gold eyes.

"There is nothing wrong with my face."

"Oh no, it's perfectly normal to let your eyes roll to the back of your head."

"You're annoying," she hissed despite the smile she fought to hold at bay. Randy patted her arm empathetically which only annoyed her more, much to his amusement.

The only member of the group she recognized was Caleb's aunt Ressa, which wasn't exactly a comfort. Beside her stood a grizzled man, his skin tan and wizened like an old apple, with brown hair shot through with silver. He laughed a bit too loudly, but was by far the more patient member of the group.

"That is Lord Elber, a friend of my aunt's." Caleb whispered in her ear. Kenna glanced at Randy, fighting the urge to roll her eyes once more, his cheek twitched while he suppressed a smile.

"The woman there is Lady Signe, a diplomat from Vontrakal."

The diplomat he named was a lovely woman. Dark-blonde hair rippled down her back in soft waves that completely devoured her narrow shoulders. She was shorter than Kenna's five feet eight inches, with a slender if not muscular frame that was uncommon for a high-born lady. Large mahogany eyes against cream-colored skin gave her a soft, doe-like look which she employed shamelessly while she listened to the intoxicated Lord Elber. Kenna smothered a snort at the unabashed use of the other woman's feminine wiles.

"That would make a nice rug." The crag-faced Lord rumbled when he spotted them.

Kenna went rigid at his words, and the drone of the crowd fell away, the sudden silence punctured by the foreboding rumble of Leara's growl, and perhaps her own. Before Caleb could soothe her, Kenna lashed out at the man, teeth lengthened into fangs that promised violence. "It would be the last thing you ever tried to do," her tone dripped venom. Elber stepped back in shock, the wrinkles of his face lessened by his wide-eyed expression while he stumbled back. Kenna watched him balefully, her feet branched apart while her body radiated energy, ready to spring.

Ressa watched Kenna with mild annoyance, her thin lips pressed into a pale line of distaste. Caleb's touch was gentle as he squeezed her shoulder. She glanced up at him and saw a muscle in his jaw flutter, only to be stilled by a soft smile. Shame seeped through the rage and stilled the wolf within her. Kenna made her form fully human, then returned her attention to the group.

She stepped back beside Randy and was once more swamped by the hum of the chamber full of decadent nobles. The soft sway of fabric mingled with the rasp of slippers and boots on stone; an undertone that hissed and sighed in time with the music. Kenna observed the trio before her through copper lashes and cringed internally at the upheaval she had caused.

"Please excuse her Elber, she has country manners." Ressa drawled. Elber eyed Kenna, mumbled that he needed another drink, then left. It was clear what he thought of Kenna and her "country manners." She inhaled, a contrite response ready to breach the chasm she had caused, but hesitated when the stone-enhanced drone of the room rose to a painful volume. An ache grew behind her eyes and she stood silently, her fingers purposely limp at her side while she resisted the urge to massage her temples.

"I thought it would be nice for Kenna to meet someone from a different country." Caleb remarked, he smoothly bypassed his aunt's excuse for Kenna's behavior.

Lady Signe smiled charmingly.

"You flatter me." Her smile grew cooler when she acknowledged Kenna. Kenna focused on the woman before her despite the insistent ache due to the noise. "I hear you come from the forest up north. What a secluded, simple life you must have had. It sounds lovely to be so out of touch with society."

Kenna bristled at her implications and grappled with her raw nerves. She glared at her companions, calm and composed, if displeased with the turn of the conversation. *Does no one hear it?*

Ressa laughed quietly which drew Kenna back to the conversation in time to see her sooth her mirth with a deep drought from her goblet. Kenna pressed down her annoyance and smiled.

"It is a very different lifestyle, yes, but the company is rather more pleasant." Her tone was honeyed daggers. The point had not been lost on Signe, her once doe-like eyes now sharp when she continued.

"It does boggle the mind though that one can live with beasts," her tone breathless. "I would be terrified of catching fleas." Signe's laughter chimed like brass bells.

Kenna inhaled through her nose as she controlled her emotions that roiled within her too-tight chest. She cast a glance at the dancers, still in perfect harmony with the music that filled the room. *How does no one hear it?*

The ache behind her eyes intensified, and she clamped her hands into fists so she would not cradle her head.

"I wouldn't worry my lady, I hear that fleas aren't fond of cold-blooded creatures." Caleb interjected, his voice tight with thinly restrained anger. "Now if you will excuse me, I tire of such bland company."

He pulled Kenna towards the swirl of dancers at the center of the hall without a backward glance. She was about to remind him they had left their friend with a pair of harpies when she paused. His jaw was clenched tight, his temple flexed as he gracefully guided her through the crowd. The ache in her head eased, and perhaps it was due to the improvement in company. Or perhaps her concern for the man before her, she could not tell, nor did she care.

"That was worse than dealing with Von." Her voice held a hollow sense of cheer.

"I'm sorry, I had no idea they would behave that way. Are you all right?"

"Yes, it wouldn't be the first time someone said something nasty about me. Though, no one has ever been so polite about it." Kenna's laughter was forced, she glanced at Caleb sidelong only to see his face was vacant, his features cut in hard angular lines while he swept her across the polished floor in steps she did not know. She wished she could pull away his mask, yet did not know where the strings were hidden; Kenna danced with a stranger.

The glow of the evening began to fade with a determination that Kenna felt with every fiber of her being. The night wore on her, each person that greeted her with arched brows, every bit of gossip and forced courtly laughter, it was insufferable. She sucked in a deep breath through clenched teeth while she scanned the kaleidoscope of a crowd. Despite the late hour the hall was still pressed with people, the air thick with warmth and perfume. She whispered her intentions in Caleb's ear as he conversed with his cousins; she slipped through the crowd, eyes locked on the glass doors on the far side of the room that reflected the candle light in bursts of pale gold.

Kenna stepped through the gilded portal and felt the tension in her temples ease. The warm breeze sighed against her, rippled the soft fabric of her dress when she strode towards the balcony rail. She unbraided her hair and massaged her scalp with claw-like fingers, eyes closed while shivers racked her spine. Kenna leaned against the rail and scanned the night with hungry eyes; she tapped into the molten well of her magic and felt the shapes of the beasts flex and strain beneath her skin. Kenna soothed them, her lips tilted up in a feral grin, then tailored her eyes from human to lupine.

Ice-blue eyes that flashed with magic in the starlight, the night sprang into sharp relief below her. She tucked a tendril of hair behind her ear that had tapered to delicate points tufted with cinnamon sable fur. Kenna watched the horses meander drowsily through the pasture, the sounds of beasts and insects floated up to her while her mind wandered back to her studies.

"Even on my day off," she muttered against her palms as

she rubbed her closed eyes. The sound of the gathering swelled behind her, only to be hushed by the soft click of a latch.

"What about it, pupil?" a voice purred behind her.

"Even on my day off I can't stop thinking of your blasted lectures. It's bothersome." Kenna responded, unsurprised by her mentor's sudden company.

"That's what makes you a good student." Isabella leaned her hip against the rail and

Kenna cast her a sidelong glance before she once more watched the horses.

"Not worried your dress will get dirty?"

"A little dirt would do me good honestly." Isabella sighed, then turned towards the pastures and forest beyond. Her ivory gown was soft as starlight, so pale against the long, coiled curls of her midnight hair.

"I can't remember the last time I slept under the stars. It feels like it's been centuries."

Kenna hummed sympathetically beside her, her own heart forlorn at the loss of wild nights beneath the celestial bowl of the world.

The two women stood together in companionable silence, the music inside the castle a faint melody on a balmy breeze. Isabella's voice broke the velvety silence, her angular features softened by shadows and moonlight.

"So how are you adapting?"

"It's been interesting to be sure, and I don't know if I'm made for this place. Caleb makes it seem so effortless."

"I understand, the capital is a challenging place. I know I had a hard time."

"Isabella, you know everything about me, more than even I know I imagine..." she trailed off under Isabella's direct gaze. "Can you tell me something about you? I hear the strangest rumors." For a long time the werecat was silent, her eyes shrouded in thought.

Kenna looked away, shoulders hunched. *Does everyone wear a mask here?* At last the woman spoke, her words slow and quiet.

"Kenna, I am rather old and have done a lot of things in my life. That is the reason that the Crown trusts my advice." Her elegant fingers twisted a dark curl, her eyes vacant as though she looked into the past. "Once, when I was considerably younger, I had a hand in civil change in Alearian. A few centuries back there was a family that ruled this country named the Glosters. They were running it into the ground, and something had to give. So when the people began to gather I helped overthrow the Glosters, then helped place the crown on a new head; Sandros Vimcor The First." Isabella paused, her lips twitched while she watched Kenna's wide-eyed expression.

"Do you want me to keep going?" Mirth filled her voice.

"Yes."

"Well, with the new family in place things did not settle down right away. In order to protect the new Royal family I decided there needed to be a contingency in place, so I created The Order of The Black Sword."

An image of the castle's flag sprang to Kenna's mind, a black sword wrapped with a white rose.

"So that, the flag, the family, it was all you?"

"No, of course not." her laugh was breathy. "I just had an influential hand in it."

Kenna watched her mentor with a newfound respect. After a long moment of silence she grinned.

"Well I have to say you look amazing for a woman your age." Isabella yelped, then lurched forward to swat her student. "Thank you for telling me... I'm guessing that you keep a lot of this to yourself. So are you immortal?"

"No. My kind isn't immortal, though we are close to it. As long as no one kills us with a weapon or poisons us, we will live an incredibly long time," she answered dryly.

"I wonder how long I will live." Kenna mused.

Isabella gave her a strange look that she could not decipher, her pale green eyes seemed awash with pain. Before Kenna could ask what was wrong the werecat touched her hand gently.

"Don't worry about such things. It's late, perhaps we should retire." They walked back into a less clamorous party and parted ways. Kenna watched her mentor leave, and a shadow over her shoulders formed from the painful look she had been given. A deep sigh rattled through her as she turned towards the sprawl of the hall.

She saw him before he caught sight of her; his laugh was effortless, it filled his chest and crinkled his eyes, it was contagious. A soft smile curved her lips. *How could one not smile in the face of such unabashed joy?* As though he felt her gaze Caleb turned towards the doors, and laid his evergreen eyes upon her. A shiver slid down her form when their gazes met, when he left his companions and strode towards her with a confidence that demanded recognition.

She watched him cross the marble floor with long, powerful strides; he did not slip through the crowd, they parted before him: Caleb Devoney. A warmth built beneath her skin and chased away the shadows that had clung to her. He reached her and his lips parted on a soft inhale when his hand clasped hers; her heart strained at the emotion that radiated from him, she squeezed his calloused fingers, and couldn't imagine a life without him by her side.

His hand cupped her cheek and she pressed a soft kiss into his palm, so wonderfully textured against her silken lips.

"Time to go?"

"Yes," she whispered while she leaned into him, her lungs filled with his scent and she sighed.

"You two look bored to tears."

Kenna could hear the smile in his voice, even with her eyes

closed she could see that lopsided grin. His body shifted and she straightened when he reached for Leara, her velvet-soft ear massaged, tail limp and golden eyes closed with comfort. Kenna glanced up and smiled, he still wore the smile of a small child, eyes bright with wonder while he caressed the dangerous beast before him. Seeing her tired look he wrapped his arm around her without a word and escorted her through the crowd.

Her hands wrapped around his arm in a gentle tug. "Let's go."

"Of course." They ambled through the hall, past the opulent dancers, the swirl of perfume-infused air saturated with laughter.

"Don't you have to say goodbye?" Kenna queried.

"I see those louts often enough, they don't need any more of my time."

"You're the worst."

"I'm the best."

Kenna snorted then snuggled closer to his arm. Finally alone in the corridor Kenna watched Caleb with new interest, her mind once more on her conversation on the balcony. The resemblance between Caleb and Isabella seemed all the more possible now that she knew how old Isabella truly was. *Stranger things have happened...But wouldn't he know about it? These nobles love their family trees.* She was unsure, but the possibility nagged at her with the persistence of possibility. Her brows knitted severely, a heavy crease marred her pale skin.

"Caleb, do you know anything about the Black Sword?"

The knight stopped, his body suddenly and completely immobile. It took Kenna an additional pace before she realized he was no longer beside her.

"Where did you hear that?"

"Isabella." She could see him visibly relax and her curiosity grew unbearable at the sight of such a tell. Caleb closed the

gap between them, his expression unusually stern.
"The Black Sword isn't something you should bring up in the hall Kenna."
"It's on your flag," she countered when they began to walk again, annoyed at the reprimand.
"Yes, but most people don't know why."
"But you do." She could smell the secret on him, and she hungered for it.

By this time they had reached her chambers; Caleb stood pensive before the heavy oak door, his gaze roved her face in search of something she could not place.
"Kenna," he stroked her cheek, "there is so much I would tell you, but I don't know if the stories are mine to tell."
She grabbed his hand, held it close while concern outweighed curiosity.
"You can tell me anything Caleb. I think after everything we have been through together, despite the short amount of time it's been… I think it's safe to say we are Pack. And Pack shares the burden and never betrays one another. No matter what you tell me, I am here." She kissed the inside of his palm, her eyes locked on his.

He inhaled a soft breath while his thumb moved across her skin.
"I will never get used to that."
Her brows pulled together once more.
"Get used to what?"
"The way your eyes light up when you are truly yourself, when you are being raw and honest with me. They are the most frigid, and beautiful shade of blue." Kenna lowered copper lashes over the flash of lupine light that now shined there. His fingers curled under her chin.
"Don't look away, they are stunning, wolf, and so beautiful." He leaned forward and kissed her softly. "Just beautiful."

He kissed her deeply; she could taste the spiced

wine on his lips, smell the heady, delightful musk of his body. Kenna pressed herself against him in a supple arch; she was pleased to feel him harden against her, so long and thick where it strained against the taut fabric of his breeches.

She ran a palm over its edge and felt him shiver beneath her touch. His own hands were upon her, eager in their exploration of her supple and soft form. Her body quivered as her skin tightened at the touch of his calloused fingers against the smooth skin of her breasts. Caleb's eyes focused hungrily on Kenna's creamy skin as her bosom heaved against the fabric of her gown with each fevered breath. They stumbled back against the smooth oak of her door, Kenna found herself trapped between the cool surface and Caleb's molten body.

His lips and tongue traced lines of lightning down her neck and shoulder that wrenched a soft moan from her parted lips. Caleb's nimble fingers found her key in the tuck of her gown, his other hand splayed across the small of her back while he held her close and unlocked the portal. Their lips curved while they kissed, a giggle bubbled up from Kenna only to be swallowed by Caleb's delicious tongue and lips. They stepped into the dark parlor, still tangled in one another's embrace. Caleb kicked the door shut behind them and pulled Kenna close, then skillfully loosened the laces of her gown; she glanced down while his fingers worked her gown, at the swells of her breasts that brushed against his hands with each eager breath.

She shivered when the silken fabric slipped from her shoulders in a whisper that exposed the cream and pink skin of her naked form before it settled on the curve of her hips. Kenna began to pull off the rest of her gown but froze at the deep growl that rent the darkness behind them. A different type of flush rushed across Kenna's body as she quickly yanked her dress back into place.

Caleb struck a match then lit the candle by the door, it bloomed into life and chased away the shows with soft aurelian light. Kenna turned slowly, her pulse a steady buzz that thrummed beneath her skin. The Pack lounged on the thick decorative carpets, on the silk and satin sofas across the parlor, a parlor bedecked by luminous eyes of amber and gold. *Great Divya save me!* Kenna's body was consumed by a feverish heat, not only at the sound of Throv's snarl that rent the darkness, or the gleam of his fangs in the dim glow of a singular candle flame; but the laughter that sputtered from Caleb behind her.

She clumsily pulled her dress up over her bare torso and yanked the laces tight, perhaps too tight.
"I'm sorry Caleb, but you have to go," she said as she turned back to him. The heat of embarrassment was quickly chased away when she saw his emerald eyes flashing with laughter.
"Yes of course. Your father does not seem pleased." His lips twitched as he set down the candle.
"It's not funny Caleb!" Kenna pushed him into the closed door.
"Give me a moment and I'll let myself out." Caleb protested when she pushed him once more against solid oak. He pried the door open to ease free of the chamber, only to feel a sharp jab to his side. "You're quite the ruffian aren't you." He laughed as she elbowed him in the right direction. He entered the hall and turned to kiss her good night, but she didn't give him the chance.
"Thank you, now goodnight!" she slammed the door in his face.

His laughter floated to her through the seams of the door and she cringed, her knuckles white against the oak. Hands clenched, she rested her warm brow against the cool surface while she gathered the tattered remains of her dignity. Kenna straighten and shook back her hair in defiance. "I will not speak of this." Head held high, she strode to the safety of her bed chamber.

The next morning Kenna was pleased to see that the Pack was no longer in her parlor. The wolves had figured out how to pull the lever of the garden door to come and go as they wished, and she could not be happier for that fact. She grabbed her bow and quiver and smoothly shrugged the weapon into place across her back, a comfortable weight against the thin cotton of her shirt. Kenna ambled through the chambers of her suite determined not to let the night before affect her present day.

She flipped her heavy braid over her shoulder and swung her parlor door open. Her fingers ached with how tightly they held the lever, the breath still in her lungs. Caleb stood in the corridor, and for the first time a small part of her did not want to see him. The recognition of that shamed her; she knew how hard he tried to see her each day, due to their duties to the crown they were often apart. His words shattered her thoughts.

"You're coming with me love."

"I have my lessons."

"Yes, well you can skip the first one and be back in time for Isabella's. Let's go."

Kenna bristled at his demand, but she followed

him down the corridor nonetheless. Her lips parted on a sharp inhale, words ready to fly, until she caught sight of his movements. He hummed softly while he pulled a plum from his pocket.

"I thought you might be hungry little wolf."

Her only response was to take the plum and take a juicy bite of the succulent fruit, her eyes dared him to comment when her tongue flicked across her lips to gather the sweet drops that slid towards her chin. Content, she licked her sticky fingers while she followed him to the stable yard. Caleb let loose a long, high-pitched whistle. Kenna watched him, perplexed, her boot resting lightly on the bottom horizontal post of the split-rail fence.

Rich meat devoured, she tossed her plum pit and wiped her fingers on her breeches while she waited. Zane soon cantered into view, his sleek black flanks dusted with yellow pollen. The equine thundered towards his master, then slid to a halt before him in a bloom of sweet grass and golden flower dust.

"Last night you said I was part of your Pack." His voice was low while he stroked the warhorse's velvet muzzle. "If I have earned the right to be part of your Pack, then you have earned the right to know my secrets." For a long moment Caleb was quiet, his gaze locked on the warm brown eyes of his horse.

It was as though the pair spoke to one another in a manner similar to Kenna and her pack; similar to her with any other beast, yet Caleb had disclosed no magical predilection. *Perhaps this was one of the aforementioned secrets?*

Kenna watched them with interest, unwilling to interrupt their intimate moment. At last Caleb spoke again, his voice snapped the tether of tension within her.

"When you deal with Zane does he feel different from other horses?"

Kenna thought for a moment, sifted through her memories and settled on the night of the raid.

"Yes, he feels more...human." She fumbled for the right words to explain the vibrant textures of the stallion's thoughts. Caleb nodded, his expression oddly grim, thoughtful.

"The reason for that is he is specially bred. Zane comes from a long line of horses carefully selected for their physique, as well as their minds. More than that they are imbued with magic while in their mother's womb. His mind is much sharper than he allowed you to know when you made contact."

Kenna watched him, her expression creased while she grappled with his words. *These people magicked a baby horse…*

"I know that it sounds crazy, but Zane needs to be as intelligent as possible. The horses that belong to the Black Sword are as important as their riders."

"How do you know all of this?" Kenna asked, her chest tight while she waited for an answer she already knew. Caleb sighed, his expression impossible for her to decipher.

"I know all of this because I am part of The Order."

"Why are you telling me this now?" A painful mix of emotions swirled through her too tight chest; curiosity, concern, and the sharp tang of bitterness.

He had left her in the dark this whole time while she had repeatedly exposed herself to him; had given herself to his world, to his royals, and to him. Kenna clamped down on the emotions, pressed down the magic in her belly that called her beast to wake and stretch inside her skin. Her jaw clenched with the effort, until his voice slipped through the haze of her thoughts.

"Trust," he turned toward her, grabbed her warm hands. "Because I trust you. Maybe more than I have trusted any- one, and I want to open myself to you in every way." The rounded ridge in his throat bobbed while he swallowed, Kenna traced the movement with eyes that burned. He seemed as hurt by this as she was, that The Order was a burden he did not wish to bare.

"I want there to be trust between us, Kenna. Not secrets."

He reached up with a hand that trembled and smoothed a stray strand from her face. She closed her eyes to the gossamer touch, and felt the tension in her body ease. "The way I became involved was due to a blood oath made by my family centuries ago. The first-born child in each branch of the Devoney line must swear their loyalty to the Royal family and join the Black Sword. It is an honor that one cannot refuse."

"It would seem more of an honor if it was chosen."

A muscle in his jaw ticked at her words, and a flash of shame seared her, yet she held true to her words. His fingers squeezed hers while he inhaled deeply through his nose.

"Some days I may agree with you, but I must follow the oath in my blood. It binds us, and bids us to follow the call." There was a shadow in his eyes that made Kenna's heart ache. "We are not meant to share this knowledge with anyone, but since Isabella saw fit to share some of it with you... I thought I should finish the story."

Kenna reached up with her free hand to cup his face and smiled softly when he leaned into her touch. Heavy lashes lowered while the strain eased from his features. A submission, a declaration of trust. Her thumb caressed the plane of his cheekbone for a moment longer before she let her hand drop against her thigh. His gaze followed her fingers with a slight downward tilt of his lips.

"Did you know that Isabella is the founder?"

"I do."

"Does anyone else know?"

"Only the Royal family."

"Then how did you find out?"
"I'm rather good at my job," he answered, a mischievous grin creased his eyes with such familiarity she could not help but mirror his expression.

Again silence fell between the pair, this time it was peaceful, gentle like the breeze that played with their hair.
"Is Von part of this?" Kenna glanced up at Caleb while he leaned against the pasture rail.
"He is but he does not know about Isabella." He had guessed Kenna's train of thought. "I don't know how he would respond if he knew how old she truly was." Caleb chuckled. Kenna snorted,
"I think he would faint, he is—"

In the distance bells rang out the hour and the smile faded from her features.
"Sounds like it is time for your studies."
"It seems so."
"Thank you for coming out here with me." Caleb spoke in a distant tone, his eyes vacant while he leaned forward on his forearms. Kenna felt a wave of unease, but stifled it as best she could; she could only hope he had shared all of the trust with her. Trust. He wanted trust, so she would have to trust in that no matter how it riled her. Her braid slid forward when she tilted her head, eyes full of questions while she looked up at Caleb. The tightness thrummed in her chest.

Hands clenched she stood on tiptoe and kissed her knight briskly before she left him to brood with his horse.

Kenna rushed down the hall in a futile attempt to make it to Isabella's chambers on time.
The need for her to remain on someone else's schedule still sat poorly with her, yet she could do nothing but comply with the wishes of the crown; this was not to say there had

not been benefits to her, but alas, she only truly recognized one pair of alphas in her life in regards to the mortal plain. Buried in the tangle of her thoughts she felt a slight pressure at the base of her skull, her nape grew cool, and her skin prickled with the sensation.

The hum felt familiar in some ways, yet a wrongness settled over her. Kenna's steps had not faltered, and glanced around the corridor in search of her mentor. Perhaps in her agitation at Kenna's tardiness the tone of her magical imprint had shifted.

She turned while she walked, her fingers fiddled aimlessly with the position of her quiver while she looked over her shoulder in a guise of unawareness. Kenna was alone; the only presence that accompanied her was the steady clack of her boots against limestone floors. The deeper into the stone monolith she went, the stronger the sensation became.

Her pace slowed marginally while she focused on the sensation, and realized there was a subtle variation to the hum; the energy gave off a different texture, a different tone. Kenna's brow creased with this realization which was only made worse when she realized that the subtle drone's source was behind her. Her back tensed while she fought the urge to turn around and draw her bow. If someone truly followed her it would be painfully obvious she was aware of them if she suddenly strung her weapon in the middle of the castle corridor.

Instead she tapped into her magic and lengthened feeble human nails into deadly claws that curved and darkened at her fingertips. *I wish I was better with a sword.* She suppressed the growl that brewed within her; sweat began to gather on her brow, small drops slid between her breasts while her heart thrummed wildly in her chest.

Kenna turned a corner of the hall, limestone smooth beneath her boot, then slid her bow over her head and into a ready position. Her muscles knew the movements, drill after drill made them smooth and warm with action. An arrow sat in the well-worn groove while she kept the missile pointed low; she drew a ragged breath, sweat slicked her brow while she listened for the telltale sound of steps. Her thoughts shivered, then fragmented as the drone overwhelmed her mind with its unbearable volume.

Her magic quivered in rhythm with the noise, it responded to the rush of blood in her veins, and the danger of the sound inside her head. A beast stretched and shifted beneath her skin while her veins burned with copper fire.

Kenna stepped from her cover, and in tandem with her stride swung her bow up; only to find the hall empty. Confusion bloomed while she scanned the corridor, then felt the pain behind her eyes gradually fade. Not only the pain had left her, but the insufferable drone that had caused it. She exhaled heavily while she lowered her weapon, then slowly released the tension. Kenna returned her arrow to her quiver with fingers that ached with restraint, then slung the bow over her back, agitation filling each movement. Kenna stood rooted in the hall, every sense on high alert, yet she was alone; the only sound that accompanied her was her own soft breath.

She sniffed the corridor then snarled as the scent of granite and dust filled her nostrils, only the faint aroma of sweetness lingered in the balmy air. She let that sweetness roll over her tongue and its taste nagged at the edges of her mind. Kenna snarled with disgust; She glanced down the hall, her mind on pursuit and she took a slow step, then paused when the boisterous chime of bells rang through the castle. *I will find you sweetling,* she promised, then turned towards Isabella's chambers.

In the safety of Isabella's parlor Kenna sheathed her savage claws. The woman saw the transition and raised a delicate brow.

"Someone, or something was stalking me in the halls."
Isabella's mouth tightened slightly as she asked,
"How do you know?"
"I felt this strange sensation in my mind, not like with animals. It reminded me of you at first, but it didn't quite feel right." Kenna struggled to explain while she settled on the overstuffed velvet couch. Isabella was silent, her normally smooth face lined with dread. A curiosity tinged with trepidation crept over Kenna's senses.

The shifter walked into her study without a word and Kenna obediently followed, her curiosity piqued by the sudden departure. Isabella walked around the room and gathered objects from the shelves, first a silver bowl, a pitcher of water, then a small assortment of oils. Kenna shrugged free of her weapons then leaned them in a corner while she watched with interest from a stool across the room.

It was rare that her teacher did magic in front of her, more often than not Isabella was more interested in her pupil's abilities than flaunting her own. Isabella was silent while she poured the water, then oil into the silver dish before she began to stir the contents carefully with a crystal wand. It hummed sweetly against the rim of the scrying bowl.

"Why do you add oils?" Kenna asked. She could no longer watch from the sidelines and had joined the werecat at the table.

"It will intensify the magic...The creature I seek is heavily shrouded," she whispered, eyes intent on her work. Though she had answered her, Kenna felt Isabella wasn't truly aware or focused on her presence. What she saw in those waters Kenna could not discern, but her sense of dread grew with each note that sang from the bowl.

At last Isabella waved her hand over the liquid while her lips moved rapidly as she invoked an incantation under her breath. The surface of the water began to ripple as beams of light glowed within its depths. While the lights grew brighter the surface of the water became still, then smooth like the glass of a mirror.

The figure of an old man slowly took form. He sat on his throne, his shoulders hunched forward while he brooded, his stare vacant and cold while it watched the unseen things that dwelled in the distance. His left eye was disfigured by a grievous scar that rendered him blind, the orb but a dismal pale-gray version of its former self. He seemed indifferent to the man that stood before him; a figure with midnight-black hair cropped close to the pale skin of his skull.

Kenna felt herself shift in a fruitless effort to get a better look at the man, something about him made her skin tighten, her belly churn with discomfort. The man walked towards the King and stood by his shoulder, then turned and revealed a face that made Kenna shudder. His skin was pale, nearly translucent; the only contrast of color was the gray of the tattoos etched across his cheekbones and the bridge of his nose. His eyes were entirely dark as though his pupil had consumed his eye altogether.

She stepped back from the image.

"Who is that?" Kenna asked softly while she watched the water, her fur rippled down her back.

"His name is Maeghnor. He is Hrothgar's right hand and a very powerful sorcerer." Her voice was grave while she watched the oil-speckled water.

"Don't tell me he was in the hall with me?"

"Goddess no, if he had been then you would be dead."

"Thank Divya for small favors." Kenna mumbled.

"My fear is that he sent someone with special gifts to spy on us, a mage perhaps. It would explain why we cannot catch the culprit. Hrothgar is mad, but Maeghnor is no fool. If indeed he did pick the spy then you will have your hands full trying to catch it." Isabella released her spell.

The water clouded for a moment then cleared, the image shattered into fragments of every color before they returned to a translucent state. All that was left was a dish of clear water with bits of glossy oil on its surface.

"Makes me all the more eager to meet my little friend in the hall." Kenna laughed weakly. *Where was Aden when you needed a real laugh?* Isabella grabbed her hand in a rare display of affection, sympathy in her almond eyes.

Kenna grew tense beneath her touch, unease heavy in her bones.

"I wish I had something better to tell you, but with the abilities you have you may be the only one suitable for this particular job. I'm sorry Kenna, I doubt this was what you thought would happen when you left your home."

"No, I can't say that it is. On the bright side I have a new horse." Kenna stated, abruptly, her comment outlandish to the present conversation.

"Yes, well there is that."

Silence settled over them, each lost in their own thoughts until Isabella rose from the table. Her fine jaw was set with determination, her shoulders held back while she pulled books from the shelves and hoisted them onto the table.

"We carry on as planned. Leaving you uneducated and ill-prepared won't help anything." She tapped a tome with a manicured nail. "Start here."

Kenna slid the text from the stack wearily. She could sense the tension that rippled off her mentor in warm waves that shivered through the air. Any comment would only earn a rebuke, and the literature based in natural design or her studies pressed upon her instead. Kenna went through the motions but could not focus wholeheartedly. *Not only do I have a mysterious stalker that makes me feel like a bee is rolling around in my head, but now there is a dark sorcerer helping a mad man. How terribly cliché.*

Kenna's brow furrowed while she gnawed her lip, an unpleasant suspicion gradually took form in her mind.
"Isabella."
"Hmm?" The feline continued to organize her beloved books.
"Has Hrothgar always been mad?" Her mentor paused, her serene face clouded over in thought.
"I don't think he was. Why do you ask?" She now faced Kenna directly.
"When did it all start going wrong?"
"About three years ago?" she answered slowly, a query in her voice.
"And when did this," Kenna waved vaguely, "Maeghnor fellow come about?"
"There had been whispers of him for many years. I would have to say the first rumors of his presence in Vontrakal started about two years ago, and weren't confirmed until fairly recently."

Kenna absorbed the information silently, her sharp teeth worked her lip raw while tension tugged at her entrails.
"Why do you ask?"
"No reason."

The next few days slid by, thick with heat that dragged on the castle residents, their movements sluggish like ants that crawled through honey. Despite the weather Kenna was determined to make herself a more formidable opponent. She stepped onto the flinty surface of the practice grounds and scanned the small crowd of men and women, resolve a heavy weight beneath her sternum.

Those gathered contained people of all ages and stations, which gave Kenna the sense that she belonged. On this dusty ground under the watchful eyes of the arms masters, they were all equals. At last she was rewarded by the soft shine of Randy's flaxen mane, a nimbus of light in the morning sun. Before her archery mentor could catch her she dashed through the crowd to the agitation of those around her.

Her breath came in rapid pants as she stepped up to Randy's shoulder, then grabbed his muscular arm to turn him toward her; where most would have been defensive, perhaps violent even, Randy was calm. His gaze fell upon her and he smiled, honey eyes warmed while they creased sweetly at the corners.
"Hello there, don't you have archery in the morning?"
"Yes, yes, but I have a favor to ask of you." She slid the

back of her hand against her brow, then licked already dry lips.

"Of course, what can I do for you?"

"I want to know how to use a sword." Her mouth was a firm line that dared him to challenge her.

Instead she was greeted with a heartfelt smile that left her oddly dazed.

"It would be a pleasure to teach you. Is there any reason why you are interested now?" he asked, walking towards the weapon wall.

"Nothing in particular." Kenna evaded while she watched him amble among the tools of warfare.

Now and then he would glance back at her, his eyes roved her body as he sized her up against the swords.

"Can I ask you something else?"

"I don't see why not."

"Are you always so polite?"

He turned towards her suddenly, laughter heavy in his voice while his teeth flashed in a broad smile.

"Do my manners bother you Kenna?" She rubbed the back of her neck, heat prickled her cheeks when she answered.

"It can be…"

"Can be?"

"Bothersome."

"Bothersome?" Randy's lips twitched.

"Well exhausting really," Kenna exclaimed. "I mean it's better than Aden, which is obvious, but sometimes I wish you could just spit it the hell out!"

Her face was on fire, if she touched it she was convinced she would sear her fingers. If Randy was offended he didn't show it, instead a soft chuckle left him while he turned his attention back to the wall of weapons.

"I'll try to keep that in mind."

I'm an ASS. Kenna berated herself while she waited for what felt like an eternity for his choice. At last he chose

one, a long masterful creation, its steel blade reflected the harsh summer light in silver flashes. Kenna went to grab the weapon, eager to feel its cool form against her own flesh. Randy snatched it back.
"What do you think you're doing?"
"You said you would teach me."
"Not with this I won't! Do you want to be cut to ribbons?"
"Well of course not!" Kenna tossed her hands in the air, exasperated with her companion.
"There is a method to the sword Kenna. I grabbed this weapon so you may understand it, not use it. This is a longsword, also known as a hand-and-a-half sword."

He swung the blade in slow circles as he spoke, its edge flashed in time with each arch; the control it deployed appeared effortless, but required strength and precision to move with such fluidity. Kenna was entranced.
"It will take time for you to wield this with any kind of skill, but I think you will enjoy it." He rested the sword's tip on the toe of his boot.
"The blade is long and slender with sharp edges on either side. It makes it perfect for slicing or stabbing one's enemy. The long cross guard protects the owner's hand when they block an attack, and the elongated hilt allows a swordsman," he saw her raised brow, "or woman to use either one hand or both when a greater amount of force is desired. The ridges along the hilt provide a better grip. In combat either sweat or blood can make handing a sword challenging."

Kenna listened with rapt attention to his monologue
"And that shallow bit there?" Kenna gestured to the long, shallow indentation that ran down the center of the sword.
"That allows the blood to flow so the sword does not get stuck in whoever you strike."
He stepped forward and thrust the weapon before him to impale the wraith of his enemy.

"When you impale someone thusly, your sword can become trapped by the pressure of their body. That groove prevents that." He returned to his relaxed stance. "Another great thing about the long sword is that it can vary in weight without affecting its quality. For you and those gummy arms I would recommend a sword weighing around two and a half pounds. Light and efficient, a perfect weapon for you."

"Well besides the 'gummy arm' bit, I am very eager to learn. May I hold it now?"

Once more she reached for the sword.

"No you may not." He turned and re-racked the weapon. "You may hold this." He faced her with a pitiful wooden sword in his hand.

"You have got to be kidding me! How am I supposed to learn how to use that," she pointed at the sleek steel, "with that!" She gestured with disgust at the wooden imitation.

Randy laughed at her indignation, raised his own hands palm out in a gesture of peace.

"I know it seems insulting, dear one, but this is how everyone learns. It is much safer. Once you have learned the proper motions and stances we can eventually move up to very dulled swords, and then at last into a battle-ready blade. It takes patience and practice." Kenna begrudgingly looked at the pathetic splinter he held out to her with a grin that both encouraged and annoyed. Kenna snatched it from his hand and shook back her braid.

"Well, let's have at it then."

Round after round the pair danced, wooden blades crossed in the fever of mock battle. Randy instructed her with a soft yet merciless voice; any error, any misstep, he corrected either with words or a smack of wood that resounded through her slick muscles. Sweat dripped into her eyes and with each blink they stung with the lick of salt. Dust clogged her throat, each breath a labor while she kept her eyes on Randy. He stood before her, calm, his golden hair darkened to amber around his neck and throat that glistened in the morning heat.

Kenna lunged, and faltered. She knelt in the dust and leaned against her splinter of a sword while she panted heavily. Randy grabbed her shoulder.
"Again."
"I don't think that I can."
"In battle you have to push past the pain, past the fatigue. If you want to master the sword you must first master yourself. Now, again."
A savage growl rasped her chapped throat as she struggled to her feet.

The pair matched blades, aurous eyes met blue; they stepped back and circled one another, each strove to find the opening in the other's guard. Kenna knew she was outmatched but she would not roll over without a fight, her determination undid her. Patience lost, she lunged for the knight while she slashed at him fervently. He blocked the blow with a flick of the wrist, then stepped to the side while she stumbled past.
"Focus Kenna." Once more they circled one another, one calm, the other trembled. This time Randy went after her, his movements slow and deliberate.

Though she had every moment to gauge his action, her arms could not seem to move fast enough. His blade smashed into hers, and under the weight of his restrained blow Kenna's tired fingers went numb, and released the object with a will of their own. Again she slid to her knees, fingers half curved, palms up against her thighs. Randy knelt beside her.
"I think that's enough for today."

Kenna flexed her fingers then grabbed her wooden sword that now seemed to weigh more than its steel master,

before Randy dragged her to her feet.
"I would go rinse, and then take things slow. Do you have studies with Isabella?" He guided her to the water bucket. He grabbed the ladle then gathered her a generous scoop of the restorative liquid. She slurped down every drop before she gathered another ladle full.
"I don't think I will ever wash the dust out of my mouth." They both laughed as she passed him back the ladle.
"You did well, I promise it will get easier." She grimaced in response.
"We'll see. Thank you for the lesson."
"Anytime." He waved at her while he grabbed a true sword from the rack, then stepped into the elegant yet deadly motions of his drills.

Kenna hobbled into her chambers and was relieved to see that the maids had beat her to the bathing room. The beast, as she referred to her tub, was full of water so warm it produced a cloud of steam that billowed inside the tiled chamber. Water beaded the ivory stones to sluice the ground and drip from the ceiling. She peeled off her soiled garments then tossed them in a rumpled heap in the corner. Kenna padded across the cool tiles towards the tub, the fragrance of lavender and roses wafted to her on the steam.

A soft smile curved her lips before she submerged herself in the bliss of liquid heat. Water swirled around her battered body while she cataloged her injuries. *Not as bad as I thought it would be.* She thought glumly as she counted the scrapes, lumps and bruises along her arms, shoulders and ribs. *Randy is wicked with that little tooth pick.* She laughed, and the water rippled around her. Blessedly clean she dried off and slipped into a comfortable cream gown.

Kenna ran her fingers through her damp hair, her nails sharp against the delicate skin of her scalp. Shivers wracked her spine while she surveyed her still wolf-less quarters, before she left to meander down the hall to the library. Isabella's lesson about the Vontrakalian King and his soulless adviser had not sat well with her, she hoped that the royal library would hold some forgotten secrets.

She pushed against the heavy oak doors polished smooth by decades of touch. She stepped into a vast chamber with reverence, a forest made by man; towers of wood that glistened, adorned with millions of leaves formed by colorful covers and ivory pages. Slender ladders attached by heavy brace brackets and small wheels adorned the shelves.

More shelves branched from the walls that created tall aisles that reached toward the center of the chamber. Three thick stone pillars had been built in single file down the center of the room, containing a cavernous fireplace. The hearths were cold due to the thick summer heat, but in the winter they would each house a small inferno. Kenna's steps were light against the polished stone. The room held the delightful scent of paper, glue, cedar and a bit of dust. She strolled past aisles while she scanned brass signs with interest.

Bold script flowed past while she strode down the seemingly endless array of bookcases. Annoyance creased her brow as she stepped past yet another unrelated topic, until she at last caught sight of the tarnished sign she desired. *Histories of Foreign Lands.*

Kenna gripped the sleek wood and stepped into the aisle with long strides that carried her past countries displayed in a combination of gilded and plain text. Unknown lands were a blur, *Conska...Tenabros...Leala... Vontrakal...* Kenna stopped, perhaps not all unknown. Her head tilted, her hair a soft sigh of movement in her left ear, as she carefully read the titles. A rather new text bound in light-brown leather with black print along the spine. *The Reign of Hrothgar.* Kenna slid the small book from its slot on the shelf with a cautious index finger, then found her way back to the tables.

She settled her tender body with care, mindful of every welt and tender inch of flesh, then thumbed through the pages until she found the most recent passage.

Year 824: Hrothgar is a fair King... his interests revolve around farming and he is often seen in the fields, toiling in the sun alongside his people...

Kenna read through the book with entry after entry of the mundane activities of a country that struggled to claw a life from a cold, ruthless ground. Boredom softened the sharp edge of suspicion, but doubt kept her in her seat.

From what she had learned of the human world; a desire to farm could be reason enough to attack one's neighbors, yet Hrothgar never had. Then all at once things changed, yet Hrothgar did not take Alearian land, he destroyed it. A Land Healer had to be called north after every interaction, and even that was not always enough. The residue of a dark magic was often found deep within the soil, twisted down toward the bedrock.

For one who loves farming, that makes no sense.

She glared at the page as she read another entry.

Year 840: The king is aging but well-loved by his people...
Year 845: Hrothgar looks abroad for an eligible marriage for his son...

So far this all seems normal enough. Yet Kenna could not ignore the tension that gnawed at her entrails.

Year 849: King Hrothgar refuses to leave the castle... His accident was grievous.
Year 851: ...a new adviser stands beside the King...

That must be Maeghnor. She thought with dread as she turned the page only to find it empty; not a single drop of ink. She flipped ahead and found the same thing, nothing. The rest of the book was simply a cluster of blank papers, yellowed slightly around the edges. Though the book said nothing in particular about the adviser she could not help but wonder if it was the dark sorcerer.

Kenna closed the book with a deep sigh, her fingers pulsed in small circles against her temples as she closed her eyes. *Something had happened to Hrothgar, this was not the man his people had known and loved.* Kenna pushed the book away with fingers that trembled then stood with a yelp. Muscles that had gone stiff while she hunched over her text, now attempted to stretch, each fiber laced with fire. She stifled a groan, her fingers diligent along the smooth column of muscles along her spine, down her pelvis. The pain dulled to a subtle ache that allowed her to retrieve the foreign text.

Kenna walked back into the aisle and slipped the book into place. With aimless steps she wandered the shelves with a sightless gaze. All she could see was the endless, pitch gaze of the sorcerer Maeghnor. A chill ran down her spine with satin fingers encrusted in ice that spurred her steps down the dim path of the library. Left, then forward, right, then deeper; Kenna plunged deeper into the shadows around her, driven by the darkness that seeped from the pages behind her.

She paused before a shelf bedecked with gold- and silver-etched books, each cover a different color of dyed leather. She slid out a supple text of sky blue, with silver letters free of its companions; her index finger gentle as she spread the pages. Her aquamarine eyes roved the delicate cream pages as she turned from one to the next, when a soft sound whispered between the shelves and caught her ear. She hovered near the towers of oak, then waited. Silence. With a one-shoulder shrug, Kenna tucked the book under her arm in preparation to retrace her steps. She meandered down the aisle, fingers soft while they trailed through thin layers of satin-soft silver.

Steps light she paused, there it was again, this time more distinct, more familiar somehow. Kenna followed the sound, her satin slippers as silent as wolf paws. Voices whispered quickly, perhaps in an argument.

"I'm tired of hiding," a woman hissed. "It isn't right, I won't do it anymore."

Kenna stopped, she was wrong, she did not know this voice. Shame seared her cheeks while she turned back the way that she had come.

"I can't tell them. Please, you just don't understand." Sophie pleaded. Kenna hesitated.

"Are you ashamed of me?" The woman's voice sounded broken, thready with tears.

"I'm not, I swear." There was a heavy pause interrupted by the soft rustle of fabric. "I'll find a way, I promise." Sophie whispered. "I promise."

Kenna turned back towards their voices and crept closer, her palms hot against the wood as she leaned around the corner. Sophie embraced the other woman, kissed her softly with lips that trembled. Her ivory fingers cool against her lover's tawny skin before they tangled in thick sable hair. Tears laced the woman's cheeks as she pulled Sophie closer, breath heavy as silken lips trailed her slender throat.

Kenna retreated behind the shelf then quickly retraced her steps through the library. Her heart beat rapidly while she recalled what she had seen. Those dark lashes so wet against amber eyes, how they hungered for Sophie. How they spilled over with… love? A heat consumed Kenna that she quickly tried to smother. That was not for her to see; it was too intimate, too heartfelt.

She pushed the scene from her mind and rounded the final corner to her table then froze. Sophie flashed again in her mind as Kenna gazed at the jade-eyed beauty's reflection, with one distinct difference.

"You believe in unicorns?" his rich voice purred against

her ears while he gestured toward her. She looked down at the forgotten weight in her hand, and the confusion cleared from her mind. *Of course.*

"Don't you?"

"I wouldn't know." Von stepped around the table and pulled out a chair; Kenna took it.

"I've never seen one," He answered from behind her shoulder before he once more stepped into view.

"There is more to life than seeing. They say the unicorn is the most cherished creation of the Great Goddess." She stroked the spine with damp fingers, her pulse a thunder in her ears. "Isabella has a horn in her room, I had always wondered how she got it," she added, her voice smooth despite her core that trembled. Kenna turned the page and was pleased to see a wine-red dragon that produced a torrent of fire. *This artist is amazing.*

"I would love to see a dragon, they are both ferocious and intelligent."

The entire time she spoke Von watched her with shrouded eyes.

"Is everything all right?" A cold finger dragged its way down her spine.

"You are lucky to be around her." Kenna released a mental sigh, *Isabella*, then flinched with regret at the sorrow in her companion's eyes.

"Why do you love her so much Von?" Kenna pushed the book aside, its cover dragged against the wood in a sigh that rasped softly.

"Besides the obvious beauty?" He chuckled. "I love her kindness, her intellect. She never seems to care about the nonsense that most court women obsess over. Unfortunately, she is out of my reach. Her status as the King's High Adviser sets her above even the highest ranking noble."

"Have you ever tried? I'm sure the King would give her

leave to choose anyone she wants. It's not like she has a family holding her back." Kenna's smile was greeted with a frown.

"How can you love someone you don't truly know, Kenna? Perhaps my love is simply admiration."

Kenna leaned across the table to clasp Von's hand tightly.

"I don't know a great deal about the affairs of love Von, but I think even simple admiration is a good place to start." At that moment she desperately hoped that Isabella was not related to the Devoney line. "Perhaps you should keep an open mind, or if you feel she is out of your reach then release her. There are many young ladies that I have seen first-hand howl over you."

Von's eyes lit up with the familiar gleam of trouble. "Howl over me, do they?" He flashed her a toothy grin.
"Oh yes, like a bunch of bitches in heat."
"Kenna?!" Von exclaimed, his morose mood shattered by mirth. "Such language from a lady!"
She grinned, "I am no lady." The pair chuckled together for a moment longer before they settled into a companionable silence. Kenna watched Von with interest while he thumbed through her book on mythical creatures.

His long black hair tumbled down to shade his jade eyes like onyx wings. His skin was darker than most of the Devoney's, a lovely bronze that warmed his otherwise midnight colors. A grin curved his full lips, and the gentle expression made Kenna smile herself.
"Thinking of trading my cousin in?"
"Excuse me?" she squealed.
"I see you eyeing me there, did you have a nice look?" he flirted shamelessly.
"And here I was feeling bad for you! You vain little peacock!"

He grabbed at his heart, then frantically clutched at

his tunic as if to pull a weapon from his wounded breast. "You wound me." He looked away with mock shame. "Though I do agree that I am quite the specimen." Von continued, his expression roguish while he wiggled his eyebrows at her.

Kenna reached for the book as a missile. Retaliation anticipated, he snatched the volume out of reach.
"Now now!" he tucked the would-be weapon beneath his arm. "Play nice little wolf." Kenna raised her hands palms up, then slowly returned to her seat while Von slid into his own. "Really though," he asked once settled. "How are you and dear old Caleb?" For a moment she did not respond, instead she twisted a small piece of hair into a slender braid.

She was not sure if she wanted to broach the subject with her sweetheart's cousin.
"We are well," she answered softly.
"Only well?" The laughter left his eyes as he scanned her face, the book forgotten on the table between them. Kenna waved his concern away.
"No, not like that. We are happy when we are together, it's just getting to the 'together' part that's difficult. Between his work and my studies we are apart more often than I like." She thought of the way he always tried to meet her at her door, so they may at least have that small walk with one another.

Von nodded sympathetically.
"You both are on complicated paths. Caleb, as the first-born son, had to take on much more responsibility than the rest of us. As for you, I hear you may be in the employ of the King?"
"How did you hear about that?"
No one was meant to know.
"Don't worry, if it's something more important than being 'Horse Mistress,' no one knows." Von soothed. *Horse*

mistress? She frowned. *I suppose that explains why I never really get the same horse twice. It's an interesting ploy, I just wish they had let me in on my cover story.*

Before she could respond Von stood with a languid stretch.

"It's been lovely seeing you but I have to be off." While he spoke a young boy slipped into the library, clothed in blue linen with the Royal Crest embroidered on his chest in silver. "And it would seem you have somewhere to be yourself."

"It would seem so." She grabbed the book from Von as he walked past.

"If you would leave your book mistress, his Majesty would like to speak with you."

"Yes of course." Her pulse quickened as she returned the text into Von's expectant hand.

"We had better be off then." Swallowing past the sudden dryness of her mouth she followed the boy to the King.

Chapter Six:
A Truth To A Lie

Kenna glanced at the golden doors carved with the world tree that towered before her. Her brow furrowed when they walked past it. "Where are we going?"
"To the King's study mistress." Tom flashed her an odd expression. Kenna dismissed his look, more concerned with the King's sudden summons than the boy's annoyance with her lack of knowledge about the castle layout. *He has left me alone for weeks, what could he want now?* she thought glumly as she trudged after the dandelion-bright boy before her. Tom slowed his pace with Kenna on his heels, and her stomach did another mutinous flip. At the end of the hall they were hailed by two stout guards.
"I am here with the mistress Kenna, she has been requested by the King."

Kenna was impressed, though his voice was high

with boyhood it rang clear and firm. The man that wielded a battle axe with unconscious ease fought back a grin, his thick mustache twitched with the effort. Without a word the guards turned, then pulled the dark chestnut doors open and revealed a narrow, pale-blue hall. Tom swept past the men, his small legs pumped furiously across the wooden floors that gleamed with age and citrus-scented oil. At the end of the corridor there was another set of doors, more simple than the last, where another man, clad in navy blue encrusted in silver, stood guard. The brunette carried a short sword on either hip, and a black staff tipped in pointed steel in his right hand.

He opened the doors to a well-lit parlor, hazel eyes watchful of Kenna as she strode past. The room smelled of leather mixed with the faint tinge of fresh tobacco. Her nose twitched while she grew accustomed to the uncommon scent. Tom melted against the wall, his tunic a subtle blend against the upper half of the room's wall. Kenna surveyed her surroundings with an expression that belied the turmoil in her mind. To her surprise the parlor was modestly furnished; a plain, low-set table straddled a faded carpet with two faded gray couches, behind them a large window that faced Sapphire Bay. Kenna relaxed within the comfort of the small room, lulled by the sound of a coastal breeze and muted chatter of the docks.

A narrow door swung open on generously oiled hinges, and in that absence of oak stood the King, Alaric Vimcor, first of his name. The air rippled in response to his power that shuddered through both Kenna and the young boy beside her. It was then that Kenna realized the king was also a powerful mage, a notion that struck her roughly; how he had masked such power left her unnerved. She swallowed against the dryness of her mouth, her tongue sticky against the roof of her mouth. If Alaric was aware of her intense disquiet he made no remark.

Before she could speak he raised a hand, "Tom, you may go. Thank you for your services."
The boy bowed, blond curls a heavy curtain around his small face, then he left the room.

Kenna watched him leave with a distinct feeling of loss, her tongue slid across her lips.
"Have a seat, Kenna." He gestured to one of the faded couches, his broad hands unadorned, with the exclusion of a thick gold band inlaid with a sapphire on his left hand. He claimed a seat on the couch opposite from her, his hazel-gray eyes veiled while he assessed her. The deep bass of his voice added a rich depth to the raucous calls of sea birds. "I hear your studies are going well, Isabella speaks highly of you."
"Thank you, your Majesty."
"That is not necessary here my dear, I would like you to be comfortable, and formalities such as titles are not comfortable for anyone." His eyes twinkled with mirth at her surprise.
"Of course your ma-, Alaric." She corrected herself with a wolfish grin. A sense of delicious tension settled in Kenna's belly, anticipation as she went nose to nose with an alpha.
"Much better. Now that that's settled I think it's time we discuss the true reason for your employment." Alaric leaned forward and rested his elbows upon his silk-clad thighs.

Silk; Kenna's soft mouth twitched at the sight. Somehow he seemed out of place in such fine clothes; perhaps it was his thick hands, or the fine sun wrinkles that creased the corners of his eyes.
"As you know we desperately need to find Vontrakal's spy. There have been rumors that Conska may be shifting their alliances, which if that proves true, shall be intensely troublesome for this country. In times past they have been a solid ally, but the new king is young and untried. He may be more easily swayed by fear of

Hrothgar and his lackeys than loyalty to a friend."
Alaric leaned into the padded back of his chair, tension heavy on his brow.
"My lord." Alaric raised a brow. "Alaric." Kenna corrected with a stifled sigh. "I have no way to know who the spy is as of yet, but perhaps if I leak some information..." her tone heightened with the intention within her words.
"That is what we are trying to avoid my dear," he answered while he stroked his goatee. Kenna cleared her throat, her palms warm against her thighs as she bit the inside of her cheek against a sudden tick. *My dear?*
"It doesn't have to be accurate information, just something enticing." The corner of his lips kicked when he gathered the true sense of her words.
"Yes... that could work quite nicely."

    Kenna felt herself mirror his expression, her head tilted unconsciously while she watched the sovereign—a sovereign yes, but never hers.

    For a time he was silent, his high brow creased in thought, until at last it smoothed with decision.
"I have a small lie for you to set in motion. It is very simple so do not be overly excited," he cautioned when he saw the eagerness that lined her body while she leaned forward. "A certain lord is being chosen, a Viscount named Barkus. Release the words and see who acts on it."
"How does this help our cause though? It just seems like nonsense if I'm being honest."

    Her ears tingled with heat at the realization that she had casually dismissed a royal's. Alaric was gracious enough to ignore her blunder, an overtly bland expression plastered to his face.
"It is nonsense. I don't dare leak something that could lead to the truth. The point of this is to see who spreads the rumor, to see who shows the greatest level of interest. Also, we will see what gets back to the North my dear."

Kenna clamped down on the inside of her cheek with a sharpness that captured her attention. Alaric stood and Kenna stood with him. She absentmindedly smoothed her tunic while she gazed out the window toward the waters beyond that glittered with unabashed beauty. What she would give to be out there, not inside the King's chambers with its tired lies and those that carried them.
"You will plant this lie tonight." His voice washed over Kenna with a firmness that snapped her back into their conversation. Her mind rushed to process the words she had hardly heard.
"Tonight?"
"Yes, tonight. We are having another gathering to celebrate the season."
"You nobles truly enjoy your parties." Kenna commented dryly.

The king grabbed her shoulder gently, his smile free of joy.
"Yes we truly do. I expect to see you in your finest." With a final squeeze he released her and returned to the ivory door he had once passed through. Kenna watched the portal close quietly behind him and took a deep breath to sooth the tension in her chest. *This is it. It's time to get to work.*

She rushed through her chamber door and stepped into an empty parlor. The garden door stood open, and a cool breeze swirled among the sheer curtains in a flurry. Kenna swatted them aside, her skin prickled with cold, and latched the portal. Based on how cold her rooms were the pack had been gone some time, perhaps they hunted in the woods that were now dappled with gold, red, and amber. She turned from the view in favor of her bed chamber and was surprised to find a burgundy dress spread delicately across her velvet coverlet. *He works fast,* she thought dryly while she lifted the garment, smooth and heavy in her hands, then dropped it once more to peel off her dress.

Kenna sucked in her breath sharply while she moved and stretched, her body was a bruised and battered masterpiece thanks to Randy. Once free she then slipped into the King's selected gown, quickly tied up the laces, and ran her fingers down the soft swells and dips of her form.

While she managed her hair she heard the click of the parlor door, and with the late autumn breeze at her heels, Leara strode towards Kenna. Their minds brushed against one another's softly, then the wolf curled around her human sister's feet, golden eyes half-lidded. Finished with herself Kenna stooped down and ran her fingers through ivory fur. "Let's go," she whispered. With a deep breath she opened the door to find Isabella, hand raised, in the hall.

Isabella greeted her student with a smile dazzling, Kenna glowered in return.
"That's a lot of teeth Isabel."
"Are you ready?"
"Yes, but why are you so excited?" Kenna had never been flashed such charm from her mentor, and at her discomfort that smile widened further. "Now you are just being creepy."

The werecat laughed unabashedly and pulled Kenna from her doorway.

"Come on then, you have a full night ahead of you."

"He told you then?"

"Of course he did, Alaric tells me all the ins and outs of the country. If he didn't, and my sources didn't," she winked, "then I wouldn't be as useful as I am."

Kenna made a noncommittal sound, her attention divided between the woman who clutched her arm, and the crowd that still skirted Leara in the confines of the hall.

They entered the grand hall, their names and titles rang dully in her ears while they immersed themselves into the mass of nobility that swirled around the dance floor. Isabella's jade eyes glittered with amusement when she took in Kenna's hitched shoulders.

"It will be fine." She shook her companion's arms into fluidity before she pulled her protégé from the stairs. The ball room was brightly lit, candles and elegant torches sent rays of light across jewel-toned dancers in a display that mesmerized the watcher. Kenna gazed at the dancers with a dull ache in her chest; she was graceful in the woods, but out there she was as leggy as a newborn colt. A gentle tug on her fingers drew her attention, and she dutifully followed Isabella while they wove through the tangled masses of the crowd.

They found a quiet spot beside a marble pillar wrapped with flower garlands while Kenna found her bearings. She surveyed the faces of those around her in hopes of something familiar.

"Stop fidgeting like that, just go out there and start talking." Isabel chided.

Without a word Kenna strode into the crowd, an ivory wolf at her side, and with each step she opened her mind a little more. She hungered for the thrum of another mage, perhaps someone like herself. Whispers of magic sighed through her thoughts, yet none matched what she remembered, that particular tenor of vibration that played within the confines of her consciousness.

While she walked she felt the press of those around her, and shifted to find her friends. A quick scan rewarded her with a view of broad shoulders and tousled onyx hair. Kenna wove through the crowd, but when she drew closer she saw that something was amiss. His shoulders were taut, his ever-present smile absent, replaced instead by a grim press of lips and clenched jaw. Those before him parted without comment, his dark mood billowed before him and blew them away while he cleared the hall and disappeared between two silver framed doors.

Kenna altered her path to join him, her hand hesitant on the lever, then slowly pushed open the glass doors. Caleb leaned against the rail, the breeze pulled strands of hair free of the black silk ribbon at the nape of his neck; he did not turn to face her. She stepped to his side and silently laid her hand atop his on the rail, his knuckles were hard ridges against her palm.

"Caleb, what's the matter?" She tilted her head to see his face, it was a dark mask, unreadable and cold. "Caleb?" The moments dragged on with unbearable slowness until his sightless eyes at last rested on her. Fraction by fraction they began to soften, then fill with pain as he reached for her, cupped her cheek. Kenna leaned into his touch.

"I have to tell you something." Caleb's voice was low and filled her with a dread that settled tightly in her belly. "I have to leave."

Before he could say more Kenna interrupted him, her body flushed with shock.

"What do you mean?"

"Alaric needs me up North. Things with Vontrakal are getting worse, and he needs me to create a protective barrier between the nearest villages and the border. I don't know how long I will be gone." She didn't feel them, the tears that streamed down her face, not until he wiped them from her skin. He kissed her then, with a slow, soft caress of lips that made her ache inside; not with lust, but with something that she could not quite explain. That sensation was soon snuffed out as her mind turned to the fires that had raged around Blackwood, the blood that had soaked the grass.

The north would be worse, instead of a random raid, it would be warriors hardened by death, and honed into flesh and bone weapons. She pressed her brow into the curve of his neck while she breathed him in, that heady blend of skin, leather, and wood smoke. He reminded her of simpler times, and in some ways of home. Caleb stroked her hair down her back in long fluid sweeps that slowly drained the tension from her body, until at last she could look at him with a smile that trembled.
"No matter where you go, know that I will always be here for you."Her smile began to brake.
"I love you Kenna."
"Caleb, I…" Caleb pulled her close and lifted her off the stones and into his embrace. *Love,* her thoughts fractured around the word, made her feel cold and unworthy. Fresh tears welled only to be blinked back by shame.
"I know wolf girl, I know." She glanced up at him with some difficulty. *Do you?*
"We had better get back," he murmured then laid his lips against her hair.
"I suppose we should."

The pair walked back into the bejeweled circus that was the ballroom. As the hour grew later the guests became louder as wine, mead, and ale took hold of their patrons. Kenna glanced at Caleb, and then away, her heart a tangled mess. She caught her reflection in the glass panes of the door and sighed, no matter how she felt, she had a job to do. She scanned the room and quickly found a cluster of women.. With a squeeze of her fingers she detangled herself from his hold and strode toward the women with a confidence that she did not truly feel. The noble women stood in a tight-knit circle, their backs to the room and Kenna as she approached.

A plump brunette noticed her first and raised an abnormally thin brow, derision in her gaze. Kenna forced a smile to her face while she frantically searched her memory for the woman's name. *Beth... Bertha...Ann?* She smothered a groan of defeat and greeted the ladies when they turned to face her.

She ignored the skeptical look from a mousy blonde and took a deep breath,
"Hello ladies, you all look so lovely!" Her tone was far more cheerful than she thought possible as she plunged into her role. Fanning her face with an exaggerated sigh she continued. "I just don't know how you all stay looking so fresh with this heat." Kenna paused anxiously and waited for their response, thankfully the women seemed to soften with her graciously spread praise.
"Well, it just takes some practice." A blonde with tightly woven curls tittered, her lace fan snapped in punctuation. Kenna relaxed a fraction despite the looks they cast towards Leara at her side.
"You will just have to tell me your secrets."
"Doesn't she get your dress all furry?"
"Seems unpleasant if you ask me," another quipped. Kenna looked at them, her brow furrowed in bafflement.
"I've never paid it any mind."

They looked as confused by her as she was by them, and for a time Kenna listened to the women talk while she waited for the perfect moment to plant her so-called "information." Her face ached with forced smiles, her tongue laden with useless words; she narrowly resisted the urge to crawl out of her skin. *Or maybe I will just shift, that might shut them up.* They spoke of silk, jewels, and the most recent scandalous affair.

"Well, what did you expect? I could not believe her father married that poor girl off to the hide-bound old man," a rotund blonde commented.

"I would never do such a thing to my girls." The brunette, Tessa, jumped back into the conversation, her venomous mouth hidden behind her fan.

"Yes, but now her marriage is ruined! With no reputation, who would have her?"

This was her moment. Kenna licked her lips and braced herself to drop her bit of knowledge.

"I wouldn't know who would take her, but the bigger question is, have you heard who is taking Princess Ena? Apparently, he is a Viscount from Conska, a Lord Barkus I believe. Wealthy enough to entice the Crown."

The women fell silent, and though that had previously been Kenna's prayer, she sensed she had kicked the hornet's nest. Suspicion lurked beneath their oiled lashes, that fragile sense of acceptance shattered.

"How could you possibly know that!" hissed the mousy blonde. Kenna hadn't bothered to learn her name since she was distinctly unpleasant.

"People in the stables talk," Kenna shrugged gracelessly, "the servants hear everything."

"So that's the kind of girl you are? A low-class gossip. How you must love your new home at court? Don't think we don't all know that mountain dung heap you hail from," the blonde sneered. "Whatever choice their majesties make is not to be judged by the likes of you."

Kenna breathed shallowly around the inferno in her chest. "I see," she responded demurely, her tone belied her rage. "It would seem I've spoken out of turn. My apologies."

"Why don't you and that mongrel move on."
Gertrude interceded. "Now, now, Veronica, don't be so harsh." She flashed Kenna a look that scathed, then turned her companion aside. Kenna accepted the curtain call.
"I'm sorry ladies, it was a pleasure to meet you."
About as pleasant as kissing a viper.

Within a few heartbeats she had disappeared into the crowd. Well, that was a disaster, she thought while she sat down; she wound her fingertip in Leara's coarse fur. *I'll have to do better next time, or I'll have the king breathing down my neck.* Kenna caught sight of Caleb and quickly joined him, her arm wound through his while she listened politely as he finished his conversation. It didn't take long for him to look down at her miserable expression.
"That bad?"
"That bad," she answered with a sigh, her head on his shoulder. "I just have to keep trying."
Caleb kissed the crown of her head softly.

The night wore on in a weary cycle of gossip and false pleasantries. Kenna found herself leaned against a pillar, her face pressed against its cool surface. While she rested she felt an unpleasant pull on her mind, perhaps a terrible headache. Despite her fatigue she grabbed a strand of magic and allowed the foreign presence to apply pressure to her mind. She twisted that thread until it glittered, strong and thick; then slid it along the connection and began to seek out the source of power in the room. Mind after mind, hampered her thread as it attempted to find the hostile source that now stabbed at her mental barrier.

Sweat slipped down her sides while she closed her eyes to the chaos, until at last she felt the source of the malevolent magic. A surge of power rippled down her thread, she almost had it. She began to see a hazy image of the user; red and auburn… golden eyes… and then it was gone. Kenna smacked the pillar with a heavy clap that sent lightning though her hand and wrist. She hissed with pain and rubbed her fingers. *I was so close,* she seethed and looked at the crowd with fury.

The noise, the heat, the smell of bodies, perfume and wine; it nearly overwhelmed her. Kenna rushed towards the balcony, to the upset of more than one noble in her struggle for freedom. Once through the double doors she inhaled the pine-spiced air, yanked loose her laces and slipped free of her gown. She tossed the garment across the rail, wriggled free of her shoes and shift, then leaped.

As her bare feet left the cold stone of the rail she plunged into her magic and felt the ecstasy of her wild form. Fur rippled across her body while her limbs lengthened, her hands turned to paws and her spine into a luxurious tail.

Her paws hit the ground, and she ran.
Kenna howled for her pack with voice and mind; she felt their answer in her bones and propelled herself towards the woods. A moment later Leara struck the earth beside her, her powerful shoulders rippled with impact, then she matched her gait to the cinnamon wolf before her. Cool grass caressed their paws as they cleared the pasture fence, the forest so close they could already see its midnight depths.

Her pack howled for her and she sang back, the stress of the night melted away with each stride. That was when she remembered, Caleb. Her pace slowed enough that she could look back toward the windows that glinted like shards of ice in the ivory castle. Stillness found her, ears laid back, torn while she watched the light from the human world. Her pack called for her again, and a war raged inside of her. She bared her fangs at the monolith then ran for the woods.

The forest enveloped Kenna; in that moment when

the trees swallowed the stars, when she was bathed in darkness, she was home. She opened her mind and felt each creature that dwelled within it as sparks of blue, green, and gold. Her magic flowed ahead of her in search of the Pack. She leapt over a fallen tree consumed by iridescent mushrooms and landed with a heavy thump, the thick heady scent of wood rot and pine needles perfumed the air. Kenna howled with joy when she glimpsed flashes of white through the tree line. Leara surged ahead of the shifter, within moments the Pack was upon them. They ran with wild abandon.

Kenna woke that morning covered in damp leaves that clung to her chilled skin. She pulled grass from her hair and stretched; muscles clenched in warm pleasure as she examined her surroundings. She stood up and shook the forest from her and opened her mind to see how far from the castle they had gone the night before. To her relief she was less than a mile from the royal pasture, she could hear the horses when they whinnied groggily for their morning meal.

    Kenna watched the slumbering wolves, not truly ready to leave. The moments ticked by, and as glad as she was to watch each ear twitch, or a wolf roll in it's sleep. The press of her human life began to weigh on her; Kenna touched the minds of her family, not enough to wake them, but enough to let them know that she would be gone when they awoke. Kenna quickly reached the tree line which proved to be a problem in and of itself.

She was naked and didn't think that she could make it across the pastures without a scene. She grasped her magic and considered different forms that she could take, then settled on a small, discreet creature that she had grown fond of since her stay at the castle: a cat. She slid under the lowest rail and purred when the wood nibbled into her back. Once immersed in the tall grasses she angled toward her chambers. With an eye out for sharp hooves, she made good time across the pastures.

All the stable hands saw was a long-haired tabby sprint through the fields then disappear into the garden. Once in the moderate shelter of roses, crocuses, and other vibrant greenery Kenna slowed her pace, and was enveloped by floral scents. Her whiskers twitched while she wound her way through the plants until she came to the twisted steel staircase that led to her chambers.

At the narrow glass door she shifted back into her human form and fumbled with the latch; her feet and hands were pink and tingled slightly from the strain, it had been a long time since she had been so active on all fours. Kenna slipped through the door and into the soft, filtered light of her chamber.

"What are you doing here?!"

Lounged elegantly across her couch was Randy. His amber eyes sparkled with concealed laughter while he watched her scramble to cover her naked form. Ever the gentleman he turned his back to her and explained.

"The maid let me in. I wanted to talk to you, though I didn't mean to intrude." The amusement was poorly concealed in his voice. Kenna rolled her eyes while she dashed for the safety of her chambers. Once the door was closed behind her she quickly pulled clothing from her wardrobe then returned to the parlor, still agitated she took a seat on the couch opposite him.

"You realize it's just after dawn." She combed her hair with tender fingers as she waited for his response.

"This war that Alearian is heading towards… where do you stand?"

Kenna's movements stilled; her mouth suddenly dry. She had never thought about what she would do if Alearian went to war. Yes, she was in the employ of the king, but would she go to fight over it? She dropped her hands in her lap gracelessly, her expression earnest.

"I don't know, I don't have any interest in war." Somehow the words seemed deceitful, guilt washed through her in waves that scalded. Her new friends and their kindness flashed through her mind along with the horrors of battle. *Can I truly leave them to fight alone?*

"I understand. You don't exactly have the same stake in all of this as we do." He stood, frame weary in the pale light. Kenna watched him while her mind filled with the faces of those she now cared for.

"I wouldn't say I don't have a stake in it… things have changed."

"Then why do you fight?"

Silence took hold of the pair. What could she say? She rose to her feet, crossed the space between them, and firmly took his hand; it was cold as though he had been outside all night. She pulled him back down to the sofa with her, her bruised hands warm against his skin.

"I fight because I don't accept the other option. Though I don't fully believe in this war, I won't lay down or turn aside as someone threatens the home… and the people I now hold dear. I fight because I would rather fight than be afraid. Wolves don't back down when someone threatens their pack, I don't back down either." Randy squeezed her hands before he pulled free to lay his head back against the sofa with a heavy sigh.

Kenna watched him while he rested; he was so weary, his shoulders nearly sagged beneath the weight of his unseen burden, stubble glowed dimly in the dawn, gold against his fair skin. Though fair no longer seemed the word anymore. Ashen, that was closer, his inner flame nearly snuffed out.

"Randy," she whispered his name. Somehow a full voice seemed too harsh for the fragile air they breathed. "What's wrong?" His eyes opened, soft and unfocused before he returned to himself.

Then the flame bloomed and chased the shadows from his gaze, he graced her with a smile.

"Let's eat and talk about other things."

"Eat?"

"Yes," Randy walked to a nearby table laden with fruit and pastries. "I brought us a snack."

Kenna ate with him quietly while he steered the conversation in any direction he liked, it was all rather meaningless until Sophie's name caught her ear.

"What was that about Sophie?"

"Oh, just that Sophie and Aden are having a bit of a falling out."

"How so?" Kenna put her apricot tart down. Randy leaned closer despite the vacant room.

"He asked her to marry him and she said no."

"That seems like more than a 'bit of a falling out' Randy."

"The love is still there," he responded softly. "There are just other complications to the matter." The memory of the library filled Kenna's mind; the smell of books, the sound of tears, that passionate kiss.

"Randy," she couldn't find the words.

"Yes?"

"I don't know how to ask this, or if I even should."

"We won't know if you never ask."
"How long have you known about Sophie?" The words came out in a rush.
"For as long as Sophie has known, maybe even longer."
He knew!
"But you don't say anything?"
"It's not my place to say anything," he countered softly.
"Wouldn't Von want to know? Does he know?"
"Kenna," Randy sighed, his narrow frame etched with sorrow. "I want to tell you a story."
"About Sophie?"
"About me."

The silence was heavy between them while Kenna waited; Randy had started a fire, his face a shadowed mask as he went about the chilled chamber. She could smell the pain, hot beneath his skin, and deeper still the bitter tang of shame.
"When I was younger, I had a problem with bullies. One summer it finally boiled over into something more."
Kenna nodded sympathetically but remained silent.
"It was at a small lake near Pernak, hardly little more than a pond, that we used to play in as children. As was normal Caleb and the twins were visiting for the summer and for the first time, so was Aden. I had made it to the swimming hole first and waited for them to join me beneath my favorite apple tree, it had the sweetest fruit. It was there that they found me, not my friends but the others. Their ringleader John hated me the most, on a personal level it seemed, and took the most pleasure in tormenting me. It did not matter that I was the Lord's son, and John was careful

and always knew where to strike or when to be far from me so no one would believe my accusations."

Randy took a breath that quivered, the embers glowed in his amber eyes; so dark they looked like rust… the light had fled their honeyed depths and Kenna could not recognize their hollowed reflection.

"It was there beneath my favorite tree that John grabbed me. He struck my head against the bark and my vision blurred red as blood streamed down my face. I did not scream; I would not scream. So, he struck me again and this time my vision went dark. I could still hear him though, taunting me. 'Was that too rough for you? I bet you like the lads to be gentler don't you, fagot?'"

Kenna cringed when the words left Randy's lips with such harshness, he didn't sound himself. She reached out to stop him; she didn't have to know, he didn't have to tell her this, but he shook his head slowly then continued.

"I could feel them kicking me, each time I felt the bite of their boots and lights flashed against the darkness. At last, they stopped and I could catch my breath while they jeered at me, but I could see again through one eye at least. 'Are you going to cry, little fairy? Cry for your sweetheart?' I was drowning in their laughter but I would not cry and that made him angry. Grabbing my hair, John dragged me to the waters and I fought him every step, but I was much smaller then and only hurt myself with the effort. Soon I felt the water, cold against my ankles, then my knees as he pushed me deeper. Now I cried. I could taste my tears mixing with my blood.

"And just like that he let me go. I couldn't believe it and I nearly fell into the lake as I turned to see what had changed. It was Caleb, he had John by the front of his tunic, twisting it so tight I could see the veins in John's face swell as he fought for air. Throwing my would-be killer to the shore, Caleb dragged me from the water holding me close against him while he shoved the others away. I can still remember the rage in his voice as he half carried me to safety. Sophie waited for me at the water's edge, tears running down her face while Von and Aden fought off the other boys. It was a mess. That's how Aden broke his nose, the first time at least. After that they never left my side and John was too afraid to challenge them."

Kenna could hardly breath, what could she say? She reached for his hand, so hot and moist against her own, while she struggled to find words that could ever soothe such a wound. The problem was those words didn't exist. Instead she laid her head on his shoulder and watched the embers as they cradled his fractured heart. At last she whispered into the silence,
"I love you Randy, and I understand. I am so sorry." Salt laced her words, and silver rimmed her eyes.
"Sophie will speak of it when she's ready. The world is not always kind Kenna, as I'm sure you well know. It is full of two types of people; those that would see you drown, and those that would save you from the darkest waters."

Chapter Seven:
Immortal

The dawn gave way to day, yet the coldness had not left Kenna even with the exuberant warmth of the fire. Pain, always so much pain. Wasn't there more to life than that? She stood, limbs stiff with misuse and begrudgingly returned to the recesses of her chambers. Kenna dressed slowly after she washed, only to be interrupted by a knock. She exhaled explosively and set down her brush, then she strode from the chamber and was greeted by a parlor full of company. Kenna was both startled and slightly annoyed that her friends had entered her den unannounced. A smile plastered to her face, she greeted her guests. Aden leaned against the mantle, his ivory tunic vivid against his warm skin, while Sophie sat stiffly in the overstuffed chair, Randy and Von lounged on the same sofa that had become a place of heartbroken secrets. *So many guests today,* Kenna thought with a twinge of exhaustion.

Caleb stood to greet her, his grin faltered a fraction when he noticed her tension.

"We thought we would take you to the beach before I leave," he said before kissing her softly. Kenna's tension evaporated when she recalled the mysterious salty waters that she had longed for since her arrival at Sapphire Bay.

Her eyes shined when she looked up at Caleb, round and luminous with joy.

"Do I need anything?"

"I would change, the salt will ruin your nightgown." Sophia called from across the room before Caleb could respond; Kenna wasted no time with a response, instead she bolted for her chamber. She returned in an undyed tunic, breeches, and leather sandals, her hair loose and wild around her shoulders.

Once in the paddock the party mounted their ready horses, saddle bags bulged with blankets, drinks, and food. The ride to the beach felt endless to Kenna while she listened to the roar of the ocean that mingled with the breeze. Finn pranced anxiously down the cliff trail in response to his rider, bits of sand and gravel slid down the slope with each step. Kenna leaned forward to stroke the stallion's neck while she touched her mind to his. Under her gentle touch his strides smoothed into a long, elegant gait.

"You're becoming quite the horsewoman." Caleb commented from her side. She responded in a droll tone, "Yes well, I am the local Horse Mistress, haven't you heard?" Caleb laughed heartily.

"Sweet Kenna, I do believe that was sarcasm." Her only response was an embellished wink that brought another peal of laughter from him.

Finn stepped onto the sand without hesitation, his muscular shoulders rippled when he sank into the shapeless earth. The sand gleamed softly in Kenna's mind as though it still carried the essence of life from the depths of the ocean, and perhaps in some ways it did. She released her magic in waves and pulled in a sudden breath; millions of small and microscopic beings lived mere inches beneath the surface, then crawled, burrowed, and surged around a cold, dark world.

The closer their band came to the waters the farther she reached, and marveled in the multitude of lives, and forms she felt within the waves. Kenna slipped from the saddle, her face a mask of adoration, while she walked through the cool sand and stepped into the frigid waters of Sapphire Bay. The brine-filled liquid lapped at her ankles eagerly as it drew her deeper into its embrace, within moments Kenna was up to her chest in salt water, her lungs tight with shock, waves battered her when she strove to join the souls that lived beneath the surface. *If only I could reach them.* She took another step and dropped off the edge.

Shock slowly rippled up her spine when she felt the earth slip away. She broke the surface, gulped in air, and looked at the sky with vacant eyes. One final breath… Kenna succumbed to the darkness below.

Kenna drew her arms close to her body while she let herself sink beneath the waves. She opened her eyes as well as her magic and embraced the gloom around her. Her magic leaped away from her with a sheer, raw power that she had never felt before, and under its touch she felt things awaken. Kenna quivered when a dark mind responded, and she swam towards the creature, but her lungs began tighten painfully. With a grimace of despair she kicked to the surface and gasped for air. Kenna looked back at the beach, her friends were accompanied by the horses and all stood at the water's edge, both human and beast called to her. A part of her wanted to return to them, and yet… she could feel that impossible creature come towards her, lulled into wakefulness by her call. How could she ignore him?

With a deep breath she dove. Kenna casted about the twilight waters and swam with great strokes towards the broad mental presence. She could feel him in her mind; dark, ageless, cold, and unchanged. In the near distance she saw a magnificently large shadow that surged toward her. Its neck was long and slender with an arrow shaped head that focused on her with an unbreakable intensity. Kenna's stomach twisted with fear and elation, made her ignore the signs of panic that scorched her frame.

The beast drew closer, its large body became more defined; Its torso, impossibly long, was shaped like a reversed arrowhead, whale-like flippers graced its sides directed by a slender tail that worked as a rudder. Kenna was mesmerized by its green-gray skin, so smooth. Kenna had not realized she now floated, suspended in opaque shadows, her limbs swirled sluggishly with cold. She touched its mind and shivered, it was emotionless like no creature she had encountered before, fear bloomed in her breast when she realized that she was defenseless and alone. The sea consumed her just as the creature intended to.

She looked over her shoulder and fought back the urge to scream; he was close behind her, his wedge-shaped head open as he revealed wicked fangs. Kenna's lungs burned while they struggled to absorb the little oxygen they had left. She lashed out at the beast with her magic in an attempt to turn him away, yet he swam closer, unfazed; the creature came from a time before magic and was unaffected by its use. Kenna cried unseen tears of frustration, the edges of her vision began to blacken as her body gave way, she was going to drown. The murky world began to flicker, she could no longer feel the beast behind her though her tired mind assured her he was still there. Kenna tried to touch the minds of her pack, her family, yet she could not reach them.

Her movements slowed, then stilled; her heart gave a stuttered rhythm, so slow she could hardly move, perhaps she would die before it reached her.

Cold hands gripped her arm firmly and pulled, Kenna opened her eyes slowly to an echo of shock that rippled through her. Large brown eyes gazed into hers from the depths of a pearlwhite face. The woman's black hair engulfed them both as her momentum shifted the water. Without a word she pulled Kenna close and kissed her deeply while she passed her breath between them. Kenna's vision cleared with the heady breath, and with the clarity of her vision came the memory of the creature that hunted her. She tore her lips from the woman and looked past her with a flash of fear tempered by confusion; the beast's shape undefined with distance.

Kenna turned to the woman, and was surrounded by smooth freckled creatures; their short fur coats were like oiled velvet in the water when they slid across her skin. They swam around her and the black-haired woman before a larger animal slid beneath her belly and wriggled against her. Nestled close to the warm form she felt the water rush around her while the seals propelled themselves towards the shore. Kenna bared her teeth in a triumphant grin then caressed her aquatic mount. It took what felt like mere moments before they burst through the surface of the water, Kenna gulped down air in ragged breaths then slid from the animal's back.

She slowly found her feet and burrowed her toes in the sand. Kenna stood less than a quarter mile down the shore from her companions, she felt a pang of guilt when she saw them, many soaked up to their waists from the sea. She turned her gaze back to the dark-haired woman that had breathed her back to life.

The woman stood naked, her skin calm and smooth despite the frigid temperatures; her muscles long and slender. Ivory skin gleamed in the sunlight and had the slightest hint of transparency that gave her a blue hue. It was her eyes that captured Kenna, large and richly brown, they were reminiscent of something she could not quite place. She stepped forward and pushed back the stranger's heavy black tresses, then smiled.

"Thank you, you saved my life." The woman kissed her once more; her lips held the salt of the ocean in a delicious moderation that made Kenna's lips tingle.

They parted slowly then the woman stared into Kenna's eyes with an intensity that demanded words, yet none were spoken, instead she released Kenna and slipped back into the sea. The seal's small faces blinked out of view while they submerged and left Kenna alone in the shallows.

Kenna stumbled from the water, every muscle strained with fatigue, one more slap from the waves and she would tumble to the ground. Her sodden clothes clung to her with a heaviness she could not stand, and she clutched at it to drain the water away, yet as she worked water cashed against the back of her knees. Kenna stumbled forward, her hands and knees ground into the waterlogged sand painfully. With a growl she swiped sand and salt from her hands and face, then jerked when she was lifted by gloriously warm hands. Her relief quickly dissolved into trepidation when she saw the hard set of Caleb's jaw, Kenna quickly found her feet and slipped free of his grasp. *Perhaps I was safer in the water.* She wrapped her arms around her middle and stared at the cliffs, her heart pounded wildly in a chest that still ached.

Caleb didn't say a word, only stood by silently while Kenna was surrounded by their friends and the horses. She did not hear their words, and hardly registered their gentle touches, her focus instead on Caleb who stood behind them, his expression thunderous.

"What were you thinking?" His voice had the low pitch of a hunter about to strike, and Kenna raised her chin, though it trembled slightly, in response.

"I felt a call, I was just trying to answer." Her words sounded feeble, even to herself.

"Oh, is that it then? That's your explanation?!" The storm within Caleb broke loose.

"What kind of a fool are you? Did you want to die?" He yelled. Kenna stood her ground, shoulders hunched against the looks of their companions. "I have never in my life seen someone behave the way you did. You just slid off your horse and disappeared into the ocean like a mindless puppet! Have you any idea what could have happened? And you had the nerve to look back at us without a word, though I know you heard our call, and disappear. You are lucky we didn't call the King's guards. Alaric would cast you from Sapphire Bay if he knew of this! We can't have a mindless mage running loose." Caleb clenched his jaw in an effort to stop himself, a muscle ticked with the restraint.

Von stepped to his side just as Sophia stepped to Kenna's, Caleb shook his cousin off.

"That's enough Caleb, we were all scared. You have said your piece now let it go." Sophia interrupted softly while she pulled a handkerchief from her bodice and dabbed a tear from Kenna's cheek. "Take him for a walk. He needs to cool off." Von reached for his cousin once more and with a muttered curse Caleb walked away, his back a ridged mass while he stalked down the beach.

Sophie pulled on Kenna's numb fingers.

"Come on, you need to rest before you fall down again." Kenna followed mutely, Randy and Finn in tow towards the pile of blankets and saddle bags that had been dumped onto the sand. Once seated Sophie wrapped Kenna in a dry blanket, then sat beside her. Finn slowly lowered himself to the ground behind her, his form warm against her back where she leaned against him.

"Well, I can't say I've ever seen him lose his temper like that. Not since we were children." Sophia commented casually. Kenna closed her eyes to Sophie's words while she fought to catch a steady breath. "He was only so angry because he had been terrified. He swam out so far and still couldn't find you, when he came back from the water he looked as though you were already dead." Sophie glanced at Randy who sat quietly beside them, his skin pale, eyes ringed with red.

Kenna did not fill the void that they left, instead she lost herself to the sounds of sea birds and the brutal waves to their left.

"I've never seen a man with such a broken heart." Randy's words ripped a ragged wound in Kenna's chest.

"Will he forgive me?" Her voice trembled.

"He already has. Just let him cool off." Sophia interjected. Kenna looked at Randy for confirmation but found his stare doggedly locked on the horizon.

"Now come on, let's not waste the day. Stretch out and enjoy the sun, you look half frozen." Kenna thought of the black water and shuddered. *I was nearly worse than frozen.*

For a long while they didn't say a word, simply listened to the world around them as the sun soothed their wounds. Kenna's mind drifted from one topic to the next in aimless circles, until it landed on Alaric, what he would do if he found out what happened. *How could the king hold any faith in me to find a spy if I could not even stay in control of my magic?*

Kenna turned her thoughts to the members of the Alearian court.

"What do you know about Lady Signe?" Kenna asked. For a while Sophia did not respond and Kenna half wondered if she had fallen asleep. Long black lashes caressed her skin, her gaze shut to the brilliant light.

"Honestly," her tone breathy, "no one really knows much about her. She came down from the north fairly recently and only speaks with the older nobles. We 'children' are not appropriate company." Sophie cracked open a jade eye at Kenna to emphasize her words with an overly sophisticated tone. They laughed, their voices mingled with the waves and wind. Kenna winced while rubbing her sternum, but she chuckled nonetheless.

Caleb and Von returned when the sun began to descend towards the horizon. Kenna watched them through her lashes in a halfhearted attempt to catch Caleb's eye; he glanced her way once then stepped further away. The group chatted quietly as they built a fire on the shore, its flames cast a circle of light as the sea swallowed the sun. Kenna cradled her sorrow while she watched the fire consume the brittle, brine-encrusted driftwood.

The temperature continued to plummet and drew the circle closer. Kenna tried to seat herself between Randy and Von but found her efforts thwarted, the only space available was near Caleb's side. With a deep breath to calm herself she sat in the cool sand, every muscle taut. Her companions' words merged with the drone of the night while she existed, until she felt a light touch at the small of her back. She glanced up at him and smiled awkwardly, her lips were too tight, too many teeth were showing, but the warmth that spread through her when he smiled in return made it feel all right.

Then Caleb leaned closer, his lips a finger's breadth from her ear.

"I'm sorry," his hand gripped hers, "I thought I had lost you." Caleb rested his brow against her collarbone. Kenna glanced at her friends and saw that they had seamlessly turned their backs to the pair, deeply engrossed in their conversations. Caleb wrapped his arms around her waist and pulled her to his chest. She softened against him, the unbearable tension inside of her uncurled as his forgiveness washed over her along with the warmth from his broad chest.

"I'm sorry too, I honestly don't know what came over me."
"It's all right. Perhaps you should bring it up to Isabella in the morning." His voice caressed her ear pleasantly. Kenna nodded then pressed her lips to Caleb's throat and reveled in his touch when he squeezed her tighter.

The horses picked their way up the cliff path undisturbed, each rider immersed in their own thoughts. At the crest of the cliff Kenna looked back at the waters, now black beneath a starlit sky with a sense of defeat. It was a relief to see the stable yard, and she quickly slid from Finn's back, then passed his reins to a plain-faced groom with a broad smile; Kenna returned his expression feebly, then made her way towards her garden stairs. Caleb stopped her with touch upon her arm, his eyes were black, indiscernible, Kenna looked away first.

"You're leaving then."

"I'm just very tired, if you want, you can come over once you are done."

"Then I'll come with you now."

"No, stay with them. They miss you and I know they are concerned with you leaving so soon." Kenna took the hand that rested on her arm and kissed it softly. "Come and see me later. I just need some time to myself."

Kenna stepped away but was quickly pulled back into Caleb's embrace. He kissed her deeply, his lips warm and firm against her own, his tongue a smooth caress. She shuddered against him, already weak from the sea; her pleasure threatened to shatter her control completely. At last he released her.

"I will see you tonight then." His voice was husky and it sent a thrill through her, her toes curled in her sandals.

"I look forward to it."

Kenna ambled through the garden in a daze, her fingers tangled with velvety petals that released a sweet perfume into the cool evening air. The gravel crunched pleasantly beneath her sandals, and at last she could take a breath that felt steady. Despite this, something nagged at her mind, almost like a forgotten thought that grew until it was an unbearable itch at the base of her skull; Kenna bared her teeth when the itch turned into a familiar buzz.

She delved into her core with an eagerness to fight, a chance at victory. Her lips pulled back in a wolfish smile that grew until it faltered; her reservoir magic was empty, only the barest glimmer stirred within the dulled glow of embers. She would fight as she was then; her fingers curled with the memory of claws, then she flexed them straight and grasped for a weapon that was not there.

Kenna prowled through the narrow gravel paths and silently cursed the noise beneath her feet. She curved around a bend ready to spring, only to find the garden was empty. Her body warmed with tension as she strained her eyes against the darkness, a thin sheen of sweat glossed her limbs.

It struck her then, a pain that blinded with its intensity; Kenna gasped and nearly stumbled, and there, beneath the roses, sat a red fox. Aquamarine met amber and the pain increased like a bolt to the head. Kenna reached for the creature with body and mind and was rejected in an acidic wave, before the vixen darted from reach and into the woods.

She watched the creature go with a sigh of relief as the pain ebbed from her mind, then turned back towards her stairs. Every step she took raised the sense of tension that loomed within her, the hairs on her arms rose, skin tight. She fought the urge to look over her shoulder and quickened her pace until her breath plumed against the glass of her chamber door.

Kenna fumbled with the handle and it released with a click that allowed her into the dark parlor room. She then latched each window, drew the drapes, her spine stiff with the distinct sensation of being watched. Kenna walked to her room, eager to see the pack, and slipped free of her salt encrusted clothes then crawled into bed.

Her skin stuck to itself when she curled into a ball, so she stretched out instead, the sheet tucked between her thighs, and fell into dreams of murky water and wicked fangs. She woke with a start; a cold nose bumped the small of her back, she recognized the soft touch of her mother, the same gentle touch that woke her from nightmares as a pup. Finna joined her beneath the covers, her fur pressed against Kenna's clammy skin. She buried her face in her mother's neck, and unbidden tears trickled into the wolf's fur. Finna's mind brushed against hers, but Kenna shrank away, her mind shut tight against the wolves.

So gentle, the subtle caress of callused fingers down her cheek, her neck and bare shoulder; pleasure stirred beneath her skin and blazed a trail beneath the touch down to her fingertips. Kenna stirred slowly and inhaled a deep breath that shuddered through her while she stretched beneath the tangle of sheets.

Blankets shifted and she moved aside on instinct, eyes half lidded against the silver light that slipped between the curtains, and felt a thrill when she heard the whisper of cloth against the floorboards. Caleb slid under the covers beside her, the blankets pooled around his hips, his chest was warm beneath her fingertips except for the scar that stretched across it, cool and bright as quicksilver.

Their gazes met and Kenna shivered at the hunger she saw there, at the tension that pulled low in her stomach, and the warmth that bloomed at the apex of her thighs. She wriggled closer to him with a sigh of pleasure when his skin kissed hers. She captured his lips, with gentle nips of teeth then licked the small hurt her bite had caused. Thier kiss deepened and the tip of his tongue grazed the roof of her mouth, she shivered at the sensation.

Caleb held her tightly against his frame. His shaft was a long, hot pressure against her stomach, hard yet smooth like silk upon her skin.

Wetness glazed her center and sent a shiver of

pleasure through her when she shifted up higher. The tip of him grazed that slick, warm flesh and pulled a moan from her. Caleb growled against her lips, his own hips worked against her while he nudged at her entrance.

"Do it," her words tangled with their tongues and breath. "Please."

His eyes were feverish with desire when he pulled back to look at her, scanned her face for an ounce of doubt. "Are you sure?" Kenna arched her back and spread her legs, a wordless invitation he could not ignore. His eyes focused on the soft, glistening opening and with a growl grasped her thighs, and pulled her towards him. Kenna gasped at the sharp pain, then pleasure that followed his thrust when he slid into her and groaned.

Caleb lowered his chest to hers, his forearms braced around her. His kissed her softly while he withdrew his length then plunged deeper. Kenna arched beneath him, her now swollen lips pressed into his throat while he ground into her. With greater speed he thrust into her, and she followed his rhythm to meet each thrust until a pressure built low in her belly. She persued that ache, her hips rising to meet his thrust, harder, faster, her thighs slick where they wrapped around him.

Her moans filled the chamber, throaty and desperate for release. Caleb's own low groans mingled with her voice until he pushed up and away from her. Cool air kissed her slick skin, nipples erect, her breasts shined softly in the moonlight with their perspiration. She watched hungrily where their bodies were still joined, caught those glimpses of his wet shaft. That ache overtook her, she cried out as release washed through her frame in a hot wave that tingled beneath her skin.

Caleb continued to pump into her, harder and faster, she clung to him and called out his name in ecstasy until his voice mingled with hers while he came. His arms wrapped

around her once more while he burried his face in her hair, both of them spent. He gently pulled out of her then rolled to her side and held Kenna close, his breath a soft caress upon her shoulder.
"Are you all right?"
"Yes." Her voice hoarse, "Just tired, I can hardly move."
Caleb chuckled and pulled her closer.
"Then rest darling."

She rolled over as a small smile tugged at her mouth, and in those moments before sleep claimed her they exchanged gentle touches, and sweet kisses until she was lost to a dreamless night.

Chapter Eight
Magic Be Thy Master

Sound by sound the day washed over her, birds chirped, horses whinnied in the pasture, a soft breath sighed beside her own. Kenna rolled over, careful not to disturb his arm around her waist. His eyes were closed yet a smile already curved his lips.
"Good morning." His gaze met hers as he pulled her close for a chaste kiss.
"Morning." She twitched beneath his touch, her back stiff, then she sat up in bed. She glanced out the window, her face placid despite the way her fingers fidgeted while her mind scrambled for something to say that wasn't an echo of his words.
"We could—"
Kenna threw the covers back.
"I'm going to miss my classes!" She glanced at the sun again for a miserable confirmation, late was a mild way to

describe her tardiness.

She dressed quickly and ignored the eyes that danced with mirth while they followed every step of her performance. Caleb sat against the headboard, his face a pitiful mask of severity as he fought back a grin.
"It's not funny Caleb, I completely missed it."
Exasperation made her fingers clumsy while she struggled to braid tangled hair. "I've got to go."
With a quick kiss she fled her chambers.

Kenna rushed into the hall, frantic to find a page to send a message to her arms teacher. It did not take her long, the halls always crawled with messengers and servants, this time to her benefit. With her message sent, Kenna made her way to Isabella's study with a mix of dread and annoyance; she was sure a lecture waited for her. Brow furrowed, she let herself into the parlor, drawn deeper by Isabella's voice.

Her tone undulated through words Kenna had never heard before, and curiosity drew her deeper into the dwelling. The werecat was busy at her work table, ebony hair pooled on the surface as she bowed above her pestle. The floorboards creaked beneath Kenna's boots and drew the sharp jade gaze of her mentor. Kenna grinned.
"You're in a good mood."
"I am, I have some new spells to show you. I think you'll enjoy them."

Kenna's stomach lurched when she realized she would not be able to comply with the task. Before she spoke, she reached for her magic, it was a shrunken ember that flickered within its domain. Kenna heaved a sigh then settled at the table; Isabella paused while she poured fresh herbal powder into a bottle with a wax-coated stopper.
"Is something wrong?"
"Unfortunately… Perhaps we should sit down."

Before she sat, Isabella poured them each a cup of tea, the mild scent of mint and chamomile seeped into the cool morning air, its steam billowed softly. For a long while the mages sat quietly, Kenna's hands curled around the porcelain cup while she gathered her words. Isabella sat tranquilly opposite her, her shoulders loose, eyes settled on the horizon through a steel-laced window.

Kenna she gulped down tea that was so hot it scorched her throat, blinked back the pain and confessed. "Isabella, I can't do magic with you this morning. I don't know when I will be able to." Kenna glanced at her mentor and was surprised to see she was calm, her only expression a delicately arched brow, so she continued.
"Yesterday, when we all went down to the beach I was called by the water, or maybe not the water but what lived inside of it. I couldn't control myself even though there was a part of me saying to turn back. I just couldn't. My magic was ripped out of me! I didn't mean to cast out so far, I only wanted to touch the creatures close to me but when I opened my magic… it wouldn't stop flowing, that's when I touched it."

She stared at her hands with vacant eyes while she remembered the cold embrace of the water and the malevolent beast that hungered for her.
"What did you find?"
"I don't know what it was, but it was old. Its mind felt like nothing I had ever touched and it was so dark. At first it called to me and I couldn't help but swim closer, then I saw what it truly was. This beast with an arrow of a head and fangs that looked like they would go right through me, but the worst was its eyes. It knew that it had me, that I was trapped and it took joy in that."

Kenna glanced up, a humorless smile on her lips. "It made a cat look loving towards its mouse." Isabella watched her closely, her lips pressed into a thin line. "Since then, I haven't been able to use magic, there isn't anything to use." Kenna spread her fingers wide, then dropped them in her lap.

"What you encountered in the water was immortal, like a dragon, and creatures of that sort. With your mind still so untrained it seems the Norigal latched on to your magic and followed it like a beacon. It has been at least a hundred years since one has come so close to shore. How did you escape it?" She poured out more tea.

Kenna took a sip to hide her blush even though it burned her tongue.

"Well there was this woman, she and her seals saved me after she breathed air back into me."

Isabella's eyes danced at her pupil's embarrassment.

"It's good luck to be kissed by a Selkie."

"Then I'm doubly lucky." Kenna mumbled then clapped her hand over her mouth.

The werecat laughed as she shook her head.

"My dear child, you have so much power, more than you could ever imagine." The joy had faded from Isabella's eyes while she regarded her student, such melancholy Kenna had never seen. Kenna leaned back against the comfortably worn chair and brandished a smile she did not feel.

"What is it Isabella, you can tell me. It can't be much worse than what I did yesterday."

"I don't know how to start. It's not an easy story to tell."

"Well," Kenna ventured, "who is the story about then?"

The werecat's eyes were pained when she looked up. "It can't be that bad..." Kenna's smile faltered when Isabella would not look at her, instead her soft voice rose just above a whisper, and voiced words that Kenna had not expected.

"The story is about you."

"What could you know about me that I didn't tell you?" Kenna countered with false bravado while she gathered her wits.

A knock at the door stopped whatever Isabella was about to say, and Kenna felt the heat of shame chase away her relief. If the werecat insisted that she knew a story about her, it could only mean something dark had attracted her attention in the first place. Kenna lurched for the door and bumped her hip sharply against the couch as she made her escape. She rubbed the lighting out of her joint while she pulled the bolt free with her other hand.

An unfamiliar face greeted her just beyond the threshold; mouse-brown hair cropped close to the scalp was the only bit of color in the man's dour face. Pale-gray eyes regarded her coolly.

"Mistress Kenna, your presence has been requested by Lord Caleb. He and his men wish to depart." The man gave her the slightest of bows, his shoulders tense as they protested the courtesy he showed her. A new concern enveloped her mind while she turned back to the table.

"Isabella I—"

"Yes of course, go and say your goodbyes. You can have the day to yourself after that."

"Thank you." Kenna bowed her head then quickly left the chamber.

The servant was clearly a no-nonsense sort, he bustled down the halls on spider-like legs, and even with her long gait she was pressed to keep up with the man. *Just what I wanted to look like before Caleb leaves. A sweaty mop.* She pushed her hair behind her ears with agitation. At last they reached the entrance to the stable yard where Caleb and his soldiers waited in an approximation of double columns. Despite the straightforward excuse of his departure and the cool effortless smile he bestowed on her when she worried, Kenna knew the mission was a cover.

Caleb was too valuable to send north, any army captain or knight could go to the villages and help reinforce them against Vontrakal, yet it was him that would go.

She stepped into the courtyard bathed in buttery warm light and swallowed against a suddenly tight throat. Caleb sat elegantly astride Zane, stallion and rider were perfectly matched, black hair gleamed in the sunlight while both watched the road. As though he sensed her presence he turned in the saddle, his evergreen eyes settled on her in a heartbeat, then a moment later he swung down to earth with the soft clank of mail and strode towards her. Before she could say a word he swept her into his arms and placed his mouth upon her own.

Kenna's cheeks burned when she heard the whistles and chuckles of his men but he would not release her, and despite herself she melted against his frame, his scent so familiar in her nostrils. With a satisfied grin he let her go, if only at arm's length.

"I'm sorry I couldn't go find you myself, but I had to ready the men."

Her eyes stung as she tried to speak, she could not trust her voice and pressed her palms to his face instead, her thumb trailed across the skin of his cheekbone, then she pulled him to her to kiss him once more. His lips were soft against hers, even as salt mingled between them. Kenna pulled back and laughed softly while she dashed away her tears with careless hands.

Caleb grabbed her fingers, and kissed each tip that trembled while he traced every line of her face with his eyes.

"Don't cry for me, love. I'm just helping some locals."

"We both know that's a lie," she whispered furiously. Caleb's deep chuckle washed over her as he drew her close. She breathed his scent in on an inhale that trembled, she didn't want him to go; every fiber of her being wanted to drag him back to her chamber and bolt the door, king or no. Yet, she knew she had to release him, and she didn't want him to have to say it. With a heavy sigh

Kenna pulled away, looked into his smooth suntanned face, and fought to mirror it.

She wanted him to remember her fondly, not like those lace-wrapped mice that lived among the castle nobility. She glanced at his men and saw that they had moved into an organized formation, with a string of heavily built war horses tethered at the end of the line.

"Why don't you have a warhorse?" she asked, relieved to hear her voice was steady. Caleb smiled at her change of topic.

"I don't need one."

"Every knight needs a warhorse."

"I'm not every knight, my line of work is a little different. A horse like Zane is my best fit, it's why the order breeds them so." His voice was gentle, low and soft for her ears alone;

Kenna sighed with the realization that he spoke in such a way to keep her calm. He kissed her a final time, his lips as desperate as her own.

"It's time for me to go." His lips brushed hers, then her brow, his hands cupped her face for a final moment before he stepped back, then with a smile that didn't reach his eyes, he swung up into the saddle.

"Be safe," she whispered the words past a too-tight throat.

It was three weeks later when Kenna received her first letter from Caleb. He had ridden far north to a small town by the name of Summer Set, only a few scant miles from the Vontrakalian border; she was lucky to receive word from him at all, the missive itself was strained and creased, its corners worn thin. Kenna laid on her bed with Leara while she rifled through the pages for the second time with a sigh, no matter how many times she read the message she found she desired more; more pages, more words, more of him.

She folded the pages with care then slid them into her nightstand drawer.

"I really should drag myself to the stables." Leara's velvet ears twitched in response. "Here we go." Kenna dragged herself from her down-filled bed, then pulled on stockings and soft leather boots, smoothed her fawn breeches and left the room through her garden door, Leara still sprawled across the emerald coverlet. She clattered down the steel stairs then landed in the rose garden with a soft thump.

Kenna searched the tree line, her fingers tangled in strands of hair that swirled around her face. The day was lively, a crisp autumn breeze blew through the gilded trees, her boots crunched pleasantly across the gravel path while she reached the small gate at the edge of the garden.

Her fingers released the latch and she was nearly knocked to her knees by a pain that blazed in her left temple. Kenna gasped for air, her arms wrapped around her head in a feeble attempt to protect herself from the unseen onslaught. Sweat beaded her brow as she braced against the gate, knuckles white, and scanned the fields only to find she was alone.

Sweat stung her eyes and her head and neck were seared with a pain that shuddered through her. She nearly lost her grip on the wrought iron while she turned to survey the castle windows and found them vacant of figures.

Desperation began to take hold as the pain increased; Kenna casted out with her magic, her pain and fear soaked through her bonds while she succumbed to the agony within her skull. Blood trickled from her nose and filled her mouth with bitter fluid, Kenna swayed, her vision blurred as she stumbled to her knees. Somewhere in the distance wolves howled, but their voices began to fade, smothered by the pulse in her ears.

Gravel bit into the tender flesh of her palms and knees when she sank toward the ground, darkness overtook her, and she collapsed. The small pebbles of gravel dimpled her cheek, dust coated her tongue with a dry film as she panted against the stones.

Her vision flickered in and out and she could see the edge of blood creep into her line of sight, could taste it purge the dust from her mouth. Her shattered mind latched on to odd things, a stone, the gloss of crimson fluid, a beautiful vixen that watched her from within the shadows of hydrangeas.

Kenna shut her eyes and could still see the creature, and somehow that enraged her; something about the fox felt familiar, yet her battered mind could not grasp it. Darkness curled around the corners of her vision, eager to take her back; Kenna welcomed it with relief and felt the pain slacken. A small breath escaped her in such a weak plume that dust no longer settled upon her, such peace she would find, and in answer the pain calmed further.

Her tranquility was disturbed by some noise that would not stop and steadily grew louder; eyes still shut Kenna's brow furrowed, for with the sound came the pain, it seared her insides and she opened her eyes to curse the cause of the sound. Isabella ran towards her and a distant part of her mind registered the sound of shattered glass. The assault on Kenna redoubled.

Kenna gritted blood-stained teeth and struggled to

her elbows; Isabella ran down the spiral stairs, Leara before her in a blur of ivory marred with red. Kenna was enveloped by green fire, a dome of translucent jade that was a manifestation of Isabella's power spell, and was nearly brought down once more by the weight that lifted from her form in the absence of pain.

Isabella ran towards her, palm aglow with light and stretched before her like a beacon. Kenna struggled to her knees and looked at the flowers in search of the fox, but found she was gone.

She turned in time to register Leara, but not fast enough to brace herself when the wolf crashed into her; the wolf knocked her back, her tongue and teeth gentle as she licked and nipped every exposed inch of Kenna's neck and face, she whined all the while, her tail tucked tight. Kenna pulled back hands streaked in blood that was not her own and fear flooded her dulled senses, Leara's form was covered in a multitude of shallow gashes.
"Oh Leara, look at you. It's all my fault." The wolf ignored her and proceeded to lick the blood from her face.

Kenna looked for Isabella and found she was surrounded by a menagerie of animals from across the castle grounds. *I've done it now,* she thought while she looked at the beasts around her.

Isabella struggled to get past two draft horses, then pulled Kenna to her feet. She leaned against the werecat and smiled feebly.
"Thanks for the help." She glanced back at her chambers, gauze curtains fluttered in a tattered display of white encased by jagged edges of glass that glittered in the morning sunshine. "I don't know how to pay for that."
"Don't worry, I'll handle it. Now you have to come with me to my chambers. First, shoo away your friends." Isabella said, her lips twitched as her weary eyes twinkled with mirth.

Kenna waved to the animals,
"I'm fine, thank you for coming dear ones, but Isabella took care of it." While she spoke she washed the animals in a wave of magic to give weight to her words, shoulders slumped beneath the weight of relief when they returned to their homes.
"I'm sure there will be some interesting talk going around."
"I can't believe my magic got away from me like that." Kenna's mind flashed to the dark waters and she shivered; Isabella squeezed her hand.
"Your magic is growing within you, flexing as it changes. In times of stress it can escape one's hold. I'll teach you how to control it." The pair mounted the stair trailed by wolves.

On their way to Isabella's chamber the werecat passed to converse with a servant, Kenna couldn't hear their conversation, but she assumed it was about her window. She walked up the stairs, pushed through the heavy oak door of Isabella's chamber then dropped herself unceremoniously on the couch, the pack streamed into the room behind her and settled on the thick, ornate rugs. Kenna jumped at the soft click of the latch when Isabella entered the room.
"I'm glad to see you getting some rest," she murmured while she walked to her shelf laden with herbs, powders, and tonics; she selected a small canister and sprinkled its contents into a porcelain pitcher full of cold water.

She murmured softly and the water began to steam, the room filled with a floral scent under laid with sage and peppermint. Pitcher in one hand and two cups in the other she strode to the couches and doled out the restorative liquid.

Kenna sipped her tea, her thoughts hazy and unfocused. Things between Kenna and Isabella had been strained since Caleb left; Isabella seemed unsure, she often gave Kenna intent looks or made odd comments about her power. Studies had gone on as usual which allowed Kenna to ignore the constant pull of loneliness not only for her sweetheart but for her second mother Jan; the pack was still close to her but her presence in the human world strained her, with the absence of those that were most familiar, she longed for the solitude of her home forest.

"About that mage craft out there." Isabella said abruptly. "I don't know of anyone with that kind of power nearby, I would have felt it. The only thing I could think of is they used a charm to enhance their abilities. Whoever it was sees you as a very real threat." Isabella's words sent a chill through Kenna; the mage had meant to kill her, and nearly had done the job. "I think you had best take the day off."

    She stood with boneless grace, patted Kenna's shoulder then took her cup. Kenna wordlessly stood, then left the chamber without a backward glance.

    She walked through the halls in a daze, one foot slid into place after the other. A member of the pack pressed their cool nose into her clammy palm which momentarily startled her into alertness, alas the clarity was brief and she quickly succumbed to the dull haze of her mind. Her pack herded her down the corridors, a gentle presence on either side until she stood before her chambers.

    Kenna fumbled for the key then stumbled through the threshold. Throv and Baylor pressed close on either side, their muscles bunched against her fatigue. Her toes scuffed the thick rugs, fingers fumbled with latches then clothes; exasperated she collapsed fully dressed onto her bed and drifted into the void.

A steady throb in her temples woke her; she rolled over with a moan, her eyes slanted against the pale moonlight that filtered through the drapes. Sleep gradually released its hold and her mind cleared, the throb became louder, a steady knock upon her parlor door. With a growled curse Kenna slipped from the bed and wove around the pack, her room looked as though it was full of fireflies, amber and gold flecked the shadows.
Kenna passed a mirror and grimaced; her collar was encrusted with blood stains gone black with age, a bleak reminder of her mortality.

    She opened the door with clumsy fingers, a frown creased her face at the volume of voices on the other side of the oak panel and was disappointed to see a boisterous Aden fill the frame. She plastered a smile on her face, swung the door open, and stepped back. Aden and then Randy entered her suite. Aden nearly tripped and fell over the heavy edge of her rug while he made his way to a sofa. "Blast it all Kenna!" he exclaimed while he flailed to catch his balance. "Would it kill you to light a candle in here?" The moonlight hid the blush that crept over his stubbled cheeks.

"Sorry lads, I was sleeping," she answered, then lit a branch of candles.

"Sleeping? What made you go to bed so early?"
"Had a bit of an accident down by the garden."

Kenna sat beside Baylor, the great wolf rested his sable head in her lap. Both men sat down gracelessly, Kenna was certain they were drunk.
"What happened?" Randy asked, his aurelian eyes filled with concern. He began to lean forward then tilted awkwardly while he reached for her hand from across the small table. Aden punched his shoulder.
"I'm sure it was nothing a night on the town couldn't fix, am I right?" Aden's crooked nose wrinkled slightly as he smiled with far too many teeth.
"Sorry, I don't know if I'm up for that."

The large brunette groaned as though someone had run him through.
"Oh come on Kenna, all you do is study and train and ride and hole up in this dungeon of yours! What do you do with your time?"
"You just explained exactly what I do with my time," she drawled in return. He snorted then he tossed a pillow at her, she was too exhausted to dodge it.
"You know what I mean! You never have any fun anymore."

Kenna didn't look up, instead she traced the delicate embroidered lines of the pillow that now rested in her lap.
"Is it because you miss him?" Randy's voice was as soft as candlelight.
"That's a small part of it, yes."
"And the other?"
"I don't really know, I just don't feel right amongst all the court folk I suppose." Her excuse sounded pathetic even to herself, but her friends were kind enough to let it stand.
Aden stood and dragged the smaller knight up beside him.
"I don't know much about feelings, not like you delicate lot." His eyes glittered wickedly as he needled her. "But a

night at the Silver Sparrow raises my spirits like nothing else." Now it was Randy's turn to groan, Kenna laughed despite herself, Aden's joy was always infectious.
"That bad huh?"
"That good!" Aden exclaimed when Randy opened his mouth to protest. "Come on," he pressed further, "Just one night on the town, then we will leave you to your own bland devices."

Kenna rolled her eyes but felt her smile broaden.
"All right, let me just change first."
Aden whooped in victory while Randy mumbled a final protest.
"Another one lost to this brute."
"Lost to glory you mean?"
"What you do is far from glorious sir." Randy responded with airy detachment.
"Now listen here, there is nothing wrong with..."
Aden's words were silenced by the thick oak of Kenna's chamber door. She peeled off clothes stiff with sweat and blood and tossed them into a dark corner, then she grabbed a cloth, dipped it into the basin and scrubbed herself beneath her arms, face, and neck. Moderately cleaner she pulled on a fresh tunic and
breeches.

Kenna glanced out the window and watched as a breeze shook leaves from the nearby trees and decided to grab a coat from her oversized wardrobe. She stepped back into the parlor to be greeted by the raised voices of Aden and Randy while they bickered.

With their attention so focused on one another they did not see her grab an apple from the bowl on the table, nor did they brace when she hurled it at them.
"Well, are we going or what?" All eyes turned to her, both man and beast while she strode towards the door. Aden retrieved the apple and took a ravenous bite.

"A Lady with drive, that's my kind of woman," he declared with a mischievous grin.

Kenna and Randy rolled their eyes.

"I'm no lady."

"Even better!" Aden hugged her shoulders roughly. Kenna reached the glass door and hesitated as a memory of the morning flashed through her mind, her hand hovered above the silver lever. She shook the ice from her veins, snatched the door from its frame then strode into the night.

The trio quickly made it to the stables where their horses stood tacked and tethered, even Finn. Kenna glared at Aden who only shrugged away her annoyance.

"You had Finn ready?"

"I knew you would say yes."

"Ass."

"Indeed," Randy chimed in. Aden ignored them and sauntered towards his gelding, a well-muscled bay with black socks.

Once mounted they made their way to town at a brisk trot, a cool breeze caressed the companions while they traveled the starlit road that led to the Silver Sparrow. Kenna rode behind her friends with some difficulty; normally well-behaved Finn struggled to stay at the back of a group and attempted to steal the bit from her more than once. She adjusted her reins and deepened her seat, Finn responded and slowed while Kenna's thoughts wandered north.

Caleb's letter had been kind and heart felt, yet light on the details of his mission near the border; Kenna flicked Finn's mane from side to side with impatient fingers while she ran through the possible reasons he kept the secret from her. She didn't feel that Caleb was a dishonest man, but it left her on edge to know he purposely left her in the dark. A twig snapped in the shadows to her right which pulled her from her thoughts with a jolt; warmth spread across her body as she changed her eyes and ears to those of a nocturnal predator.

The men went on ahead of her, their postures loose and relaxed while they rode. With a subtle cue she slowed Finn's pace till his hooves were a mere whisper on the soil, his ears tilted forward as he sensed the tension in her form. Leaves rustled, adrenaline made the nape of her neck prickle; she glanced up the road and saw that Aden and Randy had gained substantial ground on her. Those two must really be drunk if they don't notice I'm not there.

Kenna snarled, her fangs long and pale, then leaned forward in the saddle and squeezed her mount into a loose canter. Shame burned her throat and face, but she was in no condition for a fight, sometimes even a wolf must run.

Kenna clattered into the Silver Sparrow's small courtyard, clean despite the crowd it attracted; she slid from the saddle then handed the reins to a thin boy with heavily worn clothes. Kenna dug a silver coin from her purse, it was more than the lad made in a month, but she still didn't quite see the value in the small object. His brown eyes widened as he licked his lips nervously.
"My Lady, that is too much."
"I am very particular about him, make sure you hang his tack up carefully, and you put the saddle bags in the stall with him." She turned to go then paused, "If you could give Finn some grain I'm sure he would be grateful."

Kenna sighed as she turned toward the pub when the plain wood door swung open and bathed her in golden light, softened with smoke and laughter. A small part of her cowered, she longed for the cool darkness of the shadows, but she could only run so much in one night. Kenna fastened down on her control and stalked toward the Silver Sparrow with a determined grit.

The tavern door swung shut when she neared it, closed her off from the noise and light; she grasped the latch and shoved her way into the establishment, then blinked against the smoke and torch light, the roar of laughter, song, and the occasional shouts that filled the room. With a quick look around the tavern's common room she found her companions. *Some friends—they haven't even looked back since they dragged me out of bed.* Kenna strode towards them, hackles raised as she struggled to ignore the lewd stares and foul words drunk men directed her way.

On the verge of anger she turned toward the strangers and caught sight of a man with black hair; for a moment her heart quickened but it took only one inhale through altered senses to realize he was not Caleb. In that instant Kenna's anger evaporated and left her deflated and alone.

She slid into the space beside Randy with a sense of dejection, amplified by the dark liquid in the goblet that awaited her. She watched the room and listened to the constant rumble of voices that was occasionally punctured by a belligerent shout, or a bray of laughter. She took a swig of her drink then glanced at her cup, lips pressed tight against the bitterness that cloyed to her tongue; with determination she finished her cup and was rewarded with another.

Five cups in Kenna sat silently at the table, the sounds around her indistinguishable; Randy and Aden were deep in conversation with a guard from the lower districts, and she squinted at him with blurred eyes. With a groan Kenna pushed her cup away and rested her brow in her hand. A thin dew of sweat began to form between her palm and face. Bored of her human company she searched through her bond for the pack, their response was swift and the swath of woods they showed her was familiar and close.

Glee bubbled up inside of her with such force she hiccupped then stood from the table. All she craved was the cool grass between her toes and the whisper of a breeze between the boughs of ancient pines; home, that's what she truly needed, and with the realization came a pang of guilt. Kenna pushed the feeling away and stepped over the stool with a renewed sense of energy accompanied by a dizzying swirl of her senses.

She giggled at the sensation, her hip against the table. Aden turned to her and smiled.
"At last! A little joy out of you!"
"Are you leaving?" Randy asked.
"You can't go now, you just began to have a good time." Aden complained with mournful eyes.

Randy glared at him over his shoulder then turned back to Kenna with hazy golden eyes. Kenna clasped his hand with a smile,
"I will see you boys later." A final squeeze then she strode to the tavern's front door and brushed her mind against Finn's.

The hair on her arms stood up and thickened, it sent a shiver through her as the tail within her began to wag; Kenna quickened her pace then grabbed the door's latch with clawed fingers that gouged the well-worn wood. She choked down a giggle that was more of a growl and burst into the night.

Her breath billowed in pale plumes before her as the first flakes of snow began to fall, Kenna relished the cool kisses against her face; delighted in the tension that rippled through her when a wolf made of copper fire clawed its way towards release. Kenna's joints popped in expectation of the change, her gait wobbled and altered while she walked to the stable. Clawed fingers curled around the doorframe and over bright eyes rested on Finn, she made a dash for his stall and winced when her claws bit into the supple leather of his saddle when she lifted it from the rack.

The stallion stood patiently while she slung the blanket, the saddle over his back, with elongated fingers she stroked his red coat. Kenna bit the inside of her cheek in an attempt to manage her magic; she was more wolf than human in that moment, a Lycan of sorts; a snarl of frustration escaped her and she pulled the saddle from Finn's back, slung his bridle over the horn then hefted it onto her shoulder. She ran from the stables with the stallion on her heels and scrambled on misshapen legs towards the tree line.

The throaty baritone howl of her alpha shivered through the night, her excitement at the sound undid her and released a flood of magic that toppled her to the ground, a tangle of clothes, claws, fur, and tail.

A cinnamon-coated she-wolf wriggled out of the tack and clothing, her tail wagged and she yipped at Finn then dashed into the forest's undergrowth. They pounded through the leaf litter that released a pungent musk of earth, grass, moss, and leaf rot; a complex smell that filled her nostrils and filled her to the brim until she raised icy blue eyes skyward and howled. Within moments her pack's voices mingled with her own and a surge of speed overtook her.

She wove through the undergrowth like a specter and soon heard the soft rustle of leaves that held the promise of wolves. Within three heart beats she saw her father break through the tree line, her mother right beside him; the small glen filled with wolves that howled and yipped with pleasure while they rubbed against one another in a swirl of coarse fur. The pack joined their Luna Wolf in her run of freedom, and the hunger of the hunt.

Kenna opened her eyes with caution and soon regretted the deed; pain dragged through her mind with hooked fingers and her stomach lurched dangerously. Eyes closed, she breathed slowly through her nose while she struggled to ignore the sharp pain in her back, despite her best efforts she could put aside the ache no longer and with a groan rolled over and dislodged the rock. Kenna's stomach rolled with her which made her mouth water in anticipation of a good retching.

  She opened her eyes just a sliver then crawled toward the shade and took in her surroundings. *Oh Divya have mercy!* Kenna's eyes watered at the violent pulse that pounded in her temples.

  She inhaled deeply then grimaced at her odor; sweat and dried blood coated her body along with an obscene amount of mud, she gently placed her hands on her head and was further dismayed to find leaves mingled with her snarled hair. *What happened last night?* She wondered in horror as she attempted to remember but it was all a drunken blur. Slowly she rose to her feet, hand braced against a tree and caught sight of Finn by a small stream.

  She turned toward him quickly and nearly fell over as the world spun on its side, her stomach had had enough. Kenna braced against a tree and vomited up the remains of

two rabbits, wine, and something she could not quite place; a fact that disturbed her deeply. She pinched her nose then kicked dirt over the mess before she stumbled to the stream. Finn nickered at her softly, his large eyes filled with amusement at her expense.
"I don't want to hear it," she mumbled as she pushed past the stallion, then dropped to her knees to rinse her mouth.

Refreshed, she took a hesitant sip, the cold water settled in her stomach like a kick to the gut that threatened to give her mouth a second rinse. Kenna swallowed hard then slipped into the river, she was relieved to feel the fog lift from her mind in favor of the frigid sting of icy waters that braced her, then dulled the ache in her head. Kenna slogged out of the water to Finn and groaned, the ground was still dusted in patches with snow, it clung to her toes then melted into droplets.

She drew on her magic and altered her skin enough to tighten and retain heat, it kicked her body temperature up so that she would not freeze. Her palm rested over her heart that now beat faster to accommodate the change.

Warm and steady on her feet she surveyed the small clearing and noticed her tack was long gone, left behind when the change had overtaken her. Kenna accepted the loss with little regret, a small smile tucked the corners of her mouth, then swung onto Finn's warm back; her grin quickly faded while she wriggled with discomfort to adjust her seat to no avail, reconciled to her situation she nudged him into a brisk walk, the pack asleep in the frosted grass.

The ride to the capital was long and unpleasant, and the closer she got the more concerned about her nudity she became. Kenna urged Finn into a faster gait and hoped there would be no one in the stable yard to see her; the day was young yet, she may have a chance. Though her head split with each leap Finn took over the six pasture fences, it brought her that much closer to the sanctuary of her chambers. She leaned close to his neck, her heart pounded at the sight of the small garden beneath her rooms, then beat all the harder when a group of stable hands ambled to their work.

"Faster Finn!" she cried, then she hid her face in his mane, her cheeks stung with each sharp swat of his stiff hair.

The stallion's gate elongated still, devoured the ground at a breathless pace, he slowed slightly to make his final leap before they landed on a path of soft soil.

They cantered around the bend just as the stable hands came into view, then clattered through the gravel paths of the garden. A spray of small stones heralded their arrival and Kenna slid from Finn's back with a pang of guilt; his coat was dark with sweat, his nostrils distended with heavy breaths. Her brow furrowed while she rushed to his and pressed her brow to hers, then gave him a kiss before she retreated to her chambers.

Hardly two steps into her rooms she was bombarded by a frantic knock on her parlor door, Sophie's voice called from the hall.

"Kenna, what are you doing in there?! We have to be in the courtyard immediately!"

Divya save me. Kenna walked to the door with leaden feet that still felt tender from her nocturnal activities, she opened the door gingerly.

"Kenna! What happened to you?" Sophie grabbed her, nails a sharp pressure that dimpled Kenna's shoulders.

"I'm fine."

"You don't look fine."

"I just need to wash off." Kenna gestured lazily at the flakes of crimson that clung to her.

"You're welcome to wait out here if you like."

"We don't have that kind of time, you need to get dressed now." Sophie took in the other woman's figure in quick

glances, her cheeks touched with a rosy hue.
"Most ladies would be more modest." Kenna spoke softly, her shoulders tight.
"So it would seem."

Sophie looked at Kenna with guarded eyes then took her hand and walked to Kenna's bed chamber. Past the threshold Sophie let her go and walked to a small table with a wash basin and a pile of washcloths. Kenna stayed by the door, her eyes locked on her bed. Water splashed against the porcelain while Sophie swirled the cloth in cool water before she returned to Kenna, hands glossy, knuckles white.
"Wash up." She extended the rag, it dripped lazily onto the thick rug. "But if you're too slow I'll give you a hand."

Kenna's brows rose, unsure if she had been challenged or tempted; wordlessly she took the cloth and brought it to her skin in a soft, wet caress.
"So why are you here?"
"The Prince is coming."
"What Prince?" Kenna tossed the cloth aside in favor of clothing.
"From Vontrakal, he is here to try for Ena."
"Ena is already betrothed to Lord Barkus." The lie was effortless, and a part of Kenna cringed from that realization.
"Yes, but nothing is set in stone and Prince trumps Viscount." Sophie tossed a tunic at the woman.
"Yes, but why do we have to be there?"
"It is a sign of respect."
"But I don't respect him."

Sophie stared at her in exasperation.
"Where did my cousin find you, under a rock?"
"Basically." A smile passed between them before Sophie grabbed a brush.
"This is hopeless." she sighed then piled Kenna's hair in a bun and wrapped it with a ribbon. "We must leave!"
Kenna yanked on the rest of her outfit.

"We'll make it Sophie."

The women ran recklessly as they made their way to the fore of the castle, then slid to a stop when they nearly crashed through a narrow side door. Yelps and laughter echoed through the hall accompanied by matronly looks of disapproval from older court ladies, Kenna smothered a laugh that made her fragile stomach quiver. *Never drinking with Aden again.*

She followed Sophie into a small alcove that led into the courtyard. A crowd thronged the path of crushed pink gravel that looped before the castle, the tall fountain at its center nearly obscured beneath the individuals that used it like a stage. The women nudged their way through those gathered, Sophie's cold stare a firm deterrent for rebuttal; they settled themselves in time to witness the Prince of Vontrakal when he dismounted his bay charger and strode towards the King and Queen.

Alaric's eyes were cool while he watched the northerner approach, his hand casually rested on his sword, his arm extended as a brace for his Queen's delicate hand. The court in attendance was hushed, voices and expressions weary as they murmured; in anticipation or distaste, Kenna could not tell. She craned her neck to get a better look at the man; he had a coldly handsome face. Dark blonde hair fell back from a high brow that was accented by even darker eyes, eyes that twinkled with thinly veiled disdain for those around him.

He spoke to them in his native tongue, his lips tilted with condescension when they did not respond to his guttural language. Kenna touched her magic lightly to alter her senses but found it muddled from wine and exhausted from the previous night's excursions. With a curse she stepped onto a bench for a better view of his actions if not his words.

"What are you doing?" Sophie hissed. Kenna ignored her while she watched Princess Ena enter the courtyard, her stride graceful, chin held high as she walked to her parents' side.

The Vontrakalian prince took Ena's hand, his scarred fingers closed around it with a dominance that made Kenna's spine stiffen. She scanned the crowd for signs of unrest and saw furtive whispers, furrowed brows; the prince was far from welcome, his very presence was a reminder of the war that loomed heavy over Alearian heads, of the deaths of those already lost to thoughtlessly brutal border skirmishes.

Kenna ignored it all, instead her gaze rested on the rigid figure of Lady Signe. The northern woman seemed unhinged at the sight of her prince, as though she felt her gaze, Signe looked up and caught Kenna's stare. Their eyes met for one tense moment before she disappeared in the crowd. Kenna inhaled deeply, her discomfort forgotten; Signe smelled like prey.

Chapter Nine:
The Burden Of The Blade

A husk of humanity stood weakly, chained to a stone wall. His body sagged, strained against the chains that bit deeply into his wrists. He was naked, his skin streaked with red and dripped with sweat that cut paths of semi-clean skin from the grime that coated him. His eyes were covered, which left him alone in the darkness though the heat of the flames licked him passionately through the shadows. Mercifully, the heat subsided and the blindfold slid away; the prisoner felt a glimmer of hope, the meager light brought tears to his eyes while he tried to focus on the dark figure before him. As quick as his hope came, it abandoned him.

The man before the prisoner stood before the fire, his stance predatory, ready to spring while he watched his captive. His expression was cast in shadow, yet the sword slung across his back gleamed with red and gold light. The prisoner glanced away frantically, eyes wide and bloodshot in the gloom, then shuddered at a sight more gruesome. A heavily built man with a black shroud stepped forward, a double-headed ax swung in lazy arches in his callused grip.

With a speed made all the more deadly by the darkness that surrounded them he swung his weapon towards the prisoner's head; it all ended with a mighty chop. The captive screamed only to find metal bit into wood, not flesh, with such force it reverberated down his spine.

Without a word the shadow man left the room in a flash of light that blinded the chained man, then left him with his would-be executioner. He stooped then, formless face still trained on the pathetic sweat and filth-soaked inmate, and hefted a large bucket of water and melted snow.

The captive tensed in expectation of pain against his taut skin; instead the water was flung against the flame, and the coals hissed in anguish while they drowned; another flash of light then the door slammed shut. Then there was nothing, only the darkness that swallowed him whole.

Caleb leaned against the wall of the corridor, clean and cool against his back, and drew an uneven breath. He pushed sweat-soaked hair back from his brow with a grimace; he could hardly stand the smell of that man's filth a moment longer. *I can't do this, no one deserves this.* Yet he knew he didn't have a choice. The King had given his orders and he could not refuse. Caleb strode down the hall, past the small clusters of soldiers, and was soon met by Von. The two men matched stride, Von bowed his head but not before Caleb saw the tension that wreathed his pale-green eyes.
"There are two bands north of the border ready to move.

The men await your orders."

"We cannot move until I get what I need." Caleb answered tightly; the silence that followed was tangible, laden with worries, anger, resentment.

The cousins had always been close but Caleb's methods in the chamber had made them share more than one sharply worded conversation. Von knew where Caleb had just come from, he could smell the filth and fear that steeped the fine winter cotton just as easily as Caleb could see the shame in Von's rigid form.

They rounded a corner and Caleb stopped at his chamber door. *Sanctuary at last.*

"That will be all for tonight."

"Understood." A curt nod, then Von left him to his darkness.

Caleb stepped into the room and grimaced, on his desk was a fresh pile of documents that waited for his approval, many of which pertained to the activities of their northern neighbors. He ambled towards the desk with reluctance then thumbed through the parchments, a frown marred his features.

Anyone who thought war was simple was a fool; there was an unnatural amount of paperwork and plans that went with it, a war was not a bar brawl as it were, and Caleb was knee deep in the plots of Alearian's next struggle.

He dropped the forms without looking where they landed and walked to his bed then began to disrobe. Caleb sat, elbows rested on his knees, head bowed; he breathed deeply through his palms, one ragged breath after another while his mind grimly accepted his duty in the name of the Crown.

Caleb set the forms on the table with a sigh through his nose then rubbed tired eyes that still blurred with words. His thumb brushed the coarse stubble along his jaw and chin while he watched the wall with sightless eyes; the sun had risen only an hour before, its rosy hue reminded his body of aches and fatigue, that he should be sprawled out naked beneath his sheets. Caleb glanced at his bed in disinterest; he had no wish to rest while the sun rose higher and bathed his room in pale gold and amber. How many times had he caressed copper strands in that sweet light? Had trailed his fingers across cream and silk skin that glowed beneath his touch.

He reluctantly roused himself from his stupor then grasped the long tasseled rope near his desk; two brisk tugs, then he stood. The light scuff of footsteps announced his page before a timid knock echoed through the bare chamber.

"Enter," Caleb called as he shook the weakness from his limbs and gathered the appropriate forms. While he rustled amongst the documents and tossed this one or that to the side with a grunt, Raoul entered the room.

"Have you eaten my Lord?" Caleb did not turn, a deep chuckle filled the room, his laughter surprised him and then he let it go with a sigh; how he missed her laughter.

"No Raoul, I haven't the time."

"Would you like me to fetch you something?" A slight whistle escaped him while he enunciated the 't h'.

"No," Caleb pinched the bridge of his nose, he grounded himself in the tension he found there. "Put your arms out kid."

Within moments the freckled brunette was laden down with reports, maps, and strategy details. Nose wrinkled in protest he asked,

"Is this all my Lord?"

Caleb arched a brow while he debated if he would give the boy something to truly complain about, then thought better of it. Instead he grabbed a mug from his desk and drained the stale cider with regret. "Dismissed." Raoul ducked his head in acknowledgement then hurried out of the room.

He stepped into his narrow bathroom and quickly cleaned his mouth then ran water through his hair. Drops sprayed the small mirror when he flipped his hair back from his face, his skin tightened when water languidly trailed its way down his back. Pale square features, peppered jaw, vacant eyes; he hardly knew himself. *When your hands are not your own.* The grim words drifted in the dark recesses of his mind. Caleb quickly finished his morning routine and headed out the door, his steps clipped, rapid while he made his way to the center of the fortress.

His boots on the hard floor echoed the tempo of his troubled heart; would he torment that man today? *Did the poor wretch even deserve it?* There was nothing else he could do, his duty outweighed his personal desires, and with bitter reservation he laid his conscience to rest in a bed of ashes. Caleb stood before the narrow door that served as the prisoner's cell, an old room that was forgotten in the center of the small castle; its prison cells below had collapsed decades ago and had never been replaced, Caleb was thankful for the heavy oak door that smothered the screams with ease, the screams he caused.

The guard at the door watched Caleb with a mild expression, his squared-off features bland even when he was engaged. Donald casually grasped the hilt of his sword, with a subtle nod he stepped aside to allow Caleb access.

Caleb stepped into the chamber and was overwhelmed by the odor of prolonged captivity. The northerner was slumped against the wall, chains wrapped around his wrists in a merciless embrace, for a long moment Caleb watched the captive with mild indifference while he considered his method of approach. He stepped closer and his boots rang out coldly against the stone before he grasped the unconscious man's hair.

Strands of filth withered against his palm then

bloodshot eyes met his own, glazed and unfocused, it was clear the northerner did not recognize his assailant. The moment of confusion was brief before fear crept into his eyes; his neck tensed then he feebly tried to pull away from the dark figure's grip to no avail.

With a smile that never reached his eyes, Caleb released him. The man scrambled away as a spider, slender limbs and bulbous joints that flailed in his panic. "Now that I have your attention, I thought we could talk." His voice a low purr. The prisoner watched him with large glassy eyes, pupils wide, nostrils flared. Caleb could nearly see his pulse pound against the thin skin of his throat. "Come now, let's be civil." Again the captive did not speak, only bared his teeth in protest, more than one was missing. *Was that us or Hrothgar?* Caleb wondered, his method already altered with his chain of thought.

Caleb crouched in the filth, his boots squelched in gods knew what but he refused to let his revulsion show. "I know things have been hard for you. Not just here but in the North," No answer. "But it doesn't have to be that way any longer. I just need your help with something. It's a trifle really." He came closer. The captive began to pant, his eyes darted wildly like that of a savage animal; Caleb's resolve quivered.

He stood and gave the man his space, nearly to the door he paused. "You could go home, you know? If that's not what you want, I can make sure you are free, truly free. Anywhere you wanted to go I could get you there."

The prisoner groaned, his chains rattled in rhythm with his fractured spirit. Caleb looked over his shoulder, "I could do this for you, if you would simply do this favor for me. Or," he grabbed the cell door. "You can stay here and rot."

Darkness swallowed them both.

Caleb wasn't alone long, he could never just be alone. A messenger walked toward him, his lean frame bobbed with blasted purpose, and Caleb's back tensed in anticipation of more bullshit. Jaw clenched, he slowed his pace and straightened his path, they very nearly collided in fact. Sweat dripped down tawny skin, a faint musk of perspiration lingered around him while he gathered his thoughts.

"Excuse me sir, I've a missive for you," he explained while he pulled a creased vellum from his inner coat. Caleb nodded his assent then he took yet another form. A heavy seal with a sapphire ribbon dangled eloquently from the missive, the only fool who seemed enamored with such elaborate messages was the governor; the attendance of so many Lords in his domain, livery, horsemen, it had gotten to his head.

Caleb slipped his thumb through the vellum's seams, thick wax chipped then released, and he scanned the letter swiftly. Aware of the man beside him that breathed heavily while he resisted the urge to mop his brow, Caleb suppressed a grin that was a mixture of amusement and sympathy.

His gaze returned to the parchment in hand and his good mood evaporated, they had moved up the war

meeting. He leveled a look at the messenger that stilled the man's butterfly fingers, then allowed his lips to curve in a slow and beguiling smile. A part of him reveled in the confusion he saw flash across the younger man's face.
"Now when did this come into your hands?" He folded the form while he kept his gaze locked on his counterpart. The messenger straightened, the nob in his throat bobbed while he swallowed.
"I got it thirty minutes past, sir."
"Interesting." Caleb's shoulders squared with resolve then strode past the messenger.

Grimly the knight strode down the corridor, his breath a metronome that focused his thoughts. Many moved out of his way, mumbles of respect filled his ears while whispers of his methods hissed at him in derision; his knuckles showed white against the hilt of his sword. *I already know what they want from me...* yet that knowledge did not make the answer any simpler.

Snow slid silently against the narrow windows of the fort and bathed it in splashes of pale light; shadow to light, light to shadow. How familiar, that ever-present dance with darkness. With one forever at your fingertips it was easy to make the wrong choice; Caleb felt that balance, that comic display of energy, it never took more than a nudge to tip the scales.

Caleb paused before a set of double doors, the muted tones of raised voices could be heard through the dark mahogany; palms flat he leaned his weight into the felled giants before him until they gave way with a low groan. At his entrance those gathered fell silence, the rustle of cloth filled the void along with the crackle of fire.

His hands still gripped the seams of the door which he swung shut behind him as he strode into the cavernous chamber.
"I hear you have all been waiting on me, I do apologize for

the delay. It seems there was a miscommunication with a messenger." His gaze slid to the governor before his attention returned to the men that bracketed the oblong table; yet he did not miss the widened eyes, or how the man licked thin lips. *Little rat.* Caleb's own mouth twitched while he fought dark humor.

There were four other men in the room aside from Caleb and Clyde—the Governor of Summer Set—two of whom wore the Alearian Military Crest, the others were lords local to the town that had joined the fray in an attempt to stave off invasion of their own lands. The point was moot to Caleb; Pernak laid north but against the black waters of the coast. He could almost hear the ever-present sigh of the ocean against his skin, he blinked back the memories then smiled with false gaiety.

"Shall we cut to the point? I know what you all want from me, and as much as I understand your need for resolution, my answer is no." The finality in his tone left no question.

Sneers or clamped lips met his words while those assembled struggled with his declaration; one in particular with dull blond hair and the shadow of a beard eyed Caleb with hostility.

"You're not the only one with rank and experience here son," his tone carried scorn. "So what makes you think you can make all the decisions? If you're afraid to take the chance I'd be happy to take point."

"As gracious as that offer is, it is highly unnecessary, Captain. I have it well in hand."

"By means of that little rat of yours?" Clyde muttered; the Lord beside him smirked.

With practiced charm Caleb turned his attention to the two louts.

"That 'rat' of which you speak could have useful information. If we actually suspect that Maeghnor or any of his personal guards are near we need to be more than careful,"

"Ha! Scared like I thought. Why not let a real soldier handle this?" interrupted the Captain. His companion nudged him knowingly, broad white teeth flashed against olive skin.

"As I was saying. Maeghnor and his men are nothing to trifle with. Their reputation of being enhanced by the mage is not false, so rushing in won't do any good." Celeb retorted. He could feel the vein in his temple jump as his pulse quickened, his temper burned away his restraint with hungry flames.

Jaw clenched, he stepped forward.

"This discussion is over, by order of the King we are not to move until I give the signal. Any move against me is a move against the Crown, insubordination will not be tolerated." Silence, bitter and resentful followed his words. Regret crept in; he had new enemies, of that he was sure, but the damage was done.

"If I have no useful information in the next forty-eight hours I will give you the order to move. We can't linger here much longer."

A weight settled over him, so thick and heavy it threatened to submerge him. His muscles flexed to fight the weakness that seeped through his limbs while he turned, but not before he saw the satisfied leer of the captain.

Caleb left the chambers, sweat slicked his skin and clung desperately to the cotton of his tunic; without thought he changed course and headed deeper into the compound, a vein pounded vigorously against his throat while he walked, and though he displayed an expression of calm he was made of fire. Another guard was on duty and this moment of change caused Caleb to pause.

Sweet air filled his lungs and cooled the fire within, his mind cleared. He could not take his rage out on that pitiful creature; yet a dark piece of him knew that while the hours slipped away the man would feel the agony of his urgency. *You have to be calm. To be in control. Be calm.*

Unbidden images of home slipped through his thoughts like waters; not Pernak, that was not where his heart was anymore, but with her. Sheer linen curtains fluttered like butterfly wings in the breeze, wolves spanned the room amongst a mingle of potted plants and colorful rugs. Tempered glass softened the summer sun as it set the sitting room ablaze with auriferous light that caressed her. *Her...* Red hair smoldered in the light where she lifted her head from a cotton pillow. The warmth that spread from her smile to aquamarine eyes was for him and him alone. *That was home, she was home.*

He could almost feel her next to him, warm and soft, forever pliant to his form. Someone cleared their throat, the guard perhaps, Caleb was pulled to the present and smiled.

"Apologies, you seem to have caught me dreaming. What is the status of the prisoner?"

"He is well enough, my Lord."

"I'm sure." Caleb drawled. "Open the door, I will be going in."

Almond eyes widened a fraction, the only sign of hesitation, before he reached for the keys at his belt and unbolted the door.

"I will stay close if you need me, Sir."

Hinges moaned and vile air passed through the opening like the sickly breath of the decayed. Caleb bolstered himself, hid away that part of himself that cried out at the injustice of his actions, and let the darkness within his weary heart unfurl; all for the good of the Crown. *The good of the Crown.* He stepped into the cell and the door slammed shut behind him which woke his captive. A hollow gaze met his own.

"Please don't," he whispered, "he will kill me if I talk."

"Who says I won't kill you if you don't." A subtle shift; Caleb walked the walls of the room. A small fire crackled and painted the walls in red, amber, and gold. Hung prom-steel hooks pounded into the mortar between stones held a multitude of tools: cuffs, knives, hammer, hooks, pliers, and prongs.

Another shift, stronger this time; he ran his fingers down the length of a curved blade and felt a thrill. His blood thrummed hot and hungry in his veins while he pulled the weapon from the wall. There it was, that last release, he relinquished himself to it with the relief of a coward, then

Caleb delved into the darkness where the light could not reach.

Chapter Ten: How The Glitter Hides The Rot

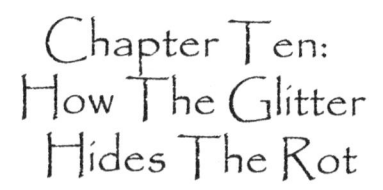

It was something about him, the way he moved, smiled; the way his voice rolled across you like waves in the sea. *Despicable*. Kenna watched the northern wolf around her princess with distaste, magic tumbled through her chest as it responded to her emotions, another lash of fire, another heartbeat missed. Kenna stifled a cough in response to the butterfly palpitations.

A firm hand on her shoulder drew her attention and Kenna turned, hackles raised as she felt the anger rush out of her. Isabella smiled,
"I know it's hard but try and control your temper. What would Caleb say if you mauled Prince Goran?"
Kenna scanned her features while heat crept over her own until she saw the twitch.
"Oh stop it. We would all enjoy it." There it was, the release of that smile, Kenna's expression mirrored hers

while Isabella took a seat beside her. "I do need to calm down though." Her hand rested against her heart, voice soft.

"What's been happening? I could feel your magic lashing out. You need to be more careful, there could be people watching you even here."

"I know, sometimes it's just hard. Before, if I was this upset I would just shift and run it out."

"That definitely can't happen here."

"I know that," she snapped then glanced at Isabella sidelong, apology in her eyes and continued. "That is part of the problem for me, I miss being able to do what I want, when I want. It's nice here, and I love those I've met, but sometimes I wonder if it's worth it."

"Would you really leave them all behind?"

"Them or him?" she countered.

"Would you?"

"No."

Kenna looked out across the room to the North, winter light gilded the pastures in amber and gold. "No, I couldn't." The pair sat quietly in the swirl of courtiers and ladies, but she was somewhere else, somewhere more like home. Safe in her mind she could truly rest beneath those shady pines, dark and rich with memories; nestled close Kenna could hear his heartbeat, feel the smooth cool skin of his silvered scar beneath her lips. Pressure on the tips of her fingers brought her back to the present.

Without hesitation Kenna found Ena and the prince near the Eastern corner of the room, alone in a mass of people there was something different; Ena was pale, with anger or fear Kenna could not tell. She leaned forward subtly.

"Are you listening?" Isabella whispered.

"I'm trying to," she hissed.

"Then *listen*." Kenna glanced over, Isabel's face was tranquil despite the message in her eyes.

Kenna reached into her magic and spun loose the thinnest of strands; it glittered in her mind's eye like a spider web, one moment it shimmered the next it was gone. She pulled it through, her body then reshaped her ears, words warped with unfamiliar depth, their complexity grated on her newly formed eardrums. Cool fingers slipped through her hair and broke her focus.
"Easy," a breathy whisper in her ear.
"What are you doing?"
"You forgot to hide their shape, slow the change."

Isabella pulled her hair close to Kenna's face to hide her ears, once concealed Kenna leaned her chin into her palm as her eyes lost focus; a picture of boredom that belied her true motives. She gazed casually around the room until she once more found the royal pair.
"Come now Ena, don't be ridiculous. We both know there is nothing that can be done."
"I don't know what you are talking about, and it's clear you don't either." Ena retorted. A rosy wash crawled its way up her neck. Goran grabbed her, her delicate wrist swallowed roughly.
"Don't be coy."
"Unhand me." No one but Kenna would have heard the tremble.
"Come now," he pulled her close, her pale chiffon skirt crumped against him. "If you accept it now it will be easier. I promise I will take care of you."

It was clear others had begun to notice their exchange, yet Goran proceeded unruffled; he adjusted his grasp upon her from one of restraint to unabashed seduction. Callused fingertips caressed the porcelain skin of her wrist, then he bowed and kissed her fingers chastely.
"Forgive my forwardness my Lady, I was not raised around

such enchanting beauty. I was swept away by it."

The sighs of fools whispered through the room when Ena succumbed to a charming blush, only Kenna knew it was anger, not flattery that colored her so. She relinquished her magic and without the fire of its touch, her temper soothed enough to look at the pair once more. Ena smiled at her fellow monarch,
"You flatter me my Lord." She curtsied then stepped away, white knuckles stark against her lilac skirts. Whispers hissed through the room when Ena departed and resentment seeped through the shifter while she watched those around her, their judgment a malicious poison in the air.

Kenna rose without a word and followed the princess into the hall. The younger woman had not gotten far, her bravado had quickly failed her without the eyes of courtiers to bolster her resolve. A few effortless strides brought them together, Kenna reached out.
"Ena, take a moment." The princess was pale, her sable lashes fluttered while she held back tears.
"It doesn't matter what I want, I have to put up with him. I can still feel him, Kenna." She rubbed her arm fervently, face stained with hot salt. "I can feel him." A sob broke from her, Ena embraced Kenna who held her tight.
"I won't let him have you."
"There's nothing you can do."
"Nothing can be done when one gives up."
"You don't understand." Her lips quivered. "I have to choose him. My parents told me of the Viscount but if I take him instead of Goran..."

Guilt washed through Kenna, she had played her part in Alaric's lie, and it had seemed harmless; yet the pain she saw in the other woman's eyes called her a liar. To Ena, Lord Barkus was real, the threat of Goran was real, and she had become a pawn in her own home. Kenna dropped her hands as though she'd been scorched.

Released, Ena fled, and Kenna watched her go. In her heart she knew the plan was right, that the happiness of one girl was nothing if her sorrow could save the lives of thousands; grass absorbed tears so much better than blood…

Kenna departed the castle and angled towards the stables, soft grass bent beneath her boots, the air cool and crisp against flushed skin. Lost in thought she nearly missed the subtle gasp on the other side of the hedge.
"You know what you're here for. Stop playing a fool." A strangled breath,
"I'm doing all I can. I can't help that she is there, around every turn."
"Does she know who you are?" The gasp hitched beneath a merciless grip; with each ragged inhalation Kenna crept closer, her own breath silted. "Well does she?"

Kenna's hackles rose as she fought the heat in her limbs, she knew exactly who was on the other side of the hedge: *Goran.*
"No my Lord, she doesn't know." Doubt tinged the woman's voice.
"She had better not. Get the job done." There was a shaky inhale followed by the clip of boots on cobblestones. "I'm

tired of this simpering court."

Kenna crept closer while the tread of steps grew dim, Goran was gone, along with his informant. She abandoned the alcove and filled her senses with the scent of the woman; so familiar, that crisp, sweet almond. She sprinted through the courtyard only to be met by a hall that split into opposite directions. Eyes closed she tilted her head and listened for that ragged breath, searched the air for that other body.

Magic shimmered beneath her skin while she dove deeper into the sensation, then took a step to the right; all the noise, the laughter, yet beneath it all Kenna heard her. A growl escaped her before she darted down the hall, servants parted, and the curses of nobles were ignored as her nostrils filled with the scent of her quarry. She could hear the woman's heartbeat stutter when she realized she was being pursued, smell the tang of fear in her sweat; it only spurred Kenna on.

Down the narrow hall the cloaked figure turned and though her face was shrouded in shadow they watched each other. Kenna could hear the staccato rhythm of her heart, and nearly taste the bitter wetness of the woman's blood. One step was all it took, the stillness shattered and the woman fled. Kenna sprinted around the bend then gasped when her legs were consumed by fabric. She skidded to a halt and caught herself against the corridor, her palm pulsed with the promise of bruised flesh.

She looked down and snarled, knuckles white while she pulled the cloak from her entangled legs. Kenna glanced up and caught sight of her missed quarry amongst the soft rustle of leaves that swallowed red fur along with the sweet scent of almonds and musk.

Chapter Eleven: What Binds Us

Blood pooled on the stone, edges black and sticky as the moments ebbed on.
"Come now, aren't you tired of all this? Tell me the location and I can make this all stop. Send you home, or far away with a small plot of land. Live your life in the light friend," Caleb leaned closer, his dagger traced another tender line down tattered ribs. "Or let it end in this darkness." A sudden jolt of pain when metal penetrated tender flesh.

The man screamed, spittle coated his cracked lips. Caleb watched a near black substance trickle from the wound, how the gloom hid the horrors of it all, that wicked touch in the darkness.
"If I tell you I'm a dead man."
"You are dead if you don't, I grow weary of caring for you little rat." Caleb perused the wall laden with tools that

gleamed dully, the steel held hues of red and amber reflected from the subdued flames behind him. "Pick the day of your death and stop wasting my time." The only response was the heavy, rapid breath of his captive, the man had little left in him.

His ribs threatened to tear through his tissue-paper skin, the cuffs that bound him had worked their way nearly to the bone; if Caleb did not kill him soon, he would die any day in such a state. *Perhaps I should just end him. Puncture too deep, the light is dim… I could make an error. It could be a mercy to us both.* His mind flashed to the chamber once more. Smug smiles grated against him while they called him a coward. *If only they knew what they were truly up against, Such darkness…* Caleb glanced at the prisoner. *Such suffering…how much longer can we do this despicable dance?*

He could almost hear it, that sweet tenuous sound of the other's soul breaking. *Ahh friend, how mine shudders with yours.* Caleb released the clamp, his boots squelched through filth until he and the prisoner were nose to nose, vacant eyes met his own.

He was a broken man, and no promise of freedom or land would ever heal him. He was dead already, only his animated flesh remained.

"You'll make it stop?"
"I promise."
"They are headed south, toward the farthest corner of Vontrakal."
"Why so far? Ravenwood is a large enough city to supply them through siege."
"He doesn't want the north. It's the waters he needs."

Caleb stepped back, shadows hid the glint of steel.
"What would Hrothgar want with the Sea?"
"Not the forgotten King, new blood is new wars. The water gives us a way."

Goran then.
"Where is Maeghnor?" The shackles were cold in his hand.
"The last I was told he was in Maniet... I do not know."
The captive exhaled in a way that left his form hollow, he had nothing left to give.

Caleb released the chains, gripped instead the hollow jaw of his rat, their eyes were empty as they met. "Then you are free."

The blade slid between brittle bone and punctured the heart that fluttered beneath its paltry cage. Tears welled and added a light to brown eyes that had long since gone dark, yet it was not his tears that spilled over; one bitter drop escaped Caleb while he ended their pain. He released the limp form that hung suspended from the chain, it sagged against the damp stones of the wall, skin waxy and dull.

Caleb dropped the knife on the gore-slicked floor, then left the chamber. *It was all for naught, Maeghnor is still unknown, and this had been my last chance to find him, to protect these war hungry men.* The blood would not stop no matter how he tried to staunch the flow.

A sweet suspense, the tenuous tension of the hunt; ever alert she waited for a sign that her prey was near. Laughter floated over her for the dozenth time before it faded into the shrouded halls, it was the last bit of laughter from one with too much wine. She could hear his soft breath while he blew out the last candle, then retired to his bedchamber, then silence. Kenna let her magic lap languidly at her senses, icy blue eyes watched the halls while her ears picked up the soft shuffle of leather on stone; her fangs descended when she caught the subtle whiff of sweet almonds.

Kenna glanced at the Viscount's door then turned her back to the moonless night; the woman drew near and a moment of doubt flickered tightly beneath her breastbone, perhaps the guards should have stayed closer.

She rolled her shoulders and took a soft breath, pulled her hood further over her head, and allowed her nails to lengthen into claws. Her slender form bunched with newly created muscle while she rode the line between wolf and woman, the other could not know of her until it was too late. Her mind buzzed with the presence of the other shifter who began to work the lock of the Viscount's chamber.

The woman was inside the room, then quickly slipped into darkness and Kenna pulled a small mirror from her pocket. She quickly slathered the glass in an enchanted oil while she whispered words of power; the guard commander Ambrose's face came into view, with a silent signal given, she stuffed the mirror away. Kenna crossed the hall and slipped into Barkus's chambers.

The parlor was quiet, only the soft breath of one deep in sleep whispered against her ears. She wrinkled her nose at the mingled scents of musk, wine, almonds, and man; it made the wolf within her shiver while she stalked the shadow deeper towards its prey. A black figure swayed beside the Viscount's bed, a soft glow emanated from her skin. Kenna could hear the soft thud of boots down the hall which pressed the wolf inside her closer to the surface.

Magic crackled at the woman's fingertips as Barkus' eyes opened; he grunted in shock, his shoulders pressed into his mattress as Kenna leapt forward, then ripped the assassin from the Viscount's bedside. They rolled to the floor, one shifter slammed against the other. Fingers coated in a pale glow gripped Kenna's throat, the barest touch seared her skin; she screamed and then the shift overtook her.

Consumed by fire Kenna shivered into her lupine form, thick fur soothed the heat that scorched beneath her jaw. Saliva dripped from her lips while she lunged at the woman beneath her, the spy cursed then attempted to throw Kenna off to no avail. Her cloak slipped down and revealed a familiar oval face; Kenna snarled as recognition washed over her. *Signe*.

She lunged and gripped Signe's shoulder, fangs punctured deep, blood spurted against her tongue in hot metallic waves. Signe screamed when Kenna's fang clipped bone, her shriek reverberated against the walls so shrilly Kenna's eardrums trembled painfully, but no matter what happened she could not release her hold. The hiss of steel surrounded her, and in her rage Kenna bared her fangs while sweet blood dribbled from her lips. *Such fools!* She clenched her jaw and felt bone fracture beneath the pressure, a resistance then the faintest sound and a give beneath her fangs.

Satisfied she released the woman and shifted; her magic swelled beneath her skin in a warm wave, then she slipped back into her human form. Many guards stepped back, while others made the sign against evil over their hearts, Kenna had known their like her whole life and ignored them in favor of the commander; only he remained calm. He sheathed his weapon then stepped forward as Kenna released her pelt and slipped back into human form.

Blood streaked her breasts and abdomen while she stood, head held high, her eyes still shimmered with lupine light.

"About time you got here, Ambrose." Kenna addressed the commander. Ambrose removed his cloak, eyes quick to take in Signe's bloodied form that quivered atop a rug. "She'll be fine. Drama is her specialty after all."

He strode closer, his boots tapping wetly through the blood that had seeped free of the thick fabric beneath Signe, then swung his cloak wide to encompass Kenna. The scent of adrenaline tinged with fear filled her nostrils. Saliva pooled in her mouth while the wolf within scratched at the surface, she leaned in and inhaled the heady scent of his amber skin, a muscle in his jaw jumped; he caught her eye while she leaned away.

A swirl of emotions consumed her, Kenna pushed her wolf deeper then stepped past the men, they parted before her silently. Faces weary they rounded the shifter to collect the prisoner and fallen Viscount who had fainted in his bed. Kenna left them, she padded softly down a hall with the echoes of Signe's screams at her heels.

Snow encrusted the leather of his black gloves, a light dust that collected while Caleb settled into the night. A night so still that silence lingered in the frigid air, only to be marred by the soft sigh of falling snow, and breath of beast.

They had been in position for nearly an hour with no sign of Northern troops; any longer and he could give the order to turn back. *If we make it out of this I owe Tanna a silver coin.* The thought echoed through his mind hardly a moment before a nimbus of light consumed the company's left flank; there would be no silver for the luck Goddess that night.

Bloody limbs splattered the snow as the night erupted in flames. Caleb wheeled his charger then pelted down the line.

"Fan out!" His order was swallowed by a ball of light that blazed and roared through the air, another dozen men, gone.

Their charred remains sank into the melted snow and mud. The Northern soldiers spilled from the trees while Caleb barreled towards a small cluster of his men, a circle protected two battle mages who flung lightning into the night with grim desperation; Alearian soldiers riddled the field in a macabre display of limbs and organs.

Those that remained had scattered in an attempt to find shelter in the trees. Caleb reached the mages then slid from the saddle, Zane circled the man, teeth bared, ears pinned while he guarded his rider.

"We need to get them out of here! Put up a barrier." A flurry filled his vision as another explosion rocked through the clearing, the forest echoed with its thunder and the cries of dying men. "We'll do all we can." Such easy, hollow words.

Caleb watched while his scattered men fled, and a fury consumed him. The darkness that had stolen so much of his soul… all to prevent this. Pain wrenched his chest, failure; he had failed his men, and he had failed himself. The screams grew dim around him, his ears filled instead with the steady beat of his heart while the decay seeped further toward his core.

Men fell, maimed beyond repair while other bodies ran while set ablaze, then collapsed in a blackened heap that sputtered in the snow. All that was left behind was a blistered pulp that steamed softly in the mud. The Alearian forces broke, and the mage fire ceased. Caleb blinked against the sudden gloom, then caught the glint of chain mail and bared swords as the Northern forces descended on the clearing through the trees.

Caleb hacked at his enemies with a numb mind, blood bathed him in spurts while his sword greedily tore the flesh of those before him. Another fell only to be replaced, it was only a matter of time before his body failed him. Crimson snow slipped beneath his boots, a fatal mistake; his enemy swung, sword high overhead, a grin of victory on his face, quickly it was broken by a steel-shod hoof that smashed through his chest.

Caleb stumbled, his limbs heavy while he watched Zane paw the crumpled man into the soaked soil, then bolstered himself against the saddle.
"Get out of here Zane, go home." The stallion nickered softly, his eyes human in the shadows while he lipped Caleb's sleeve, the same gentle pull he had done since he was a colt.

The man patted his midnight neck, a bitter smile on his lips.
"Together then, friend."

Carnage consumed them all as Alearian soldiers succumbed to the North, there were so few of them left. *Where are the barriers?* Caleb scanned the clearing for mages, but only one remained. His bearded face a bloody grimace as he gripped the stump of his right arm. Magic flickered from his fingers while he feebly cast spells to bat aside any man foolhardy enough to come near, with each release blood spurted from his ravaged limb, his side black with it.

Caleb and Zane slashed and kicked their way to him, then Caleb wearily walked to a tree and slid down the coarse bark of a pine. Caleb smiled as the man; spite and pain, rage and fear a brand against his heart.
"Hell of a night, good as any other I imagine."
A bark of laughter met his remark.
"You and I have different ideas of a good night, sir."
"Maybe so… I must admit I've had better."

His gaze wandered the clearing studded with the guts and gore of his men, so few Northern scum had fallen. He shook his head then reached up to pat his charger.
"Last chance friend."
"Last chance for what sir?" The mage blasted through a soldier that covered them in bits of flesh and splinters of bone. Caleb flicked a finger off his thigh then drew up a leg, he rested an elbow on his knee.
"You 'bout to write some poetry?"
Caleb laughed. "What's your name mage?"
"Eric."
"Caleb."
"I know."
"I'm aware."
"Do you have something to go back to?"
Caleb closed his eyes.
"I have someone. She's home if I can make it there."
"Good luck with that sir."
"Fuck luck."

The words hardly left his lips when a light filled his eyes, it was all he could see. *Fuck.* Before he could take another breath the heat seared his skin then it all blazed to nothing as it consumed them all. The night echoed with the screams of incinerated men.

Kenna held Signe down, she fought hard despite the shackles that bound her.
"You don't understand! I didn't have a choice." Tears glossed her cheeks while she fervently shook her head. Isabella stepped closer, eyes dark as she gripped the other woman's face, her lips moved yet no sound was uttered. Kenna felt the werecat's power, it pulsed between them and Signe's body became stiff then began to tremble, then her eyes clouded over into ivory orbs. Kenna
shivered in the face of the unworldly stare.
"Kenna, I need to draw power from you. Her mind is shielded." Kenna placed her hand on her mentor's shoulder and opened her magic, a cold sensation crept over her hand, then arms while Isabella siphoned her energy.

Signe went rigid and screamed, Kenna's hand pulled back, and the circuit between them dissipated.
"Get a hold of yourself girl," Isabelle snapped. "We don't have time for this!"
"I don't believe in this!"
"I don't care."
They stared at one another coldly.

"You aren't a wolf Kenna, you're human and humans get their hands dirty. You have already mauled her, stop playing innocent. Now lend me your magic."

Kenna gripped the werecat's hand and sent out her magic with such force it burned them both, Isabelle tempted to pull away only to be held in place by a clawed hand.

"You wanted this, now do something with it!"

Signe's head snapped back, smashed into the stone wall when magic flooded her system, blood and strands of golden hair stuck to the stone. She shuddered then begged, "Please don't do this to me."

"We don't have a choice."

Isabella's eyes shifted rapidly under closed lids while she scanned the unseen thoughts, Kenna held down Signe with her other hand until her joints ached, then held on still. A shriek escaped the blonde, then she slumped to the floor.

"It's not him." Isabelle muttered.

"Who?"

"How could it not be him?" Her voice was soft as she turned from her pupil.

"Who are you talking about?!" Kenna blocked her companion's path. "Isabella, what is it?" At last the werecat saw the other woman, her shrouded eyes cleared while she took Kenna's hand.

"It's not who we think, but it can't be right."

"What's not right?" Kenna asked softly.

Isabella glanced at Signe.

"I must speak to the King." She pulled her hands free then left the chamber.

The image shivered as he sat back.

"Your Halfling won't save you, sister. No one can," he said while he traced his finger over the surface of water, the scene shivered then scattered into fragments of light. As the bowl cleared, black almond eyes looked back at him in a face that was once a perfect ivory, now the flesh was translucent, ashen where it stretched over angular bones.

Maeghnor stood, his gaze roved about the chamber languidly while Hrothgar lounged in a chair next to him, the mage grasped his boney hand.

"There's nothing she can do. Even if she suspects me, she won't be able to stop me. A little sibling rivalry at its finest." Maeghnor chuckled then he flung the king's hand, Hrothgar's skeletal jaw swung wide in a dead man's grin. "That's it, have a laugh with me." Maeghnor chuckled humorlessly then turned his back on the ruler's remains. "Oh my sister… How you have always tried to help these pathetic wretches. Your human toys will be the end of you."

Kenna slumped to the floor beside Signe. The broken shifter trembled beside her, hair clung to her damp face as her lips moved wordlessly.
"Why would you do it?" Kenna's voice was soft, yet Signe closed her eyes to the sound. A spark of anger flared within Kenna, but it burned itself out. "You must have known it would end this way? It all fell apart when he came, or perhaps when I did." She glanced sidelong at the Northerner, her glassy brown eyes were open again, but sightless.

She took a deep breath.
"Whatever reason it was, I truly hope it was worth it." She stood, her body stiff after the violent purge of magic for Isabella's disposal. She grasped the prison cell's door then paused, unsure. A broken voice cracked the silence.
"I did it for my son."

With those words Kenna's heart shattered.
She turned slowly and walked back to Signe, her boots scuffed the granite floor.
"Where I come from, the living is hard, the land unforgiving. So, I took my child to Maniet. I figured there was more food, more work; a better chance at life for us both." She closed her eyes while Kenna slid to the floor

beside her. "I was wrong. My work in the castle seemed easy at first, but it brought me closer to him."
"Gorin?"

A laugh more akin to a caw escaped the prisoner. "He is a brute and a pawn. No, it brought me closer to—" The door slammed open, Kenna snarled as claws erupted from her fingers.
"It's time to get out. I have business with her." The guard eyed Kenna with revulsion. With reluctance Kenna retracted her claws, an image of her claws in his belly flashed through her mind before she looked back at Signe. A part of her wavered.

Blonde hair hid the woman's face where she had crumpled against the wall, she was so still Kenna would have thought she was dead had she not heard her ragged sigh of resignation.
"What will you do with her?"
"None of you concern. Now get out, I do the King's work." His broad frame blocked her view as she backed from the room. Her last glimpse of Signe was her being pulled to her feet, body limp before the guard slammed the door shut.

Kenna descended the stairs with a dull, heavy ache within her chest. *She had a son, a son that no longer has a mother.*

A fire cracked softly while she watched the first snow dust paths of stone and mortar; the sun was gone but a soft glow remained which left the world suspended in time. Kenna rubbed Leara's muzzle with absent fingers, her eyes locked on the horizon. As the last rays of light left the sky her gaze did not falter, instead shifted from sea green to icy blue while she longed for the night. A soft click of a latch, a weight beside her on the sofa.

"You can't hide here forever."

"Maybe… maybe not."

"Kenna."

She turned lupine eyes on him. A smile met her gaze, soft and warm as honey.

"I hate the way they talk about me."

Randy gripped her hand.

"People fear what they don't understand." He squeezed her hand then he stood. "Take a walk Kenna, you shouldn't coop yourself up." Randy left her to her darkness. For better or worse, that darkness was a comfort, her solace, in a way no human could hope to provide.

Kenna listened to the silence that followed him, the castle was restful, hardly a sound echoed through its halls. With a heavy sigh through her nose, she left her chambers with the white wolf in tow. She wandered the halls aimlessly, her steps accompanied by the faint clack of Leara's claws on stone; then without intention found herself before the library.

She stepped into the dry warmth of the cavernous chamber, small fires burned in the hearth of each column which lit the shelves in an amber glow. Kenna wove deeper into the labyrinth; the air permeated with the smoky scent of pages, laced with vanilla, a woody tone under it all.

Kenna breathed deeply, the knots in her shoulders

rolled free; it was then that a rustle reached her, muffled. She left the glow of the center path, through the dark corridors of books and wood. Kenna crossed smaller paths that led to the corners of the library and caught the glimmer of aurelian light. Strangled sobs filled the halls as Kenna stepped into an alcove laden with leather chairs, a circular table marred by ivory wax sat in its center. A figure curved in on herself while her body trembled with smothered tears, Leara whined then quickly crossed the space between the women.

Ears flat she tucked her muzzle under the other's elbow, then bumped her embrace open until her face was exposed. Kenna closed the gap between them.
"Sophie, what happened?" She sat on the floor, hand extended before she let it fall in her lap, her fingers clenched tight.
"I told him everything." Sophie's voice cracked. She covered her face and mumbled into her palms. "I told him... I told him *everything*."
"I'm sure whatever it is, he will forgive you."
"Oh, he won't, Aden is too proud for that. He'll act like it's nothing, but he won't ever forgive me."
"What did you tell him Soph?"
"Amira... I told him about Amira."

Beautiful bronze skin accented by amber eyes filled Kenna's mind while realization settled over her. She took Sophie's hand, hot to the touch where it trembled against her lap, then spoke slowly.
"You can't keep hiding who you are. It will only hurt you and those you love."
"I did love him... just not in the way he needed." She took a breath that shuddered. "If my family finds out about us they won't accept it, but if Amira's family finds out," Sophie shook her head. "Kenna, I've ruined us both."
"Then you'll both start over."

Sophie scoffed, "It's not that simple." There was doubt in her voice as she gazed with vacant eyes at the books. "I don't know if she will go with me."

"Go?" Kenna stood, heat flashed through her. "I didn't mean leave. I meant start your life over your way, choose a different path."

Sophie gripped Kenna's hand, then tugged her back down with her onto the settee.

"I know what you meant, I am choosing a path, it's just not one that will keep me here."

"Where will you go?"

"Vintra perhaps."

"You intend to leave before they get back?"

Sophie smiled softly, her chin trembled, over bright eyes surveyed the room.

"Caleb will understand."

"And Von?"

"That vain peacock won't even notice I'm gone," her voice stiffened with aristocratic disdain, but her tears betrayed her. "He will understand, eventually. He'll have to."

"When will you leave?" Kenna watched the other woman, a dull ache throbbed against her sternum.

"Tomorrow, if Amira will come. The sooner we leave the safer she will be."

Sophie rose, Kenna's hands held in hers while she pulled the woman to her feet.

"This feels wrong, you shouldn't have to leave." Kenna's lips trembled.

"No, I shouldn't and yet I must. I will miss you, Kenna." Their eyes met; a gold fleck glittered beneath a sea of tears. "I pray we meet again. Take care of the boys for me, they are hopeless." She leaned forward and kissed Kenna's cheek softly, then with a final squeeze she left the island of light.

"Divya be with you." Kenna whispered.

Cotton rustled as she slid to the floor, Leara curled around her while her vision blurred, and pale silver laced her cheeks.

Chapter Twelve: Darkness

She watched from the shadows and counted the six Royal Guards lined against the chamber door; this was the third time she had counted their number. The men were well seasoned, handpicked by Alaric himself, yet Kenna could smell the tang of apprehension in their sweat.

Her skin prickled when the lead guard gripped the burnished lever before he swung the door wide, their torches high.

"Prince Goran, in the name of the Crown and by order of the King you are under are—" His words turned into choked gurgle, he stumbled back in a slow arch towards his comrades, a small throwing ax lodged in his throat.

Goran burst from his bed with the ferocity of a wild cat, teeth bared in defiance, then lunged for his sword against the mantle. The guards ran towards him, bare steel glinted in the slivers of moonlight that pooled through the curtains onto thick decorative rugs. Kenna watched it all unfold from the hall opposite the chamber door, cloak pulled low while she harnessed and restrained the change.

Alaric's guards tightened their circle around Goran who now stood sword in hand before a lifeless fire, his eyes, his smile malicious and feral; this was no man, but a cornered wolf ready for a fight.
"Goran, you are under arrest. Lay down your sword!"
"And let you run me through? Not a chance," he snarled, then he lunged forward. The lead guard parried, yet Goran did not stop, he pivoted on bare feet and punched the nearest man.

A wet crunch followed the contact as bone crumpled. The guard stumbled back, blood spurted from his broken nose, temporarily blinded by unbidden tears as his body reacted to the trauma. Goran strode into a flawless maneuver, his sword ached above him then swept down, its edge cut through the black leather armor of another guard; ribs splintered as steel bit deep.

Kenna released more of the change, ready to step in, and crossed the hall. She paused; her senses overwhelmed by the metallic scent of blood, her mouth pooled with saliva while she fought down a surge of hunger. Her fingers dug into the doorframe while she steadied herself, and watched the men tighten their circle on the foreign prince.

Goran turned and searched for an exit, and Kenna saw it when he did; a small space between his captors that he could slip through. Her fingers flew to the clasp at her throat just as he slipped in a pool of blood, his bare feet slick against the stone.

Goran flailed in a desperate attempt to right himself, only to crash against the floor. The guards kicked away his sword, it sparked and rasped against the stone, it sent shivers down her spine. She stepped back from the door as the guard with the broken nose dug his knee into the center of Goran's back, then roughly pulled his arms behind him. His wrists were bound so tightly the cord dug deep, his fingers pale with blood-loss.

He was pulled to his feet between two guards and dragged towards the exit, Kenna quickly backed away, her grip tight around the brim of her hood.
"You can't do this!" he yelled while he hurled his weight from side to side in a ploy to free himself. "The North will crush you for this!" He began to laugh, deep manic laughter that echoed through his chest. Goran was taken down the hall, his cackles a trail of madness behind him.

Kenna watched them go, then returned to Goran's room; the fallen guard laid upon the rug now stained black, a pool of precious liquid sprawled around him. She released the change and watched the clarity of the room soften with relief, with a murmured prayer she closed the door and made her way down the hall.

The chamber glowed with a soft aurous light that shifted against the wall, torches sputtered softly yet their flames offered nothing more than light. Goran knelt in the center of a small chamber without windows, the stones were large and roughly hewn, the chamber cold and barren. He was held in an old section of the castle, far from prying ears. His pale hair covered his face now marred by sweat and blood, his mouth bruised, lips split where a guard had demanded silence.

The flames swayed when the door opened and Alaric entered the room, face grave as he stepped towards the imprisoned prince. He waved his hand in dismissal of the small attachment of guards at his back, they discreetly tucked themselves between the torches.
"This is not what I intended for you."
Goran spat on the stones between them. Alaric stepped over the saliva and firmly grasped Goran's blood-encrusted face.
"Careful boy, you are in deeper than you think."
"I'm not afraid of some silken king. You're soft just like this pathetic country."

Alaric smiled grimly then stepped away; he was in a position no royal wished to be.
"Your trial will start shortly, Goran. You will wait here in the meantime." Goran laughed; a dry, humorless sound.
"A trial? You southerners have no balls. You are hiding behind others so you don't have to make the bloody choices yourself."
Alaric paused, his calloused palm loose on the latch.
"You have forced my hand." The Alearian King stepped through the doors, his guards in attendance, while his captive spat curses at his back.

Crows cawed raucously while they flapped across a steely sky, then landed on ledges, feathers fluffed against the bitter cold. Snow fell softly, an ever-present sigh that mingled with the hushed whispers of the crowd. Sapphire Bay's citizens gathered thickly in the small courtyard, never before had they seen something like this.

Even the elders crossed their thresholds for the sight, boney fingers trembled while they clutched their shawls, thin silver hair scattered by the breeze. Kenna stood under a tree north of the stage, she would savor this, the sweet success of a finished hunt.

She pulled her cloak tighter against the chill then tucked away a tendril of hair; what a sweet moment indeed. He was quiet now as they walked him up the stairs, one guard on either elbow, each dressed in black. A masked figure waited for them on the platform, silent and still. Goran's eyes were vacant while he crossed the worn wooden planks; a plain white tunic hung loosely from his shoulders, spread wide to reveal the prickled skin of his neck.

Does one register the cold at such a time? Perhaps the senses are heightened even more in the face of such finality, that even the chill breeze that bit the flesh was a desired sensation, a pleasurable caress. Goran knelt before the block, his eyes roved over the executioner's sword with bitter admiration.

"This will be your undoing, at least my end will bring about yours," his words echoed over a silent courtyard. Everyone held their breath as Goran spoke his piece to their king. Alaric regarded the younger man with eyes of flint.

"That shall be my burden to bear, beneath the weight of my crown. Be thankful you are spared such an obligation."

Goran smirked, then laid his throat against the cool hollow of the block. He closed his eyes to the simple pattern of the wicker basket before him, his pulse thundered through his limbs.

Though he could not see Alaric's nod to the executioner, he could feel the shift in the air; hear the shift of fabric as the executioner took his stance. Well-crafted steel had a way about it, that it could cut through the flesh, through the bone; the impact was sudden, final. Alearian steel bit through the prince to bury its bloody maw in oak. Goran's head toppled into the basket, soaked through the wicker. The stump of his neck pumped, blood spurted feet from him while each pulse loosed across the wooden boards. Without a head his flesh lost meaning and his body slumped from the stand.

Kenna walked away while the crowd rose in one voice; cries of fear, cries for war; they all mingled in a bitter wave that sent the crows to the sky. Kenna's steps slowed before the pale bare feet, blue around the tips, that dangled so near her line of sight. She could not bear to look up into Signe's face, twisted in a mask of pain where she hung suspended from the courtyard's tree.

A hollowness filled her; how she had craved the sweetness of this moment only to find a bitterness upon her tongue. She remembered the tears of Ena, how she longed for those tears now, she would let them rain down on the fields and forests if she thought it would help. Tears would not save them from the blood that would come; a blood that was no longer sweet, a blood she no longer craved, yet it was a taste that would wet her mouth all the same.

Acknowledgements

First and foremost I want to thank my husband, and best friend, Matt. You pushed me to finish this story when I continued to stall, I was scared to finish this book and share it with others. You supported me, let me use you for storyboarding, fixed my action scenes with a soldier's eye; I couldn't have done it without you, and I am eternally thankful for you.

Then I would like to thank my other best friend Kim for being willing to read the messy draft that even my editor never saw. Your support meant the world.

After that I would like to thank my editor April, and each friend that read my drafts. I appreciate all of you. Also, thank you to my wonderfully kind and talented cover artist, Marry. You gave my dream a face.

Finally, and with all of my gratitude, thank you to each person that picked up this book and gave it a chance. You have helped breathe life into my dream, a dream I have carried with me since I was a young girl. Child of The Pines means so much to me, and I look forward to sharing more of Kenna's journey with you in Children of The Moon.

Eternally thankful,
Hales McInerney